WAR ALERT!

The clearly audible explosive boom was followed by a massive swell of agitated water that smashed into the bow of the submerged *Phoenix*, tossing the 18,700-ton vessel like a feather in the wind. In the submarine's command center, the unfortunate sailors who didn't have a secure perch found themselves thrown off balance. Several men crashed to the floor while others found themselves flung into the compartment's equipment packed walls.

"What in the world hit us, Skipper?" the executive officer shouted.

Blake shook his head. "Damned if I know."

A radio transmission fresh from the decoding machine was placed in Blake's hands. The words *COCKED PISTOL* were typed neatly in the paper's center. Blake's gut turned sour as he turned to his exec, and his words rang out apocalyptically.

"My God, Pete. *It's started!*"

THE
PHOENIX ODYSSEY

RICHARD P. HENRICK

ZEBRA BOOKS
KENSINGTON PUBLISHING CORP.

ZEBRA BOOKS

are published by

Kensington Publishing Corp.
475 Park Avenue South
New York, NY 10016

First printing: March 1986

Printed in the United States of America

Special thanks to Scott S. for his belief, Tim L. for his patience, and Nancy and Harold for making this all possible.

Had the fierce ashes of some fiery peak,
Been hurl'd so high they ranged about the globe?
For day by day, thro' many a blood-red eve,
The wrathful sunset glared . . .

St. Telemachus
Alfred, Lord Tennyson, 1892

Chapter One

Approximately two-thirds of the way between Hawaii and New Zealand lie several relatively small outcroppings of volcanic basalt known collectively as American Samoa. The largest of the four islands comprising this chain is Tutuila, famous for its capital city, Pago Pago, and it was because of the excellent layout of this village's harbor that the U.S. Navy first showed an interest in occupying this remote island kingdom. With the blessings of the local chiefdom, the navy built a coal depot and a small dock here. This complex grew rapidly during World War II. It wasn't until the cessation of hostilities that the base at Pago Pago was abandoned, and the responsibility for governing the island was transferred into the hands of the Department of the Interior.

Because of the island's strategic importance, the modern navy of the 1980s decided to once again occupy Tutuila. This renewed presence took the form of a single, one-man research station, located on the island's westernmost edge. Situated in the midst of a stand of majestic coconut palms, the station occupied a simple, native structure known as a *fales*. This oval habitation was designed around a large room, set on a wooden platform and sheltered from the elements by a thick, thatched roof. With year-round temperatures averaging well into the eighties, it needed no walls. Instead, blinds of woven leaf were much more practical in keeping the tropical showers out and allowing the cooling trade winds in. They also allowed for a splendid view of the nearby beach at Cape Taputapu, and the crystal-blue Pacific beyond.

To most of his countrymen, Lieutenant Thomas Kraft appeared to have the ideal duty. Responsible for the day-to-day monitoring of the various electronic consoles set inside the hut, the thirty-two-year-old naval officer had been stationed here since the station's inception, five months ago.

From the moment he first received his present orders, he had looked upon this assignment in the South Pacific as a dream come true. As a geophysicist with the Office of Naval Research, he had drawn previous duty in such locations as the Aleutian Islands, Greenland, and the barren wastes of Canada's Northwest Territory. When the orders had arrived sending him to American Samoa, he could hardly believe his good fortune. Without a regret, he had traded in his gloves, parka, fur-lined boots, and long johns for a set of tropical khakis.

Because he had no surviving family members, and had remained a bachelor throughout his years, Thomas had had few people to say good-bye to in the States. An instinctual loner, isolated outposts such as this were ideally suited for him. High profile, beaurocratic assignments, like those available back in Washington, D.C., would probably be better for his career's advancement, yet they certainly weren't for him.

The first three months in the South Pacific had passed quickly. Most of this time had been spent at sea, aboard an oceanographic research vessel. Some four hundred miles due south of Samoa was the Tonga

Trench, a unique geological feature formed where two immense crustal plates met. Separated by a ridge of subterranean volcanic mountains, the Trench penetrated depths of over 30,000 feet. Kraft's mission had been to place a complex grid of seismic sensors on the seafloor here. These devices were connected to the monitors that occupied the majority of the interior space of the fales, which also served as his primary living quarters.

This period at sea had been a most exciting time for Thomas Kraft. With the ship's experienced crew comprised of a mix of navy and local civilian personnel, he had received his initiation into the region's rich history and fascinating customs. And as supervisor of a work crew made up of a half-dozen rugged Samoans, he had soon learned why their island was referred to as the "Ireland of the Pacific." Though these men were generally a hard-working, dedicated bunch, they remained totally unpredictable. Subject to constant, seemingly unprovoked mood changes, the big-boned islanders could be charming one moment, and in a bat of an eyelid, turn completely uncooperative. The rascals also had a irrepressible propensity toward stealing. Thomas had learned this trait the hard way, for on his very first night at sea he had lost his compass, a fountain pen, and a prized pair of compact binoculars to these compulsive thieves.

It had proved to be the captain, a Navy veteran of thirty years—most of which had been spent plying these waters—who calmed Kraft down. Over a snifter of brandy, he had explained the Samoans' utter disrespect for personal property rights. This wasn't meant to be spiteful, it was just their way of life. He had cautioned the young lieutenant to accept his losses, and to be more careful with his belongings in the future.

Thomas had listened carefully to the skipper's advice. And the next morning, he hadn't gone up on deck until his belongings were locked securely in the bin located under his bunk.

A day out of Pago Pago, the ship had passed a series of tiny, uninhabited coral islands. Thomas had stirred excitedly as he observed that their origin was certainly volcanic. Volcanology had been his major interest in college, and the sighting had been his first actual view of a type of island he had previously only read about in textbooks.

Formed by immense volumes of hardened basalt, whose origins were deep in the earth's mantle, the islands took form as various coral polyps drifted in and attached themselves to this rock. Since corals built vertically, the fringing reefs took shape over a period of hundreds of years.

One of the Samoans had told a tale of actually having seen such a volcanic island rise from the watery depths. Waving his hands emotionally, he had described the rounded cone as it rose upward, capped by long ribbons of venting steam and immense, exploding fingers of fiery lava. He had gone on to voice his puzzlement upon returning to the exact spot several weeks later and finding the new island nowhere to be seen.

In reality, Thomas knew that such an incident was a common occurrence, especially in this particular region. The trench that they were littering with seismic sensors was a hotbed of volcanic activity. The geophysicist was well aware that the Tonga region was but an extention of the infamous Ring of Fire. Enclosing an area of over seventy million square miles, the Ring was characterized by a series of constantly shifting fault lines. It could be followed by tracing the shoreline of the Pacific northward from the tip of South América, up the Andes, and then over the Cascade Mountains of

America's Pacific Northwest. Here it arced westward, through the fiery Aleutians, turning south over Russia's Kamchatka Peninsula, and continuing down through Japan, Eastern China, the Philippines, Indonesia, and New Zealand.

The energy stored, and occasionally released, along the Ring was awesome. Not only did it take the form of powerful earthquakes, but over three-quarters of the earth's active volcanoes were located here. Thomas knew that a proper monitoring of quake activity here would allow him to further study several popular theories in relation to a field of science still in its relative infancy.

Of course, the U.S. Navy had a much more practical reason for placing the sensors on the floor of the Tonga Trench. Although the true purpose was veiled in secrecy, Kraft was able to determine that his assignment involved a newly activated, submarine refitting installation placed somewhere in the waters between American Samoa and the Tonga Islands. This base was supposedly situated inside the hollowed-out base of an extinct seamount. Apparently, his services were needed to relay back to Naval Command in Pearl Harbor any evidence of geological disturbance that could possibly threaten this top-priority installation.

Thomas couldn't help but admire the type of foresight responsible for such a plan. He knew that such a base would be of instrumental importance, especially in the event of a full-scale nuclear war. With their home ports certainly targeted for immediate destruction, the surviving subs would need someplace to refit their stores of supplies and weapons. What better place to do so than a top-secret, underwater pen, protected by an entire seamount?

Unfortunately, the navy had picked one of the most geologically unstable areas on the planet. The unusually high levels of seismic activity taking place on the Pacific seafloor had been apparent from the moment Thomas had first completed the attachment of the sensor monitors. For the past two months, barely a day had gone by without a tremor of at least 4.1 on the Richter scale occurring. Inevitably, this signaled that a quake of major proportions was about to occur, or possibly that a volcano, either already existent or newly formed, was about to erupt. Either one of these events could destroy the navy's supposed base with a single, massive shake or blast.

Thomas Kraft was aware that such a cataclysm could take place at any time — within the hour, or possibly not for an entire series of decades. All he could do was watch the monitors, to insure that nothing out of the ordinary was presently taking place.

It was well past five P.M. by the time Lieutenant Kraft finally pulled himself away from the chattering seismograph indicator, and left the shelter of his fales. Outside, he had a clear view of the sun as it began inching toward the western horizon. The sky was a vibrant blue, with not a cloud visible. Thomas stretched his cramped, five-foot, seven-inch frame, relishing the fresh trade wind that blew in even gusts from the east.

His stomach growled, and once again he was aware that he had worked throughout the entire day without bothering to break for lunch. This disinterest in feeding himself was one of the reasons he had stayed so thin throughout the years. Absent was the familiar paunch, which extended the waistline of the majority of his similarly aged coworkers.

Focusing his deep-set sea-green eyes on a school of dolphins who had just swum through the reefline,

Thomas found himself thinking again that he had never fully appreciated life until he had landed here. With his full, bushy brown beard and deeply tanned skin, he looked like a native. Now, an inner transformation was making the change complete. He was beginning to understand why so many westerners found it so hard to leave the South Pacific once they had a taste of these islands.

As was his late-afternoon habit whenever work permitted, he seated himself in one of the two rattan lounges placed on the porch. Continuing to study the antics of the frolicking dolphins, he gradually emptied his mind of the day's monotonous duties. It took only minutes more for the soothing surge of the surf to lull him fast asleep.

When he awoke, it was well past sunset. Over the ever-present crash of the waves, he heard someone moving around inside the hut. His heart pounding, half expecting to find a crew of natives busily stripping the station of his belongings, Thomas rose cautiously. Lit by the golden afterglow of sunset, he peered through the structure's exposed blinds. It took him a full thirty seconds to locate the intruder.

She was visible from the rear, standing over the central seismograph unit. Her long, flowing dark hair cascaded over bare brown shoulders, falling to a tight waist. Below, a pair of long, slender legs were covered by a brightly colored, lavalava, wraparound skirt.

Deeply engrossed in the monitor before her, she didn't notice as Thomas Kraft soundlessly entered the room. She became aware of his presence only after he snuck up behind her and grabbed her shoulders. She jumped, startled with this touch, as the lieutenant spun her around.

"Can I help you, young lady?" Thomas asked sternly.

13

As their eyes met, all the tension in the young woman's stare instantly dissolved. Seconds later, she was in his arms.

"Thomas Kraft, you scared the dickens out of me! What do you mean, sneaking around in the dark like that?"

"I was only protecting my government's property, Telsa," returned the officer with a playful wink. "Since when have you become so interested in the equipment?"

The twenty-two-year-old Samoan beauty answered defiantly. "Often when you're not around and I'm cleaning, I watch the instruments in your place. Grandfather still says that the writing which needs no hand to sketch it is *aitu*, but we know differently, don't we, Thomas Kraft?"

"This seismograph certainly isn't run by magic, little lady. Now, what brings you out here so late in the day? I wasn't expecting you until tomorrow."

Picking up a piece of folded cheesecloth, Telsa Vanua, eldest daughter of the *matai*, or chief, of the nearby village of Amanave, began to dust the equipment-loaded table before her. "Tomorrow is a sacred day, dedicated to Pele, the goddess of the fire that created our island. Since I won't be able to come and clean as usual, I didn't think you'd mind if I fulfilled my duty today."

Thomas watched the Samoan continue her work. Though the room was rapidly darkening, and they had yet to flick on the fales's single electric bulb, she efficiently proceeded with her dusting. How fortunate he had been to find a gem like Telsa to give him a hand with the station's upkeep! Not only was she extremely conscientious with her chores, a trait most unusual for an islander, but she was also one of the most passionate, beautiful woman he had ever met.

14

It had been her village's responsibility to ready the station for the navy's use. Along with the fales and the beach that surrounded it, the citizens of Amanave had offered the services of a combination cook/housekeeper. When he had learned of this, Kraft's first impulse was to graciously refuse the chief's generous offer. A nosey woman poking around was all he needed. In fact, he had been on his way to the village to convey this wish personally, when he had first met Telsa . . .

Having spent the night before in Pago Pago, and anxious to settle into his new station, he secured a motor scooter for the fifteen-mile drive from the capital city to the beach at Cape Taputapu.

His first impression of the island of Tutuila was that of encountering a virtual paradise. Pago Pago's excellent harbor and quaint Colonial-style architecture gave way to miles of dazzling, pure white beaches as he proceeded to the southwest. Ringed by fringes of majestic coconut palms, the virtually uninhabited expanses of sand overlooked a huge, crystal-clear lagoon, protected from the surrounding Pacific by a curved ring of brightly colored coral. As the asphalt roadway turned inland, he found himself crossing acres of dark-leafed, scarlet-podded cocoa trees. This plantation bordered another containing thick stands of breadfruit and coconut, all thriving on the rich volcanic soil.

While mentally recreating the series of violent, geological events that led to the island's creation tens of thousands of years ago, Thomas passed through the tiny towns of Futiga and Leone, soon finding himself at the road's end on the island's westernmost tip.

He found the deserted fales housing the new naval station without a problem. Satisfied with his quarters, he parked his scooter, and making sure to lock it securely and pocket the key, began the short hike to the village of Amanave.

The path was narrow, though easy to follow. While halfway through a field planted with taro, a sweet-potato-like tuber, he first set eyes on the shapely figure of Telsa Vanua. She was just emerging from an opposite stand of coconut palms. The lieutenant's first impression was that he had to be dreaming. One thing that was certain was that a gorgeous creature like the one who was approaching him only served to make this tropical paradise complete.

Tall, lithe, and lean, she walked with a dignified, fluid grace, more characteristic of a dancer. Though her hair flowed in two long, thick ribbons over each shoulder and down to the waist, it was obvious she wore nothing but her bright red lavalava. As she drew nearer, he couldn't help but admire the full rising of her pert breasts. To his utter dismay, all that he could coax from her was a shy nod of recognition as she hurried past him without halting.

Continuing down the path, Thomas soon found himself passing the dozen or so fales that comprised the village of Amanave. There, the chief met him as if he were the most honored of guests. Before he could explain the purpose of his visit, the lieutenant found himself accepting an invitation to a feast to be given in his honor that very evening. The chief then asked him if he had happened to encounter a young woman on the path up from the beach. When Thomas remarked that he had, the chief explained that this was his daughter, Telsa, Thomas Kraft's new housekeeper. The naval officer found himself unwilling to convey the original purpose of his visit. After all, he didn't want to insult the chief. Surely, he could try the girl out for a little while. Lord knows, he could use a decent cook.

And then, if she did turn out to be a nuisance, he would somehow find a way to send her back.

Standing inside the darkened fales, watching Telsa in the midst of her cleaning, Thomas forced back a smile. To think that he had actually been worrying that his housekeeper would get in the way! As it turned out, he was finding he didn't know how he could manage to live without her.

Telsa's voice brought Kraft's imaginings back to the present. "Tonight we will be holding the kava ceremony. This precedes tomorrow morning's sacrifice to the goddess."

"Didn't your father promise to invite me to the next ceremony? I'm anxious to see what this ritual is all about."

Telsa responded carefully. "I'm afraid tonight's activities are for the elders only. Father will let you join the circle as soon as it's permissible."

"Is the kava really as potent as I've heard? One officer who tried it admitted that he had strange hallucinations for at least two days afterward."

Kraft watched as the Samoan dropped the dusting cloth that she had been so diligently utilizing and came to his side.

"Would you like to try some for yourself, Thomas Kraft? I don't have to be back to the village before midnight, and I just happen to have a sample with me."

Illuminated by the bare light of the remaining dusk, Telsa's exotic features beckoned seductively. The lieutenant found himself unable to resist.

"I'd love to try it, as long as it doesn't interfere with my duties."

"Which duties are you referring to?" cooed the Samoan, as she brushed up against him and gently cupped his crotch. "It is childish to fear the kava. It will take you only as far as you wish to go."

Breaking away from him, Telsa sauntered to the kitchen counter and began fumbling through her large, straw handbag. Meanwhile, Kraft pulled the cord leading to the socket of the room's single, seventy-five-watt bulb. The flash of the sudden light stung his eyes. His pupils had barely had time to adjust when Telsa's voice boomed out authoritatively:

"Please, my love, no artificial light. The kava is only comfortable with the glow of a candle, or that of the stars."

Shrugging his shoulders, Thomas pulled the cord, and the room was engulfed by total darkness. It took almost a full minute for his pupils to adjust to the abrupt change in lighting. Once he could orient himself, he proceeded to pull out the candles, which he kept nearby for stormy evenings when the station's fragile electrical current was interrupted.

With a brass candlestick in hand, Kraft walked over to the kitchen counter. There, the slender taper showed Telsa intensely involved in her preparations. Having placed a kettle of water on the stove to boil, she was in the process of emptying a pouchful of a whitish, pulp-like substance into the bottom of a large coconut cup. Carefully, she poured the hot water into the cup, allowing the ingredients to steep.

Telsa looked up and spoke proudly. "As my village's *taupou*, I am in charge of preparing the kava for the elders. This is a responsibility of great honor. It is my duty to dig up the root, wash and dry it in the sun, then chip and grind it. I then prepare the drink, like I have this evening, and serve it in the ceremonial manner. All this is done with an exactness prescribed by generations of ancestors."

She stirred the cream-colored brew with a wooden

18

spoon, and then, gripping the cup with both hands, brought it to her lips and consumed the barest of sips. Satisfied, she handed the cup to Thomas, along with the following instructions.

"It is our custom for the kava drinker to pour out a tiny portion of the cup's contents before draining it. Spill out a few drops before you, and say the word *manuia*. This will bring you good fortune. Also, take care not to drain the cup completely. Fling the remaining portion over your right shoulder. This sacrifice will insure that the goddess will respond favorably to your most fervent prayers."

Mindful to carry out the directions exactly as they were conveyed, Kraft consumed a hearty gulp of the lukewarm brew. Though its taste was somewhat alien, his first impression was that of sampling a type of watered-down milk, seasoned with pepper and cloves.

"It's not anything like I expected," Thomas remarked with a smack of his lips. "In fact, it's downright tasty. Are you going to join me?"

"I'm afraid my duties later tonight must keep me from doing so," the Samoan said. "Let me fix you another cupful."

Without waiting for a response, Telsa emptied a pouch of kava pulp into the polished coconut husk, and added a portion of hot water. Thomas watched her, a bit apprehensive.

"Are you sure I can handle the aftereffects, Telsa?"

"Come now, Thomas Kraft. Do you really think I would ever give you anything that would cause you the least bit of discomfort? The teenage boys of Amanave are allowed to consume a similar portion at the time of their initiation into manhood. I guarantee that this additional cupful will only serve to make you that much more receptive to the demands of the goddess."

Sensing the seriousness of her words, and aware of

no apparent side effects from the amount he had just consumed, Thomas took the refilled cup.

"*Manuia*," he replied, spilling a few drops of the milky liquid before him. Draining the peppery brew with a single gulp, he took special care to make sure to leave a small amount behind. As he tossed these remaining drops over his shoulder, a sudden, tingling warmth shot through his stomach. This was followed by a slight wave of dizziness. All of these sensations were quickly forgotten, as Telsa sensually rubbed her body up against his side.

"Welcome to the kingdom of the kava goddess," purred the Samoan. "As long as you relax, and flow in the direction that Pele calls, no harm would dare befall you. Now, come to me, my hairy lover from the land of the sunrise. Wrap me in your arms, and shoot your seed deep."

Thomas Kraft felt enchanted. Inflamed by an inner radiance that he had never experienced before, and with his Samoan beauty locked securely in his arms, an entirely new sensory dimension opened up before him.

The touch of Telsa's warm, smooth skin produced a delight beyond comparison. Soaking in her sweet natural scent, Thomas felt the frantic urge of true desire. Aware of the rising heat of passion, he allowed his love to guide him outside. Standing on the fales's narrow porch, the sounds of the island encompassed them. Mesmerized by this surging call, needless pieces of clothing were soon abandoned, and the two sprinted, hand-in-hand, over the soft sand. Seconds later, they plunged into the warm waters of the lagoon.

Once again the lovers faced each other and embraced, this time cooled by the salty Pacific. Thomas stood on the firm, sandy bottom, while Telsa straddled his hips with her long, slender legs. As their lips met, and their tongues began their mad probing, the two became one. No guiding hand was needed to direct Kraft's erect manhood into the smooth, tight channel that he craved so. With short, teasing strokes, he prepared his love to take him. When this was given, Telsa reacted with long sigh of delight.

Barely conscious of any other sensation but the feel of Telsa's depths, Thomas pulled his hips back, then plunged them forward. Time after time, he repeated this instinctive movement, until his mate was trembling in the midst of utter ecstasy. Aware of his own gathering climax, Thomas increased the frenzy of his coupling, and the water that surrounded them seemed to boil up in response. Tightening his grip on her shoulders, he grunted in sheer pleasure as his seed began pumping its way homeward.

Never before had Thomas Kraft given of himself so completely. Never before had he received so much in return. Drained and totally satisfied, with Telsa straddling him, her arms draped contentedly around his shoulders, Thomas looked out at the surrounding waters. Several hundred yards away, he could just make out the frothing line of white water that marked the lagoon's encircling reef. Beyond lay the dark void of the awaiting ocean, and just above the Pacific, rose a spectacle he would never forget. Like a returning sentinel, with a brilliant radiance all its own, a golden full moon was rising over the eastern horizon. The crater-scarred orb seemed close enough to reach out and touch.

Telsa was aware of Kraft's sudden preoccupation, and turned her head to see what was holding his attention. Upon setting her eyes on the reason for his distraction, a wise smile broke her lips.

"Ah, I see that the goddess has finally arrived. Are you satisfied with your first experience with the kava spirits, Thomas Kraft?"

Abruptly broken from his trance, the bearded American looked away from the lunar surface, focusing his full attention back to the woman he had just made love to. His response was soft and sincere.

"I'll tell you one thing that I'm certainly satisfied with."

He followed this remark with a full kiss upon her moist lips. Just as the hot flame of passion once more rose in his loins, Telsa's legs lost their hold on his hips. Standing on the seafloor before him, she took his hand and began leading him back toward the shoreline.

"The hour is getting late, my love," she explained as they made their way onto the beach. "All too soon it will be time for me to return to my duties in the village. Sit with me on the porch of your fales, and I'll share with you the legend of the goddess who brings us together this evening."

Thomas, who had felt weightless and fully vibrant while standing in the lagoon, found himself feeling unusually leaden as he crossed the narrow strip of sand. Climbing up the steps of the hut was an exhausting effort; he found himself completely drained of energy by the time he plopped onto the rattan lounger.

"Take it easy, my love," cautioned the Samoan, who sat by his feet. "Don't fight the kava. Instead, let yourself flow in its current."

The lieutenant listened to these words and gradually found himself relaxing. Lying on his back on the comfortable couch, his line of sight once again held on the rising moon as Telsa continued:

"Tonight, the goddess Pele walks the earth in judgement. It is on her behalf that this evening's kava is sacrificed. Though the beautiful goddess can be as calm and gentle as a nursing mother, she is also subject to fits of murderous rage. This anger is spawned during her annual visit to the earth's surface. Arriving

22

with the full moon, Pele searches humankind's hearts. If she finds the majority of mankind coexisting peacefully in a world of equality and charity, the earth will be spared. Pity the poor planet if she finds it otherwise!

"It is waste, greed, and envy which provokes her anger. The calamitous price Pele extracts from her subjects takes form as she stomps the ground, sending forth powerful earthquakes. She follows these tremors with waves of boiling lava, summoned from the underground. Many are the legends of the elders, which tell of actually seeing the goddess riding the currents of bubbling rock, screaming curses and hurling fiery boulders."

Thomas was fascinated with Telsa's story. With his weary eyes still locked on the moon, he summoned the strength for a single question.

"Can Pele's judgement be influenced before her wrath is needlessly provoked?"

Telsa bent forward and kissed him gently on his cheek. "That is the purpose of tonight's ceremony, Thomas Kraft. The elders shall draw the circle and beg the goddess to be merciful. We hope to appease her with gifts of sacred kava. It is time for me to go, my love. May your sleep be sound and your dreams be pleasant ones."

Another kiss followed, and then Telsa quietly entered the fales to collect her few belongings. His eyelids heavy, Thomas was sound asleep by the time the Samoan left the hut. She took one last fond look at her slumbering love, and proceeded toward the narrow trail that led back to Amanave.

The naval lieutenant was generally a light sleeper, yet this evening proved an exception. Caught in the grasp of a deep, dreamless slumber, he was oblivious to the sound of the crashing surf and the rising howl of the gusting trade wind. It proved to be the shrill ringing of an electronic buzzer that eventually woke him from his nap. Struggling to open his eyes, it took him several seconds to orient himself. Looking out over the railing of the hut, he noticed that the moon was no longer visible, having long ago risen in the heavens. It was with the realization of the hours that had passed while he slept that his mind cleared. His stomach tightened when he identified the persistent buzzing as emanating from inside the fales. Sitting up with a start, he momentarily swayed back dizzily. But the dizziness quickly passed and he stood up stark naked, and went inside.

He pulled the light cord, squinting as his eyes adjusted to the glare of the single, bare bulb. Then, after throwing on a pair of skivvies, he rushed to the digital monitor.

His first task was to disconnect the incessant warning tone. Next, he switched on the desktop computer, and, utilizing its keyboard, instructed the device to identify the cause of this disturbance. The monitor came alive with a long series of coded, telemetry coordinates. This was followed by data which confirmed his greatest concern. Somewhere, beneath the waters south of Tutuila, a series of massive earth tremors were occurring. The largest of three quakes measured 5.1 on the Richter scale.

To locate the exact epicenter, he began the complicated process of isolating each one of the one hundred and fifty seismic sensors they had recently implanted on the seabed. It took him over an hour to complete a preliminary scan. Since the devices were set down in a line roughly parallel to that of the north-south meander of the Tonga Trench, Kraft needed only to activate every fifth sensor to determine the area where the quake was most active.

It proved to be the northernmost sensors that showed

the majority of the activity. This meant that the focus, or subterranean point of origin of the disturbance, was approximately three hundred miles to the south of Tutuila and some fifty miles to the east of the Vavau Seamount. Thomas instructed the computer to draw up an intricate relief map of that particular area of the Tonga Trench. The rendering showed it to be a particularly rugged sector, characterized by a wall of steep, underground mountains, many over thirty thousand feet tall. Several of these seamounts appeared to offer the perfect site for the navy to have chosen to place the rumored submarine refitting pen.

Although a reading of 5.1 on the Richter scale indicated a strong tremor, Thomas knew it was far from a major one. The disastrous San Francisco quake of 1906 had measured 7.8, while the great Alaska shake of 1964 had scored a whopping 8.4. To determine the exact nature of the disturbance, Thomas needed additional information. Was it caused by a mere rubbing of the two, massive crustal plates that met here, or did this point to a phenomenon of an entirely different nature? The answer to the question centered around the existence of accompanying harmonic earth tremors. If this condition was present, Thomas could be certain that the quake was being accompanied by tons of molten magma released from deep within the earth's mantle. And when this liquid rock poured through the earth's crust at the spot of least resistance, one of nature's most awesome events would take place—the birth of a volcano.

No seamount could protect man from a volcanic eruption if it took place anywhere in the near vicinity. Responsible for hundreds of thousands of human casualties, a volcano was one of man's mightiest adversaries. Only today was its workings beginning to be understood.

Kraft had been one of the fortunate geophysicists at Mount St. Helens during the weeks that preceded the mountain's major eruption. The spring of 1980 had been an important one for the young science of volcanology. At that time, much theory became proven fact as forecasters successfully warned of an imminent explosion. One of the devices responsible for this knowledge were specially designed seismic sensors, created to trace the vibrations caused by rising magma. The detection by the sensors of harmonic tremors proved that an eruption was almost certain.

Over two dozen of these expensive instruments were scattered over the floor of the Tonga Trench. These sensitive scanners operated on a different power source and relay frequency than the normal seismic sensors. This meant that a special portable system had to be designed to individually activate them. Unfortunately, the range of this remote control device was limited. To determine if harmonic tremors were present, and that a volcanic eruption was inevitable, Thomas would have to sail into the region to trigger the sensors and make a proper evaluation.

As luck would have it, the research vessel responsible for conveying him into these waters was presently in dry dock at Auckland, New Zealand having a propellor shaft straightened.

Hastily, Thomas reviewed the evening's unusual seismic activity. Years of scientific training had instilled in him the discipline to carefully interpret all the facts, and to be hesitant in becoming an alarmist.

After counting over three dozen tremors measuring 4.5 or below in the last six-hour period, his instincts cautioned him that something out of the ordinary was taking place. The conditions were similar to those that had preceded the explosion of Mount St. Helens on May 18, 1980. Yet, he knew he couldn't sound a full-fledged alert, at least not until he had a chance to activate and study the data that the special harmonic sensors would provide.

Cursing the misfortune of having his boat out of commission, Thomas made his way to the porch. As he looked out to the sea, and then set his eyes on the crystal-clear full moon soaring high overhead, a flood of recently experienced memories filled his consciousness. Was it really only a few hours ago that Telsa had shared the dusk with him? It felt like it had occurred a lifetime ago! How different his contemplations had been. Telsa's telling of the story of the goddess Pele had been delivered with true conviction. He wondered what her reaction would be if he explained that a real volcano was very possibly forming on the seafloor to the south of Tutuila, at this very moment. Would she attribute this to the goddess's magic.

Kraft had seen Mount St. Helens explode firsthand, and was aware of a volcano's potential danger. In fact, a colleague had been one of the eruption's first victims. Recalling the sheer magnitude of the damage inflicted that day, the naval officer decided it would be best to follow his hunch, and give Pacific Fleet Command in Pearl Harbor a call. Though he couldn't prove his suspicions, at least he could share them with his superiors. When dealing with an unknown factor such as a volcano, it was better to be safe than sorry — it was one lesson he had learned well in Washington in the spring of 1980.

Chapter Two

One hundred and forty nautical miles due north of the island of Tutuila, the Ohio Class submarine USS *Phoenix* cruised deep below the water's surface. Over five hundred and sixty feet from its blunt bow to the conical, tipped stern, the massive, 18,700-ton vessel was headed southward, on a patrol route that neatly cut through the South Pacific basin. Specifically designed to carry the Trident ballistic missile, the sub carried twenty-four of these highly sophisticated weapons, whose range allowed them to be targeted on coordinates 4,000 miles distant.

Seven days out of its home port of Bangor, Washington, the *Phoenix* would remain at sea for two and a half months. During this time, it would be responsible for enforcing the most survivable arm of America's defensive triad. Commanding its complement of one hundred and fifty-seven officers and seamen was Captain Charles Blake.

An Annapolis graduate, Blake had been in the navy for twenty-three years. The majority of this time had been spent aboard submarines of the attack and missile-carrying varieties. The slender, six-foot, two-inch, blond-haired officer was well liked by his men, who respected his quiet, reserved demeanor. This low profile masked a hard working, highly efficient administrator, who demanded a one-hundred-percent effort from his subordinates.

Having just completed an eight-hour duty segment, the captain found himself looking forward to the cramped confines of his private quarters. It was shortly after midnight when he transferred the helm to Pete Walsh, his executive officer, and made his way below.

Veiled in a twenty-four-hour mask of perpetual darkness, the *Phoenix* produced an artificial environment all its own. Blinded to the rotation of the sun, moon, and stars above, it was up to each individual submariner to establish a daily routine. After more than two decades of service beneath the seas, Charles Blake rarely found himself disoriented by the disappearance of day and night. He had learned to accept it, just as he accepted the fact that he had spent half of his adult life in such a Stygian netherworld.

He had resolved earlier that before hitting the sack, he would complete the letter to his wife, Susan. Although it was doubtful he would be able to mail it in the foreseeable future, at least he could record the inner thoughts that had haunted him so this past week.

The month leave just completed had made it obvious that their twelve-year relationship was in serious trouble. Cold and distant, Susan had treated him like a virtual stranger. Aware of the subtle changes in his wife's personality these past few months, Charles had attributed them at last to her plunge into middle age. Yet, as her depression deepened, it was apparent that the cause was more complicated.

Still a spotless housekeeper and a dutiful mother, Susan's inner anger seemed to be directed solely toward him. Ignoring his presence as if he didn't exist, she went about her daily chores in a world of her own. When they did talk, she complained that he had

29

become to narrow-minded and stubborn-hearted.

To take his place, she had focused her entire life on their children. Mark, ten years old, and Cindy, seven, certainly weren't hurt by the additional attention. Instead, they seemed to thrive on it. Charles was the one who was being driven from the family. And any attempts on his part to plan outings to include them all had met with one or another of Susan's endless excuses.

Less than two years ago, they had been the tightest of families. His returns from the sea were met with joy and celebration. Camping and fishing trips were much anticipated and enjoyed by all, and made up for the hundreds of hours Charles was absent from the family circle. Recently, though, when he had suggested a trip into the Cascades, Susan mumbled something about it being too dangerous, and had recommended that if he wanted to go, he should do so with one of his buddies.

This same coldness was apparent in their sexual relationship. She had long since stopped acting like she enjoyed him. Laying back expressionless, she seemed to merely tolerate his touch. This lack of response in itself was enough to turn him off completely.

Although he preferred to keep his personal problems to himself, the responsibility of his command demanded that he have biannual psychological checkups. It had been during his last session, two weeks ago, that his domestic problems had come out into the open. The navy analyst hadn't seemed shocked by Susan's symptoms. Apparently, such a withdrawal was extremely common among the wives of sailors on frequent, extended assignments. To alleviate these natural feelings of alienation, the doctor had recommended that she attend one of his weekly group-therapy sessions held at the base. Hearing the anxieties of other navy wives would help make Susan aware that her problems weren't that unusual.

But as he'd expected, Susan had immediately balked when he mentioned the "shrink's" recommendation. She hinted that perhaps their frequent separations weren't the source of their problem. Had they fallen out of love? If this was the case, it certainly wasn't by his choice. Susan had been the only woman he had ever known or needed. No, his long tours of isolated duty had to be the reason for the marriage's deterioration. To set the record straight, he had made a drastic decision. He would relate this to her in the letter he would now write.

Seating himself at his small, wall-mounted desk, he readied his pen and paper. But just how did one go about explaining in a few pages that he had failed as a husband? Charles decided it would be best to not dwell on his past mistakes, but instead, to concentrate on expressing the sincerity of his feelings, and how he planned to address the problem. His course of action would be simple and straight to the point.

This would be his last cruise for the navy. At the end of this assignment, he would hand in his letter of resignation, and then seek employment in the private sector. Only with such a drastic move could he be assured of his family's survival.

While concentrating on the words he would employ to best express this plan, his eyes strayed to the framed photograph that hung on the wall before him. The colored snapshot had been taken last summer. It showed his family, seated in their backyard around a redwood picnic table. Freckled, red-haired Mark looked devilish in his soiled baseball uniform, while pony-tailed Cindy sat posing proudly in her "cabbage-patch" jumpsuit. Beside her, Susan faced the lens, her expression etched with bored indifference.

This year would mark their eleventh wedding anniversary. Married at the ripe old age of thirty-four years, Charles knew little else about life but his family and his naval career. After graduation from Annapolis, he had gone immediately to submarine school in New London, Connecticut. His first assignment had been as the junior sonar officer aboard a nuclear-powered, Skipjack Class attack sub. As the first underwater vessel to incorporate a teardrop hull design, these boats were capable of submerged speeds of well over thirty knots, a heretofore unattainable velocity. It was aboard a Sturgeon Class sub that he had seen action off the coast of Viet Nam. This traumatic experience prepared him for his first command position on a Lafayette Class strategic-missile submarine. Armed with sixteen Polaris A-3 nuclear-tipped missiles, such boats were the predecessors of the larger, more sophisticated Ohio Class subs, such as the one he presently commanded.

Fondly remembering each of these assignments, as one does a long-lost friend, Blake found his thoughts slipping rapidly into the past. It proved to be the soft electronic beeping tone of his room's comm line that redirected his attention. He picked up the telephone handset on the third ring.

"Captain, here."

The deep, familiar voice of his executive officer answered him. "Skipper, I thought you'd be interested in the Austere ELF page that we just received."

"Go ahead, Pete."

The XO cleared his voice. "We've been instructed to head with all due haste to a surface rendezvous point eighty-five nautical miles due north of the Manua Islands in Samoa."

"Are you sure that those orders indicated surface rendezvous coordinates?"

"The page was repeated three times, Skipper. We copied each transmission loud and clear."

"It's mighty unusual to draw us needlessly up out of the water like that," Blake replied, genuinely puzzled. "What's our E.T.A. to the rendezvous point at top speed?"

"We should reach it by 0700 hours. I've already instructed navigation to draw up our most efficient course and speed."

"Very good, Pete. Clear our baffles, and then get underway. I'll join you in the command center. I couldn't sleep, anyway."

"Aye, aye, Skipper."

Hanging up the receiver, Charles found his thoughts focused on the strange message that the *Phoenix* had just received. The Austere ELF communications system was a relatively new device, to be utilized in emergency situations only. The extremely low frequency transmission had originated in the state of Michigan, where a fifty-eight-mile-long antenna, hung above the ground like a telephone wire, was situated. Able to send limited, coded messages, such a system allowed the *Phoenix* to receive orders while cruising deep below the ocean's surface, with only its antenna trailing in the water.

It was the ultimate destination of these orders that disturbed the captain the most. Only rarely were missile-carrying subs called to the surface. Such vessels relied upon the cover of the ocean's depths to veil them from the ever-probing eyes of the enemy. A situation of extreme delicacy must have occurred to warrant such a risky move.

It was while standing, to begin his way upstairs to the command center, that Charles became conscious of the blank piece of stationery that lay on his desk. Though his intentions had been sincere, his present duty was once again calling him away from completing the letter he knew he would have to face eventually.

Like a prisoner on death row who had just received a temporary stay of execution, he could postpone expressing his commitment, to leave the navy after this cruise, to another day. Once this promise to Susan was on paper, he knew he would be bound by it. Taking a last look at the family photograph on the wall beside his desk, Charles found himself with no time to question the direction of his difficult decision. At the moment, there was a responsibility of an entirely different nature to concentrate on.

Two floors above the section of the USS *Phoenix* that housed the crew's living quarters was the sub's command and control center. Located directly beneath and forward of the boat's twenty-five-foot-tall sail, this equipment-packed compartment was the heart of the vessel. Dozens of manned digital consoles directed the sub's sonar, fire control, propulsion, and navigational capabilities. Bisecting this mass of brightly lit dials and monitors were a set of periscope tubes.

The command center was alive with the muted, chattering of the targeting and navigation computers when Lieutenant Commander Pete Walsh entered from the adjoining radio room. The muscular, solidly built six-footer took up a position behind the three crewmen responsible for manning the boat's sonar console. Each of the sailors wore a set of sensitive headphones, and were fully absorbed in the bright monitor screens before them.

Lieutenant Junior Grade Anthony Canova was the sonar officer responsible for this current shift. Seated at the center console, the bald-headed, pot-bellied New Yorker was in the process of switching the frequency selector to concentrate on the patch of ocean directly behind the *Phoenix*, when the exec tapped him on the shoulder.

"What have you got, Tony?"

Turning down his volume feed, Canova shook his head solemnly. "I'm afraid our uninvited guest is still with us, sir. Our climb through the thermocline seemed to fool them for a couple of minutes. Unfortunately, they just came up to one hundred and seventy-five feet, and are presently right on our tail."

"Have you got a definite sound I.D. on them yet?"

"When they changed depth, we were able to pick up a decent screw signature. It's the Alfa, all right. That damn Russkie has followed us all the way from Juan de Fuca."

"Well, I've got a feeling we're going to have this sea all to ourselves soon." Patting the sonar officer on the back, the XO added, "Hang in there, Lieutenant, and call out the moment we give our Soviet comrades the slip."

"Will do, sir," Canova said as he reached forward to turn up the volume on his console.

Behind him, Pete Walsh was making his way around a massive wall of humming computers to the control console responsible for diving operations. The tense expression etched on his face eased as he saw the tall, blond-haired, lanky figure of Charles Blake emerge from an opposite hatchway. Meeting the captain with a relieved salute, Walsh briefed him regarding their present situation. His superior reacted to this sharing of information just as he had expected.

"If we're going to make our rendezvous this morning, Pete, we'd better do something on the double about losing that Alfa. Sure wouldn't want to surface with a Soviet attack sub on our tail. How about putting a knuckle in the water, and saying good-bye to our Russian friends once and for all?"

"I'd say that's just what the doctor ordered, Skipper.

Will you take the helm?"

"You can do the honors, Pete. Let's just get moving. We've still got some traveling to do if we're going to reach that rendezvous point by 0700 hours."

Buoyed by the captain's confidence in him to carry out the difficult escape maneuver, Walsh seated himself behind the three diving operators. With his hands firmly gripping the steel rail separating him from the crewmen, the exec barked out his orders.

"Mr. Peterson, sound general quarters. Helmsman, prepare us for a tight spiral dive. Level out at seven-five-zero feet and begin a course change of one-two-zero degrees, followed by a run at full power."

As the helmsman repeated the instructions, the compartment filled with the harsh, persistent beeping tone that sent the crew scurrying to their action stations. Seconds later, the *Phoenix* was sealed, buttoned down, and ready for combat.

"Planes down, dive!" cried the XO who watched as the helmsman pushed forward on the steering yoke.

The results were instantaneous. As each of the sixteen-foot-long, twelve-foot-wide diving planes set into each side of the sail bit into the surrounding water, the sub's nose angled sharply downward.

Seated in his command chair, directly behind the executive officer, Charles Blake felt the gathering g-forces as the boat shifted sharply to the starboard. Shoved forward and to the right, the captain hung tightly onto the section of railing that surrounded him. One eye on the crew and the other on the damage control board, Blake felt the *Phoenix* shudder as the boat rolled on its side.

Charles visualized the tight, corkscrew route the massive vessel was taking. Because such a maneuver would leave a vortex of swirling water in their wake, the Alfa's sonar would be practically useless. Such was the captain's hope, when a loud, piercing electronic tone sounded throughout the command center.

"We show a minor seal failure in the forward torpedo room!" warned the damage control officer.

"Contact Chief Crowley and have him size up the situation," ordered the captain. "Pete, what's our depth?"

"We just passed the five-hundred-foot mark, Skipper," the exec answered. "Shall I abort the dive?"

A few anxious seconds of strained silence followed, punctuated only by the persistent ringing of the damage control indicator, and the far-away humming of the boat's single propellor shaft.

"Cut off that infernal warning tone!" Blake shouted impatiently.

When the irritating ring abruptly halted, the captain continued more calmly. "We've committed to this depth; let's follow on through with our original plan, at least until we hear from Crowley. Any word from the chief yet?"

The damage control officer, who had been speaking into his headphone-mounted transmitter, answered with a breath of relief. "Mr. Crowley's initial inspection shows an O-ring failure on the inner seal of the number two tube. Water leakage has so far been minimum.

With this report, Blake caught his exec's concerned stare as the sub again canted hard to starboard.

"We're approaching six hundred feet," Pete Walsh observed dryly.

Suddenly aware of the fact that he had been gripping the support rail with more than enough pressure to counter the pull of gravity created by the dive, Blake loosened his grasp and wiped off the band of sweat that had gathered on his forehead. It was then he became cognizant of the distant sound of straining carbon steel. Charles knew that this was caused by the great pressures of this depth as the seawater compressed itself around the *Phoenix's* one hundred and thirty-nine internally reinforced, welded hull cylinders. Although their operational diving limit was considerably greater than the depth they hoped to attain, this was a portion of the ocean that demanded respect. Knowing full well the great risks involved, Blake's heart quickened as his XO reported passing the seven-hundred-foot mark.

"Prepare to level out at seven-five-zero," Walsh added expectantly. "Break from spiral on preprogrammed course change at full throttle."

The last few feet seemed to take an eternity. Then the diving officer's excited voice broke the tense atmosphere. "Pulling back on planes. Neutral bubble in two-five seconds."

"Reactor room is standing by for full power, sir," added the engineering officer.

Again, Charles Blake caught his exec's glance. This was followed by a simultaneous movement of their heads as both men looked down to their watches.

"Ten seconds to neutral bubble," advised the diving officer.

An electronic buzzer sounded, and Pete Walsh sat forward, fully alert. The orders that next flowed from his lips were given with pure satisfaction.

"Full throttle, engineering. Let's get the hell out of here!"

Propelled by more than 60,000 shaft horsepower, the *Phoenix* surged forward with an incredible burst of speed. Minutes later, the sub was doing over thirty knots and still picking up speed. Satisfied with the boat's performance, and his exec's handling of the maneuver just accomplished, Charles Blake stood and joined the lieutenant commander beside the diving console.

"Good job, Pete. Do you think our little knuckle did the trick?"

Walsh answered carefully. "That depends on how sharp that Soviet skipper is. Let's check with Canova."

Both officers made their way to the sonar control panel. There, the three crewmen responsible for monitoring the operation of the BQQ-6 system were busy manipulating their frequency selectors. It proved to be the hefty individual occupying the center position who finally turned around with a satisfied grin.

"That dive was a beauty, Skipper. We left more noise behind us than Times Square New Year's Eve. Those Russkies aren't anywhere in the neighborhood. I guarantee you they'll be chasing their own tail for at least the rest of the night."

"Well, I hope your observations are correct, Lieutenant," returned the captain. "Do this paranoid old man a favor, and remain on alert for the rest of your shift. Let me know immediately of any suspicious sensor readings. It is most important for us to have the ocean all to ourselves for the next couple of hours."

"Will do, Captain," the bald-headed sonar operator said with a wink. "You can be assured that Tony Canova and company won't let you down. Don't you worry."

As the lieutenant returned to the sonar panel, Blake turned to his exec. "So far, so good. We'd better get over to navigation and pull all the charts corresponding to that rendezvous point. Before we go poking our heads out of the water, I want to know just what the seafloor looks like beneath us."

"Any ideas, Skipper, what's waiting for us there?"

Blake shook his head. "You know the navy, Pete. Lord knows what they've got in store for us. Six more hours and we should have a better idea. Meanwhile, let's pull those maps and then I'd better grab some shut-eye. I've got a suspicious feeling in my gut that we're not going to have much time to rest these next few days."

Following the XO's lead, Charles Blake turned to begin his way to the chart room. He was barely conscious of the sub's forward movement as the USS *Phoenix* broke the forty-knot threshold, moving ever southward, seven hundred and fifty feet beneath the South Pacific.

Captain First Rank Victor Kalinin couldn't believe his rotten luck. For the past week he had followed his orders perfectly, trailing the American Trident submarine all the way from its home port in the state of Washington. For over four thousand miles, he had kept the pride of the U.S. Navy practically in his torpedo sights, only to lose it with some sort of trick maneuver. And the loss of contact had come at the worst time imaginable. With Operation Lenin scheduled to begin in barely eight hours, he knew the task he now faced was a formidable one.

As commander of the Alfa Class, nuclear attack sub *Magadan*, he was well aware that the responsibility for relocating the American vessel rested solely on his shoulders. Yet, he couldn't help but be enraged with his senior lieutenant's complete incompetency. Why hadn't the fool awakened him when the Yankees initiated their sudden crash dive? As it turned out, by the time he arrived on the bridge, the trail was long cold.

Now, with their sonar inexplicably useless, tracking down the Ohio Class vessel would be an almost impossible task. One advantage they still held was the Alfa's excellent speed. Kalinin was utilizing this quality to its maximum, having just implemented a comprehensive zigzag search pattern at full power.

Nervously pacing the narrow corridor that split the cluttered control room in half, the captain failed to notice the arrival of a visitor from the sealed hatchway behind him. Immaculately groomed and uniformed, the *Magadan*'s zampolit, Sergei Vengerovo, entered and approached Kalinin. Oblivious to the salutes of the various seamen manning the control room's consoles, the political officer confronted the captain as he reached the corridor's end.

"Comrade Captain, I understand your concern regarding the loss of the Americans, but is this a logical reason to so needlessly threaten the safety of all those aboard the *Magadan*?"

Victor Kalinin, who was no great fan of the zampolit in the first place, retorted angrily. "Whatever are you babbling about, Vengerovo? Have you already forgotten who is in command here?"

The political officer sensed the captain's mood, and diplomatically softened the tone of his response. "I am not questioning your ability to run this vessel, Comrade. I only desire to know why you're so insistent at running at top speed. Surely you've read the safety reports."

Kalinin, his face reddening, could hardly believe what he was hearing. "So now you've added nuclear engineering to your ever-broadening list of expertise. Comrade Vengerovo, I promise never to question your knowledge of political matters, as long as you allow me to run my boat as I see fit."

"Easy now, Captain. I was only issuing an innocent inquiry. Run this vessel as you see fit. Who am I to tell you otherwise? May I ask, though, why Senior Lieutenant Gribovka has been placed in detention? The men are most curious."

Kalinin scowled, hesitant at first to answer. "The imbecile failed in his duty. I can not afford to have such

41

a man in a position of command. Next time, his misjudgment could be instantly fatal to us all."

Vengerovo smoothed down his shiny blond hair and shook his head compassionately. "Surely his failure to immediately awaken you was an innocent mistake. What could you have done, anyway? The Americans dropped from sight so suddenly that even our sonar was useless."

The captain squeezed his pained temples. "I must remind you that there is no such thing as an innocent mistake aboard an attack submarine, Comrade Zampolit. Each second that we fail to react can take us farther away from our elusive quarry. I have witnessed such a maneuver on the part of an American sub once before. I believe they call such a move "putting a knuckle in the water." At the first hint of such a maneuver, we should have crash dove ourselves. Only by staying parallel with them, could our sonar have remained effective. Now, who knows what direction they've sped off in?"

Once more aware of the enormity of the task that faced him, Victor Kalinin resumed his nervous pacing. Following at his side, was the slightly smaller figure of the political officer.

"I didn't realize that it was possible to counter such a maneuver," Vengerovo offered humbly. "And what will become of us if we don't locate the Americans by the time Operation Lenin begins?"

The captain didn't hesitate. "For all of you, life will merely go on as usual. But for me, I'll be lucky to secure duty aboard a tugboat on Lake Baikal. Admiral Kostromo is all but deaf to excuses. What he demands are results!"

"But this is only an exercise," justified the Zampolit. "Surely the admiral will understand the circumstances, if we don't stumble onto the Yankees soon."

Captain Kalinin didn't even bother to respond to this remark. Instead, he walked silently over to the navigator. Looking over the chief petty officer's shoulder, Victor studied the computer-enhanced, three-dimensional map of the section of the South Pacific they were currently sailing through. Having just passed Swains Island, they were presently entering the sector known as American Samoa. At this point, the Trident sub could have sneaked off in a variety of directions. By initiating an easterly heading, they could be on their way toward the myriad of sheltering islands belonging to the Polynesian chain, while a turn to the west would take them into the Melanesian Islands. The maneuver could also have been a masking tactic to cover a turn back northward, to Hawaii. Or had they sailed southward, toward New Zealand, to take advantage of the deep waters of the Tonga Trench?

Since the vessel he was tracking was a missile-carrying boat, Victor doubted the Yankees would position themselves any further from the Asian landmass than was necessary. In the event of a missile launch, it would be most advantageous for their Tridents to have as short a journey as possible, to guarantee the survival of the warheads. Thus, he doubted their course would take them any further eastward. Instead, he found the Mindanao and Mariana trenches, located west of Melanesia, a much more attractive patrol station.

With his eyes glued to the lucite map, Kalinin attempted to second guess the route the American captain would choose to penetrate these waters. Following their present position southward, it was most apparent that the Tonga Trench would offer a convenient deep-water corridor into more open waters. A turn to the northwest would allow them to penetrate the South Fiji Basin, cross the Coral Sea, and, skirting

New Guinea, lead them directly into the deep, quiet trenches bordering the Philippines. Though it was all speculation, he gambled that this was the American's plan. If lady fortune was with them, Victor knew there was still a chance to tag the Trident before Operation Lenin was scheduled to begin.

Turning to inform the helmsman of this new course, the captain traded glances with the *Magadan*'s political officer. Victor knew this was a dangerous individual to alienate, yet he wasn't about to put on an act just for his benefit. Breaking eye contact, Kalinin emptied his mind of any such needless worry. At the moment, he had only one concern: to find the Trident sub before 0800 hours.

From the other side of the cramped control room, Sergei Vengerovo looked on as the captain proceeded to confer with the helmsman. It was obvious from the anxious look in Kalinin's eyes that the man was under incredible pressure. The next few hours would show what the line officer was really made of.

As political officer, it was Sergei's duty not only to direct all ideological indoctrination, but also to monitor the political reliability of the officers and men. The captain's disinterest in Party affairs had already been noted. Yet, until this present crisis, his skills as a sailor couldn't be questioned. Now, an entirely new dimension of the captain's personality had been revealed.

Sergei had been on the bridge when the captain arrived earlier and was informed of the American's disappearance. Never before had he seen a man so enraged. Though it was probably true that the senior lieutenant had made a mistake in judgment by not calling for Kalinin sooner, this was no reason to castigate the young officer before the rest of the men and then send him off to be confined to his quarters. When the captain ordered an immediate search pattern to be initiated, propelled under full power, the zampolit, backed by a majority of the others, had seriously questioned the wisdom of such a move. Though known as the fastest underwater vessels in the Soviet Navy, with speeds over forty knots, the Alfa Class subs were notorious for reactor malfunctions after such runs. This fact, coupled with the knowledge of the radioactive core's improper shielding — an effort to save weight — genuinely upset the crew. A desperate captain was not the least bit conducive for a crew's morale, and it was in this area that the political officer was directly responsible.

Sergei understood that Kalinin had been under strict orders to have the Trident in sight when the operation began. Yet, mistakes happened. Wasn't this what naval exercises were all about?

For the rest of their voyage, Vengerovo knew he would have to continue to watch the captain closely, taking care not to needlessly antagonize him. His superiors would be most interested in these observations. An unstable line officer could have disastrous implications for them all. When the imperialists finally gathered their nerve to attack, the Soviet Union could only afford to have their best men serving on the front lines. Here, beneath the world's oceans, the true conflict would take place. In such a liquid battlefield, the fate of the entire planet could rest with a single vessel such as the *Magadan*, whose purpose was to track down and destroy the enemy's floating missile pads before they launched their loads of death and destruction.

Chapter Three

For Thomas Kraft, this had been a most memorable dawn. When he first left the shelter of his fales, barely an hour ago, the sky had been pitch black, with only an inkling of bluish-gray light painting the eastern horizon. From his present vantage point six thousand feet above the Pacific, the entire horizon was now filled with a golden radiance as the newly arrived sun inched its way upward. To the muffled chopping clatter of the Sikorsky SH-60B Seahawk's rotor blades, the geophysicist contemplated the strange sequence of events that had brought him here.

It had all started with last night's call to Commander Walker back in Pearl Harbor. As chief liaison officer with the Office of Naval Research, Walker was the individual Thomas was directly responsible to. When informed of the unusual earthquake activity taking place on the seafloor, approximately three hundred miles south of Tutuila, the commander had given Kraft his full attention. He seemed to be especially interested in the fact that the focus of these quakes had been traced to the northern sector of their sensor grid, some fifty miles to the east of the Vavau Seamount. Thomas had next expressed his desire to be allowed to travel down to this area, to trigger the remote-controlled sensors that would indicate the presence of harmonic tremors, and thus signal the eventuality of a possible volcanic eruption.

Promising to call him back shortly, Walker had

explained that he would have to notify Admiral Burnhardt, Commander-in-Chief of the entire Pacific Fleet. The next hour had been one of the longest of Kraft's life. While waiting expectantly for his phone to ring, Thomas returned to his data, to make extra certain that his analysis was a correct one. Walker's desire to immediately inform the admiral of the tremors certainly confirmed his suspicions of the importance of his assignment. Somewhere in the vicinity of the Vavau Seamount, a top-secret naval installation was being threatened.

When his phone again rang, Thomas had found his orders puzzling. He was merely instructed to pack his instruments in a seabag, along with enough personal gear to see him through the rest of the month. After explaining that the surface vessel assigned to his station was off in Auckland being repaired, Kraft had received a veiled response. The navy would see to his transfer southward. All he had to do was sit back and go along for the ride. Once he arrived in the active sector, he was to activate the remote-control device, assess the situation, and get back to Walker immediately. Without any additional information, the commander had wished him good luck, and their conversation was ended.

Barely conscious of the late hour, Kraft had gone about the task of assembling the gear he would need for the job. With the assistance of a large pot of strong black coffee, he worked diligently through the early morning hours normally reserved for sleeping. He had just finished packing his personal effects when a distant, chopping sound signaled the arrival of his transportation.

The white Navy Seahawk had angled in over Cape Taputapu and landed in the small sandy clearing between his hut and the lagoon. With its two, 1,690-

horsepower, General Electric turboshaft engines still grinding away, the fuselage hatch had popped open to discharge a jumpsuited figure. Greeting Thomas, who still stood on his fales's porch, was the chopper's ATO, or air-tactical-control officer. Using a minimum of words, he had introduced himself, asked Kraft which gear he desired to take aboard, and beckoned the young lieutenant to follow him. Minutes later, they were airborne.

Inside, the vehicle was packed with a variety of sophisticated digital equipment. After stowing his duffel bag, the ATO had introduced him to the pilot and the sensor operator. Looking out the wide front window, Thomas studied the predawn sky, and noticing the endless expanse of water below, realized that they were heading northward.

Aware that the voluntarily tight-lipped aviators weren't about to divulge their destination, he gathered the courage to ask just where they were bound to. Surprised to learn that Kraft had no knowledge of their destination, the ATO explained that they were off to a rendezvous point of 13.50 degrees south latitude, and 170.42 degrees west longitude. This corresponded to a spot in the open ocean, some eighty-five miles due north of Tutuila's sister island, Manua. He was informed that here they would hopefully link up with Kraft's next means of transport, the Trident missile-carrying sub, USS *Phoenix*.

Astounded by this revelation, Thomas found it hard to accept the validity of this disclosure. Making his way back into the chopper's interior cabin, he sat down and tried to make some kind of sense out of just what was happening here. He knew that his mission was more important than he had previously realized, yet just how significant it really was had finally hit home. For the navy to risk one of its Trident subs, it was evident that the nation's security was somehow on the line. Exactly what were they so concerned with, situated under the waters, three hundred miles to the south? It was while he was in the midst of this contemplation that the ATO emerged from the cockpit and sat down on the bench beside him.

"Ever been inside of a boomer before, Lieutenant?" queried the tactical officer, his powerful voice rising over the noise of the swirling rotors.

"A what?" returned Thomas, not sure what the aviator was talking about.

"Boomer is navy slang for a missile-launching submarine," retorted the ATO.

Kraft shook his head.

"Well, then, you're in for a special treat. I got to tour the USS *Ohio* the day she first arrived in Bangor. That sucker is awesome! You certainly must be one very special VIP."

Thomas couldn't help but smile with this observation.

"How long have you been stationed in Tutuila?" continued the aviator.

Kraft had to practically scream to be heard. "Six months, now."

"Well, you certainly look the island type," observed the ATO.

Suddenly conscious of his full, bushy brown beard and longer-than-regulation haircut, Thomas shifted uneasily. The ATO sensed this discomfort and replied accordingly.

"It's cool, Lieutenant. Samoa isn't exactly the Pentagon. Our chopper just got placed on Manua, and I can't wait to go native. Seems we're going to be one of the first ASW Seahawks permanently linked to a ground station. Sure beats the hell out of trying to land one of these babies on the rolling deck of a frigate in a

49

sea state of five. We don't have much further to go, so just relax. I'd better get on the job and see if we got any unwelcome visitors prowling down below."

Standing, the jumpsuited officer walked over to a bank of sensors, donned a set of headphones, and began scanning various frequency channels. For several minutes, Thomas watched the ATO at work, then found his gaze drawn to the portion of the dawn sky visible through the cabin's single window. Aglow in bright bands of blue, violet, and an ever-rising gold, the eastern horizon shone, awash with color. Captivated by this spectacle, Thomas allowed his thoughts to wander. Spellbound by the sight of the sun as it broke from the far-off sea, a single vision flooded his weary consciousness. Beckoning him to follow her into the sea was his beloved Telsa.

Was it really only a few hours ago that they had made love in the lagoon before his fales? Revisualizing that blissful joining, as if it had taken place only seconds before, Thomas felt a surge of sexual longing stiffen in his loins. And what of the kava cult, that she had at long last initiated him into? Was this potion really responsible for the magical moments that had followed? Smacking his lips, as if he could taste the milklike, peppery substance as it passed into his mouth, Thomas Kraft slipped off into a sound, dreamless sleep.

After what seemed to be an eternity's passing, the lieutenant awoke to the sound of a piercing electronic tone that rose above the constant chopping of the rotors. Quickly reorienting himself, he caught sight of the ATO and the sensor operator as they worked in front of a large, digital transmitter. It was from this console that the alien noise was emanating. Standing to join them, Kraft stretched and yawned fully.

"Welcome back to the land of the living," greeted the

ATO. "You've been out a good twenty-five minutes. We're just warming up the ELF transmitter, in preparation to let the *Phoenix* know that we're here. Are you ready to get your feet wet?"

Kraft smiled at this last statement, which he took as an obvious figure of speech. Taking a second to think it over, he asked a basic question which had slipped his mind before.

"Speaking of the devil, how are you going to go about transferring me down to the sub? I didn't think that the Seahawk had amphibious qualities."

Grinning from ear to ear, the ATO answered, "We don't. Ever use a case-vac sling before?"

Having only seen such a device in use during basic training, Kraft's stomach turned.

The tactical officer seemed to be enjoying his role. "Easy does it, Lieutenant. It's not as bad as it looks. We'll set you down on the *Phoenix* as gently as a mother robin sits on top of her newborn chicks. You've got nothing to fear."

Just as Thomas was about to respond, the Seahawk's intercom chattered. Above a line of crackling static rose the contained voice of the pilot.

"We're approaching the rendezvous sector, gentlemen. Deploy the antenna and activate the ELF transmitter. I'm certain that Lieutenant Kraft is anxious to complete the transfer, so let's get snapping!"

Accepting a wink from the ATO, Thomas watched him begin unreeling the handle of a circular, metallic canister placed at the cabin's rear. As he finished this procedure, the sensor operator started to slowly increase the transmitter's volume gain. Meanwhile, the geophysicist noticed that the helicopter was now flying in a tight, circular bank.

"Why fly in a circle?" he questioned.

"Because it's the most efficient way to contact a

51

submerged sub," answered the sensor operator. "By trailing our antenna behind us, our signal will be able to penetrate the first hundred or so feet of seawater. Flying in a bank will keep the wire pointed downward. The more powerful TACAMO EC-130s utilize a similar system to contact submarines thousands of miles distant."

"Let's just hope that the *Phoenix* is able to make the party," added the ATO. "Calling in a boomer on such short notice isn't such an easy trick in itself."

As the two men continued working on the transmitter, Thomas cautiously walked over to the fuselage window. Holding back his weight, he looked down to that portion of the sea that they were currently circling. Only several thousand feet distant, the water surged a deep sea-green, topped by an occasional foaming whitecap. It didn't take him long to spot the first fin. The triangular, slate-gray patch cut neatly through the ocean, several inches above the water's surface. Focusing his gaze, to try to identify the body of the creature to which it belonged, Thomas soon caught sight of several dozen similarly shaped dorsal spikes. With a jolt of awareness, he knew that the fins belonged to a pack of marauding sharks.

With spellbound eyes, he watched the swift, sleek creatures in the midst of their never-ending hunt. As the helicopter banked to the east and blocked the direct sunlight with its fuselage, Kraft was able to make out the shadowy body of one of the huge predators. From his vantage point, it appeared well over seven feet in length. Chilled with this observation, the geophysicist found his thoughts returning to a time ten years distant, when he had viewed a very similar sight.

Just out of college, with the ink of his Bachelor of

Science degree still wet on its parchment, Thomas was preparing to join his parents for a month in the Florida Keys. Because of a Naval ROTC commitment, this would be his last free couple of weeks as a civilian. Prepared to make the most of this time, he anxiously packed his bags and flew down to Miami. A rented car brought him safely down to Key West. On the way, he soaked in the spectacular scenery created as U.S. 1 arched over the islands bordering the Straits of Florida. He also had his first tasty sampling of conch chowder, green turtle steak, crispy corn fritters, and key lime pie.

Once down to the highway's end, he went about tracking down the office out of which his folks were currently working. As freelance geologists, whose specialty was the location of petroleum deposits beneath the ocean's surface, the Krafts were employed on a contract basis. Their present assignment was with a large, Texas-based oil company. Shocked by the recent OPEC embargo, such American corporations had begun looking closer to home to satisfy the country's insatiable energy appetite. For the Krafts, business was never better.

From their letters, Thomas knew that they were presently involved with the sinking of a test hole in the Dry Tortugas Islands. This tiny chain of islands was some seventy miles due west of Key West, and accessible only by helicopter or boat. Thus, he didn't find it unusual when he arrived at the main office and was informed that his parents were still out in the field. With a promise to check in later, he parked his car and began a walking tour of the colorful, quaint town made so memorable by such legendary figures as Ernest Hemingway.

It was later that evening that he started to become concerned. His folks had yet to return, and hadn't even called in to check if he had arrived safely. This was not like them at all, especially since their previous letters had anticipated his visit so. Finding the secretary at the oil office completely uncooperative, Thomas checked into a nearby motel room, and spent a restless, disturbing night.

Bright and early the next morning, he returned to the office. Parked in front of the building were a pair of Highway Patrol cars. He swiftly entered, and after introducing himself to the worried officers who waited inside, found out the reason for their concern: The helicopter carrying his parents was several hours overdue, and presumed down at sea. The Coast Guard had been informed, and the first search teams were already scouring the area.

With this disclosure, Thomas felt his stomach sour. Even though his parents' work often took them to obscure parts of the earth by such means of transportation as small planes and helicopters, the possibility of a disaster occurring had never entered his mind. Unable to accept the reality of such a tragedy, he begged the patrolmen to allow him to assist in the search.

His previous ROTC experience was most helpful in convincing the commander of the Key West Coast Guard station to allow him to accompany them on one of their rescue flights. In fact, it was from the observation window of a Guard Sikorsky "Pelican" that he got his first sight of a circling shark. Their route had taken them over the crystal-blue waters to the west of Marquesas Key, a miniscule coral mass halfway between Key West and the Dry Tortugas. It was one of the guardsmen who identified the predator as an eight-and-a-half-foot hammerhead. The sight of this savage beast sobered Thomas. In the hours that followed, he viewed dozens of other sharks of a number of different varieties, yet not a sign of the helicopter that had been carrying his folks.

The official search ended three days later. Because no wreckage had been spotted, Kraft hired a pair of fishing boats to continue a sweep of the nearby waters. For an entire week, he searched in vain. Frustrated, tired, and sunburnt, he only gave up after a visit by the Guard commander emphasized the futility of his efforts.

The day that he left Key West for the long drive northward, signaled the beginning of a new chapter in Thomas Kraft's life. Alone, except for a handful of distant relatives, he began the difficult task of filling in the void that the loss of his parents had created. It proved to be the navy that served as his unlikely savior. Literally throwing himself into his new duty, the scars slowly healed, as new purposes and goals emerged.

His memories of that dark time had gradually faded, to be awoken only on the rarest of occasions. Though the waters he currently flew above belonged to a different ocean on the other side of the globe, the sounds of the chopping rotors, the rolling seas, and darting fins were all so familiar. Yet, how very different was the object of their current search!

As if awakening from a vibrant dream, Thomas gently backed away from the Seahawk's observation porthole. Turning, he fully returned to reality as he crossed the fuselage and approached the two khaki-clad figures perched before the transmitter. It proved to be the somber-faced ATO who greeted him.

"I told you linking with a boomer wasn't going to be an easy task. We've been broadcasting for over fifteen minutes now, and still not a sign of them."

"How much longer until you're forced to return to Manua?" quizzed Thomas.

The tactical officer checked his watch. "We've got another half-hour left, at the max. That would leave us with just enough fuel to get us back to base safely."

"Sir, I'm going to try increasing the frequency range," interrupted the sensor operator. "They could be down there but deaf to our call."

"Give it a shot," replied the ATO. "I'm going forward to check with the commander to find out exactly how much longer we can stay out here."

While the heavy-shouldered officer squeezed his way toward the cockpit, Thomas returned to the observation port. He had barely settled into a comfortable position, so that he could resume his study of the sea, when an alien, thin line of white froth became visible. Expecting to next view the thick fin of a huge shark, Kraft could hardly believe his eyes when the rounded tip of a periscope clearly broke the water's surface. Excitedly, he called out so that the entire crew could hear him.

"It's them!"

Several seconds passed as the pilot set his eyes on the scope and guided the Seahawk out of its tight, monotonous banked turn. Following the sub, whose course was due southward, the chopper hovered in the air, several hundred feet from the rolling whitecaps.

With his eyes still glued to the sea, Thomas looked on as the bubbling trail the sub was generating gradually thickened. He soon saw for himself just what was creating this additional disturbance as the vessel's black, tear-shaped sail penetrated the surface. Dominated by a pair of rectangular diving planes, the sail rose skyward as the rest of the immense vessel began to take shape.

Larger than he had ever imagined, the sub appeared as a huge, black behemoth, looking more alive than manmade. It's symmetrically rounded, blunt bow smoothly knifed through the water, an occasional wave smashing white upon the sail that followed. Set behind this towerlike structure lay the majority of the sub's length. This part of the boat featured twenty-four circular indentations, set twelve abreast, barely visible on the steel deck — Thomas assumed these were where the Trident missiles were nestled. After this point, the width of the vessel gradually narrowed, finally terminating in a spikelike tail. All together, it was fully ten times as large as the Seahawk helicopter, and even from the height from which it was observed seemed to fill this entire portion of the sea.

The sub took on additional detail as the chopper began to descend. Thomas was able to get a clear view of the top of the sail, and a square opening on its forward section became visible. Filling this space were three, blue-capped, khaki-clad individuals. While one of these figures checked them out using a pair of binoculars, the other two snapped the Seahawk a smart salute.

As if on cue, the ATO suddenly appeared behind Kraft. In his hands, he held a sturdy canvas shoulder sling. Securely attached to this harness was a length of coiled steel cable.

"Well, Lieutenant, it looks like your ride showed after all. Those types hate to be kept waiting, so if you'll just step into this rig, we'll have you on your way."

With the tactical officer's help, Thomas soon had the harness fastened. Making his way over to the exposed hatchway that the sensor operator had just opened, the geophysicist peeked downward. The submarine looking just as impressive as it had from the porthole window.

"Where in the hell are you going to set me down?" screamed Kraft over the roar of the chopper's engines.

The ATO winked. "I'm afraid there's only one area

of the boat that will safely allow such a transfer. We're going to drop you right into that opening in the sail, where those three officers are standing. That way, you won't even get your feet wet. I just hope she's one of ours. You ready, Lieutenant?"

Thomas swallowed hard. "Let's get it over with. Say, what about my seabag?"

"We'll drop it as soon as you're down," answered the tactical officer. "Just hit that red release lever when you're ready to break contact. Good luck, and don't worry — we've yet to lose anyone during such a drop. Of course, this is the first time anyone's been foolish enough to give this procedure an actual try."

Beaming a sarcastic smile, the ATO beckoned Thomas to have a seat on the floor of the open hatchway. The scientist did so, dangling his feet into the open air. Aware of the tightening sensation behind his shoulder blades, he supposed this was due to the pull of the steel lift cable as the slack connecting it to the motorized winch was pulled in. A hard tap on his right shoulder followed, and the next thing that he knew, his entire body was outside the helicopter. Here, the clatter of the Seahawk's engines roared even louder as he was buffeted by the rotor's downdraft.

Though the relatively tiny hole in the sub's sail looked like an impossible target to hit, he could see that the boat had practically stopped its forward momentum. Pounded by an occasional wave, the vessel bobbed innocently in the turbid waters. While only five hundred feet from the safety of the conning tower, Kraft laid eyes on the first of the gray fins, which cut through the water on each side of the inert sub. Called from the surrounding depths, the sharks appeared to be waiting for a meal that they somehow sensed was imminent.

This terrifying sight was followed by a sickening

lurch as the hoist cable slipped, dropping him downward over four hundred feet in a matter of seconds. Closing his eyes tightly and holding his breath, Thomas expected the worst, when all of a sudden his shoulders jerked upward, and his uncontrolled drop abruptly halted. When he again opened his eyes, he found himself staring at the forward edge of the sub's diving plane. Just as he realized how close he had come to being smashed upon the flat surface of this sixteen-foot-long steel appendage, the hoist cable once again tightened. Sixty seconds later, a pair of strong hands gripped his lower body and pulled him into the narrow aperture cut into the top of the sail. Another set of hands did the honor of triggering the harness release.

Weak-kneed and dizzy, he barely remembered looking up to see the Seahawk in the process of lowering his duffel bag. This transfer went much more smoothly. Only when his bag entered the firm grasp of one of the submariners did Thomas exhale a full breath of relief.

"Welcome aboard the USS *Phoenix*, Lieutenant," greeted the big blond-haired officer who stood on his left. "I'm Captain Charles Blake. Behind you, is our XO, Lieutenant Commander Pete Walsh. If you don't mind, we'll continue these intros downstairs. This sub has seen enough daylight for one cruise."

Taking a last look skyward, Kraft watched the Seahawk tip its fuselage, initiate a wide, banked turn, then dart off to the south. Not really sure what he could expect next, Thomas followed the captain down a flight of narrow metal stairs.

Behind him, a deep voice boomed, "Dive! Dive!" This was followed by the piercing wail of a claxon.

As the hatchway sealed shut above him, the geophysicist found himself in a vastly different world than that he encountered topside. Lit by powerful banks of pulsating red lights, the vessel was filled with the sound of rushing water as the sub took on additional ballast. Only when he stepped down into the command center was he aware of the forward tilt of the deck, indicating that the *Phoenix* was already plunging back into the veil of the ocean's depths.

Surprisingly enough, he faced a rather spacious compartment, filled with computerized equipment more indicative of a well-stocked scientific laboratory than a ship of war. Staffed by over a dozen seamen, the various consoles contained the latest in high-tech digital software. He felt instantly at home. The captain seemed to notice this, and approached him, smiling.

"Some boat, isn't she? We'll give you a full tour as soon as you've settled into your new quarters. Lieutenant Commander Walsh has been good enough to offer you the spare bunk in his room. You know, we still don't know your name."

"I'm sorry, Captain," stuttered the distracted newcomer. "Lieutenant Thomas Kraft, requesting permission to come aboard."

Returning his salute, Blake answered. "Permission granted, Lieutenant Kraft. Now, how about getting you settled in, and then you can let us know what this whole pick-up is all about."

"You mean that you know nothing about my mission?" returned Kraft, genuinely shocked.

"That's correct, Lieutenant. All we received were these rendezvous coordinates. Whatever you're up to, you must be one hell of a hotshot to have the navy use one of its Tridents for taxi service."

"I never thought that was the case, sir, but I guess my research was pretty important after all."

"I'll say," responded the captain. "Pete, take the lieutenant down to your quarters and show him where to stow his gear. We'll all meet in the wardroom in fifteen minutes."

Accepting the XO's salute, the captain watched the two officers disappear on their way downstairs. Blake found himself left with the impression that the lieutenant they had just picked up was actually just as innocent and humble as he appeared. Upon receiving the initial ELF page, he hadn't known what to expect. Now, he was even more puzzled. Anxious to find out the bottom line, he checked his watch, then proceeded to cross the room toward the bald-headed, hefty figure seated at the sonar station.

"Lieutenant Canova, anything in the vicinity that could give this old-timer some additional gray hairs?"

The junior officer looked up alertly. "You can rest easy, Skipper. It sounds like we got these waters all to ourselves. I'll bet those Russkies in that Alfa are halfway back to Pearl still searching for us."

"I hope you're right with that one, Lieutenant."

"My hunches have been right on, so far. What's our new passenger like?"

Blake answered carefully. "He seems like a regular enough guy. Could use a good haircut and a shave though. Must have drawn island duty. Keep me posted, son."

"Will do, Captain."

While Anthony Canova went back to his headphones, Blake's next stop was at the adjoining diving console. "How's she handling, Mr. Peterson?"

The young officer, who was presently responsible for the boat's helm, was quick with his reply. "Like a dream, Captain. We're running on a southwesterly course at two hundred feet. If we continue at our current speed of two-zero knots, we would be passing Manua Island in four more hours."

"Very good, Lieutenant. Say, have you given any more thought as to whether or not you'll be signing those re-enlistment papers when we get back from this

61

cruise?"

The helmsman stirred slightly. "I'm still kicking it around, Skipper. My wife is due with our first child sometime next month. I promised her that I'd make a definite decision by the time we returned to Bangor."

"Well, if it's any consolation to you, I know how difficult such a choice is. I've faced it several times myself. One thing for certain is that it would sure be to the navy's detriment if we lost you, lad. You're doing one hell of a fine job."

Blushing, Peterson replied. "Why, thank you, Captain. The Service has been good to us so far. I'm proud to serve aboard the *Phoenix*, yet I'd sure like to know what's going on back home."

"We'll be headed back to port before you know it. Until then, try not to count the hours. Time has a funny way of dragging its feet when you're conscious of it."

Blake left the helmsman with a neat salute. After passing through the radio room, he ducked under an open hatchway and proceeded to make his way down a narrow, metallic stairway. Once on the floor below, he took a minute to survey that portion of the vessel reserved for data processing. To the chattering sounds of the massive equipment at work, he studied the six-man detail responsible for their operation. They were supervised by a studious-looking young officer, who was completely absorbed in his duty.

The captain couldn't help but get the impression that this vital area of the boat appeared more like it belonged in a modern office building than a submarine. There was no doubt that the *Phoenix* would be practically useless without the help of this machinery. It was here that the tens of thousands of bits of information from each of the sub's various operating systems were funneled. Like a complex human brain, the computer readily answered each request demanded of it from the operational consoles throughout the boat.

For some reason, Blake always felt like a stranger in this compartment. He supposed this was due to his rather limited knowledge of the intimidating technology involved here. Faced with a problem in such areas as the engine room or reactor compartment, he could rely on his own troubleshooting ability to solve it. Yet if he was confronted with a breakdown here, he would be practically useless.

Thankful for the thorough competence of those men who worked before him, the captain climbed down to the next floor. This level was reserved almost exclusively for the crew's living quarters. Charles was most aware of the fact that this area's roominess was one feature of the *Phoenix* vastly different from other classes of submarines.

Crossing a tube-lined corridor, he stepped through a hatchway and passed by the boat's spacious mess. To the smell of frying bacon and fresh-perked coffee, he took a quick glance at the dozen or so seamen who sat four to a red-checkered, tableclothed booth, obviously enjoying their breakfasts. Charles wondered if the majority of these sailors appreciated the fact that an attack submarine's entire mess would fit easily inside the Phoenix's galley.

Blake next passed the crew's dormitory. Whereas other classes of subs were fitted with crowded, Pullman-type bunks, the Phoenix's living space was partitioned into units holding nine men. Each of these individually curtained sleeping stations had a large locker fitted under each bunk, and included hanging space for all uniforms. They also were fitted with small booths which functioned as desks.

Set between this dormitory and the officers' mess was a fully equipped recreation room, complete with a built-in stereo system, television monitor, a videotape player, free jukebox, ping-pong table and an ice-cream machine. This compartment also included a gym crammed with body-building equipment. For those sailors with more scholarly interests, there was also a thousand-book library and a study area.

As Charles continued toward the sub's bow, he mentally recreated the cramped confines of the vessel on which he had undergone his first cruise, over two decades ago. At that time, boats the size of the *Phoenix* could only be dreamed of. The navy had certainly come a long way in addressing the comforts of its men. This fact was even more obvious as he crossed into that section of the *Phoenix* reserved for the officers. It was toward the wardroom that he was drawn. Upon entering the simulated-wood–paneled compartment, he found two men seated at the room's central conference table. With mugs of steaming coffee before them, Pete Walsh and Thomas Kraft welcomed the newly arrived captain with a salute.

"I hope I haven't kept you two waiting long," greeted Blake, as he poured himself a cup of black java and seated himself at the table's head.

"Not at all, Skipper," returned the exec. "We just got here ourselves."

"Are your quarters sufficient, Lieutenant?" questioned the captain.

Kraft nervously cleared his throat. "Thank you, Sir, they seem most comfortable."

"Good," returned Blake, who intently studied the tanned face of the man sitting on his left. "Now, perhaps you can tell me what this little rendezvous is all about."

Again Thomas cleared his throat. "Believe me, Captain, I'm just as surprised as you regarding my presence here. As I was just explaining to Lieutenant

Commander Walsh, I only learned that I would be transferred to a submarine within the last hour. This whole morning has been simply incredible!"

Noticing the way Kraft's hand shook as he picked up his coffee cup, Blake sympathetically lightened his tone. "As I'm sure you understand, communications to a submarine are kept to a minimum whenever possible. Several hours ago, when we received the page sending us to pick you up, all we were informed of were the rendezvous coordinates. I can only assume that the navy has one hell of a good reason to bring us together. We're relying on you, son, to explain just what that reason is."

Having taken an instant liking to the shy lieutenant, Pete Walsh added, "Why don't you start by describing your duty at the time you received the chopper pick-up orders."

Thomas took a deep breath and responded fluently. "This whole thing revolves around my present assignment with the Office of Naval Research. I'm a geophysicist, stationed at one-man observation post on the western coast of Tutuila. For the past six months, I have been involved with the placement of a series of seismic sensors on the seafloor, beneath the waters bordering the Tonga Trench. Last night, several of these sensors, laid on the Trench's northern extremity, relayed back to me knowledge of a series of fairly moderate earth tremors taking place there."

"That would put the quake near the Vavau Seamount," interrupted Walsh, who caught his captain's concerned glance.

"That's correct," answered Thomas, who continued without further prompting. "My chief responsibility is to report back to Pearl Harbor regarding any seismic activity in this sector that I deem unusual. Although the tremor's magnitude really wasn't that significant, the dozens to severe aftershocks that accompanied it indicated that a geological disturbance of a much greater nature could be in the works. Such an event could take the form of a full-scale volcanic eruption."

"I didn't realize that it was currently possible to actually forecast such a phenomenon with any degree of certainty," the captain observed cooly.

Kraft looked Blake full in the eye. "The science of forecasting volcanic eruptions, though still in its relative infancy, has progressed greatly in the last few years. It has taken great bounds ahead, particularly with the recent Mount St. Helens eruption—which both myself and hundreds of fellow geologists were privileged both to witness and subsequently study. Incidentally, it was at this time that a new seismic sensor was developed to monitor the presence of harmonic tremors, caused by the rising of magma on its way to the crust's surface. The presence of such tremors, caused by the rising of magma on its way to the crust's surface. The presence of such tremors almost guarantees that a volcanic eruption is about to take place.

"Several of these sensors were subsequently buried in the floor of the Tonga Trench. The current state of the art requires them to be triggered by a remote-control unit, which must be positioned in the nearby waters. The surface vessel assigned to this task is currently out of service. Earlier this morning, I informed Pearl Harbor of the tremors in the northern Tonga region, and expressed my desire to travel down to this sector to trigger the harmonic sensors. The orders, requesting me to ready the remote-control triggering device and a month's worth of personal gear, arrived not too long afterward. I was merely informed that a means of transportation was being arranged, and that I was to sit tight to await its arrival. I assume now that the USS

Phoenix has been provided to fulfill this task."

"It indeed appears that way," responded Charles Blake thoughtfully. "Pete, we'd better get up to navigation and chart a course into the Tonga Trench on the double."

"About how long will it take us to reach the Vavau Seamount Sector?" queried Thomas, who followed this question with a wide, uncontrollable yawn.

Pete Walsh was quick to respond. "We're approximately four hundred nautical miles due north of that sector now. With a little luck, we can be there by dusk."

"You look beat, Lieutenant," added the captain. "I imagine that you didn't get much sleep last night. Since we're going to need you bright-eyed and bushy-tailed the moment we enter the Tonga region, why don't you go and catch some winks. We'll wake you in plenty of time to grab some chow and ready your instruments."

This suggestion sounded perfect to Thomas, who again yawned, suddenly conscious of the great strain he had been under these last few hours. "Thanks for your patience, Captain."

"And thanks for yours," added Blake. "Now, are you going to need any help in finding your bunk?"

The geophysicist rose stiffly, suddenly aware of a dull pain in his upper back where the Seahawk's harness had been fastened. "I think I can manage okay," he mumbled, while slowly approaching the wardroom's exit.

"It's the second stateroom to your right," reminded Pete Walsh. "Sweet dreams!"

Both officers waited in silence a full minute and Kraft had disappeared from their midst. Their faces heavy with concern, it proved to be Blake who rose first. Walking over to the wall-mounted telephone, he picked up the handset and punched in two digits.

"Mr. Peterson, it's the captain. Draw us up a direct

course to the Vavau Seamount in the Tonga region. Until further ordered, continue on present heading, with a speed change to three-zero knots."

Hanging up the handset, Blake turned and faced his exec, who remained seated. "Jesus, Pete, do you believe that story we just heard?"

The lieutenant commander hesitated a second before answering. "Other than being a bit confused and rightfully nervous with his first sub ride, I'd say Kraft was telling us everything. Apparently, he genuinely has no knowledge of Delta Bases's existence inside the Vavau Seamount."

"Well, if his suspicions prove legitimate and there's even a hint of the possibility of a volcanic eruption nearby, I can understand the treason we were called in for taxi duty. With the fleet visiting Japan, there's not much in the way of other available ships in this area. I'm just surprised that word of Delta didn't leak out to him. After all, he has been poking around on the seafloor there for the last six months."

"Skipper, you know that Delta's existence was on a need-to-know basis only. In all my years of service, never have I known such an installation to have kept its cover so completely. Our own navigators don't even know that hollowed inside the Vavau Seamount is a fully equipped, submarine refitting station."

Blake reached down for his coffee cup. "No project stays top-secret for long, Pete. Surely he must be asking himself what's so darn important in that region to risk sending in a nuclear sub just to trigger some sensors. To tell you the ruth, I really have a hard time believing that even the Soviets don't already know about Delta. Their satellite recon had to pick up a portion of its original installation."

"I thought we covered that by reporting a major oceanographic research project in the Tonga Trench at that time," countered the exec.

Blake took a full sip of coffee before responding. "Oceanographic study — you don't think that the Soviets really bought that one, do you?"

Pete pushed back his chair abruptly stood. "I was sure hoping that they did, Skipper. If it ever comes to a shooting war, and we escape initial destruction, I was certainly counting on Delta to provide a much-needed refit of stores and weapons. I seriously doubt if there will be much left of Bangor or Kings Bay."

"Or any other major naval installation on this planet," added the captain grimly. "Let's just pray that we never see such a day come to pass. In the meantime, let's get topside and check out our choice of courses southward. Once we round Manua, we'll have plenty of water to hide in. I still think, though, that we'd better clear our baffles before definitely committing for the Trench. I'd sure hate to lead that Alfa right up to Delta's front door."

"I'll agree with you on that one," returned Pete Walsh, who led the way out into the hallway.

Blake followed closely on his heels. As they turned to the left, and began the way toward the crew's quarters, the captain found his thoughts centered around a single question. Even if Thomas Kraft's predictions did prove correct, and a volcanic eruption did seem imminent, what could they possibly do to save Delta Base anyway? Charles decided that he would face this problem when and if it was necessary.

Chapter Four

The sun had risen well into the sky by the time
Deputy Defense Minister Mikhail Antonov finally
boarded the Ka-25 Hormone helicopter, which had
been stationed at the Cam Rahn Bay airport. With his
mind still occupied with last night's activities, he was
barely aware of passing the smartly uniformed, Vietnamese honor guard that lined the red-carpeted walkway leading to the dual-rotor, triple-tailed Hormone.
Entering the stubby, inelegant vehicle, he found himself in an equipment-jammed compartment, whose
length was lined with a single, uncomfortable-looking
bench. After being introduced to the three-man crew,
he gratefully accepted the offer of the copilot and
settled into the high-backed leather command chair,
that graced the right-hand side of the cockpit. Thankful that the pilot was a man of few words, Antonov sat
back and watched him coax the vehicle skyward,
pointing its rounded chin toward the southeast.

Though the loud roar of the chopper's twin
Glushenkov turboshaft engines at first disturbed him,
Mikhail gradually found himself getting used to the
steady chopping sound of the rotors. Now, if only the
aspirins would finally go to work on the throbbing ache
that pounded in his temples, perhaps he could yet

70

salvage some sleep. He had certainly gotten very little rest during the previous night.

Antonov nodded diplomatically as the pilot informed him that they faced a flight of approximately two hours. Since the weather was good over the South China Sea, he didn't foresee any difficulties in reaching the aircraft carrier *Minsk*, their immediate destination. There, Admiral Alexis Kostromo would be anxiously awaiting their arrival. Already an hour late in leaving, Mikhail wondered if the crusty old naval commander would find fault with the excuse for this tardiness. As the deputy defense minister remembered, Kostromo had been quite a "stick man" in his day. A legend amongst the men for the supposed length of his manly tool, Mikhail had actually seen him at work the night they shared a pair of busty, long-legged German hookers. He had found that the legend was most true.

That incident had taken place over four decades ago. In the years after World War II, the two men found themselves working closely together, rebuilding the military might of their bruised and bloodied homeland. Today, their duties brought them together only several times a year. As Deputy Defense Minister, Antonov was based primarily in Moscow. Spending the majority of his time fighting for increased appropriations, he had become more of a politician than a military man. In contrast, Alexis Kostromo had been able to keep relatively free from such political intrigue, relying on men such as Antonov to do the fighting for new funds. Thus, he could spend the majority of his time at sea, with his men. This, he insisted, was the place a true naval commander should be.

Mikhail realized that a smile had broken out on his face as he mentally recreated those earlier days spent with his old comrade. Glad that they would soon be together again, he looked out the Hormone's side

71

window. No longer was the lush, green, palm-tree-lined coast of Viet Nam visible. In its place, the whitecap-topped South China Sea surged to the far horizon. Only an occasional sampan broke the monotonous expanse of deep blue water. Calmed by this sight, his weary eyes closed and his thoughts returned to ponderings of a more recent nature.

Mikhail had been in Viet Nam for two days now. His presence was a gesture on Moscow's part of goodwill and respect. The country was celebrating a decade of independence since overthrowing the yoke of imperialist aggression. It had been nearly that long since he had last visited Southeast Asia, and Antonov had found the country vastly changed from the emergent, war-torn nation he had initially inspected.

Almost completely purged of the decadent Western ways that had crept into every crevice of Vietnamese society, the new Marxist order had finally taken hold. Today they were one of the Soviet Union's closest allies. Still faced with threats on its western and northern borders, Vietnam relied on the U.S.S.R. for protection and guidance. In return, not only did the Soviets have a shining example of the benefits of communism at work, but they also had the use of excellent military installations, such as the one they had just taken off from.

Dredged and developed initially by the United States, Cam Rahn Bay offered the Soviet Union a much-desired warm water naval port. At the generous offer of the Vietnamese government, this facility was presently open to Soviet vessels of every type. The battle flotilla to which the *Minsk* currently served as flagship, had set sail from this very port only a week ago. From what he could determine after yesterday's hasty meetings with naval authorities, the battle group's visit to this new facility had worked out excellently. As it appeared, a permanent Soviet naval presence here was almost inevitable.

While Mikhail had been in the midst of inspecting the city that surrounded the western edge of this harbor, he was afforded the opportunity to leave the confines of his Zil limousine, and actually walk the streets. When visiting foreign locations, the deputy minister found this the only way to get a real feel for the natives. The six-foot, four-inch, white-haired Siberian had proved quite a contrast to the dark-skinned, small-boned local population that swarmed about him. Excited with the alien sights and sounds that soon overwhelmed him, he had agreed to accept the services of an interpreter/guide and to continue his tour in the evening. Mikhail smiled now as he remembered what had happened.

Led back to his hotel, the sixty-nine-year-old civil servant was allowed time for a short nap before his guide was scheduled to arrive. Mikhail reflected on the fact that upon waking from this all-too-brief rest, he wished that he could have called the unofficial tour off. The exhausting effects of the time changes that he experienced on his recently concluded flight from Moscow were finally catching up with him. The old-timer wanted nothing better than to slip back under the silken sheets and sleep through to the next morning, when he was scheduled to fly out to the *Minsk*. He would have done so, if his new guide hadn't personally knocked on his door to summon him.

When this person entered his suite, Mikhail spoke out from between the covers, expressing his desire to cancel the tour. Only when he heard the guide's sultry response did he bother to open his eyes to see who this voice belonged to.

The woman who stood before him was easily the most exotic creature he had ever laid eyes on. It was her tall, shapely figure that first caught his attention. Clothed in a tight, silk one-piece dress, a provocative slit in the material showed off a pair of comely legs, leading to a tight, narrow waistline. A plunging neckline also favored a most ample bust. This doll-like figure was capped by an exquisite face, the type that only the Far East could produce. She seemed to sense Mikhail's interest and subsequent approval. Throwing back a long ribbon of jet-black hair, which had fallen over her shoulder, she smiled, exposing a set of perfectly formed, white teeth.

"Hello, Comrade Antonov," she greeted in excellent Russian. "My name is Black Jade. Are you certain that you can't summon your strength so that I can show you our illustrious city? I can show you sights that you'll never forget."

Certain of this fact, Mikhail managed to sit up. As the sheet fell to his waist, he exposed his naked chest. Proud of his excellent physical shape, he watched the woman's eyes quickly take in his solid pectoral muscles.

"I guess I'm not as tired as I originally supposed," the Deputy Minister returned with a wink.

Conscious of the fact that he was holding his stomach muscles unnaturally taut, Mikhail felt like a lad again. When an alien stiffening began forming beneath the sheets at his lap, he knew this transformation was complete. It had been much too long since he had felt like a real man. He relished the moment, then swung his legs off the bed, and, flaunting his gathering erection, sauntered over to his clothing.

Oblivious to any apparent embarrassment, Jade sat on the corner of the bed and the two began animatedly conversing. Praising her excellent command of his native language, Mikhail soon learned that her father had been a full-blooded Russian. An officer with an army engineering battalion, he had met Jade's mother while she was living outside Hanoi. Though they were never officially married, he supported his new family for the duration of his stay, which was over nine years. It was under his tutelage that she had learned Cyrillic. The last she ever heard of him was when his unit had left for duty inside Cambodia. To the best of her knowledge, not a single member of his battalion survived this reassignment.

Jade had seemed to accept this fact without too much bitterness. Taking advantage of her natural intellect and excellent language ability, she had applied for a scholarship at the People's University. Much to her amazement, she had been accepted, and had thus achieved her current employment.

They had finished the good part of a fifth of Russian potato vodka by the time they finally left the hotel bar and hit the streets. Comfortably seated in the back seat of a bicycle-powered rickshaw, Jade began their tour. They started in the section of town closest to the water. There, amongst the rat-infested wharves and crumbling warehouses, Jade pointed out the sleazy honky-tonks that seem to grace every port city. This neighborhood was also home to hundreds of gaudily dressed whores. They stood in the alleyways and doorways, brazenly displaying their sexual wares. Many looked like mere children.

Jade explained the State's attempt to put these girls out of business. Yet, every time that the streets were cleared, back the girls came. Of course, it was most obvious that the demand for their services was great, for prowling these streets were packs of wild-eyed sailors, whose natural appetites were sharpened by too many months alone at sea. At present, the official Party line was to condone this decadent behavior — at least in this particular neighborhood.

Next, Jade ordered the coolie to drive them further inland. The part of town they soon entered was in vast contrast to the port area. Neat, white stucco, red-tile-roofed bungalows lined both sides of a narrow street that reminded Mikhail of the Black Sea resort towns near Odessa. Fascinated with his comparison, Jade explained that this sector had originally been designed and built by the French over thirty years ago. Today it was home to a variety of hard-working, high Party officials. In fact, her own apartment was located only a few blocks away.

When Mikhail divulged the fact that he hadn't eaten a thing since a light breakfast, Jade suggested a very special restaurant only a block distant. Completely at his guide's mercy, he instructed her to lead the way.

The restaurant's name was the Red Lion. It occupied the ground floor of a two-story, narrow stucco structure, situated right off the street they had been traveling on. Inside, Antonov found it surprisingly intimate. Lit only by candles, each of the dozen or so tables appeared filled by soft-spoken, well-dressed diners.

Jade greeted the establishment's portly manager with an innocent kiss on his cheek. Bowing toward Mikhail, the Vietnamese elder then led them to the only apparent vacant booth, set in the room's far corner. Again, Antonov allowed his guide to take over when it came time to order their food and drink.

They began with a bottle of chilled Moet Chandon champagne. Not used to such extravagance, Mikhail savored each dry sip of this marvelous tasting, effervescent wine. He enjoyed it even more when his escort told him that this was another of the gifts that the Americans had so thoughtfully left behind. Served along with this was a bucketful of huge shrimp.

Mikhail watched Jade pull off the legs, head, and outer shell of these crustaceans, then dip the remaining meat into a cup of cocktail sauce and plop the combination into her mouth. Never having consumed seafood in this manner, his first attempt was a bit awkward, yet well worth the effort. The sweet, chilled shrimp meat was accompanied perfectly by the spicy sauce, and served to enhance the taste of the champagne even more.

Following this appetizer were a half-dozen food-laden plates, overflowing with such delicacies as sweet-and-sour lobster, roasted pork tenderloin, crispy duckling, garden fresh vegetables, and mounds of steamed rice. With the help of a second bottle of champagne, they eventually put a substantial dent in this feast. Their bellies filled and appetites satiated, Jade recommended a walk to aid their digestion. Mikhail wholeheartedly agreed with this suggestion.

Outside, the night air was hot and humid. Following his guide's lead, Antonov turned down a deserted sidewalk, which climbed up a gentle rise leading to a dark complex of quiet buildings; far off in the distance, a dog could be heard barking. The deputy minister inquired where in the world they were bound for. Jade took his hand in her warm grasp and squeezed his palm sensuously. Kissing him suggestively on the lips, she added, "My apartment is up ahead. If you wish, I could brew us some tea."

Tea was the farthest thing from his mind as he embraced her and kissed her full on the lips. Breathlessly, he followed her up the stairs leading to the simple flat.

Mikhail didn't notice much about how her place was decorated. All he knew was that neither one of them bothered turning on the lights as they proceeded straight into the bedroom.

A widower for the past three years, Mikhail really hadn't felt the need for a woman—that is, until the moment he had set his eyes on Jade earlier. Since that time, he had thought of little else. Now that he was about to have her, it was as if the hands of time had been miraculously reversed. Gone were the years that lined his brow and whitened his hair. Tonight he was a young man again, as spirited as a colt about to take his first mare. With the great responsibilities of his duty far from his mind, he prepared to give her his all.

Illuminated only by the light of the full moon as it cascaded down through the room's single picture window, the lovers fumbled for the snaps and zippers that held on useless clothing. When Jade's dress finally dropped to the floor, Mikhail's groping hands shot out to touch the soft, cream-colored skin that the moonlight exposed. As he did so, a feeling as vibrant as an electric shock passed through his body. At that moment, Antonov finally knew the secret of true desire. It was a mystery that had somehow alluded him during his thirty years of marriage.

While his lips merged with those of his Eurasian beauty, her hands deftly unbuckled his trousers and began an exploration of their own. Cupping his swollen testicles, she primed him until he was fully stiff, then pulled away. Anxiously, Mikhail backed off, and seating himself on the edge of the bed, slipped out of his undershorts. As he was doing this, Jade got down on her knees and slowly crawled toward him. Like a stalking black panther, she tossed her hair back, then reaching his side, passionately kissed the skin of his inner thighs. With deliberate slowness, she worked her way inward, stopping only to tease another gasp from deep inside his throat.

When her hot breath and flicking tongue finally hit their mark, Mikhail's swollen manhood proved a more

78

than adequate target. Starting at its pulsating tip, she went on to explore every inch of the thick, throbbing erection. As the grip of her lips tightened and she began slowly pumping its length, Antonov shifted forward in utter ecstasy. Aware of the first hint of rising seed, he knew that he wanted to possess her fully before allowing himself to explode.

Scooting backward, he pulled her up beside him and laid her on her back, across the bed's width. His kisses started on her neck and worked their way down to her full, ripe bosom. He suckled the erect nipples like a baby hungry for a meal. This proved to drive Jade wild, as her cries pleaded for him to cool her burning desire. Positioning his body on top, Mikhail guided the object she craved so into her tight, wet depths. With a series of thrusting shoves, this gift was given completely. Ahhing in delight, he lay still above his love, savoring this moment of bliss. Seconds later, their mad, frantic copulating began.

Completely oblivious to the confines of time, they climbed the hills and valleys of lovemaking. Each time they reached a pinnacle that appeared to be an ultimate, a new vista beckoned and a new chase ensued. It was only after Jade's body shuddered in a warm spasm of joy, that he allowed his own happiness to come to fruition. His seed given, Mikhail's embrace gradually lessened as both lovers fell into a deep, trance-like sleep.

When he awoke, the Vietnamese sky was aglow with the first hint of dawn. Sitting up with a start, he remembered the day's duty and thus was aware once more of time's rapid passing. With this realization, the spell that had captivated him all evening abruptly lifted. Massaging the dull, champagne-inspired ache that pounded in his temples, Antonov felt every year of his age and more. The girl who still slept soundly beside him looked lovely indeed, yet surely she was young enough to be his granddaughter. What had gotten into him last night?

Silently, he crept out of bed, slipped on his clothes, and left the apartment. It wasn't hard to orient himself and find his way back to the hotel. The sun was just breaking the horizon over the waters of Cam Rahn Bay as he rushed into his room and plunged into a steaming hot shower, then hastily shaved, dressed, and packed the rest of his clothing. Without even stopping for morning tea, he was already almost a full hour late in reaching the helipad. Yet high-ranking Party officials certainly had their privileges, and this was one instance that Mikhail wasn't about to worry about arriving late. Old Admiral Kostromo would excuse his tardiness with a jealous smile once he found out the true reason for Antonov's delay.

And as for Operation Lenin, his presence on the *Minsk* was only meant as a gesture to improve morale. He would make his speech in plenty of time for the men to comprehend the true scope of the naval exercise of which they were currently a part.

Suddenly aware that his headache was long gone, Mikhail opened his eyes and squinted in the light of midmorning. He was surprised to find the sun high in the cloudless eastern sky. After checking out the seemingly endless vista of water below, his glance locked on the jumpsuited pilot who sat to his left. The red-haired, moustached young officer was in the process of pushing forward on the steering yoke. The Hormone reacted to this movement by gradually decreasing its altitude.

A crackle of electric static sounded over the steady whine of the engines and the chop of the six rotors.

Antonov traced this disturbance as emanating from the radio speakers set into the corners of the control console. He watched the pilot reach upward and increase the volume gain, which was set into the padded ceiling. A broken, male voice soon addressed them.

"Little Swan, this is Red Banner leader. Do you read me?"

The pilot flipped on the transmitter and spoke into the headset-mounted, miniature speaker. "Affirmative, Red Banner. This is Little Swan, reading you loud and clear."

The voice crackled forth once again. "Excellent, Little Swan. We have you on approach radar. E.T.A. Red Banner in two-five minutes. Good flying."

"Thank you, Red Banner. Will contact you for approach coordinates when we have you on visual. Over and out."

As the pilot reached up to lower the volume gain, he glanced to his right and noticed that his passenger was fully awake. "Good morning, Comrade Antonov. Would you like some hot tea?"

Mikhail yawned and stretched. "That sounds like a wonderful idea, Captain."

"It's in the thermos strapped to the right, bottom side of your chair."

The deputy minister poured himself a cupful of the steaming brew. Sipping from the plastic cup, he found the black tea just the way he liked it, piping hot and heavily sweetened. He responded appreciatively.

"This saves the day, Comrade. I feel more like a member of the human species already. I haven't been out for over an hour and a half, have I?"

The pilot nodded his head. "You sure have, sir. You faded out only minutes after we left Cam Rahn Bay. Surprisingly enough, when the weather's good, this

81

flying machine can be quite conducive for a little nap. Half the time, it's all I can do to keep my copilot awake."

Sampling the tea once more, Mikhail found it the perfect temperature for sipping. With his gaze focused on the portion of the South China Sea they were headed toward, he questioned, "Are you stationed aboard the *Minsk*, Captain?"

"That we are, sir."

"What's it like serving under Admiral Kostromo?"

The redhead answered carefully. "It is a privilege to serve such an illustrious personage."

Mikhail smiled at this cautionary response. "I imagine that the admiral keeps quite a tight ship."

"That he does, sir."

"Well, believe me when I tell you how very fortunate the Motherland is to have such a figure in command of its navy. Because of his foresight, the Soviet Union can hold its own on any ocean on this planet. Things were quite different when I was your age, lad."

"I've read several naval textbooks which tell of the poor condition of our fleet up to the time of the Great War, sir."

Antonov grinned and shook his head. "Those narratives only tell a small portion of the story, Comrade. When I first joined the service, in the decade immediately before that madman Hitler's rise to power, we could barely defend our own coast. You wouldn't believe the handful of crude vessels that made up our navy then. Why, we couldn't even send more than three old battleships, ten decrepit cruisers, and sixty primitive destroyers out to sea to meet the Nazis. Yet somehow we persevered, allowing Kostromo to begin completely rebuilding our fleet during the years following the war."

With the conclusion of these words, Mikhail finished

off the rest of his tea. Sitting back fully awake, he realized that men such as the young pilot who sat beside him never really could understand how very close the Motherland had come to succumbing to the German hordes. This was one history lesson that had to be continually ingrained in every Soviet citizen's mind, no matter how young, for they couldn't allow such a thing to ever happen again.

Glancing down at his watch, the deputy defense minister saw that it would soon be time for the operation to begin, which would show the world's aggressors that the modern Soviet Navy was an awesome force not to be fooled with. Anxiously, the white-haired civil servant scoured the far horizon, searching for the nine-hundred-foot vessel from which this exercise would be directed. Excited with the fact that he would soon be face to face with the man directly responsible for this show of force, Mikhail smiled contentedly. After the conclusion of this day, the planet would be a much different place to live on!

Twenty-one kilometers to the southeast of the Hormone helicopter code-named Little Swan, the flagship of the Soviet Pacific Fleet, the aircraft carrier *Minsk*, prepared to enter the waters of the Balabac Strait. Nine-hundred feet from stern to bow, the 42,000-ton vessel smoothly cut a wide patch of white foam on its way into the narrow band of sea separating the Philippine Islands and the northern tip of Malaysia.

From his high-backed leather command chair mounted in the forward superstructure's central control room, Admiral of the Fleet Alexis Kostromo looked over the heavily armed bow and studied the seas immediately before them. Barely visible on the horizon was the stern of the Kresta Class guided-missile cruiser

Vladivostok. Working in conjunction with a pair of Udaloy Class destroyers, the cruiser effectively swept the waters beneath them for any sign of the enemy. So far, they had these seas all to themselves. This was just how the admiral wanted it. When the operation began, the one thing that he least desired was a nosey Los Angeles Class attack sub nearby, monitoring their progress.

Sweeping his intense gaze to the left, his line of sight lowered to concentrate on the carrier's angled flight deck. He counted six Hormone helicopters presently parked in their landing circles. This left the space set nearest to the bow conspicuously vacant. Hastily checking the airspace behind them, he looked down at his watch, scowled, and called out angrily.

"Captain Markova, where is Little Swan? All too soon it will be time to assemble the men in the hangar, yet our guest of honor is nowhere to be seen."

A tall, dark-haired, distinguished-looking officer calmly approached the admiral. "Do not fret, Comrade. Our radar shows them only minutes away. We should have them on visual any minute now."

Not bothering to reply, Kostromo took off his gold-braided white cap and wiped a handful of sweat off his shiny, bald scalp. Appearing far younger than his seventy-three years, the admiral smoothed down his thick, bushy brown eyebrows and began a series of deep, calming breaths.

How hard he had worked through the years for this day to be possible! Like a dream come true, a lifetime's effort was about to unfold. Having faced thousands of seemingly insurmountable obstacles during his four decades of unceasing work, these last few hours of inaction moved at a snail's pace. The ships were deployed, their orders delivered. In less than an hour's time, he would see if his vision had been a worthwhile one.

Forty years ago, an exercise such as the one they were about to initiate would have been unthinkable. Even he had trouble comprehending the reality of it all. What would his father think of all this? Responsible for his initial enlistment in the navy in 1935, his patriarch, though long dead, could rest at ease. After all, wasn't it he who had instilled in him the knowledge that nothing was impossible if one was willing to make the necessary effort and sacrifices? This was a lesson that Alexis had proceeded to share with his entire country.

The only difference between the accomplishments completed by his father and those of his own was a direct by-product of the political climate each of them had worked in. First entering the navy at the turn of the century, the elder Kostromo had joined a fairly large Russian fleet, whose strength was sapped by poor morale, second-rate training, and an officer corps deaf to any calls of self-improvement. Soundly beaten by the Japanese in 1904, the fleet also failed to meet its responsibility during World War I.

"Modernize or abandon the Navy altogether" was his father's advice to Lenin in the frantic years that had followed. Unfortunately, political strife at home prompted the new government to ignore this counsel for the time being. Though his pleas met a more receptive ear when Stalin came to power, the mobilization to modernize the fleet had been too late to affect the German invasion of Russia in 1941. Soon afterward, his father died under the torpedo of a Nazi u-boat.

Four decades later, his son had at long last made his vision of a first-rate Soviet Navy a reality. Now that the exercise was about to begin that would prove this fact to the world, Alexis couldn't help but feel that his life's purpose had finally been achieved. His toil would produce a priceless legacy that future generations of Soviet citizens could enjoy. Peace of mind through naval strength was the gift he would leave behind. It was a present for which two generations of Kostromos had sacrificed the better parts of their lives.

The crackle of amplified radio static broke him from his deep contemplations, and he turned his head expectantly. While he surveyed the northern horizon, a relaxed male voice emanated from the command center's elevated speakers.

"Red Banner leader, this is Little Swan. Do you read us?"

Captain Markova spoke into the carrier's microphone, "This is Red Banner leader. We read you loud and clear, Little Swan. Go ahead with your transmission."

"Affirmative, Red Banner. We have you on visual, vector three-zero point four-nine and closing. Do we have an all-clear to land?"

Markova instinctively looked toward the admiral. Accepting his simple nod, the senior lieutenant responded, "You are cleared to continue your present approach. All air traffic has been grounded awaiting your arrival. Please complete your descent at landing position Alpha."

"Alpha it is, Red Banner. We are initiating our descent. Over and out."

As the sound of crackling static dissipated, the white-suited admiral stood, joining the captain at the observation window. Neither officer needed the assistance of binoculars to spot the snub-nosed Hormone as it swept in from the northwest. With its prominent chin radar dome and "Homeguide" Yagi antennas leading the way, the vehicle positioned itself over the carrier's deck. When it landed, it did so with a bare jolt.

Alexis Kostromo again checked his watch. "Captain Markova, it's time for all available hands to assemble in the main hangar. Please have the welcoming squad escort our newly arrived guest there at once."

Clicking his heels smartly, Markova pivoted to initiate these orders. Still standing by the window, the admiral watched as the Hormone's double-decked rotor blades slowly spun to a halt. As they did so, the helicopter's cabin door slid open. A single, black-suited, white-haired figure emerged from the doorway and carefully climbed down onto the deck. Stretching his full length, the newcomer appeared fit and most grateful to have reached his destination. The three-man greeting party arrived at his side. Handshakes were exchanged, and the foursome began their way toward the "island" superstructure.

Kostromo's old friend looked as alert and full of life as ever. Only his mass of white hair indicated that the years had indeed caught up to Mikhail Antonov. The two men had certainly gone through a lot together. Responsible for allocating the navy's desired portion of the nation's already overstrained defense budget, Antonov remained one of the few allies in the Party who Alexis could always rely on. As the decades moved on, the old guard who had lived through and fought the Great War were slowly diminishing in number and, subsequently, power. Taking their places were a new generation, whose outlooks on the world were vastly different.

What did these youngsters know of invasion, bloodshed, depravity, and strife? It was military strength that kept these conditions far from their awareness. The question now, was whether this generation was willing to pay the price such security demanded.

In the forefront of this new wave were such individuals as their present First Secretary, Vladimir Kirensk.

This dynamic Georgian had just been emerging from his mother's womb when Hitler's army swept into the Motherland. Though personable and intelligent, how could such a baby possibly grasp the larger vision needed to direct a country as diverse and complex as the Soviet Union? Why, Alexis had had to practically beg the young premier just to allow Operation Lenin to unfold. For wouldn't such an exercise prove to be a dangerous, provocative move against the Western powers, the premier had argued?

Of course it would, Alexis had replied. It's time to show the imperialists that they no longer rule the oceans. When the rest of the world realizes this, the influence and prestige of the Motherland will increase a hundredfold! And the dream of our country's founding fathers will then be that much closer to being accepted on a worldwide basis.

Although the first secretary had eventually given in and reluctantly authorized the exercise, Alexis could clearly see the writing on the wall. This was another reason he knew today's events had to go perfectly. He would have no second chance to prove his theory if things went otherwise. Allies such as Mikhail Antonov could only go so far. He would have to do the rest all on his own.

Checking his watch for the hundredth time that morning, Kostromo realized that the first vessels would already be at their action stations. It was now time to share this knowledge with his men. Anxious to do so, he turned and began his way into the carrier's interior.

Two floors beneath the stern flight deck, the *Minsk*'s central hangar was the scene of an unusual mass assembly. Over two thousand men—nearly four-fifths of the ship's complement—found themselves seated on the spotless, metallic floor. They faced a small wooden podium, set against one of the cavernous room's massive walls. Here, a large banner had been hung. On its length was etched a realistic rendering of the mustached father of communism, V. I. Lenin.

A hushed silence fell amongst this crowd when a single, white-uniformed figure entered the hangar from the hatchway leading to the pilot's briefing room. Making his way quickly up to the dais, Admiral Alexis Kostromo tapped the attached microphone to make sure that it was working. Satisfied, he took a second to survey his attentive audience as they rose to attention in unison and snapped him a salute.

The crew was dressed in various uniforms of khaki, white, and navy. Each of these different styles corresponded to the type of specialty the particular sailor was assigned to. Alexis spotted a large grouping of natty aviators situated immediately before him. Next to them were a contingent representing the ship's logistics, medical, and engineering officers. By far, the largest number of those present belonged to a mass of eager conscripts. This lot filled the majority of the hangar, spilling back into an area dotted with several dozen Hormone helicopters and Yak Forger verticallift jet fighters.

A large swell hit the *Minsk*, and the hangar rocked to and fro until the carrier eventually steadied itself. To the far-away drone of the vessel's four, 40,000-horsepower, steam turbine engines, Alexis beckoned the men to be seated, cleared his throat, and began speaking.

"Thank you, Comrades, for your prompt attendance this morning. It is with great pride and excitement that I announce the initiation of Operation Lenin, a worldwide naval exercise of unprecedented scope, of which the *Minsk* shall be an instrumental part. For the next seven days, your efforts shall go hand in hand with those of tens of thousands of your fellow sailors, as the Soviet Union demonstrates the extent of its oceanic might.

"At present, our battle flotilla is steaming into the South Pacific Basin, a heretofore unexplored realm for our navy to travel in. It will be up to each one of you to do that which is asked of you by your superiors without question. Since we are still not certain how we will be received here, the flotilla will be sailing in a state of continual alert. Only in this way shall we be ready for any contingency that might befall us.

"I now have the honor of introducing a very special guest, who has traveled many miles to be with us on this important occasion. Please welcome the Deputy Defense Minister of the People's Republic, Mikhail Antonov."

To a hearty round of applause, the admiral stepped back as the white-haired, black-suited figure of his old friend emerged from the briefing room doorway. The two men met in an emotional bearhug, kissing each other on both cheeks.

"I was afraid that you were about to stand us up," greeted Kostromo softly. "I'm sure that your excuse for this tardiness is a sincere one, though."

"Oh, Alexis, must you always be the commanding officer?" Mikhail said with a wink. "You will be proud of me upon hearing the reason for my delayed arrival. Let me get on with my speech, and then we can discuss it over vodkas."

The admiral couldn't help but smile as the likable beaurocrat rolled his eyes back playfully. This youthful exhibit was quickly controlled as Antonov turned to approach the podium. With shoulders back and a serious expression, he faced the crew. His words rang out with earnest determination.

"On behalf of First Secretary Kirensk, I than you for this warm reception. This morning, even while I speak, the naval forces of our great Republic have begun a massive, worldwide exercise, which we have labeled Operation Lenin. The by-product of decades of planning and sacrifice, this exercise, like no other yet attempted, will show the world's population the true extent of our fleet's unprecedented strength. With such a demonstration of power, the ever-weakening imperialist nations will wake up and take notice that they no longer have total mastery of the seas.

"It is as a direct consequence of the efforts of such heroes as our own Admiral Kostromo that this day had been made possible. A modern navy can't be created overnight. It takes years of development. In the last twenty years, our navy has been transformed from a mere coastal defense force into an oceangoing fleet second to none.

"Over one thousand warships flying the Hammer and Sickle are currently positioning themselves at their action stations. In the Atlantic, ships from the Northern and Baltic Fleets have moved out into the open seas to control sea lanes too long dominated by the Western nations. This flotilla is spearheaded by an offensive force of attack and missile-carrying submarines. Laying in wait off the enemies coast, the warheads of these vessels are capable of hitting major targets with as little as five minutes' flight time.

"In the Mediterranean, our Black Sea Fleet has deployed itself in sufficient numbers to create a situation of unquestionable dominance. The very belly of Europe has never been so exposed.

"Elements of our own Pacific squadron are in the midst of fulfilling an even greater challenge. Presently, we have the responsibility of policing three diverse regions of the planet. This includes the Indian Ocean, where a battle group complete with amphibious warfare capabilities is positioning itself in the Arabian Sea. In the Northern Pacific, the sub pens at Petropavlovsk have been emptied. This awesome force has a dual mission. While our missile-carrying vessels close in on America's exposed western coastline, our attack subs shall monitor each and every Yankee submarine as it leaves its port. This includes boats of the dangerous Ohio Class, Trident missile variety. This is where our particular battle group comes into play.

"Since the American Trident subs have generally chosen the deep, previously undisturbed waters of the South Pacific to establish their patrol routes, we have assembled the mightiest antisubmarine-warfare flotilla ever to sail the seas. Led by the *Minsk*, this force of cruisers, destroyers, frigates, and attack subs will track down each Trident, thus demonstrating to the imperialists that these sophisticated launch pads are far from being invulnerable.

"Operation Lenin will also include the activation of several radically new weapons systems that our countrymen have been hard at work developing. This will include the launch of a highly sophisticated missile of the cruise type, whose development, until this date, has been kept top-secret.

"Again, this show of force will be utilized in an effort to demonstrate to the world not only the might of the Soviet Navy, but also the effectiveness of the Marxist way of life. Only a system of unparalleled strength could create such an awesome war machine. In a world free of the threat of imperialist aggression, such a productive unit could be focused entirely on satisfying the needs and wants of its people. The dreams of our great forefathers will at long last be realized as the entire planet reaps the benefits of the Communist way. It is your sweat, toil, and sacrifice that makes this exercise possible. May all of our efforts not be in vain.

"To your stations, Comrades! The Motherland implores you not to let her down!"

A chorus of applause followed as Mikhail Antonov put both hands overhead and briefly waved his acknowledgments to the men. As he turned to back away from the podium, the sailors stood en masse and issued a rousing round of inspired cheers. Aware that he had apparently done his job effectively, Mikhail accepted the hearty handshake of the *Minsk*'s captain, and then that of Alexis Kostromo. With the admiral leading the way, the deputy defense minister ducked under the hatchway leading into the pilot's briefing room. Holding back a yawn, he looked forward to a quiet day in his old friend's stateroom, with a bottle of vodka between them to stimulate their conversation. And then it would be time for a real story to be told!

Was it really only a couple of hours ago that he had lain at Black Jade's side? It seemed more like a dream than reality. Antonov knew that such an affair, though tiring, had served to temporarily refresh him. Every man needed such a diversion from time to time. Surely, he deserved it. Smiling inwardly at his guilt, he promised himself that he would try to take more time out for himself once Operation Lenin was concluded. Yet, who was he kidding? — for wasn't this the very same resolution that he had been making to himself for the last two decades?

Chapter Five

Of all the forsaken spots on this planet to be, Petty Officer Second Class Vasily Chapayev could think of no worse place than the East Siberian Sea. Bordered by the Arctic ice pack to the north and the frozen tundras of Siberia to the south, these icy waters offered some of the most desolate duty a sailor could chance upon.

Why, even the bitter-cold environs of Vladivostok seemed like a virtual paradise compared to the iceberg-packed seas they presently skirted through, Vasily pondered as he hurried down the exposed stairway leading to the forward storage area. At least there, this incessant wind occasionally stopped blowing. No matter how many layers of clothing he threw on, the chill still managed to penetrate his very bones. He doubted if he would ever get used to such a harsh environment.

Born and raised in the Caucasus Mountains of Southern Russia, Vasily found himself ill-suited to adapt to these present climatic conditions. It was his blood that was too thin. Sure, they had their share of ice and snow back home, but only in moderation. Here in Eastern Siberia, such icy gusts blew 365 days out of every year. It was truly only a land fit for Eskimos and polar bears.

To top all of this off, Chapayev had no idea what

they were doing here in the first place. The *Boris Chilikin* was an underway-replenishment ship, not an icebreaker. They should be out in the Pacific with the rest of the fleet, where they belonged. But who was he to make sense out of the strange ways of the navy he served? He could but do his present duty to the best of his ability, and pray that an assignment to more southerly waters would soon follow.

With one gloved hand gripping the ship's icy railing, he prepared himself for the exposed trip up to the *Chilikin*'s bow compartment. As an angry gust of wind whipped viciously in from the north, he initiated his first tentative steps. Ever-mindful of the slippery, rolling deck beneath him, he inched forward.

Halfway down the vessel's length, he stopped briefly to regather his nerve. Looking to his right, he peered out cautiously into the thick mist that topped the turbid waters. Except for the whitecap-tossed sea, he saw little else. Half expecting to view the huge crest of an approaching iceberg, he quickly turned his attention back to the ship and once again began moving forward.

Just as he was certain that he had lost all feeling in his face, hands, and feet, he passed the twin gun-mounts that indicated his goal was nearby. Turning to his left, he managed to locate the hatchway entrance. Using the crowbar kept tied to the door for this very task, he awkwardly began the tedious process of chipping the thick ice off the steel latch mechanism. With his breath streaming from his raw nose and mouth in clouds of misty vapor, Vasily cursed to himself with each strike of the heavy iron tool.

"So this was why you joined the navy, Chapayev, to freeze your balls off in the midst of this icy hell. Curses to you, Admiral Kostromo, and to the rest of the idiots whose grand vision has sent us here!"

Fearful that his efforts would fail to open the hatchway soon enough to keep him from freezing to death, Vasily held the crowbar in his numb grasp and struck out wildly. After a half-dozen frustrated blows, a large chunk of ice covering the doorway's entire length crackled to the deck in several jagged pieces. Not stopping to celebrate, he angled the tool under the iron latch and yanked upward with all of his might. With a rusty grunt of disapproval, the hatch swung open. Seconds later, the petty officer had it rebolted securely behind him.

The first thing that he was aware of upon entering the forward compartment was the blessed embrace of warm, heated air. The second was the noticeable muting of the unceasing howl of the gusting wind. In its place rose the far-off drone of the ship's turbines, and the constant creak of the hull as it crashed through the angry Arctic sea.

With feet still numb, he shuffled down the cramped hallway toward his morning duty station. Since it was still early, the majority of the *Chilikin*'s crew were still warm in their bunks. Though this was where Vasily certainly wished he was at the moment, he found some enjoyment in having the compartment all to himself. Passing the ammunition room, he stopped before a locked doorway immediately behind it. Using his teeth, he removed his gloves, and took a few minutes to rub some warmth back into his stiff fingers. Once they were tingling pink and alive again, he was able to remove the key from his jacket pocket and unlock the door he faced. Inside, he flicked on the light switch for the cubicle, which would be his station for the next six hours.

Among Vasily's present responsibilities was to act as the ship's assistant weapons chief. Even though the *Chilikin*'s primary purpose was to carry fuel and other stores for the larger warships, she was armed with a variety of weapons systems. These included two 100mm gunmounts, a 30mm Gatling gun, and a single SS-N-2 "Styx" cruise-missile launcher. Such limited systems would allow the vessel to take care of herself it attacked by hostile aircraft or surface ships.

Vasily doubted that the *Boris Chilikin* would be able to put up much of an effective fight if she were caught out alone on the open seas in a time of war. Yet, it was somewhat reassuring to have at least some weapons available to defend themselves with. This was in vast contrast to the majority of supply ships belonging to the U.S. Navy, which went to sea practically stripped of all armaments.

"Some good our guns will do us here," contemplated the petty officer as he removed the first of his sweaters. He knew that both the cannons and the Gatling gun would be frozen securely to their mounts. That left them with only the missile launcher to defend themselves with.

Trained in all aspects of the Styx missiles' operation and maintenance, Vasily found himself wondering if the recent scuttlebutt he had been hearing was true. The rumors hinted that, during their recently completed refit in Vladivostok, the SS-N-2 had been removed, and that a radically new cruise weapon was sealed in its launch tube. If this had indeed taken place, the new missile must have a computerized target-acquisition system exactly like that of the Styx, for none of this equipment had been touched. In fact, he had spent most of yesterday programming this very console, with target coordinates given to him by the captain.

As always, it appeared that his lowly rank would make him one of the last to learn of such a systems deployment. This really upset him—for here he was, responsible for a weapon's maintenance, and he didn't even know for sure what he was taking care of. It could be a nuclear bomb for all he knew.

Peeling off his second sweater, Vasily was finally beginning to feel like a human being once more. The sensation was even returning to his cheeks and feet. Stripped down to his everyday uniform, he decided it was time for his morning eye-opener. This procedure was guaranteed to get his blood circulating.

He kept his flask hidden in the top file-cabinet drawer. Appropriately enough, it was stashed behind the file labeled "Ammunition Inventory." The pewter decanter had been given to him by his father, upon his graduation from the Nakhimov Black Sea Higher Naval School in Sevastopol. Its contents never failed to offer him inspiration and courage in meeting a new day's challenges. This morning proved no different. Yanking the cork from the flask's neck, Vasily helped himself to an adequate gulp. The cheap vodka burned his mouth and throat, finally settling in his belly like a lump of burning coal. Following this with a healthy burp, he took a second drink. This one went down much more smoothly.

He was in the process of downing his third and final swig of the morning when the door to his compartment swung back abruptly. Standing in the now-open hatchway, his beady, black eyes locked on Vasily as if he had caught the petty officer in the act of murder, was the dreaded figure of the ship's zampolit, Yuri Nevskiy. For a full minute, the scrawny political officer said nothing. His glance did all the talking necessary.

Vasily sulked backward, meekly capping his flask. Not knowing what to do with the now-sealed bottle, he guiltily placed it upon his desk and looked up for a response. All he got was a cold nod of indifference as Nevskiy swaggered into the room, shutting the door behind him.

With his hands on the back of his hips, and his chest puffed outward, the zampolit approached the desk and snatched up the flask. Popping the cork, he brought the vial to his nose, sniffed, then pulled it away, apparently completely repulsed by what he had smelled.

"At least you could demonstrate some taste by choosing a brand other than this trashy rotgut," the zampolit said with a sneer.

"I would, Comrade Zampolit," offered Vasily, "but this was all that they had for sale in Vladivostok."

Nevskiy grimaced at this response. "Certainly your black-market friends could have done you better, Comrade Chapayev. Don't look so startled, young man. We've been watching you deal with such scoundrels for some time now."

This revelation caused Vasily to suddenly blush, and the alert political officer knew that he had him on the defensive. Still holding the uncorked bottle at his side, Nevskiy cocked his shoulders back defiantly.

"If you had attended last night's Komsomol meeting, you would be aware of the danger this substance had on both your physical and mental health. The Young People's Communist Organization has decided to initiate a total ban on the consumption of such beverages amongst its members."

"Good luck with the enforcement of that directive," replied Vasily submissively.

Before the zampolit could respond, the ship keeled in the grasp of a massive sea wave. Caught off balance, Nevskiy smashed clumsily into the side of the cabin. As he struggled to regain his equilibrium, the petty officer couldn't help but chuckle. This completely infuriated the political officer, whose face turned beet red.

"I've had enough of your cockiness, Comrade!" screamed Yuri, while rubbing his bruised left thigh.

"You are a disgrace to the Motherland."

Another wave rocked the *Chilikin*, and again the zampolit found himself falling uncontrollably, this time crashing into the sealed hatchway. This caused a stream of laughter to once again pass Vasily's lips.

"Damn you!" cried the political officer while righting himself. Raising his left hand above his head, he smashed the pewter flask down onto the deck.

Vasily was completely sobered by this move. His glance angled down to take in the bottle's split side as the clear vodka it held poured out onto the wooden-slat floor. Hardly believing what he was viewing, he bent down and carefully picked up the unrepairable decanter.

The flask had been his father's. It was one of the few physical possessions that had been passed down to him. Far from being just an intrinsically valuable piece, it held memories of a much more significant nature. Not wishing to give the zampolit the satisfaction of knowing how much the container had meant to him, Vasily took a deep breath and tried to contain himself. His only desire was to get the beady-eyed officer out of the compartment before he really lost control and strangled him.

"Comrade Nevskiy, I'm sorry for drinking on duty. It won't happen again."

The zampolit was caught off-guard by this response. "So you've come to your senses, huh, lad? Believe me, you'll be a much better person if you can stick to such a decision. Your entire outlook on life will change. Just wait a few weeks and see."

With one hand steadying his body against the bulkhead, Nevskiy slowly approached the desk. He reached into his breast pocket and pulled out a small black notebook, from which he detached several pieces of paper.

"For a second there, Comrade Petty Officer, I thought I'd have to remove you from duty and put another in your place. Now, it appears that won't be necessary. You seem to be the most qualified man for this job, anyway."

Laying the lined sheets of notepaper on the desk, he continued, "I need you to make the following course changes in the SS-N-2's guidance system. You are to get to work on this at once, and to inform me personally when this important task has been completed."

Vasily issued a bare nod. The zampolit studied this meager response curiously.

"So you're worried that I'll report this incident to the captain? You have nothing to fear, Comrade, as long as you keep your promise to quit drinking. While you're at it, consider attending tonight's Komsomol meeting. Hearing the Party line on this subject, and sharing the experiences of your fellow shipmates who have shaken this demon, will give you inner strength. Your attendance will also look good on your record."

"I'll seriously consider it," Vasily said as genuinely as he could.

The political officer checked his watch. "It's time for me to get back to the bridge. Don't forget to notify me as soon as you've completed the reprogramming. Your immediate cooperation in this matter will be noted."

Throwing his head back, he pivoted and carefully made his way out of the compartment. Only when the hatch was securely tightened behind the zampolit did the petty officer issue a breath of relief. Placing the split flask on top of the file cabinet, Vasily bent down and opened the locked bottom drawer. Inside, the cabinet was jam-packed with over a dozen quart-sized bottles.

While still kneeling on the deck, Chapayev picked up one of these containers, then closed and locked the drawer. He wasted no time in twisting off the bottle's plastic cap and bringing the now-opened jug to his mouth. A long, satisfying drink followed. His lips were wet and his eyes red as he seated himself behind the desk, bottle still in hand. Downing another gulp, his glance went from the split pewter decanter to the sheets of paper his recent visitor had left him.

So, the bastard wanted him to redo the targeting program. From the thickness of these notes, it appeared to be another major coordinate change. And to think that he had spent practically all afternoon yesterday completing a similar reprogramming for the captain. Were they doing this just to keep him busy?

Certainly they weren't about to go to war. If the state of world affairs had deteriorated to such a point, the *Chilikin* would have been sent to join the rest of the fleet long ago. No, instead they must be in the midst of one of those endless readiness exercises dreamt up by the admirals to show the politicians that they were getting their rubles' worth.

The notepaper before him held another senseless series of coded telemetry information. When entered into the computer keyboard, this data would alter the cruise-missile's course by drawing up a new set of satellite-obtained topographical maps for the weapon's on-board video camera to follow. The number of additional map points indeed made it appear that either the Styx's range had been dramatically increased, or that an entirely new type of weapon lay sealed in the tube. One way or the other, Vasily knew it didn't make much of a difference to him. Nothing short of a war would cause the navy to actually launch such a missile, anyway.

In his three years of duty aboard the *Chilikin*, he had yet to fire one of the Styx devices. Except for training films, he didn't even know if the damn thing would work or not. His superiors had explained that needless, expensive tests of such weapons systems proved to be impractical. Such a policy was even applied to the 100mm cannons and the Gatling gun, whose breeches were only allowed to be tested by a live firing of ammunition less than two times a year.

So what did all this reprogramming really mean? They didn't intend to really initiate a launch. Who were they trying to fool? This was only one more instance of the officers creating pointless busy work. The way he presently felt, he wasn't in any mood for such idiocy. The admirals could keep their childish war games. The Motherland would persevere with or without such simple-minded diversions.

Remembering the broken flask, a new wave of contained anger coursed through his body. Now the imbeciles even wanted to take away the solace of vodka. How else were they to put up with the navy's inadequacies? The cramped confines of the *Chilikin* were depressing enough. Add to this the tasteless, half-rationed meals and ridiculous, meaningless duty, and you found yourself in a situation where drink was the only thing that held together one's sanity. What else was there to look forward to during the day — one of the swaggering zampolit's thrill-a-minute Komsomol meetings?

Vasily's resentment was further provoked as the ship rolled in the turbulence of another series of towering waves. He fought to stay anchored in the chair as what was left of his father's flask rolled off the desk and tumbled onto the floor. Barely able to retain his balance, he reached forward and crumpled the orders that the Zampolit had left him into a tight ball. He looked on as this ball proceeded to fall onto the deck and disappear behind the computer console.

"So much for your new target coordinates, Comrade

Nevskiy," mumbled Vasily drunkenly. "To the Motherland!"

This toast was followed by a hearty drink, as the petty officer put the vodka bottle to his lips and drained off nearly a fifth of its contents. No longer aware of the sting of the raw liquor as it tumbled down his throat, he decided that a short nap was now in order. He would then awaken in plenty of time to call the bridge and inform them that the reprogramming was concluded. Who knows, he might even receive a commendation for such exemplary behavior!

The command bridge of the *Boris Chilikin* was located on the upper edge of the vessel's raised, stern superstructure. Perched immediately in front of the single exhaust funnel, the bridge was designed to offer a clear view of the heavily rigged portion of the ship reserved for supply storage, the bow armament turrets, and the surrounding waters. On this particular morning, the heavy fog made a viewing of the rising seas they sailed upon practically impossible. Captain Petyr Timoshenko nervously paced the spacious compartment, aware that they were relying solely on their radar to keep them out of the way of the thousands of icebergs that dotted these waters. Taking care to hold onto the brass railing that lined the outer perimeter of the room, the captain knew his ship was taking a beating and that there was very little he could do about it. When their hull bit into a particularly massive wave, and the deck heaved upward, rolling correspondingly, an urgent voice broke out behind him.

"Sir," pleaded the green-faced helmsman. "Request permission to leave the wheel."

Cognizant of the conscript's plight, Timoshenko indicated his permission with a nod. As the sailor raced outside to the exposed deck, without even the protection of a sweater, the captain eased himself over to take hold of the helm. The big-boned officer was feeling a bit queasy himself, yet so far had been able to keep his stomach under control. This was not the case for the majority of those aboard, who had been almost constantly sick since entering these waters last evening.

Scratching his bushy, salt-and-pepper beard, the twenty-year naval veteran wondered how much longer they would be forced to stay here. Designed for calmer, temperate waters, the *Chilikin* was responding stiffly, primarily because of the thick coating of ice that gripped its upper deck. Since this ice added hundreds of tons of extra weight to their superstructure, the boat was dangerously top-heavy and thus was under the constant threat of swamping. And with the ever-rising seas they were experiencing, this menace was a very real one.

With the polished brass wheel secure in his powerful grip, Timoshenko focused his practiced gaze on the large compass set in the wall immediately before him. To bring them back on course, he guided the rudder gently aport. This put them heading due west, directly into the cresting waves.

As the hull of the *Chilikin* plowed bluntly into the swells, a noisy splattering of frothing sea water sprayed onto the forward observation window set in the wall above the compass. Thankful for the recently installed deicer, Petyr was able to inspect that portion of the ship still visible. Veiled by the thick fingers of swirling fog, he could just see the icicle-enshrouded refueling gantries and beyond, the square, white housing of the replenishment cranes. To his dismay, both the gun turrets and the bow itself were no longer visible.

A cold, damp chill penetrated the bridge as the outer hatch opened and quickly closed again. Soaked and shivering, yet visibly relieved, the young helmsman dried himself off with the help of a thick, terry-cloth towel. Wrapping a woolen blanket around his shoulders, he walked over to the wheelhouse.

"Request permission to take the helm, Sir."

"Permission granted," answered the captain, who stepped back to let the conscript retake the wheel. "Are you feeling any better?"

The sailor shyly answered. "A bit, sir. I don't see how there's anything left in my stomach to throw up. You know, that vomit looked completely frozen by the time it hit the sea."

"It most probably was, lad," Timoshenko returned, smiling. "Now, keep us headed due westward. I want those breakers hitting us square in the bow."

Assured that the seaman would be feeling well enough to keep them on course, the captain turned and opened the doorway set into the bridge's rearmost wall. Here, a cramped, badly lit hallway led to another sealed hatchway. Breaking open this obstacle, Petyr entered a relatively small, equipment-packed room. Set into each of the walls stretching to his left and right were two complex, digital consoles. It was toward the station to his left that he was drawn.

The radio transmitter had a single petty officer third class seated behind its controls. Busy speaking into the counter-mounted microphone, he didn't seem to be distracted by the slim, goggle-eyed figure hovering over his shoulder. This neatly dressed personage proved to be the one who the captain next addressed.

"Comrade Nevskiy, any success in reaching the *Minsk* yet?"

The political officer straightened himself alertly. "Negative, Captain. All we continue to be getting is static."

"It's this ice that's the culprit," offered Timoshenko.

"The entire communications mast is shrouded in solid ice. There's no way our satellite dish is able to properly function in such ridiculously harsh conditions."

Yuri shrugged his shoulders. "You're probably correct with that assumption, Captain, yet what else can we do?

"We can move out at once to the calmer waters to the southeast," the captain shot back. "I fear that the *Chilikin* can't take much more of this incessant pounding."

As if to emphasize his statement, the boat shifted hard aport, then rocked jerkily back to starboard. Both officers had to reach out and grasp onto the compartment's mounted electrical fixtures to steady themselves. Unfortunately, Yuri Nevskiy failed to act in time to keep from colliding with the captain. Steadying the off-balance zampolit with a free hand, Petyr kept him from falling onto the deck itself.

"One more wave like that, Comrade Nevskiy, and a very top-heavy *Boris Chilikin* could topple right over. Then, what would Admiral Kostromo have to say?"

Timoshenko's words of warning were answered by the shaky voice of the political officer. "I'm certain that the admiral didn't expect us to encounter such stormy conditions when he assigned us to this mission. Surely, you remember the exact wording of the orders we received earlier? The instructions made it very clear we were to hold this position, due west of the island of Ajon, until 0900 hours. Then we will have a forty-five-minute window in which to launch the SS-NX-12."

"But does the admiral realize that the weather here is continually worsening?" the captain persisted.

Nevskiy smoothed his rumpled uniform and checked his watch. "We have only minutes more to go until nine o'clock. We've just got to hold on until then. Just think, Captain, if this weren't an exercise. What if a global war were to break out at this very moment? Would we then be afforded the additional time to cruise to calmer seas? This, Comrade, is what tests are all about. Now, if that weakling Chapayev would only finish the reprogramming, we could be making the final preparations for the launch. Perhaps I should go down there and spur him on."

In answer to this, the ship's intercom began ringing. Timoshenko alertly picked up the console-mounted white handset on the second buzz.

"This is the captain."

Whatever he was hearing caused a broad smile to enliven his previously drawn face. "Excellent news, Vasily. It shall be noted that you have completed your task in more than enough time. Take a few minutes to put your feet up and rest your tired mind. You certainly deserve such a break before initiating your next task, which is to actually fire the cruise weapon itself."

Hanging up the phone, he faced the expectant zampolit. "Petty Officer Chapayev has not let us down. If this storm will keep from intensifying for a few more minutes, we can complete our assignment, and then be off for the Pacific without any further delay. Now, if only our radar remains operational.Shall we check the console, Comrade Nevskiy?"

Pleased with the captain's condescending tone, the political officer raised his head, and smartly nodded. His great fear of Timoshenko scrubbing the launch had passed. Even that weakling weapons chief had managed to come through. Perhaps it was his little speech earlier that had brought the lush around. Gloating with this triumph, he followed on the big-boned, bearded officer's heels as they crossed the compartment to the opposite console.

* * *

108

From the cramped confines of the *Boris Chilikin*'s weapons preparation room, Petty Officer Second Class Vasily Chapayev sat erect at his desk, wondering if he had correctly heard the captain's puzzling words. Had he really said that his next task would be to actually fire the cruise missile itself? The officer had to be playing with him!

A dull, alcohol-inspired ache pounded in his forehead as he pondered his next course of action. Looking guiltily at the computer keyboard mounted before him, he seriously considered calling the captain and letting him know of his charade. Not the type of individual who directly shirked his duties, Vasily's actions had been spawned by the zampolit's irritating arrogance. Yet, the petty officer doubted that Timoshenko would accept such an excuse. In matters such as these, officers always stuck together. He would be removed from his post, thrown in irons, court-martialed once they returned to port, and if he escaped with his life, sent into lifelong exile in Siberia.

Vasily couldn't begin to imagine an entire life spent in such a cold, icy environment. The only way he could possible escape such a fate was to act quickly. Scooting off his chair, he hastily surveyed the floor. Upon finding nothing on its length but a few shards of pewter, he scrambled over to the wall, where the majority of the electronic equipment was stowed. He had to get down on his knees to inspect that narrow, dark portion of the floorboard hidden behind these consoles. Just when he was about to stand up to seek the assistance of a flashlight, he saw the object that he had been searching for, caught underneath a thick electrical cord. With his body flush against the wall, he snaked his right hand down the length of the covered floorboard.

It took the full reach of his arm to make initial contact with the ball of crumpled notepaper. When it became apparent that he would need at least another inch to get a decent grip on it, he shoved his right shoulder behind the narrow counter and strained forward. It was at that exact moment that the *Boris Chilikin*'s hull smashed into the lip of the largest wave that they had yet encountered.

As the entire bow lifted up, then smashed downward with a sickening thud, the deck of the floundering ship rolled and vibrated. Caught unprepared by this alien, crushing movement, Vasily had just grasped the ball of paper and was about to pull it out when his body was tossed toward the deck. Still pinned behind the bank of computers, his shoulder found itself wrenched at an angle nature had never intended it to assume. Grimacing in pain, Chapayev managed to yank his entire right arm free.

Never had he experienced such excruciating agony before. Though his right hand was completely numb, his shoulder and upper arm throbbed in pulsating currents of pure anguish. Oblivious to the fact that the object he had been so desperately seeking was now laying on the floor at his side, his shock-torn mind refocused itself on a much different goal. His tear-stained eyes locked on the bottom file drawer set into the opposite wall. There he would find ample relief for the gnawing pain that racked his body.

Somehow, he managed to crawl halfway across the compartment, with his dislocated right shoulder and arm hanging uselessly at his side, before succumbing to a wave of warm, nauseating dizziness. Seconds later, he collapsed forward, his left hand reaching out vainly for the cabinet, which still stood a full six feet distant. For the time being, Petty Officer Second Class Vasily Chapayev would need no vodka to dull his hurt, as he slipped off into blessed unconsciousness.

Both the *Boris Chilikin*'s captain and political officer were making their way down the short hallway leading toward the bridge when the ship hit the massive wave that snapped the petty officer's shoulder. Awkwardly, both men steadied themselves by tightly gripping the pair of brass rails that lined both sides of the walkway.

"These seas seem to be increasing, Comrade Zampolit," warned Timoshenko firmly. "We've got to be getting out of here!"

Yuri Nevskiy was speechless at first, as he struggled to keep his balance. Only when the deck settled beneath them did he attempt to check his watch and issue a response.

"Check the time, Captain. I'd say that it's close enough to 0900 hours to launch the SS-NX-12. How about it?"

Timoshenko hastily glanced down at his wristwatch and briefly nodded. Taking another step forward, he opened the bridge hatchway, and led the way inside.

The remnants of the wave they had just hit was still dripping down the *Chilikin*'s observation window as they entered the bridge. Standing at the wheelhouse, tightly gripping the wheel, the pasty-faced helmsman looked like he had seen much better mornings than this one.

"How's she handling, lad?" the captain queried compassionately.

"Not good, sir," the young sailor said. "I'm trying to keep us headed due west, but it's a constant battle. The helm is very unresponsive."

"Well, we'll soon be saying good-bye to these cursed waters, Comrade. Prepare to swing us around to the east."

Timoshenko couldn't help but notice that this order caused a smile to break the helmsman's previously bleak face. He followed this directive by approaching the intercom mounted on the back wall. Anxiously, he picked up the handset and punched in two digits. He kept it to his ear for a full minute before disconnecting the line, punching in the same two numbers, and then getting a similar response.

"Chapayev is not answering," the concerned captain observed as he hung up the handset. "I wonder if everything is all right down there."

The zampolit was quick to reach his side. "Easy now, Captain. Most likely the petty officer is only in the head. In order to keep our delay to a minimum, why don't we launch the weapon from here. I believe the *Chilikin* has such an ability."

Petyr scratched his heavily bearded chin. "Such an alternative launching position was incorporated into the ship during our most recent refit. In fact, we've yet to give this system a try."

"Then this will serve as the perfect opportunity to do so," beamed the zampolit.

Petyr checked his watch again, then caught the political officer's anxious glance. "All right, Comrade, let's launch the SS-NX-12 from the bridge. Helmsman, turn us around one hundred and eighty degrees. Please notify us back in the control center as soon as this new course has been established."

While the young sailor strained to divert the ship's rudder to initiate this turn, the two officers once again climbed through the hatchway cut into the back of the bridge. Two minutes later, they stood behind the digital console located directly opposite the radio transmitters.

The radar screen was mounted at such an angle that both its seated operator and the two observers standing behind him could get a clear view of its face. Presently, the green glass screen showed a relatively minute portion of the East Siberian Sea located directly to the west of the island of Ajon. This area was laid out in gridded increments, with a detailed map projected above the constantly revolving, white sweep hand.

"Increase the radar scan to full intensity. Eastern horizon, between 65 and 70 degrees latitude only," ordered the captain.

The operator reached forward and punched a series of plastic buttons. As he did so, the screen went blank. Programming the desired information into the keyboard, he looked up as the glass surface began filling with an ever-expanding map segment. The white sweep hand still emanated from a portion of the sea to the west of Ostrov Ajon. Yet its length now penetrated far to the east, passing over the Chukchi Sea, the northeasternmost corner of Siberia, and extending to the middle of the Bering Strait, over seven hundred miles in total distance.

"Excellent," replied the captain, who took a step to his left.

He now faced a compact panel, filled with various digital readout counters. Utilizing a key, which he kept stowed in his pants pocket, he proceeded to open one of these counters. Inside was a device resembling the tumbler of a combination safe. Without hesitating, Timoshenko began twisting this knob in a precise series of turns. As his hand dialed the last desired number, a loud click sounded. Lifting up the tumbler, he exposed a single, half-inch-square button. Inside this plastic knob, a tiny red light incessantly blinked.

"The SS-NX-12 is now armed and ready to fire, Comrade Nevskiy. You know, in all my years of command, this will only be my second actual launch. That test was completed in the warm waters of the Caspian. Would you like to do the honors?"

Most surprised that the captain would permit him to initiate such an important task, Yuri's thick brows rose inquisitively.

"Don't tell me that you're shy, Comrade Zampolit. Merely give that red pulsating button a good push with your index finger. It will be something to tell your grandchildren about."

Never before having been allowed to be such an integral part of an actual launch, Yuri found himself excited. While he selfconsciously wiped his clammy right hand on his pants leg, the intercom loudly buzzed. It was the radio operator who answered it, shouting out so that all of them present in the room could hear.

"It's the helmsman, Captain. The *Chilikin* is now headed due eastward."

"Excellent, Comrades," Timoshenko responded commandingly. "Have him hold our present course at one-quarter speed."

"Yes, sir," shot back the communication's specialist, who went on to relay this request to the helm.

The captain patted his political officer firmly on the back. "It's your show, Comrade."

Sucking in a deep breath, Nevskiy reached forward and readied his extended right index finger. He let out his breath, then made full contact with the plastic button. As he jammed it downward, the light inside abruptly stopped blinking.

The political officer's heart was unexplainably pounding in his chest from this single exertion of energy. He looked up and noticed the captain beckoning him to join them at the radar screen.

Meanwhile, from the stern of the *Chilikin*, a ring of explosive charges activated. To a loud series of corresponding bursts, a twelve-foot-long, two-foot-wide, previously sealed, torpedo-shaped canister split neatly

114

open in a puff of thick, white smoke. Though no one on the ship would hear it, the SS-NX-12's powerful rocket engine was activated, and the sleek, finned missile climbed up its launch rail. Seconds later, it was airborne, smoothly cutting through the thick, icy mist. Its terrain-contour-matching guidance system was already seeking out familiar landmarks as it reached its cruising altitude of a mere five hundred feet above sea level, then burst eastward in a sudden jolt of blinding, supersonic speed.

On the ship's radar screen, the missile's progress was represented by a tiny, blinking red dot. The SS-NX-12 was already well to the east, rapidly crossing over the western shore of deserted Ajon island.

Timoshenko reached forward, and from the blinking dot's current location traced an imaginary line directly eastward. This course crossed Caunskaja Bay, passing onto Siberian soil south of the village of Pevek. Approximately forty-five miles east of this spot, his index finger stopped at the town of Krasnoarmejskij.

"This, Comrades, is where the cruise device is programmed to turn southward. Decreasing its velocity to subsonic speeds to save fuel, it will begin the portion of its flight which will take it snaking down the Anadyrskoje Mountain range. Here, its terrain guidance system will pick up the Anadyr River. Following this tributary ever southward, the missile will continue on down the spine of the Penzinskij Mountains, and pass over the Gulf of Penzinskaja to a splashdown point in the Sea of Okhotsk.

"The completion of such an involved route will signal a new era of Soviet technological achievement. It will also permit the addition of thousands of such relatively inexpensive weapons into our strategic arsenal."

"Could you imagine the Americans having to deal

with such a force streaking toward their territory, low over the wilds of Canada?" added the zampolit.

The captain smiled. "Even with their so-called Star Wars platform, a mass cruise attack would be practically impossible to defend against."

Stepping back from the radar screen, the bearded officer positioned himself beside the slim figure of Yuri Nevskiy. Their eyes remained locked to the monitor as they watched the SS-NX-12 approach the Siberian village of Krasnoarmejskij. Both men looked on, unblinking, as the red dot representing the missile passed over this town, continuing eastward. A full minute passed before the political officer's tense voice broke the strained silence.

"I thought the SS-NX-12 was to turn southward at this point?"

Timoshenko continued watching the monitor closely. "Give it a few more seconds, Comrade. Poor visibility is probably giving the terrain-matching system fits."

Another sixty seconds ticked by, and still the missile continued its progress to the east. The captain caught his fellow officer's concerned glance, and without further comment, his hand shot out for the nearby intercom. Hastily, he punched in two digits. With the plastic handset cradled to his ear, his line of sight went back to the radar screen. He couldn't help but notice the red dot's slight change of course to the northeast, as it began following the spine of the Ekiatapskij Mountain Range.

"Chapayev is still not answering," observed the captain, a bit more urgently. "We'd better get down to the forward weapons room ourselves, and see what is going on there."

After hanging up the intercom roughly, he wasted no time in starting on his way toward the sealed hatchway that would take him back out to the bridge. Yuri watched the captain in the midst of this unnatural haste, and a heavy feeling of nausea settled deep in his belly. Hurrying to catch up with him, the zampolit sensed that something quite out of the ordinary had happened. What it exactly was, he still didn't have the slightest idea.

The long, cold walk to the ship's bow took on an additional hazard with the presence of a sheet of solid ice covering the exposed decking. This slippery obstacle didn't seem to hinder the captain in the least. With one hand on the guide rail, he somehow managed to zip down the one-hundred-and-fifty-foot passageway without even a stumble. His figure had long since disappeared into the hatch by the time the political officer reached this spot.

Frozen and completely numb to the bone, Yuri gratefully ducked under the doorway. A blast of heated interior air hit him full in the face. Gathering his pained breath, he mentally recreated the dangerous walk that he had just finished. Thankfully, the *Chilikin* had already reached more sheltered waters. If this hadn't been the case, he didn't know how he would have ever been able to manage to keep his footing and not slip overboard.

Conscious of the urgency of their situation, he pushed himself down the interior hallway. He crossed through an open hatch and passed a padlocked iron door marked *Ammunition Storage, Authorized Entry Only!* in bright red letters. The next door down the hall was curiously wide open. Yuri would never forget the scene that waited for him inside.

Standing in the middle of the cramped compartment, in the process of unraveling a tightly crumpled ball of paper, was the captain. At his feet lay the unconscious figure of Petty Officer Second Class Vasily Chapayev. His left arm was stretched out in front of the rest of his inert body, as if he'd been reaching for the file cabinet that sat on the other side of the room when he went down. Yuri also noticed that the sailor's right arm was twisted at his side, projecting out in the strangest of angles. It proved to be Timoshenko's puzzled words that brought him instantly back to reality.

"These appear to be the new target coordinates that I instructed you to give Chapayev earlier. I found them rolling on the floor, in a ball like this, as I entered."

"Well, I can assure you that their condition was in a far different state when I indeed gave them to the petty officer," Nevskiy said carefully. "What do you think has occurred here?"

Without bothering to respond, Timoshenko stormed over to the wall-mounted intercom. Activating the handset, he spoke brusquely into its transmitters.

"What is the current position of the SS-NX-12?"

Whatever response he heard caused a grim look to etch his face. Placing the handset down on the counter, he turned to address the zampolit.

"The cruise device is continuing its course eastward. Presently, it's passing the village of Mys Smidta on the edge of the Chukchi Sea. Do you realize what this means, Comrade?"

"So, the missile has malfunctioned," returned Yuri. "This will not be the first time that a new system has failed in a test firing. Hit the destruct button, and we'll both convey the bad news to Admiral Kostromo."

"There is no destruct button," Timoshenko retorted tersely. "And the SS-NX-12 has not failed."

"What ever are you talking about, Captain?"

The bearded officer shoved the wad of crumpled notepaper into Yuri's hand. "Chapayev never reprogrammed the warhead's target-acquisition system like he was instructed to do. The missile is merely obeying the last set of instructions, which he fed into it only yesterday. We've got to inform the admiral of this fact at once!"

The political officer swallowed hard as he considered the drastic implications such a notification would entail. "Surely there must be some alternative way to terminate this flight, before we are forced to inform the *Minsk* of our blunder."

Most aware that the targeting error was completely his responsibility, Petyr took a second to rethink their situation. "There is an outside chance that one of our newly installed SS-N-4 heat-seeking, surface-to-air missiles could reach the cruise device. If only it's still within range!"

Racing over to the room's single computer keyboard, he rapidly entered a stream of request data. In response, the green-tinted monitor screen lit up with a series of complex, coded equations. This was followed by an intricate map cross-section that corresponded exactly to the rendering that had last graced the radar screen. In place of the white sweep hand and the trail of blinking dots, though, was a single red pulsating star, set on the northern Siberian coastline one hundred and forty-seven miles due east of the town of Mys Smidta.

"We can still knock it out!" the captain cried hopefully.

Reaching into his pocket, he removed a single key, then stood and took a step to his left. Before him was a compact panel filled with various digital readouts. After singling out one of these counters, he proceeded to insert the key into a narrow slot set neatly into its side. This act caused a large, square segment of the panel to pop open. Inside was a tumbler, which Petyr began twisting in a precise series of turns. As his hand dialed the last desired number, a loud click sounded.

Lifting up the tumbler, he exposed a single, half-inch-square button. From inside this plastic knob, a tiny red light incessantly blinked. Without a second's hesitation, he jabbed this button downward.

Yuri watched this frantic movement breathlessly. When the red knob stopped blinking, he noticed the sound of machinery activating above them. This dull rumble was succeeded by the deafening roar of a jet engine. The boat seemed to rock gently in response, and then, all was silent.

"She's gone!" Timoshenko reported tersely. "With a little more luck, we should be out of our dilemma in just a few more minutes. We have two things going for us. First, there is speed. The cruise device has already settled into that portion of its flight reserved for a velocity well under that of sound. On the other hand, the SS-N-4 is powered by motors giving it a speed of over Mach 5. Second, is the fact that the SS-N-4 zeroes in on its pursuer with a heat-seeking sensor. Though the cruise missile has a heat signature purposely shielded to thwart such an attacker, the absence of any confusing alternative heat sources should guarantee a kill. The only other thermal presence in those parts is that caused by an Eskimo's fireplace!"

Yuri found himself chuckling along with the captain. But their joviality was quickly stemmed when the sound of a painful groan rose from behind them. Both men turned to identify the source of this alien cry. Stiffly stirring on the floor, was the fallen petty officer.

"We'll see to that poor bastard later," Timoshenko advised, glancing at his watch. "Let's check with radar to see how our attack is progressing. It shouldn't take much longer now to get the final results."

The zampolit followed the captain, who proceeded to pick up the intercom. "How is the SS-N-4 running?" he queried into the transmitter.

Smiling with the radar man's response, he put his palm over the handset and quickly briefed Yuri. "She's right on target. Intercept is only seconds away."

When a voice diverted Timoshenko's attention back to the phone, the political officer found his heart beating away at a much excited rate.

"We've got contact!" cried the bearded officer, whose joyous expression all too soon soured.

Not having any idea as to the reason for this abrupt mood change, Yuri couldn't help but question, "What in the world is going on up there, Comrade?"

Timoshenko gave no reply, still glued to the handset and the report he was receiving from the radar operator.

"But how can that be?" pleaded the captain, whose tone now seemed resolved to total failure. "Very well, Comrade. Keep me informed of any further developments."

As he hung up the intercom, he slowly looked up to face his fellow officer. "Our radar has reported a major explosive flash on the northern Siberian coastline, near the village of Vankarem. This coincides with the SS-N-4's presumed interception point. Even though this weapon has dropped from the screen, the cruise device is somehow still flying. It continues on an easterly course, nearing the one-hundred-and-seventy-five-degree longitude point."

"Then I guess we'd better activate the satellite link-up with the *Minsk*," the zampolit sighed, his tone and expression grave. "Admiral Kostromo is going to be furious with us."

"He's going to be beyond furious," Timoshenko replied carefully. "You see, there's one additional bit of information that I failed to share with you. The course I gave Chapayev yesterday to program into the SS-NX-12 corresponded to a target over 2,660 miles distant. These coordinates are directing the nuclear-tipped warhead to a splashdown in the straits less than ten miles from the American city of Seattle, Washington."

A strained, painful groan seemed to emphasize these last words. Both men looked wordlessly down at the semi-conscious figure laying on the floor beside them.

Chapter Six

Twenty-one thousand miles above the East Siberian Sea, Defense Support Program satellite 647, or DSP North as it was known in the trade, peered down onto the bleak Siberian landscape. Nearly twenty feet long, nine feet wide, and weighing more than a ton, the platform's main load was a twelve-foot, Schmidt infrared telescope. It was the lens of this precision instrument that acted as the satellite's eyes. Impregnated with thousands of minute, lead sulfide detectors, DSP North constantly scanned a programmed patch of territory, ever watchful for the hot flame produced by an ICBM rocket-engine booster as it soared out of the lower atmosphere.

It was well into a new day, as the sun washed the cold, black void of space with its direct light, when several dozen of these lead sulfide sensors crackled alive. Quickly determining the precise location of this disturbance, the satellite's telemetry transmitter beamed this data down to the dual IBM 360–75J computers housed in the "Casino" downlink station located at Nurrungar, South Australia, three hundred miles northwest of Adelaide. With the help of another satellite, this one from the Defense Satellite Communications System, the data was then relayed to a point in North America over eight thousand miles distant.

Air Force Captain William Ford was the officer in charge of NORAD's missile warning center, whose computers were the first to be notified of DSP North's findings. The missile warning center was situated in one of the dozens of manmade granite caves carved thirteen hundred feet below the peak of Colorado's Cheyenne Mountain. The staff of two officers and four enlisted men had a single, all-important task: to receive and analyze all early-warning data before passing it on to the main command post.

Captain Ford was a heavyset, likable officer, who took his serious duty all in stride. Stationed here for the past six months, he was finally learning to adjust to the long, lonely, monotonous hours this assignment demanded. This had been quite difficult at first, as his previous tour of duty with the 600th Tactical Control Wing in West Germany had proved a most active one.

A seven-year service veteran, Ford knew he would most likely see many more posts before his twenty years were up. Thus, he had long ago resolved to take the good with the bad, flowing with the current whenever possible.

The small room in which he currently sat appeared more like it belonged in a modern office building than in a military installation. It was dominated by a wall of computer terminals, whose video screens were blank at the moment. Opposite these consoles was a wall-length display panel, containing a number of empty, windowlike boxes. Two airmen were presently working on this panel, in the process of replacing a number of blown, miniature-sized light bulbs.

Covering a wide yawn, the captain sat back in his comfortable leather chair and checked his wristwatch. Any minute now, the junior officer assigned to relieve him would be arriving. Ford had a double reason to anticipate this transfer of command. Not only was he being relieved from a tedious, eight-hour work shift, but he was also about to begin a much awaited three-day pass. He knew exactly where he was going to spend these precious seventy-two hours of free time.

Bill had met Anne this past New Year's Eve. Both of them had literally bumped into each other before the roaring fireplace of the Vail ski resort they were staying at. While wiping the hot buttered rum she had spilled on him off his ski sweater, the career officer, who was also a confirmed bachelor, had found himself infatuated with the innocent beauty of this red-headed young woman. Over steaming hot refills, they had soon been chattering on like long-lost friends.

Anne was an English teacher at the nearby University of Colorado in Boulder. Recently divorced, she was at that stage in her life where she just wanted to start over with a whole new circle of friends. As it turned out, Bill had arrived at the perfect time to help fill this void.

Later that night, they had shared much more than mere conversation. Wrapped in each other's arms with an icy blizzard blowing menacingly outside, the two had become lovers. It all happened so naturally that neither one of them felt guilty about this hasty coupling the next day. In fact, a good part of the first morning of the year had been devoted to the act which both lonely parties had been craving so.

After a shared bus ride back into Denver, the two had pledged to continue their relationship, a promise that both parties fulfilled quite willingly. Each of his hard-earned passes had been spent with Anne since then. Though often confined to "the mountain" for weeks at a time, this absence had only seemed to cause their bond to grow even stronger. And lately, this affinity had been taking on an entirely new dimension. Not knowing how he had ever survived without her, Bill was seriously considering asking Anne to marry him. Who knows, maybe he'd do so later, this very day!

Smiling inwardly with this thought, the thirty-one-year-old officer stretched his long limbs, and again checked his watch. Any second now his relief would show, and he could be off to another passionate reunion with his new-found lover. He was contemplating the day hike he had planned for them, high in the mountains above Loveland Pass, when a series of events occurred that quickly stripped him of any such pleasant imaginings.

The first stimulus to divert his attention was the harsh, metallic cry of a warning siren. This seldom-heard signal corresponded with a simultaneous activation of each of the video screens.

"It's a DSP North!" cried the young airman seated immediately before the computer terminals. Shocked into action from the paperback novel he had been immersed in, the airman sat up erect, and closely examined the readout screen.

"We show a launch!" he continued, his voice strained and unnaturally high.

Quickly at the airman's side, Ford calmly replied, "Draw up a computer-enhanced map of the region in question."

With hands slightly shaking, the airman fed this request into the keyboard. Almost instantaneously, a detailed representation of the northeastern coast of Siberia popped up on the screen. There, a single, red flashing dot pulsated from a position directly west of

126

the one-hundred-and-seventy-five-degree longitude line.

"That's the SS-18 field located outside of Vankarem!" exclaimed Ford, his words punctuated with dread. "If that heat flash is for real, it looks like the entire flight has been launched. Double-check the scan for accuracy while I inform Mr. Big."

Not taking the time to wipe off the gathering line of perspiration that had gathered in thick beads on his forehead, the captain reached over and picked up a beige telephone handset. While waiting the seemingly endless seconds that it took for his party to answer, his eyes locked on the map that pulsed before him. It was only then that Ford became conscious of the tight knot that was hastily gathering in the pit of his gut.

The main command post of the North American Aerospace Defense Command's Cheyenne Mountain facility was situated in a huge, hollowed-out cavern located several hundred yards from the separate chamber holding the missile warning center. Dominated by a massive, seventeen-by-seventeen-foot display screen, the room was laid out in two levels. Occupying the dimly lit lower level was a series of individual computer terminals, manned by a handful of hushed officers. Overlooking this work space was a relatively narrow balcony. It was here that the installation's central battle station was located. Seated at this position were a pair of blue-uniformed individuals.

General Theodore Bowman was the senior of these two figures. Commander in Chief of the NORAD installation, or CINCNORAD for short, Bowman was known for his feisty temperment and the white shock of flowing hair that perpetually rose from his scalp. In the midst of an absorbed telephone conversation on the red handset, one of five different colored phones that sat next to him, the general didn't even notice when the call from the missile warning center arrived. Picking up the beige receiver on its second ring was his assistant, Brigadier General Walter Craig.

"Attack assessment, General Craig speaking."

The strained voice on the other end spoke out clearly. "Sir, it's Captain Ford. DSP North has awoken! Target source is the Vankarem ICBM fields."

"Have you verified the accuracy of that scan yet, Captain?" quizzed Craig automatically.

Ford was quick to answer. "Preliminary check shows a positive on that launch, sir. Heat source indicates we've got a full flight in the air."

"Double-check that scan, Captain. We're going to draw up Vankarem on the big map. Keep us informed."

Hanging up the receiver, Craig hastily addressed his computer keyboard. After completing this task, he turned to General Bowman, who was still fully absorbed in his conversation. The brigadier general had to put his hand on Bowman's broad left shoulder to rouse him. Looking to his left, the white haired general could see in his assistant's eyes that something serious was occurring. He interrupted his conversation hastily, cupped the phone's transmitter, and questioned, "What's the matter, Walt?"

Bowman turned toward the massive display screen that dominated the room before them. Etched on its length was a detailed representation of the northeastern coast of Siberia. A red flashing light pulsed from the coastline immediately beside the one-hundred-and-seventy-five-degree longitude line.

"DSP North shows a major launch from the Vankarem ICBM fields," Craig advised icily. "The missile warning center is double-checking this initial scan for accuracy."

With the red phone still covered on his lap, General Bowman caught his aide's concerned glance. "I've got Peter Abrahms from the Defense Intelligence Agency on the line. They're confirming the Navy Department's earlier warning. An unprecedented ninety-five percent of the Soviet Fleet is currently steaming into the open seas. We've tagged dozens of their missile-carrying subs as close as one hundred miles from our coastline. They've even got them pulling into the Gulf of Mexico. Jesus, Walt, this looks too legit. You'd better sound the alarm and seal the mountain. Then bring us up to DEFCON 3, contact SAC, and get those aircraft off the runways. Right now, they are just sitting ducks. I'll inform the Pentagon."

In response to this directive, Craig reached forward and punched a single red toggle switch. The harsh buzz of a warning siren spurred the giant complex into action. Meanwhile, General Bowman concluded his conversation on the red phone. Hanging it up, he lifted up the black handset, whose handle was labeled "Secure." Seconds later, he had reached the National Military Command Center in Washington, D.C. to have them set up a conference call on the line. The participants of this forum would include the Joint Chiefs of Staff, the Secretary of Defense, and the President.

While waiting for this distinguished group to be assembled, Bowman held the receiver up to his right ear expectantly. Looking out over the balcony, he could see that all consoles set into the lower level were manned and activated. He was once again scanning the detailed map displayed on the room's central screen when the beige telephone began ringing. Without hesitating, he reached out and brought the receiver to his vacant left ear.

"General Bowman, here."

"General, it's Captain Ford. We've just been contacted by the Over-the-Horizon-Backscatter radar installation at Point Hope, Alaska. They show a definite on a bogey — cruise-type weapon or weapons — approaching American airspace from the Bering Strait. An AWAC E-3 Sentry out of Elemendorf confirms this detection."

Theodore Bowman's face reddened as this revelation took on a visual nature: the giant map before him was shifting to the east, in ten-mile increments, until the Bering Strait was visible. Just entering this narrow stretch of water from the west was a tiny, pulsating red dot.

"Any more word from DSP North?" the general queried adamantly.

The voice on the other end cleared itself. "Negative, sir. We're experiencing problems contacting Casino. We believe this disturbance is being caused by solar flare interference."

"Well damn it, Captain, keep on trying! If more ICBMs are on the way, we've got to know about them!"

Forcefully hanging up the beige phone, Bowman met his aide's puzzled stare. Before he could vocally respond, a familiar voice filtered into his right ear. With his eyes still glued to those of Walter Craig, he crisply spoke into the black transmitter.

"Yes, Mr. President, I hear you loud and clear."

Twenty-five thousand feet above the airspace of southern Indiana, President Andrew Lyons sat in the conference room of the modified Boeing 747 known as Kneecap (National Emergency Airborne Command Post). One of the most costly aircraft of its kind in the world, the plane was packed with sophisticated avionics, including thirteen separate radio systems. Since the E-4B was designed to protect the lives of America's top leaders in times of crisis, such an extensive communications array was necessary to permit the commander in chief to keep in touch with his troops on the ground, in the air, and under the sea. This morning, the ruggedly handsome chief executive was using a single one of these radio bands.

With the red plastic receiver snuggled close to his ear, he listened to General Theodore Bowman's precise assessment of the suspected crisis being monitored from Cheyenne Mountain. Surveying the concerned faces of the two men sitting across the table from him, Lyons shook his head gravely.

"I understand, General Bowman. It is a stroke of fortune that we were in the midst of this test run when this whole thing came down. I'm going to put this call on the squawk box. Secretary of Defense Tate and General Sachs are right here with me."

Activating the speakerphone that sat on the walnut table before him, Lyons was able to hang up the receiver and have both hands free to take quick notes on his legal pad. It was the distinguished, gray-haired Secretary of Defense who issued the first question.

"General Bowman, Russell Tate here. Could you briefly repeat our situation?"

CINCNORAD's voice boomed out clearly. "Mr. Secretary, four minutes ago, DSP North notified us of a launch flash from the Vankarem ICBM fields. So far, we have yet to pick up the number of warheads, of their intended targets. We should have this info any second now. We do know that the signature was intense enough to indicate that a whole flight was sent airborne. Less than ninety seconds ago, our OTH radar station at Point Hope, Alaska, picked up a yet-undetermined number of cruise-type missiles approaching U.S. territory over the Bering Strait. This detection was confirmed and is being monitored by one of our AWACs aircraft."

"And just what has been our response so far?" the secretary continued anxiously.

"I've taken the liberty of bringing our alert status up to Defense Condition three. SAC has just been notified to scramble all available aircraft. You are aware of the unusual movement of Soviet Naval forces worldwide?" added Bowman.

The Chairman of the Joint Chiefs of Staff, General Barton Sachs, responded to this, "Ted, it's Bart Sachs. We've been watching this deployment take shape these last couple of days. No one's ever seen anything quite like it before. If DSP North proves accurate, we could be seeing the beginning of a decapitating attack. Targets would be limited to military command posts and message-relay stations in the hopes of knocking out our ability to order a counterstrike. Those bogey subs off our coasts would serve to back up such a crippling blow. My advice is to bring us up to DEFCON Two."

"Aren't we being a bit hasty with such a move?" the president shot back. "Say this whole alert is being created by a faulty microchip."

"And what if it's not," returned Barton Sachs. "Starting this countdowns on our Minutemen and putting word out to our subs can all be justified as being but a cautionary move. These orders can always be reversed if we're mistaken."

Andrew Lyons sat back and exhaled a full breath of concern. Looking up to the presidential seal that graced the blue-and-white cabin, he was hardly aware of the fact that they were airborne. Though only on the job for a little over four months, he couldn't help but feel the tremendous strain which had caused so many other presidents to grow old before their time. And here he was, the country's youngest leader since John

Kennedy, and already he was noticing a few new gray hairs with each dawn's passing. Most aware that his word was the final say, he spoke out thoughtfully.

"General Bowman, before intensifying our defense condition, I want you to recheck all sensor systems. I've got to be positive that this alert isn't being caused by a glitch in our equipment."

"Very good, sir," answered CINCNORAD. "We are presently double-checking all computer feeds, and will notify you of our assessment at once."

As the line deactivated, Andrew Lyons sat forward. "You know, I keep waiting for one of you to tell me that this whole alert is only a practice run, to give my first ride in Kneecap an added flavor of realism."

"I wish it was," the secretary of defense said. "Even if that indication of an ICBM launch is caused by a malfunctioning sensor, I don't like the idea of an unknown amount of cruise missiles headed toward our airspace."

"Or so many of their ships, poking their noses where they've never been before," added Barton Sachs. "Mr. President, I sure wish you'd reconsider ordering a jump to DEFCON Two. It could save some valuable time later, when each passing second could be responsible for millions of lives."

With his stare still locked on the gold emblazoned seal that symbolized his office, Andrew Lyons knew the general was right. Yet, still, he wanted to be absolutely certain before needlessly unlocking the door to America's deadly arsenal of nuclear revenge. Conscious now of the far-away whine of the E-4B's four, 52,500-pound-thrust engines, capable of keeping them in the air for over seventy-two hours, the young chief executive, whose movie-star good looks had aided his rapid rise to power, contemplated his alternatives. Unbeknownst to him, a momentous event was taking place on the other side of the world that would soon make up his mind for him.

Captain Bill Ford of NORAD's missile warning center found his thoughts somehow wandering far away from those of his present all-important duty. Even with his small room buzzing with frantic activity, he was able to focus on the fact that his weekend with Anne would almost certainly be cancelled. As his eyes slowly scanned the console-mounted display screen before him, another part of his mind was aware that the target they had been tracking was gradually drifting northward. Still skirting U.S. territory, it was continuing eastward over the Arctic's Beaufort Sea.

Having had his share of false alarms in his time, Ford couldn't help but get the feeling that this would be another one. Somehow, the actuality of a real shooting war was just too horrible to comprehend. One fact that he could be certain of, was that if a nuclear conflict did ever come to pass, Cheyenne Mountain would be one of the first targets to feel the sting of the Soviet warheads.

The ringing of a harsh alarm bell redirected his attention to the wall-length display panel that had previously been non-operational. In a flash of sudden light, the boxes set into this console began filling with various combinations of numbers. From the information relayed to NORAD from DSP North, these numerals represented the number of supposed warheads belonging to the Soviet ICBM base at Vankarem. Since each SS-18 could carry up to eight MIRVs, with a yield of two megatons each, there was an almost infinite amount of attack combinations that the enemy could utilize. This board would attempt to determine exactly how many warheads were actually on the way.

It proved to be the ringing of another alarm buzzer, of a much higher-pitched tone, that brought Captain Ford completely back to reality. Sitting up erect in his chair, his fingers scurried over the computer keyboard as one of the airmen shouted out excitedly, "It's DSP South!"

Gradually, the map of the Arctic Ocean faded, to be replaced by one of the South Pacific. Approximately two-thirds of the way between the Hawaiian Islands and New Zealand pulsed a single, large red dot.

"We show a NUDET!" cried the airman.

Ford's stomach instantly tightened as his eyes confirmed that this dot's heat signature corresponded exactly to that of an actual nuclear detonation. One puzzling fact remained. This explosion seemed to have taken place in the middle of the ocean, far from the nearest landmass of any size. Guessing that it could have been caused by a submarine-launched warhead aimed at a naval surface vessel, Ford's now-icy palm shot out for the beige telephone.

Unlike the missile warning officer, General Theodore Bowman had no trouble determining the NUDET's supposed target. Aware of his heart pounding in his chest, NORAD's commander-in-chief soberly faced the brigadier general who sat to his left.

"My God, Walt, it's started. The Russkies just knocked out Delta Base!"

Gripping the black handset, he hastily initiated the inevitable call that had been an integral part of too many nightmares.

Per his request, Andrew Lyons sat alone in Kneecap's conference room. The information relayed to him by CINCNORAD only minutes ago had left him with no choice. The armed forces of the great country he led were presently being notified of a defense condition that was only one step away from a full-scale nuclear war.

From the dozens of SAC bases located throughout the nation, hundreds of B-52 bombers were scrambling for the relative safety of the air. Streaking to their rendezvous points were the KC-10 tankers, whose duty was to fill the tanks of the B-52s for the six-hour flight into the enemy's homeland.

Nestled in silos buried deep below the nation's midwest, various two-man command teams were preparing America's ICBM force for its final launch orders. With countdowns being held at the sixty-second mark, this awesome force of over one thousand missiles needed only a single coded password to send their lethal loads skyward.

And cruising silently beneath the world's seas were the missile-carrying submarines of the U.S.A's ultimate revenge force. Carrying the destructive potential of over 23,000 Hiroshimas in their holds, these vessels were currently receiving a rare, direct radio transmission. With the assistance of trailing, very-low-frequency antennas, the subs were being notified that a defense condition code-named "Cocked Pistol" prevailed. Needing no other authority to launch their loads of Trident and Poseidon missiles, the boats would now descend quietly into the ocean's depths for a prescribed length of time. Only afterward would they rise to listen for countermanding orders. Barring receipt of such instructions, the sub commanders would consider a state of war to exist and would proceed with their attack plans accordingly.

Lyons now had only to broadcast the coded message that lay in the open briefcase before him to complete the sequence that had been started in motion. This case was known as the "football." Kept always within his reach on the handcuffed wrist of a military aide, this case also held the fabled "black book." Over one hundred pages long, the book contained the various courses of actions available to him to meet a Soviet first strike. This nuclear response strategy was known as the Single Integrated Operational Plan, or S.I.O.P. for short. In effect, it would instruct him how to command America's warheads to inflict the maximum amount of damage to the enemy, with the minimum amount of risk to the U.S. Four months ago, he hadn't even known that such a thing existed.

When he had first decided to run for the nation's highest office, it had been with the sincere belief that his presence in Washington would make such a morning as this one even more of an impossibility. Sick of ever-rising defense budgets, and the constant threat of instant nuclear annihilation perpetually hanging over their heads, the American electorate had overwhelmingly chosen him to carry out this mandate.

At first glance, this chore had seemed like an easy task to achieve. Where so many others had failed by neglecting to approach the Soviets sincerely, with concrete, reasonable proposals to halt the nuclear madness once and for all, he would do otherwise. Barely a month into office, his invitation to First Secretary Vladimir Kirensk to come to Camp David had been instantly accepted. This hastily scheduled meeting had taken place over a two-day period. As the first hint of spring touched the Maryland foothills, the leaders of the two most powerful nations on this planet had sat down for a sincere meeting of the minds.

Andrew had developed an immediate affinity for the relatively young premier who had been working hard to consolidate ultimate power within his own country.

The prematurely balding, good-natured Russian agreed with him that the escalating arms race was only breaking the backs of their respective peoples. Only the naive had hoped that their initial meeting would lead to the banning of nuclear weapons all together. What the two leaders had agreed upon was a necessary first step to this eventual desired aim.

The resulting Space Weapons Treaty was currently awaiting ratification in the Congress. In exchange for both countries halting all further development of orbiting weapons platforms of both offensive and defensive natures, the Soviets promised to significantly cut back deployment of their long-range SS-N-18 ICBMs, while the U.S. did likewise with their MX missiles. Further cutbacks of a much greater number were presently being discussed in Geneva.

Beyond such an agreement, Andrew had thought that he had developed a genuine understanding of the Soviet leader. Their emotional farewell at Andrews Air Force Base had even prompted Lyons to admit that he actually trusted the man's sincerity. Like a slap in the face, this trust had suddenly come back to haunt him.

Beyond a feeling of personal betrayal was one of utter failure to his constituents. If they could only see their great peace candidate now, only a quarter of an hour away from issuing the order that could very possibly doom the entire planet! Had he fallen into the inevitable trap, just as the leaders before him had?

A pocket of rough air shook the 747's fuselage, and Andrew Lyons was once more aware of the alien medium on which they traveled. Glancing down at his scribbled notepad, he attempted to put the morning's events into their proper perspective.

DSP North's initial warning could very well be the by-product of a faulty sensor. That would be why any corresponding warheads had still yet to be picked up, directly negating NORAD's suspicions that a series of solar flares were responsible for this non-detection. Yet, how could he explain the undetermined amount of cruise-type weapons currently skirting America's northernmost border? And what of the actual nuclear detonation in the waters south of American Samoa? Why, until five minutes ago, he had never even known that such an installation as Delta Base even existed. He had no doubt that such a top-secret, U.S. sub refitting station would indeed be among the first casualties of World War III.

And then there was the reality of the massive, worldwide Soviet naval maneuvers, which the U.S. had been watching develop for the last several days. Such an unprecedented show of force went against everything Vladimir Kirensk had pleaded so convincingly that he stood for. Had their meeting been a clever political ruse to lull Andrew Lyons into a preconceived trap? If so, he had swallowed the bait hook, line, and sinker.

Well aware that the first Soviet warheads could very well already be headed toward American soil, the young president recalled General Sachs's advice as to the benefits of a pre-emptive strike on America's part. Such a launch on warning strategy could save the country's entire ICBM force from being destroyed in their silos. Added to the damage created by those B-52s that managed to penetrate Soviet airspace, and the thousands of submarine-delivered warheads, the U.S.S.R. would receive a fatal, knock-out blow that would take them a hundred years to recover from. Yet, could the so-called candidate of peace live with such a decision on his conscience? Or was he to wait until his own citizens were being incinerated before ordering the inevitable slaughter?

Sobered by the choices available to him, he realized

that there was only a single way to find out the Soviet Union's true intentions. Forcefully shutting the infernal black case that lay before him, Andrew Lyons reached out for the red telephone handset. Obtaining a direct line into the Pentagon's National Military Command Center, he initiated the series of complex procedures that would eventually allow him to talk first-hand with his "old friend," Vladimir Kirensk. With the time on the doomsday clock rapidly approaching high noon, it was now or never for both parties to put their cards on the table. For this was a game that had no winners.

Chapter Seven

Thomas Kraft couldn't help but admit that this had already been one of the most exciting days of his life. Less than twenty-four hours ago, his duty had been tinged with sheer boredom. Other than the monitoring and upkeep on the sensor equipment, and the diversions caused by Telsa and his weekly trips into Pago Pago, there had been little to do in his isolated fales overlooking Cape Taputapu. Little had he realized what the result of his call to Pearl Harbor would be. The trip by helicopter and his transfer to the USS *Phoenix* had put him deep into a liquid dimension he never even dreamed of traveling through. And adding to the strangeness was the fact that he was devouring a full-course turkey dinner while doing so.

Pete Walsh, the boat's XO, and Lieutenant Mark Peterson shared the table with this newcomer. Between bites of tender white meat, cranberry sauce, mashed potatoes, and dressing, their conversation drifted innocently.

"When's that kid of yours due, Peterson?" quizzed Walsh, whose hand went out for his coffee cup.

"Should be sometime later this month," returned the junior officer. "Peggy's so full in the belly that the doc advised her to keep her bags packed just in case it decides to pop out early."

"Is this your first baby?" Kraft inquired.

Peterson wiped his lips with his napkin. "Sure is. I've got to admit that being a papa is a bit more nerve-wracking than I expected."

The XO smiled. "Well, take it from a three-time veteran and don't sweat the details. Nature will take its course, just as it has since the beginning of mankind. Who's taking care of your wife while you're away?"

"She's staying with her parents. This is one cruise I sure wish I didn't have to make."

"She'll be fine," continued Pete, who began working on his pumpkin pie. "Say, Lieutenant Kraft, what do you think of our little vessel so far?"

Thomas pushed back his tray and patted his stomach. "With chow like this, how can I complain? I haven't eaten so good in months."

Surveying the spacious compartment, whose other tables were only partly filled, he added. "You know, I didn't expect living conditions on board a submarine to be so darn comfortable."

"Few other submariners are as fortunate as us," Walsh observed with a wink. "The naval designers really outdid themselves when it came to putting together the Tridents. For a change, they seriously considered the comforts of the men that would sail them. You wouldn't believe some of the cramped conditions I've encountered in other class vessels. Some of those subs were so packed that they even had extra torpedoes stowed in the mess and bunk areas. You see none of that here on the *Phoenix*."

Even though his appetite was thoroughly satiated, Thomas tried a bite of the pie. He found it extremely tasty and couldn't resist polishing off the rest of it. Washing it down with a mug of strong, black coffee, he found himself totally contented.

The XO checked his watch. "The Trench isn't far off now. You say that you know these waters pretty well?"

"I spent the good part of a month here," replied Kraft. "Since my assignment was the placing of seismic monitors on the seafloor, I devoted a lot of time studying the topographical maps of this sector. The Tonga Trench has some incredible geological features."

"Exactly what's it like down there?" Lieutenant Peterson asked.

Kraft took a second before answering. Reaching for his dinner plate, he used his fork to shape the remnants of his mashed potatoes into a long, thin line. At the end of this line, he positioned a sliver of cranberry sauce.

"Imagine the cranberries to represent the island of New Zealand. The potatoes become a massive underwater mountain chain that stretches for over 1,700 miles. Occupying the northern tip of this range is the Tonga Trench. Formed by a series of undersea mountains, many over one thousand feet taller than Mt. Everest, the Trench features some of the deepest water known on this planet. One sounding that we attempted took over 30,000 feet of line, and we still never hit bottom."

"I've had a good look at those maps myself," offered the XO. "This region never fails to impress me. How did you go about placing those sensors, anyway?"

"For the most part, we utilized a remote-control, deep-diving submersible. We could use divers only when working the relatively shallow waters that surrounded the seamounts."

Two soft, electronic tones sounded in the background, and the XO looked up expectantly. "Excuse me, gentlemen, but I believe they're playing my song."

The solidly built six-footer stood and made his way over to the wall-mounted intercom set. He placed the receiver to his ear, and with his eyes still locked on their bearded guest, had a brief conversation. Thirty seconds later, he was back at their table.

"The skipper wants us topside," instructed the still-standing officer. "He seems to think that it's time for us to start working off this turkey."

"What, no nap?" jested Lieutenant Peterson, who stood and stretched his stiff frame.

Thomas Kraft followed the two sub officers out of the mess hall and the stairway that would lead them upward to the command and control section.

Two floors above the mess, the *Phoenix*'s command center was buzzing with activity. In the process of making a personal round of inspection was Captain Charles Blake. The tall, blond-haired officer alertly walked the circuit of stations, halting briefly at each of the consoles responsible for navigation, diving, and communications. At the bank of instruments reserved for the sonar monitors, he addressed a balding, heavy-set individual, seated in the central position between two other operators.

"Good evening, Mr. Canova. Anything on that scan?"

The broad-shouldered lieutenant reached forward and turned down the amplifier feed leading into his headphones. "Negative, Skipper. I just finished a three-hundred-and-sixty-degree hydrophone analysis and it's as quiet as a church out there. I told you that we gave that Russkie the slip."

"That you did," returned Blake with a nod.

Before the captain could continue, Canova's hands shot up to his compact earphones. "We've got something, Skipper! Due south of us."

This warning was followed by a clearly audible, distant explosive boom. Reacting instantly to this

144

detonation, Blake called out harshly, "Hit the recorder! Sound General Quarters!"

The men in the command center were still reacting to this warning when a massive swell of agitated water smashed into the sub's bow. Tossed abruptly upward, like a feather in the wind, the 18,700-ton vessel rolled jerkily from side to side. To the blinking lights of the boat's shorted electrical system, those unfortunate sailors who didn't have a secure perch found themselves thrown off balance. Several men crashed to the floor, while others found themselves flung into the compartment's equipment-packed walls.

Charles Blake had managed to hold onto the tubular steel railing set behind the sonar console. Fighting to keep his balance, he barely had time to scan the scene that surrounded him when another concussion wave smacked into the *Phoenix*. This one caused the vessel to nose downward. As the boat keeled over on its side, the captain found his ever-tightening grip unable to keep him steady. Tossed to his left, he kept himself from falling to the deck by grabbing onto the back of Lieutenant Canova's deck-mounted chair. When the boat lurched hard to the right, he quickly widened his stance and somehow remained upright.

Several anxious seconds passed, while the captain decided that the rough waters had subsided. He didn't waste any time in barking out his orders.

"Damage control, I want a full report on all stations! Mr. Canova, are you still with us?"

The stunned sonar operator looked up sheepishly, flashing Blake a thumbs-up.

"Get us a fix on that explosion's source. Then, play it back on the tape, and see if the computer can figure out what in the hell that blast was all about."

"Aye, aye, sir."

As the sonar operator went to work, Blake stood up

erect and straightened his uniform. Efficiently, he surveyed the room. It was only then that he laid eyes on Kraft and the two other latecomers, who were in the process of picking themselves off the deck. Blake didn't waste any time getting to their sides.

"Jesus, Pete, are you all right?"

The XO stood stiffly. "I think I'm still in one piece. I'm afraid I can't say the same for Peterson here. Seems that I gave him an elbow in the nose when we went down."

Still kneeling, the diving officer was being attended to by a disheveled but otherwise healthy Thomas Kraft, who was stemming the steady stream of blood running from the lieutenant's nostrils. Utilizing his handkerchief as a compress, Kraft was able to gradually halt the blood flow.

"We'd better get Peterson down to the sick bay," the executive officer said as he scanned the control center to make sure no one else needed medical assistance. It appeared everyone else had managed to survive the ordeal without being more than badly shaken. "What in the world hit us, Skipper?"

Blake shook his head. "Damned if I know. Whatever it was, it was triggered by one hell of a blast. Hopefully, we've got it on tape. Canova is doing the tape analysis, and also a sound fix."

Both officers looked on as Thomas Kraft helped the bloodied helmsman stand. Peterson was holding the bright-red-spotted handkerchief up to his nostrils on his own now. As he caught his captain's concerned glance, he spoke out almost apologetically.

"I'm sorry for the mess, sir."

"Whatever are you talking about, Lieutenant?" Blake replied with a grin. "We can thank the XO here for almost rearranging your face. You can get even with him later. Until then, do you think you can get

146

down to the doc on your own?"

"I think I can manage, sir. Is the *Phoenix* okay?"

"It's going to take much more than a little rough water to stop this little lady," answered the captain. "Now, you just go and take care of yourself. I'm going to need you back at the helm as soon as you're able."

Returning Peterson's salute, Blake watched the young officer carefully turn around and disappear through the interior hatchway. Angling his glance back to the bearded figure standing next to his exec, the captain cleared his throat.

"Are you okay, Mr. Kraft?"

Thomas nodded and the skipper continued, "Then, let's see just how we rode out that wave. Damage control, what's our status?"

An alert voice from the opposite side of the compartment responded instantly. "Mr. Crowley reports another O-ring failure in the number-two port torpedo tube. The leak has been contained and they're presently mopping the room dry and initiating replacement procedures. Other than a few broken gauges and a bit of a mess down in the galley, all other stations remain secure."

"Any word from the doc?" Blake quizzed firmly.

Again, the damage control officer answered efficiently. "The initial report from sick bay shows that the crew suffered a few minor bruises and cuts. So far, no broken bones or any other significant injuries."

"Thank the Lord," Blake sighed under his breath. Catching the XO's glance, he shook his head.

"We were very fortunate, Pete. I think it's time to find out precisely what caused that little tumble. Shall we, gentlemen?"

Beckoning the two officers to join him, the captain moved over to the sonar console. While watching the pudgy fingers of Anthony Canova frantically feed his

147

requests into the computer keyboard, Blake addressed those who stood beside him.

"The shock waves were preceded by a single, large explosion. Though muted, it was loud enough for me to actually hear it resonate from this very position."

"Exactly where are we, captain?" questioned Thomas Kraft.

"We were some thirty-five nautical miles due north of the Tonga Trench's uppermost extremity when I buzzed you down in the mess."

The geophysicist scratched his beard thoughtfully. "That would place us near enough the area of geological disturbance to be directly effected by any major release of effluence."

"What do you mean by that?" queried the XO.

Kraft looked up with his gaze unfocused. "What I'm inferring is that both the explosion and the resulting shock wave could have been caused by an enormous, undersea volcanic eruption."

"Boy, that's a first," reacted Walsh lightly. "Could you imagine us being knocked off by a volcano?"

Thomas frowned. "Actually, such a possibility isn't that remote, especially in waters such as these."

"I've got to admit, son, that's a new one even for me," added the captain. "I've patrolled these waters for over twenty years, and have only been tossed around like that once before. At that time, it was no volcano, but a Soviet depth charge that did the shaking."

The rough voice of Anthony Canova interrupted them. "Excuse me, Skipper, but I've isolated the portion of the hydrophone tape that you requested."

"Play it back over the control room's public-address system at full volume," instructed Blake.

After depressing a series of switches, Canova sat back as a loud, rumbling explosion sounded from the room's mounted speakers. This throaty blast continued to gather in intensity until it rose to an almost-deafening crescendo. Taking another full minute to dissipate, the rumbling was still audible in the distance as Charles Blake signaled the balding New Yorker to cut the feed.

"Does the computer's memory show any I.D. on that sound signature's source?" the captain asked.

Anthony Canova swiveled over to face his console's display screen. As several lines of data flashed onto it, his face suddenly drained of all color. Blake couldn't help but notice this, and quickly bent over and scanned the monitor for himself. Shocked by what he had read, the captain turned to face his exec.

"If only that blast was indeed caused by a volcano, Pete."

The XO found himself puzzled by the captain's expression. "What's the matter, Skipper. You look like you just saw a ghost."

Blake's gaze widened to include Thomas Kraft. "I'm afraid I have. Big Brother shows a ninety-five-percent probability that the blast was of a nuclear origin. Sound signature I.D. matches it almost precisely with the thermonuclear test blast of November 1, 1952, that wiped Eniwetok Atoll off the face of the earth."

This revelation was punctuated by the harsh buzzing of a persistent metallic tone. Both the captain and his exec turned immediately toward the communications console. On the far side of the equipment-cluttered control room, a pair of sailors were busily transcribing the newly arrived VLF radio transmission this alarm announced. It took only seconds for the two officers to cross the compartment and intercept this message firsthand.

Fresh from the decoding device, the transmission was placed in the captain's hands. Though it was only a simple message two words long, the reality of their meaning caused Blake's hands to begin shaking as he handed the sheet to Pete Walsh. The XO's gut turned and soured as he beheld the words *Cocked Pistol* typed neatly in the paper's center.

Charles Blake's words rang out apocalyptically. "My God, Pete, it's started! That blast just took out Delta Base. A couple of miles further, and we could have gone with it."

Unable to respond, Walsh looked up into the eyes of his commanding officer, and for the first time saw fear. Instinctively, he found himself folding up the message and handing it back to the captain as Thomas Kraft approached them from the room's center.

"Captain, if you give me a chance, I think I can prove my theory. I'm almost certain that the blast we just heard was not manmade."

"For God's sake, man, not now!" exclaimed Blake angrily.

Sensing the captain's frustration, the XO alertly stepped in between the two men. "Lieutenant Kraft, I'm afraid that I'm going to have to order you to leave the control room at this time. I believe you know the way back to your quarters."

"But if you'll just give me a second to explain," pleaded Thomas.

"Unfortunately, I can't even give you that at the moment. Perhaps later. Now, if you'll please excuse us."

Sensing the legitimacy of the XO's urgent tone, the geophysicist reluctantly pivoted to make his way out of the command center. As he crossed the open hatchway, he couldn't help but notice that Pete Walsh had joined the captain behind the seated helmsman. The tall blond commander was barking out a long line of unintelligible directives as Kraft exited the room.

Halfway down the narrow corridor that led to the descending stairwell, he became aware of a sudden noticeable tilt of the vessel's bow. This rapidly steepening angle was accompanied by a distant gathering whir caused by the Phoenix's engines. It was most obvious that they were already rapidly gaining in both speed and depth.

Where they were off to in such a hurry, and why the captain wouldn't even bother to take the time to listen to his theory, remained an enigma. The only thing that he could be certain of was that something in that message they just received had scared the living daylights out of both veteran officers. There could be no ignoring that look etched in their eyes only seconds ago. He had seen a similar expression clouding the faces of his colleagues back in the spring of 1980. Inspired by the booming, thousand-foot fingers of smoke, ash, superheated gas, and pumice created when Mount St. Helens had blown apart with the force of over a hundred nuclear bombs, that look of terror haunted him to this day. Why it had returned to possess the officers of the USS *Phoenix* was a mystery posing a much more immediate threat.

Chapter Eight

To be the supreme leader of an entire country can be one of the loneliest occupations known to man. Empowered to direct the destinies of the masses below, such a personage had to learn to rely on no one but himself in order to do his job efficiently. Because of the scope of government beaurocracies, advisors were a necessary evil. Yet, when it came to the final say, it was the chief executive who bore the responsibility alone. This was a lesson Vladimir Kirensk had learned well during his six years as General Secretary of the Communist Party of the Soviet Union.

Too often the scope of his current position seemed almost impossible to comprehend. This evening, the immense power he ultimately wielded was much too obvious. For tonight, not only did he have the destiny of his own people on the line, but also that of the entire world.

The fifty-two-year-old politician knew that the time to make a final choice would soon be upon him. Until that moment came, he could but channel his nervous energy, attempt to clear his mind, and put the evening's events into their proper perspective. To aid his concentration, he resorted to a habit he had developed when he was only a minor official with the Ministry of

Agriculture. Cocking his hands behind his back, he paced the full length of his office, halting occasionally to glance out one of the room's large picture windows.

Clearly visible outside was one section of the sixty-foot-high, twenty-foot-thick Kremlin wall. Lit by a powerful bank of spotlights, the solid, red-brick edifice loomed with ancient splendor. Originally built by Ivan III in the fifteenth century, the outer wall was designed to protect this section of Borovitsky Hill, situated on the northern banks of the Moscow River, from invaders. Unfortunately, the advent of modern warfare had made such a castlelike rampart practically useless. One nuclear warhead, and the seat of their government would be but a mass crater of radioactive rubble. Visualizing such a scene, Vladimir realized that the very missiles set aside to accomplish this task were already being activated.

The land-based Pershings and submarine-launched ballistic warheads needed but a scant ten minutes of flight time to totally obliterate the Kremlin and the rest of Moscow. Even though their own warheads would subsequently destroy Washington, D.C., and the rest of America, he would have failed in his primary duty— which was to keep the Motherland intact. Those Russians who would be fortunate enough to survive such a nuclear exchange would find a scarred country, about as technologically advanced as that which Ivan had ruled. This was a legacy he didn't dare leave behind. Somehow, he had to summon the wisdom to make such a future an impossible one.

With his gaze set upon the copse of evergreens placed immediately before the wall, Vladimir found his contemplations drifting to a much earlier time. How innocent and naive were those days of his initial government service! Born and raised outside of Kiev, in the heart of the Ukraine, Vladimir had started life as a farmer's son. Endless fields of ripening wheat and corn were his entire world—until his above-average intelligence and leadership ability had brought him to the attention of the local Party cell. Unaware of what they had in store for him, he had accepted the invitation to attend the State University in far-off Volgograd, with dreams of returning home a man of the world. Enrolled primarily in agricultural courses, young Kirensk had found his appetite for new knowledge an insatiable one. Devouring book after book, he had anxiously soaked in the immense diversity of the great republic he lived within.

Vladmir had gotten an idea of the hugeness of his country when a summer field trip sent him far to the north. For days on end, the wide-eyed student had traveled by train, up the Urals, and into the thick woods that stretched to the Arctic Circle. Here, he had learned about forest management firsthand while serving with a lumber detachment. With the help of a sturdy axe, wood to build the Motherland's homes, fill its books, and warm its furnaces was cut and prepared for shipment. It was in such a camp that he had turned twenty-one, the same summer his shoulders had seemed to suddenly blossom. It was also at this time that his hair had begun falling out in steady strands. By the time he returned to Volgograd and the fall courses, he had been almost totally bald, yet none the worse for his summer in the field.

After graduating a full year early, Vladimir had learned, somewhat to his dismay, that he would not be going back to Kiev as he'd anticipated. Instead, he had been allowed but a week to say good-bye to his family, pack his few belongings, and take a train to the capital city itself.

The day he had first arrived in Moscow, the town was receiving the brunt of the first snowstorm of the season. Not accustomed to fighting the icy Siberian winds and huge drifts of blowing snow, Vladimir had desired nothing else but to reboard the train and make his way southward. But summoning his courage, he had decided that it would be foolish to run away, that he mustn't allow the new environs to intimidate him so. With the assistance of the city's excellent subway system, he had somehow made it to the imposing, brick structure that housed the Ministry of Agriculture. There, with hands, face and feet thoroughly frozen, he presented his credentials.

The duty officer had been a grizzled World War II veteran who had immediately sized up the young man's plight. Before sending him off to the worn desk he would occupy for the next one and a half years, the old-timer had shared with him a pint of vodka and a bowl of piping hot vegetable stew.

Refreshed, and with feeling already returning to his numb limbs, Vladimir had felt like a new person, and with renewed direction had surrendered himself to his new duty. A week later, he didn't know how he had ever truly lived in any other place than this city, which from that time onward, he was to call home.

As the weeks had melted into months, and the months to years, Kirensk at last became a man of the world. Two years after initially arriving in Moscow, he was named the Chief Aide to the Minister of Agriculture himself. This position had sent him off to the far reaches of not only the U.S.S.R., but also the world. With an alert, inquisitive eye, had he traveled to the farmlands of America's midwest, the rice fields of Southeast Asia, and the woods of Canada and the Pacific Northwest. He'd attained economic maturity by participating in an actual grain deal with the clever Americans. It was for the signing of this agreement that he was sent to Washington, D.C., and then to

New York City. The town known as the "Big Apple" had proved to be beyond his wildest expectations. Surely, never had so many people been jammed into such a tiny amount of space before! And the buildings, they were like something out of an architect's nightmare.

It hadn't been long after returning from this trip that the likable old minister who had taken Vladimir under his wing died of a heart attack. Caught unprepared by this sudden death, the government had requested that Kirensk temporarily take over the minister's duties until a proper replacement was assigned. Vladimir had done so without hesitation.

With the assistance of his secretary, Vladimir had handled the job flawlessly. It was with great satisfaction that he had initialed a copy of the most recently concluded five-year plan. Personally presenting these results to a session of the ruling Politboro, the bald-headed, young bureaucrat had reported an unprecedented harvest. Every area of agricultural output appeared on the rise, generated by a massive application of modern farm management and technology.

Vladimir would never forget the moment the legendary figure seated at the head of the table had answered his findings with a wide smile. As his bushy, black eyebrows arched upward the portly general secretary had risen and addressed his fellow Politboro members. It seemed that Kirensk's bureau had been the only one to have met its preplanned quota. Vladimir's heart had jumped with joy when he learned that the ministry's present head would be both decorated as a hero and given the position permanently.

Called before the Supreme Soviet, Vladimir had been given his medal. And a week later, he had taken his ever-faithful secretary to the altar. Since then, Olga had been his only woman for over two decades. Always at his side, she assisted him invaluably on the rapid climb to ultimate power that soon followed.

Six years ago, he had become the youngest leader in the Soviet Union's history. Tired of the worn-out, old men that had perpetually been at the country's helm, the central committee had gambled on this daring move. Slowly at first, Vladimir had worked to firmly consolidate his position of power. Many of the old-timers had still been cautious of any abrupt break from precedent, and were hesitant to accept any new policies which would upset the apple cart. Ever-conscious of this fact, yet aware of the new world around them, Kirensk had waited patiently.

The first signal of his acceptance outside the Soviet Union had come during a visit to Europe. With his fashionable wife at his side, Vladimir had been something of a media star as he toured the cities of Rome, Paris, and London, meeting the leaders of the countries. Impressed by the new general secretary's quick wit, superb intelligence, and Western appearance, the Europeans had praised him to the rest of the world.

Back home, any doubters jumped on the band wagon. Without a question in their minds, even the most sullen of skeptics had admitted that this was the type of image the Soviet Union needed abroad. Such additional support had been all that Vladimir needed.

The first of what was to be a series of new State directives had soon been released. This initial reform was in the area he knew best, agriculture. By encouraging competition between the thousands of farming cooperatives, the general secretary had caused a new spirit to possess the countryside. One-third of all production over the quota was to be the exclusive property of those who labored to grow it, to dispose of as they saw fit. To rejuvenate the country's worn soil, he had diverted millions of rubles into the development and allocation of fertilizers. An even greater amount of man-hours had been set aside for the manufacture of farm equipment, including vehicles designed to eliminate waste at harvest time and to transport the picked crop to market before it was subjected to the ravages of mold and blight.

Two years after the implementation of such policy, the crop yield had been significantly higher than ever before. For the first time in decades, the Soviet Union actually had enough grain to feed its own population. As their efficiency continued, there would soon even be a small amount available for actual export sales.

Gloating with the success of this program, Vladimir had gone on to shore up the country's sagging industrial might. With an emphasis on computer education, he'd proposed an unprecedented seven-year program, during which time an entire generation of children would become competent on the devices directing modern technology. To acquire such equipment, he had announced plans to barter oil from the rapidly growing Siberian fields to various Western nations such as England, France, and Japan.

If there was any portion of the economy that he was rumored to be soft on, it was said to be the military. Under Kirensk's leadership, few new weapons systems had been proposed or were currently being developed. Instead, he emphasized improving the country's present arsenal by stressing training, proper equipment repair, and the manufacture of sufficient numbers of spare parts. This policy had taken on an added dimension when the general secretary had agreed to meet the newly elected U.S. President, to discuss ways to begin a serious cutback of wasteful military spending. The resulting Space Arms Treaty was heralded by many as a great achievement, a first step to the eventual elimination of all nuclear arsenals. Yet to

158

others, especially within the military complex itself, Kirensk's hastily planned summit at Camp David bordered on sheer betrayal.

Of all the wasteful ways for the Motherland to apply its industrial might, Vladimir could see no more worse way to throw away precious man-hours than in military efforts. True, a strong defense was needed to keep out all aggressors. But what did the Soviet Union possibly need with an offensive force? Minor excursions like that in Afghanistan could be met with relatively small detachments of troops and weapons. It was the thousands of unnecessary missiles, planes, and ships that were draining the country dry. Why, they already had enough strategic warheads to blow up the Western nations a hundred times over. Must he listen to his military advisors and make this overkill a thousand times?

It proved to be in such an area that he and the young American president had agreed on completely. The treaty they proposed had promised to send this message to each of their country's military planners. At present, this treaty was being debated by both the U.S. Senate and his own Politboro. Being a political realist, Vladimir knew of the great clout the military had amongst the thirteen members of this all-powerful council. Still dominated by the old-timers, who had been present when Soviet soil was violated by Nazi Germany, these elders had sworn, and rightfully so, never to allow such a tragedy to befall the Motherland again. Suspicious of any cutback in military spending as indicating a soft defense posture, these hardliners had to be dealt with very carefully. Alienating this clique could doom his position of leadership as quickly as an assassin's bullet could. This was one of the reasons he listened to his advisors, and against his first instincts, had allowed Admiral Kostromo to proceed with Operation Lenin.

The logic had sounded all so legitimate that he couldn't resist their pleas. The old officer corps in the military were reaching the end of their years of useful service. The decades since the end of the last World War had been theirs to dominate exclusively. With a free hand they had wielded their power, diverting the industrial might of Russia to satisfy their hunger for new weapons systems. From the ashes of 20,000,000 dead, they had built an armed force second to none. This included a standing army of almost two million men, an air force sporting some twelve thousand sophisticated aircraft, and a navy capable of extending its control to any sea on this planet. To begin indiscriminately cutting back these forces now would be an affront to those whose vision created this awesome force. Thus, to reaffirm his intentions, Vladimir's advisors warned him to listen to the pleas of those old-timers, such as Admiral Kostromo.

Let them play their wargames, they argued. For could you imagine what it would be like to be a child who found it impossible to show his rival a cherished new toy? It would drive him wild with frustration!

Against his better judgement, he had let the admiral proceed. For the first couple of months, while the preparations for Operation Lenin began, Vladimir had indeed found a warmer reception from the hardliners. Many of them had even appeared to be seriously considering his plan to cut back on the deployment of all new offensive ICBM installations.

Sensing victory, the general secretary had recently even been considering a call to Andrew Lyons to convey this fact. As it had eventually turned out, though, the two had indeed had a telephone conversation—yet how very different the subject had been. With the President's recent words still stinging his ears,

Vladimir checked his wristwatch, backed away from the picture window, and again began his nervous pacing.

This evening's nightmarish events had all begun less than a quarter of an hour ago, when he had received Admiral Kostromo's emotional phone call. Originating on the other side of the world, where a new day had already dawned, the fifty-year naval veteran had told of a disastrous series of accidental events.

From the deck of the underway-replenishment ship *Boris Chilikin,* one of the new SS-NX-12 cruise weapons had been launched. Because of a drunken sailor's incompetence, this weapon had been improperly targeted. Attempts to shoot it down had led to the destruction of a major oil drilling rig that had been operating off the coast of northeastern Siberia, across from the village of Vankarem. Over seventy men had been killed in the blast, and the fire was still burning out of control.

Meanwhile, the cruise weapon continued its preprogrammed attack pattern. Presently, it was still skirting U.S. territory, skimming the Beaufort Sea off the northern coast of Alaska. Any second now, it was due to turn abruptly southward. Snaking down the rugged, mountainous terrain separating the U.S. and Canada, the SS-NX-12 would need less then two hours more to deliver its load of nuclear death to the American city of Seattle, Washington.

The admiral's foreboding words were still sinking into his head when the shrill buzzer of one of his desk's other phones diverted his attention. Having picked up this crimson-red handset only a single time before, he found his hand slightly shaking as he raised the receiver to his ear. The voice on the other end was calm and deliberate.

President Andrew Lyons spoke like a father who was

161

pleading with a doctor to tell him that his only child really wasn't dying. What could the Soviet Union possibly hope to gain by such a flagrant attack, he asked?

Most aware of the seriousness of the situation, Vladimir pleaded with the president to believe him. The United States was not under an intentional attack. Explaining the problems they were experiencing with the errant cruise missile, he swore that there had been no mass ICBM launch from the Vankarem fields. The heat signature their satellite was picking up was coming from a burning oil platform, not from a missile's exhaust system.

When questioned about a supposed nuclear detonation in the South Pacific, the general secretary answered cautiously. Admitting that he knew nothing about such an explosion, he urged Lyons to hold on while he attempted to find out what this blast was all about. The black phone, which he next activated, connected him with PVO Strany, the Soviet Defense Command bunker buried underground thirty miles from the Kremlin. The general in charge, unaware of the personage Kirensk was talking to on the other line, warned of an imminent U.S. attack. From the Crimean satellite ground-control station at Yevpatoriya had come a warning of a full-scale American war alert. Why, they even had knowledge of an almost-certain nuclear attack on elements of the Soviet Fleet cruising in the South Pacific.

Upon hearing this part of the report, Vladimir Kirensk hesitated. Perhaps he was being too quick to believe Lyon's accusations. Could this be a clever, imperialist ploy, to lull the Soviets to sleep while the Americans initiated their own bolt-out-of-the-blue attack? Certainly, he had to learn more about this supposed detonation in the Pacific before continuing his conversation with the president. Accepting Lyons's advice that both leaders had to keep their cool, Vladimir hung up the hotline with a promise to reconnect as soon as possible.

Before he could ring for them, his two military advisors were knocking at his door. D. F. Pavlodar and Pyotyr Altyr were two of his country's top experts in the field of nuclear strategy. Having worked with the last general secretary, they shared over four decades of international experience between them. As Vladimir instructed the two to enter, he seated himself behind his large gilded desk. He wasted no time getting down to business.

"Comrades, I have just gotten off the phone with PVO Strany. The Americans have initiated a full-scale war alert. We even have knowledge of a supposed nuclear detonation in the South Pacific, where elements of our fleet are currently sailing. How do you think that the Soviet Union should react to these moves?"

Pyotyr Altyr, who remained standing beside one of the two straight-backed chairs set before the desk, was the first to answer. "In typical fashion, the imperialists have over-reacted to the misfiring of our SS-NX-12. The first move we must make is to bring the alert status of the Motherland's strategic forces to an equal level."

"But won't this be unnecessarily provocative?" questioned Vladimir.

The hefty figure seated in the other chair replied, "It proves to be the Americans who are making the menacing moves, Comrade General Secretary. We can't afford to sit back and do nothing while their B-52s reach their fail-safe points, their Minutemen continue their countdowns, and their Tridents prepare to launch. At the very least, scramble our own forces to counter these threats."

"I'm afraid that you're both right," Kirensk observed thoughtfully. "I had hoped to solve this whole dilemma without a show of force on our side, but this is just too dangerous. I will need today's alert code to convey to PVO Strany."

Pyotyr Altyr alertly nodded. "Comrade General Secretary, I have taken the liberty of already entering the data bank and unearthing it for you. Today's code line is Red Vulcan."

Without hesitating, Vladimir picked up the black telephone. After conveying the two words that would bring the military might of the Soviet Union to a state of top readiness, he hung up the receiver and issued a long breath of relief.

"Now, what do the two of you make of this detonation in the South Pacific?"

"Obviously, the Americans are already jockeying for an advantageous position in that region," returned a still-standing Altyr. "Most likely it was one of their attack subs taking out one of our own Alfas."

"Or, it could have been targeted on one of our surface vessels," Pavlodar offered. "Elements of Admiral Kostromo's fleet are already entering those very waters. Their unusual presence there threatened the paranoid imperialists, who reacted in typical Yankee fashion."

Vladimir smoothed down the two thin tufts of hair which lay beside each of his ears. "We must contact the admiral at once to determine his fleet's exact status. Do any of you have any ideas as to how we might stop the SS-NX-12 device before this whole mess gets completely out of control?"

D. F. Pavlodar cleared his throat. "I'm afraid once the cruise missile initiates its turn southward, it's going to be extremely difficult to eliminate. The terrain-comparison guidance system is programmed to take

164

advantage of the rugged landscape that characterizes that region. By snaking its way through the various mountain ranges at an altitude of less than fifty feet, the device will be practically impossible to pick up on radar."

"Perhaps one of their F-15s will get lucky and chance upon it," Altyr suggested.

His seated coworker shook his head. "I seriously doubt it, Pyotyr. That countryside is just too vast, much like our own Siberia. Instead of gambling on such a long shot, I'd say we'd be much better off instituting an immediate decapitating attack on the Western powers. As we discussed earlier, by the use of less than fifty nuclear warheads carefully targeted on U.S. leaders, command posts, and message relay stations, their entire ability to counterattack can be negated. This, Comrades, is the way to solve our problems once and for all, with a minimum of bloodshed on both sides."

"*Nyet!*" Vladimir Kirensk responded angrily. "Such an attack will gain us nothing but a hundred million killed. It is our fault that the SS-NX-12 has been sent off-course. It is thus our responsibility to eliminate it before it completes its mission. I want that missile's exact route. Include every single turn, no matter how minute."

"Yes, Comrade General Secretary," replied a very-passive Pyotyr Altyr. "I will get you that information at once."

The sound of the black telephone broke the room's tense atmosphere. Vladimir picked up the receiver before it could ring a second time. After listening for a moment, he gave a relieved smile.

"Yes, Comrade General, please be so good as to send a copy of this picture over to my office at once. And thank you for notifying me personally."

Dropping the phone back on its cradle, Vladimir took a full thirty seconds to silently size up the information that he just received. Relishing this moment, he addressed his two curious guests.

"That, Comrades, was General Kupol. Minutes ago, the satellite relay station at Yevpatoriya received the latest recon shots of the South Pacific Basin. This series included several crystal-clear photos of the supposed nuclear detonation. Although the enormity of this blast can't be questioned, the photographs made it most obvious that the explosion was caused by an immense underwater volcanic eruption. It appears that the Americans haven't initiated World War III, after all."

Catching each other's eye, the two advisors seemed almost disappointed with this news. Both couldn't help but notice as the general secretary's right hand settled on top of the handset belonging to the red telephone.

"If you'll excuse me, Comrades, I've got a call to make. Please relay to me that information I requested regarding the SS-NX-12's exact course at once. That will be all."

Accepting this dismissal without comment, the somber-faced duo left the room. As they ducked through the doorway, a slender, attractive, middle-aged brunette passed them and entered the office without knocking. She held a single, silver serving tray.

"Olga, my dear," greeted Vladimir. "What in the heavens are you doing here at this late hour?"

"I thought some tea would certainly do you no harm, husband."

Placing the tray on the desk's corner, she filled a single china cup with tea, a dash of cream, and a single sugar cube. "From the looks etched on the faces of those two as I passed them, it appears that I got here just in time. Are things really that bad?"

Accepting the tea before him, Vladimir pushed his

chair back, stood, and warmly hugged his wife, who appeared tiny in the midst of his arms. While stroking her hair, he said, "For a few tense seconds there, I actually thought the nuclear nightmare was about to be unleashed. Now, it looks like sanity has prevailed after all."

Olga leaned back to search her husband's eyes. "What on earth has happened this evening?"

Vladimir reached down, picked up the tea cup, and took an appreciative sip. "One of our new cruise missiles is presently skirting the northern boundary of the American state of Alaska. Any second now, it will veer to the south—to complete a flight course directing its nuclear warhead to the city of Seattle, Washington. A drunken computer programmer caused this foolish mistake, which I am now directly responsible for."

"Have you informed Andrew Lyons?" quizzed Olga, genuinely shocked by what she had just heard.

"The president called me on the hotline several minutes ago. Fearing that this device was but the spearhead of a surprise attack on our part, the Americans have issued a full-scale military alert. To bring our own forces to a state of readiness, I have just issued a similar warning."

Olga took a step backward. "Surely there must be a way to stop the warhead before it reaches its target. Can't we shoot it down using our own forces?"

A flash of enlightenment lit Vladimir's eyes. "Of course! What better way to show the Americans the legitimacy of our motives than to use one of our own planes to down it. I believe that the missile is still well within our range. Surely Lyons has to trust me to complete such a vital task."

Mentally calculating the dimensions of such a venture, he knew he would make a quick call to PVO Strany first. If one of their MiGs was indeed within

167

range, he would have two significant pieces of information to pass on via the hotline. And to think that a mere volcano and a drunken sailor's incompetence had almost brought the world to the brink of nuclear catastrophe!

Twenty-seven thousand feet above the airspace of northern Indiana, the plane known as Kneecap soared in a zigzag course ever northward. While its battle staff busily monitored the defense conditions of the world's great superpowers, three tense individuals sat alone in the aircraft's forward conference room. One of these figures, a tall, handsome individual dressed immaculately in a gray pin-stripe suit, had just finished disconnecting the red telephone set that sat on the table before him. With his gaze focused on the gold-and-blue seal hung on the opposite wall, he spoke out distinctly.

"The general secretary seemed very much concerned. He fears that we're overreacting."

"That's a switch," returned the secretary of defense. "And just how would the Soviets react if it was one of our Tomahawks out there headed for Vladivostok?"

"Mistakes happen, Russell," the president shot back. "I wonder how much longer it's going to take for Big Bird to get back to us with those shots of the South Pacific?"

The uniformed gentleman checked his watch and answered, "We should have that info shortly. It sure would be something to have two bad readings in one day. NORAD could have sworn that the Vankarem flash was an ICBM launch."

"When it rains, it pours," observed Andrew Lyons. "This wasn't the first time that one of our satellites has mistaken an oil well fire for a rocket's signature, and unfortunately, it won't be the last. I must admit that this volcano bit is sure one for the record books."

General Sachs sat forward in his chair. "Mr. President, if we're indeed able to verify that an eruption is responsible for that flash in the Pacific, are you still going to allow the Russians to penetrate Alaskan airspace? I don't like the idea of inviting those MiGs in like that."

Andrew Lyons met his glance. "Neither do I, Barton, but there's not much else that I can do about it. Even you admit that using our own interceptors would present them with an almost impossible task. Without the help of radar, it would take the air force too much time to track that warhead down. Those MiG pilots will know just where to look for it, and precisely what to do to blow it from the skies."

"Something about this whole thing gives me a bellyache," the secretary of defense admitted. "Are you still certain that you can trust Kirensk? Sometimes I think that guy is merely taking us on a one-way ride."

"Come on, Russell. You were down there at Camp David with me. If Vladimir Kirensk is putting us on, he certainly gets my vote on academy awards night."

Lyons was quick to pick up one of the intercom lines when it buzzed a single time. "This is the President. . . . Excellent, give the folks down at the Johnson Space Center my personal thanks for a job well done."

Disconnecting the phone, he faced his anxious audience. "Big Bird just beamed back the first in a series of startling photographs of the waters immediately south of American Samoa. Even though they show an immense, mushroom-shaped cloud stretching some forty-five thousand feet up into the atmosphere, our analyst are positive that this is not a manmade explosion. What we are witnessing there is one of the most violent

169

volcanic eruptions ever monitored in modern times."

Sitting back heavily in his chair, a satisfied grin broke the corners of his boyish mouth. "I told you that Kirensk was talking turkey. He's just as sick of this nuclear madness as we are. I'm going to let his flyboys in to finish off that cruise missile. General Sachs, I think you'd better warn NORAD that we're going to be having a squadron of MiG-25s passing into northern Alaska shortly, with my blessings. I sure wouldn't want our own planes to shoot them down by mistake."

"What are you going to do about our present defense condition while these MiGs are on their way?" questioned the secretary of defense.

The president read the concern etched on his old friend's face. "If it will make you feel any better, Russell, we'll hold our present status until the Soviets finish their mission."

"That's a wise decision, Mr. President," commented Tate.

Accepting a nod of agreement from the general, Lyon's hand went over to the red telephone. "I'd better inform the General Secretary of my decision. We're going to have one hell of a phone bill when this is all over."

"Let's just hope that's the extent of it," added Barton Sachs as the president initiated his much-anticipated call to Moscow.

Chapter Nine

For Lieutenant Nikolai Kupol of the Soviet Air Defense Command, the morning started out as a typical one. Awakening at dawn, the twenty-nine-year-old pilot quietly snuck out of bed, careful not to disturb his wife, Ludmilla, who slept soundly beneath the thick folds of their comforter. Invigorated by the brisk Siberian air, he efficiently performed his toilet, taking a few extra minutes to shave closely and carefully comb his wavy blond hair. Satisfied with the solid physique reflected in the cracked bathroom mirror, he went on to don his dark-blue, cotton flightsuit. Before stepping outdoors, he tiptoed into his daughters' bedroom. The two rambunctious girls looked like perfect angels lying there in each others arms. Both the five-year-old and the seven-year-old had his wavy blond hair and their mother's deep blue eyes. He knew that they would be knockouts in their time, and pitied the poor boys whose task it would be to break them.

With this vision of his sleeping youngsters still fresh in his mind, he left the wood-frame officer's apartment house and soaked in his first impressions of this new day. It proved to be a brisk, spotlessly clear morning. Beyond the surrounding woods of spruce, hemlock, and cedar, the dawn sky pulsed a vibrant powdery blue, without a cloud visible. Most aware that it would be an ideal day for flying, he hastily began his exercise routine of sit-ups, push-ups, and pull-ups. Though the ground was still a bit soggy, he decided to pass up a ride in the dilapidated old bus, and jog the three miles into the headquarter's compound.

Hardly working up a decent sweat, he made his way down the narrow dirt road and passed the guard kiosk signaling the entrance to the 517th Fighter Regiment less than a quarter of an hour later. Nikolai found his stomach growling as he entered the small, red-brick building holding the officer's mess hall. Inside, the room was filled with a dozen, white, tableclothed tables, each set for four officers. Less than half of these tables were currently taken, and while returning several familiar greetings, he approached the seated squadron commander.

Colonel Valerian was a tall, red-cheeked Belorussian. Since Nikolai was the acting deputy commander of the 4th Squadron, he was assigned to share the colonel's table at mealtimes.

"Good morning, Comrade Kupol," Valerian greeted him sourly between bites of fruit compote. "A bit late this morning, aren't we?"

Nikolai sensed the commander's rotten mood. "It was such a glorious dawn that I decided to jog here, instead of taking the bus."

"Glorious morning, huh," repeated the colonel sarcastically. "If only you'd been in my shoes, you'd think differently. Why, already I've received a call from Vladivostok."

Valerian returned to his fruit while a pretty red-haired waitress set a tray of goulash, rice, cut fruit slices, rye bread, and buttermilk before the young lieutenant. While Nikolai began digging into his breakfast, the colonel continued.

"It seems that we have a most serious problem here. Last week's supply audit shows too many unexplainable shortages. In coolant alcohol alone, we find ourselves missing over fifty tons."

Nikolai used his cloth napkin to wipe a drop of the spicy stew from the corner of his mouth. "You know as well as I, Colonel Valerian, where this alcohol is being diverted to. It is a practice that's common wherever jet planes are being maintained."

"But fifty tons!" exclaimed Valerian. "This pilferage has gotten completely out of hand. I will need the immediate help of you and the other deputy commanders to halt this flow at once. Not only do we nurture a bunch of drunks here at Uelen, but also too many philanderers. The venereal disease rate has risen for the third consecutive month."

"Men will be men," the lieutenant discerned wisely.

Valerian stifled a belch. "If only they were indeed men. We have nothing here but a bunch of animals. Now, to make matters even worse, we have been instructed to prepare for the visit of another stodgy bureaucrat. Deputy Defense Minister Mikhail Antonov will be visiting the base by month's end. You know what this means, Comrade Kupol?"

Nikolai lowered his eyes. "Then there'll be no flying today."

"That's correct," shot back the commander. "This airfield looks like a pigsty. Assemble the men on the parade ground immediately after breakfast, and I'll distribute your individual chores. How are you with a paintbrush, Comrade pilot?"

Unwilling to reply, Nikolai attempted to divert his full attention to his food. Yet suddenly the meal was utterly tasteless, his appetite long gone. It was at times like this that Kupol desired nothing more than to pick up the telephone and call his father back in Moscow. As the general in charge of PVO Strany, it was important for him to know what the conditions at the forward defense posts were really like. Nikolai was no mere handyman. He was a MiG pilot, trained by thousands of hours of intense study and practice. This would make the fourth day this week that they hadn't been allowed to fly. Certainly, that was no way to run an effective air force.

Fighting to control his temper, he knew such a call would accomplish little. Unfortunately, such wasteful practices had been part of the Soviet military since its inception. Even the most important wargames were subject to postponement if a nearby crop needed harvesting. The soldiers grumbled, yet few spoke out.

Twenty minutes later, Nikolai assembled the men on the asphalt parade grounds. Occupying the first row were the pilots. Behind them were the flight engineers, their assistants, and the rest of the enlisted men. Each of them looked on with a sullen expression as Colonel Valerian assigned the day's duties, which included landscaping, groundskeeping, general cleaning, and painting details.

As per the colonel's earlier promise, Nikolai soon found himself with a paintbrush in hand. He and two other pilots were ordered to whitewash the chipped brick structure housing the latrine.

"If only my parents could see me now," jested Grigori Galick between strokes of paint. "How their eyes glowed that afternoon when the air minister pinned on my wings."

"Our duty is still better than being stuck permanently in some factory," replied Stephan Litvinov, a tall, gangly Estonian who applied his portion of paint expertly. "I only cherish that much more those precious days when we're allowed to go airborne."

"I agree," returned Nikolai, oblivious to the splatter-

174

ings of paint that dotted his forehead. "I would gladly perform the most demanding of duties just to be allowed a few hours a week in the sky. What burns me up, though, is that this all seems like such an utter waste."

Grigori responded mockingly, "But just think what Comrade Antonov would report to the general secretary if we didn't complete this chore." His voice suddenly lowered. " 'I tell you, Vladimir, the state of our air defenses is just horrible. Why, you just should have seen how badly their outhouses needed painting.' "

With this, the pilots enjoyed a good laugh. It proved to be Nikolai who spotted the rapidly approaching orderly first.

"Careful, Comrades," warned Kupol in a whisper. "Old Valerian's other eyes and ears is on his way over here."

Seconds later, the bug-eyed adjunct greeted them with a stiff salute. "Lieutenant Kupol, the colonel wishes to see you at once, sir."

Nikolai shrugged his shoulders while cautiously eyeing his coworkers. After sticking his brush back in the paint can, he turned and followed the scrawny conscript back to the concrete-block building housing the staff headquarters. Inside, he found the atmosphere unusually friendly.

"Comrade Kupol," Valerian greeted warmly. "Please step into my office and join me in a cup of tea."

Most aware that something out of the ordinary was going on, Nikolai accepted the colonel's invitation. While seated in a comfortable leather chair, sipping a cup of strong, sweet, black tea, he looked on as the commander walked behind his desk and pulled down a large, previously rolled-up map. On this projection's surface was etched an intricate representation of the eastern tip of Siberia, the Bering Strait, and the northern half of the state of Alaska.

"I have just gotten off the phone with PVO Strany. Your illustrious father sends his warmest regards. Earlier this morning, an event of the gravest nature took place in the waters northwest of us. As a result, the very security of the Motherland has been placed in jeopardy."

Nilolai anxiously sat forward as the colonel picked up a wooden pointer and traced a line from the Chukchi Sea, over the Bering Strait, and eastward over Alaska's Brooks Mountain Range. Valerian halted at this state's northernmost boundary with the country of Canada.

"I'm certain that you're familiar with the new family of SS-NX-12 cruise missiles. Less than an hour ago, one of these devices was launched from the waters west of Ajon Island. What started off as a mere test run has developed into a major international incident. Improperly programmed, the SS-NX-12 failed to make its southward turn into the Sea of Okhotsk. Instead, its nuclear warhead was armed and its targeting system directed to carry the missile to an ultimate splashdown in the harbor immediately outside of the American city of Seattle, Washington.

"Elements of the 4th MiG-25 Squadron have been called upon to eliminate this device before it causes further embarrassment to our great country. As deputy squadron leader, I have chosen you to lead a flight of three aircraft. You may choose who you wish to accompany you."

"And where is the SS-NX-12 presently?" questioned Nikolai.

Valerian made a wide circle with the tip of his pointer to include a good portion of the extreme northeastern corner of Alaska. "At last report, it had just turned southward off the Beaufort Sea. It is

176

traveling at subsonic speeds approaching the Davidson Mountains."

Nikolai abruptly stood and approached the map. "But that's American territory! No way could we cross into such a sector without first being spotted by their air defense forces. Their F-15s would intercept us before we hit the Brooks Range."

"Not on this morning," the colonel replied icily. "Through a special pact between General Secretary Kirensk and President Lyons, an agreement has been reached to allow you to penetrate their airspace. The cruise device's preprogrammed course is already being fed into your aircraft's computer. With the assistance of external fuel cells, you should have just enough fuel to proceed from Uelen at supersonic speeds, cut over the Brooks Range, and intercept the SS-NX-12 here, over Ammerman Mountain."

Studying this territory, Nikolai shook his head. "I still don't understand why the Americans couldn't accomplish this simple task."

"Simple?" quizzed Valerian sharply. "Not only is the missile flying below their radar coverage, but it also is fitted with a specially designed, top-secret heat signature deflection device. Even if the F-15s spotted it, their heat-seeking rockets could never knock it down. Only our AA-6 Acrid Foxfires can do the job. Of all of our country's pilots, it has fallen on your shoulders to do the job. Good hunting, Comrade. Now, you must be on your way quickly, before the missile is beyond our reach."

Spurred by the colonel's sincerity, the twenty-nine-year-old pilot rushed from the office. With elements of this strange mission darting through his mind, he jogged quickly over to the latrine. There was no question which two pilots he would choose to accompany him as he beckoned his comrades to put down their brushes.

"Does anyone want to do some real flying?" Nikolai questioned between gulps of air.

"All right!" cried the two pilots in unison.

Wasting no more time, Kupol briefed them while on their way to the flight preparation room. With a minimum of questions, Lieutenants Galick and Litvinov listened intently. The reality of their destination was just dawning in their consciousnesses as they donned their helmets, oxygen masks, and gloves. Each man signed for an automatic pistol, with two clips of seven rounds per pilot, and then walked hurriedly outside to the hangar area. Waiting for them there were three shiny, dark gray, MiG-25 jet fighters.

With their twin tailfins gleeming in the midmorning sun, the three, twenty-two-ton vehicles were in the process of taking on fuel, coolant alcohol, and oxygen. Nikolai Kupol walked toward the lead aircraft. Efficiently, he checked its long rocketlike nose, the short, swept-back wings, and the rear housing of the two, Tumansky R-266 engines. Satisfied that all appeared in good repair, he began his way up the fourteen-foot metallic ladder that led into the cockpit. Like a traveler returning home after a long trip abroad, he gratefully settled into the comfortable cushioned seat. Soothed by the familiar green tint of the craft's interior, he checked the various dials, gauges, buttons, and levers.

Only after the ground crew removed the engine covers and signaled that his hydraulic systems were working properly did he start the engines. He followed this procedure by speaking into his helmet-mounted radio transmitter.

"Uelen Tower, this is Foxbat leader. Requesting clearance for taxi and liftoff."

A crackle of static was followed by the familiar voice of Colonel Valerian. "Foxbat leader, this is Uelen. All traffic has been cleared for your flight. Proceed accordingly."

With this, Nikolai reached forward and changed his radio's frequency. "Baby chicks, this is mother hen. Are you ready to fly this coop?"

Two positive responses followed, one after the other. He began to taxi his plane toward the field's main runway. Without hesitating, Nikolai pointed the nose of the MiG down the smooth concrete pavement, ignited the afterburners, and with the engines squealing and the vibrating fuselage straining forward, released the brakes. A throaty roar followed as the craft surged down the runway and smoothly lifted off into the air.

Even though he was still dangerously low, he shut off the afterburners prematurely, in an effort to conserve on fuel. At the speed and altitude he would now be flying, the MiG would gulp its jet fuel with a voracious appetite. If he was going to reach his target and then have a chance of returning, he knew he would need every last precious drop.

By the time he reached 24,000 feet, the woods of eastern Siberia were well behind him. In their place were the icy, mist-covered waters of the Bering Strait. As his companions took their positions at each of his wingtips, Nikolai could already make out the rugged confines of Alaska's Seward Peninsula on the western horizon. He swallowed hard upon realizing that they were most likely already well within the airspace of the United States of America.

How many times had he dreamed of making just such a flight? Yet, in this instance, how different was his intended target! They were trained to intercept imperialist's B-1 and B-52 bombers, not one of the Motherland's own missiles.

For the Americans to have allowed such a flight, the

situation must have indeed been as serious as the colonel had explained. He could just imagine how frantic things must be at PVO Strany. Surely his father was a major part of this whole operation. There was no way that he would let either him or his country down. Whatever it took, he would track down the errant SS-NX-12 and see to its total destruction.

As his plane lurched forward at a speed twice that of sound, Nikolai could see through the bare cloud cover that Seward Peninsula was already passing well to the south. Ahead was Cape Krusenstern, and beyond was the first visible rise that signaled that mass of mountains comprising the Brooks Range. Seeing the snow-capped summits shining on the eastern horizon, he half expected to view a squadron of lethal F-15 Eagles soaring down at them out of the sun. Yet this morning, both his radar and a visual scan proved that they shared these skies with absolutely no other aircraft.

If only he could have shared the knowledge of this mission with his wife, Ludmilla. She'd probably never even believe him when he returned home later and conveyed to her his day's activities. At present, he had trouble believing his current duty himself.

Rechecking his speed gauge, he saw that he was progressing at a velocity equivalent to 1,800 miles per hour. It wasn't often that their superiors allowed them to travel at such a rate. Even though the MiG-25 was capable of speeds of over Mach 3.2, the powers that be kept them well under this threshold, with the hopes of keeping the wear and tear on their valuable equipment to a minimum.

Propelled in such a manner, Nikolai realized that he was well into the Brooks Range by now. Since a thickening band of cloud cover made a visual sighting impossible, he sat back and mentally calculated the time left until they reached the intercept point. Upon verifying with his computer that they were merely five minutes away from the spot they hoped to cut off the cruise device, he reached to his left and armed the MiG's four, wing-mounted rockets.

The AA-6 Acrid was the world's largest air-to-air missile. Designed to eliminate the proposed B-70 Valkyrie bomber, the 248-inch-long, 1,874-pound rocket worked in conjunction with the plane's look-down radar unit to blast its targets from the skies. With a speed of over Mach 4.5, it didn't have to travel far to do so.

An unexpected crackle of loud static redirected Nikolai's ponderings. "Mother hen, this is baby chick Alpha. Look-down unit has our bogey in sight. She's sixty-five miles to the northeast, at coordinates one-four-zero. Shall we go down and take a peek?"

Punching these coordinates into his computer, Kupol let out a breath of relief and briefly responded to Grigori's findings. "You get the honors, Alpha. Take us down!"

Looking on as the aircraft on his left dipped its wing and peeled off in a steep dive, Nikolai jammed his stick forward and initiated his own power descent. With the engines whining, the MiG plunged into the thick bank of awaiting clouds. Blindingly quick, the altimeter dropped over 20,000 feet in a matter of seconds. As the resulting g-forces pushed him back into his seat, he strained to determine the exact moment that they would break from the cloud cover. This occurred at a height exactly 3,550 feet above sea level.

Conscious of the rugged terrain that stretched below him, Nikolai took in the vast wilderness expanses now visible. Astonishingly enough, it appeared to exactly match similar portions of eastern Siberia, right down to the huge herds of elk he could see galloping off at the unnatural sound of their engines.

"I see her!" cried an excited voice from his helmet's speakers. "Mother hen, she's right there in front of us, at about 750 feet, following the meander of that riverbank."

When Nikolai caught sight of the SS-NX-12, his heart jumped excitedly. Looking like some sort of huge, soaring prehistoric bird, the cruise missile followed each turn of the river, appearing more alive than manmade. Over 250 inches long, its fuselage was painted in drab, camouflaged tones, with two, five-pointed red stars etched on each wingtip.

"This is Alpha, mother hen. Going in to kiss our bogey good-bye."

Nikolai quickly triggered his transmitter. "Roger, Alpha, you may proceed. Beta, please follow your brother in to make sure the wolf is down for good. I'll be on your tail."

Stephan's voice broke forth tensely. "Understood, mother hen. This is Beta, over and out."

Following closely on Litvinov's tail, Nikolai pushed his stick forward. In response, the MiG dropped down to a mere 900 feet above the rugged foothills. Concentrating to ensure they had enough clearance to pass above any surrounding terrain that might get in their way, Kupol jumped when his look-down radar unit suddenly issued a piercing, electronic hum. At this moment, his headphones filled again with Grigori's excited observations.

"I've got a lock, mother hen. Will commence firing, *now*!"

With eyes glued to the lead jet, Nikolai saw the pair of huge black-and-white-painted rockets drop from each of the plane's wings and burst forward leaving a thick trail of milky smoke. In seeming response to this, the SS-NX-12 suddenly plunged downward itself. Only a few hundred feet from the river's surface now, it snaked under a thick projecting ridge of rock just as the pair of AA-6s streaked down for the final kill. A blinding burst of light followed as the Acrid's warheads exploded almost simultaneously. To his utter dismay, Nikolai watched as the entire rock ledge fell into the river, leaving the cruise missile to continue on its way southward.

As Grigori pulled up on his stick to position himself behind the others to prepare for another run, Stephan changed his course and speed to match that of their elusive quarry. Glancing off in the direction they were now headed, Nikolai set eyes on a huge cloud of rising mist, veiling the approaching section of river valley.

"Pull up, chicks!" he cried as he yanked back on his stick. "We must find a safer spot to make our final showdown."

Over the whine of his engines, he could barely believe what he was hearing emanate from his radio speakers. "I've got the big bad wolf right in my sights, mother hen. I'm going to lay these AA-6s right between its eyes!"

"No, Stephan!" Nikolai exclaimed vainly.

Abruptly reversing his climb, he rolled to his right — just in time to see a brilliant explosion burst through the cloud of mist below.

"Litvinov!" screamed the deputy commander.

In response, all he heard was a hushed silence. When the radio again activated, it was the gloomy voice of Grigori Galick that met his ears.

"It's no use, Nikolai. Stephan smacked right into the side of Ammerman Mountain. He was just too anxious. I'm afraid I'm going to have to be leaving you at this moment also. Both my engines are seriously overheated. They are going to cut out any second now. I hope the fools who stole that alcohol choke on their own vomit. Do you think the Americans will find me before I freeze to death? Sure hope this parachute works."

Scanning the sky to get a firsthand look at Grigori's efforts, Nikolai caught sight of the big jet lumbering in the air several hundred feet above him. Just as he was about to respond, both columns of flame that had trailed out from Galick's engines cowling snuffed out at the same moment. Seconds later, the MiG's canopy popped open and the seat carrying his old friend rocketed upward. Nikolai's prayers were answered as the white chute billowed out fully, with the alert figure of Grigori Galick swinging daintily below.

"Good luck, Comrade," wished the deputy commander, with a tip of his wings. Although he would have liked to exactly mark the spot at which his coworker landed, he knew that both time and fuel were rapidly running out. If he didn't get moving immediately, Stephan Litvinov would have died in vain.

It took less than two minutes for him to again spot the ever-plodding cruise missile. Still skimming the river-bank, the SS-NX-12 was entering a broad valley, generally free from any protruding obstacles. Pushing down on his stick, Nikolai knew it was now or never. When the plane reached 650 feet above sea level, a family of four startled Dall sheep could be seen, frantically scurrying for cover. As these shaggy beasts ran toward the river, he positioned the Foxbat directly behind the missile's exhaust. Emptying his mind of every emotion but revenge, the deputy commander activated his radar scan. This time he didn't jump when a harsh tone sounded, signaling him that the AA-6s were locked in firmly on their target. Taking a deep breath, he pushed his right index finger down on the red plastic button designed to send the Acrids skyward on their missions of destruction.

Nikolai could hardly believe it when the characteris-

184

tic *whoosh* of the rocket's engines failed to sound in his cockpit. Since the plane also didn't bob upward, as it would when suddenly freed from the AA-6s' great weight, he tried depressing the launch switch one more time. Again, all was silent except for the whine of the MiG's engines, and the steady tone that accompanied the radar-lock indicator.

"Damn it to hell!" Nikolai cursed angrily as he ineffectually jammed his fist into the launch button.

Stuck beneath the wings of the plane, his AA-6s would see no action on this morning. He could think of only one thing that could be responsible for their failure to operate. An idiotic technician, most probably drunk on coolant, had failed to attach the firing pins. No matter how many times he hit the launch button, the rockets could never receive the signal to fire. And since the MiG-25 carried no guns, that left him with no effective weapon with which to knock the cruise missile down.

Seeing the SS-NX-12 slicing through the air only a few hundred inviting feet away caused a wave of frustrated anger to course through his body. What could he do now—fly back to Uelen and tell his father how very close he had come to knocking it from the skies? Some reception that report would get! Even Ludmilla and the girls would be totally embarrassed by his failure. He had come too far, with too many hopes pinned on his shoulders, to fail now. There had to be some way that he could stop the cruise device with his present load of equipment. It was while opening up the throttle, to see how close he could come to the missile, that the idea came to him.

With the assistance of the broad, level valley that continued to spread out southward, he was able to exactly match the SS-NX-12's speed and height. Nuzzling the throttle ever so slightly forward, he positioned

185

the spiky nose of the MiG-25 so that it practically ran up the exhaust manifold of the target he was sent to terminate. After completing a series of three deep breaths, he took another minute to reconsider the results of the drastic move he was about to commit.

Surely, he would have no time to hit the ejection button. Even if he did, the resulting explosion would burn him to a crisp as the canopy shot back and he was catapulted skyward.

They say a man's entire life passes before his mind's eye when he faces the moment of ultimate death. For Lieutenant Nikolai Kupol, deputy commander of the Soviet Air Defense Command's 4th Fighter Squadron, this last vision represented itself as single, vibrant mental picture. His faithful, loving wife and two angelic daughters never seemed as beautiful, as he jammed the throttle forward, sending his Foxbat's radar cone hurtling into the SS-NX-12's exhaust nozzle.

Approximately 2,470 miles to the southeast of Alaska's Davidson Mountains, William Ford was at NORAD's missile warning center's central computer screen, intently studying an exact duplicate of the scan sector being monitored by a Boeing E-3 Sentry AWACS plane. Reflected in the glass monitor was an intricate map of America's largest state, showing the portion of land stretching from the Arctic Circle northward. Though this scan was subject to frequent interruptions when the targets it was tracking dropped under the sight of its look-down radar, the captain was able to get a pretty good idea of the MiGs' progress as they crossed Alaska's northern width. In an ever-progressing series of red blinking dots, he had traced the three Russians since they had entered U.S. airspace over the Bering Strait.

Still unable to believe what he was witnessing, he could only pray that his superiors knew what they were doing. To allow a trio of Soviet Foxbats into the country was an unprecedented move in itself. Now, to permit them to shoot their rockets at an elusive quarry that darted in and out of the AWACS radar range with an unpredictability all its own, was unheard of. Of course, the events of this whole day had taken place without previous example.

When DSP North first activated, it had appeared to match exactly the heat signature of an ICBM launch. How was he supposed to know that it had only been an oil well fire? Moments later, when DSP South awoke, he had been equally certain that they were picking up a NUDET. Only minutes ago, a Big Bird recon satellite had showed this explosion to in fact have been caused by a massive volcanic eruption. This left a single positive bogey to be concerned with.

Stretching his long legs, Ford realized how very close they had come to war. Reaware of the precariousness of the fragile peace that kept the warheads from flying, he decided that he would definitely ask Anne to marry him as soon as he got out of Cheyenne Mountain. It would be senseless to wait any longer. Life in the nuclear age had to be lived to the fullest. Waiting for a tomorrow that might never come would be the ultimate waste.

It was while this decision entrenched itself firmly in his mind that the first of the dots representing the MiGs disappeared from the radar screen. Assuming that it had only dropped out of range, he hunched forward when a second flashing light also blinked for its final time. This left but two targets proceeding southward down the spine of the Davidson Mountains. He found himself rubbing his eyes in disbelief when these individual dots seemed to merge, followed by a single, powerful pulse of light, and then there were absolutely no bogeys on the map. Scanning the northeastern section of the state carefully to make sure that they merely hadn't lost the low-flying targets as they had many times before, Ford stirred excitedly. That pulse could mean only one thing: a powerful explosion had occurred, knocking both the pursuer and the pursued permanently from the air. After waiting a full minute to confirm his suspicions, his hand shot out for the beige telephone receiver.

General Theodore Bowman received the news from the missile warning center with a relieved smile. Directing his attention to his computer keyboard, he fed in a single request, and the main battle station's seventeen-by-seventeen-foot screen filled with the exact map portion William Ford had been previously surveying. This duplicate of the AWACS scan showed no unfriendlies anywhere in the area.

"The Soviets did it!" Bowman observed passionately. "Do you believe it, Walt?"

Brigadier General Walter Craig looked to the map and grinned. "It looks like they lost three very brave MiG pilots in the process, but I'd say that SS-NX-12 is down for the count."

Bowman reached over to pick up the black telephone handset whose length was labeled *Secure*. "The president was right, after all. I must admit that I didn't like the idea of inviting those Russkies in like that, but they sure did the trick. Bring us down to DEFCON 3, Walt. I'll inform Kneecap."

While Bowman began the process of reaching the flying White House, Walter Craig picked up the red phone. His call to the National Military Command

Center had two purposes. The first was to inform SAC to call back its bombers and to cancel the ICBMs launch sequences. The second directive went directly to the Chief of Naval Operations. Using the various communications means at his disposal, orders would be sent out to the missile-carrying submarines that a state of impending war no longer existed.

As he expected, the Strategic Air Command's two legs of the triad were the first to respond to the alleviation of tensions. Addressing his computer keyboard, he changed the map segment projected on the battle station's screen to include a polar view of the North American continent. Hundreds of blinking blue dots represented individual B-52s, which had fanned out northward to begin their flights into the Soviet Union.

With the red phone still snuggled up to his ear, Walter Craig studied the screen as the orders he had relayed less than a minute ago reached these aircraft. One by one, the blue dots halted their progress and turned around. When it became visibly evident that each of the lumbering bombers had acknowledged its new orders, the brigadier general received word that the country's force of ICBMs had also recognized the cessation of all further hostilities. This left only the submarine force to be heard from.

While awaiting the all-clear from the Navy Department, he couldn't help but overhear portions of General Bowman's conversation with Andrew Lyons.

"Yes, Mr. President, this one was too close for comfort. Your decision to trust the general secretary was a brilliant one . . . I'm certain that we would have most likely knocked that cruise missile out long before it hit Seattle, yet it's sure a relief not to have it breathing down our necks. . . . Now, if only their subs would pull back, I'd say we could wrap this whole thing

189

up."

Keeping his glance locked on the room's central screen, Walter Craig surveyed the portions of ocean visible on both the continent's shores. He visualized the country's armada of Ohio and Lafayette Class submarines as they plunged silently through the water's depths. Trailing their sensitive antennas in their wakes, the boats would just now be picking up the simple coded message calling them from their action stations.

To successfully contact this scattered fleet, the navy would be utilizing a variety of diverse communications systems. Powerful transmitting stations located in such locations as Michigan, Florida, Washington, and Australia would be broadcasting these orders on the very low frequency bands. To reach the obscure areas of the world's oceans that were out of any ground station's reach, a series of satellites would be beaming this same message into the depths. Serving as the ultimate back-up were the Lockheed C-130 Hercules transports, known as TACAMO, for Take Charge and Move Out. These specially designed turboprop aircraft each trailed a heavy, copper-jacketed steel wire antenna, weighing almost a ton, from their fuselages. Extending over five miles in length, these antennas would be pointed straight down toward the ocean as the planes flew in a tight circular bank.

This redundancy in communications systems practically guaranteed that each of the subs would be reached. Yet, when dealing with such an alien medium as the ocean's depths, Craig was well aware of the difficulties they faced. Thus, he wasn't particularly concerned when almost a quarter of an hour had passed without the Navy relaying to him the all-clear signal. But until such a message was received, he wouldn't be able to relax totally. Conscious of each passing minute, the brigadier general sat tensely, nervously drumming his fingers on his desktop.

"Relax, Walt," Theodore Bowman advised with a wink. "Believe me, the worst is all over. Those subs aren't about to do anything for a good five hours, anyway. We'll catch them all in plenty of time. Don't you worry so."

Craig took a series of deep, calming breaths in an effort to follow CINCNORAD's fatherly suggestion. Even with this added oxygen in his system, his stomach was still tightly knotted.

"I'm sorry, Ted. I guess I'm just turning into an old worrywart."

"Well, inflaming your ulcer sure isn't going to help matters any. The president sounded relieved. That kid is cool as a cucumber. The last I heard from him, Kneecap was headed back to Andrews. I wonder what the press is going to make out of this whole thing?"

"I can just imagine," Craig answered with a shake of his head. "The liberals will be on our asses again, crying out that our defense organization is riddled with deficiencies."

"We may have our weaknesses here at NORAD, but at the time it's the best warning system this country can field. I wouldn't trade it with the Soviets' for one second."

CINCNORAD's words were punctuated by the buzz of the black phone. "I bet you that's the navy with the all-clear," he added, as he reached out to pick up the handset.

Bowman's first reaction was a broad grin and a victorious thumbs-up. Yet as he continued to listen to his party, this grin gradually dissipated.

"Well, what about TACAMO?" he questioned firmly. "I don't give a damn about any typhoon! Get Admiral Burnhardt on the horn personally. I want that C-130 sent into the Southwestern Pacific Basin on the double, no matter what the risks are!"

Slamming down the receiver, CINCNORAD took a second to regain his composure. Aware of the concerned stare of his aide, he cautiously cleared his throat.

"That was Admiral Fletcher. All of the subs have been reached, but one. She's the USS *Phoenix*, our latest Trident boat. Their last known position was in the waters immediately to the south of American Samoa."

"That would put them in the vicinity of that volcanic eruption," responded Walter Craig, who reached forward to issue a request into his keyboard.

Both men looked up as the battle station's screen filled with a detailed map of the South Pacific. A large red dot pulsed from the waters approximately two-thirds of the way between Hawaii and New Zealand.

Theodore Bowman continued, "The *Phoenix* was headed smack dab into that disturbance. She's carrying some hotshot from Naval Research, who was going to monitor the seas around Delta Base for volcanic activity. I'd say that he's arriving there just a little bit late."

"Could the volcano be responsible for the vessel's inability to receive the cancellation code?" queried Craig.

CINCNORAD hesitated. "Though I've never heard of such a thing happening before, I suppose it could be possible. That is, if the sub even survived the initial blast."

Again the brigadier general questioned, "Suppose that the *Phoenix* received the alert orders, and then rode out the eruption—what would happen next?"

Bowman scratched his smoothly shaven jaw. "Since this is the scenario that we have to assume came down, let's draw up the sub's S.I.O.P. and see exactly what her war orders are."

The general opened one of his locked desk drawers. Inside, he removed a single, thick portfolio, closed with a red, waxen seal. Breaking this closure, he extracted a black notebook whose insides were filled with pages of coded data. After locating the section that corresponded to the precise information that he desired, CINCNORAD addressed his computer's keyboard. Because of the highly classified nature of this portion of the Single Integrated Operational Plan, he had to include several key passwords that would assure the proper security access.

By the time he completed the program request, a thin line of sweat had gathered on his bald forehead. Wiping this moisture off with the palm of his right hand, he sat back and waited for the computer to conclude its computations. It seemed that an entire eternity passed, when all of a sudden, his monitor screen began rapidly filling with information. With Walter Craig close at his side, Bowman began translating.

"Upon receipt of a Cocked Pistol alert, the *Phoenix* has been instructed to silently run to the cover of the nearest deep water, all the while keeping its communication's channels open for alert updates. She's to ascend to launch depth five and a half hours after the initial receipt of battle orders. At this time, if communications have still yet to be re-established, they're to launch the first of their Trident C-4s. This missile has been fitted with a MILSTAR advanced-fleet-communications satellite. Serving as a last ditch fail-safe mechanism, the satellite will be placed in orbit at a height of eleven thousand miles above the earth's surface. Only in the event that they still aren't contacted to do otherwise, is the skipper authorized to proceed with the launch of the other missiles.

"The rest of the *Phoenix*'s load is comprised of twenty-three Trident C4s, armed with eight Mark 4 100K-ton, MIRVs apiece. These one hundred and eighty four warheads have been targeted to eliminate Soviet air defense installations located throughout northern, eastern, and central Siberia, the Kamchatka Peninsula, and Sakhalin Island. Six warheads have been reserved for the naval installations at Vladivostok and Petropavlovsk. Three warheads apiece have been targeted on the Siberian cities of Ussuriysk, Chabarovsk, Blagoveshchenskoye, and the Manchurian rail depots at Tsitsihar and Chita.

"Because of the recent release of Defense Department directive one-three-nine, which re-emphasized the risk of a Soviet bolt-out-of-the-blue, decapitating attack targeted on U.S. communications facilities, the *Phoenix*'s commanding officer, like those serving aboard all of our missile-carrying boats, has been authorized to initiate his S.I.O.P. upon receipt of the initial war alert. His primary goal shall remain to survive for whatever length of time it takes for him to launch his entire load of missiles."

Sobered by this grim narrative, General Theodore Bowman pushed his chair back and issued a long, anxious breath. "Jesus, Walt, if the *Phoenix* is still out there, unable to receive further communications, we could be in for more trouble than we ever dreamed up in a worst-case scenario. You'd better bring us up to DEFCON 2. I get the fun job of informing the President."

While CINCNORAD went on with this unpleasant task, Walter Craig sat with his eyes still locked on the battle station's main screen. Focusing his weary gaze on the single, red pulsating dot that still graced the waters at the projection's center, the *Phoenix*'s S.I.O.P. ran endlessly through his mind's eye. Though the threat was always present, never before had one of their

194

strategic platforms failed to respond to an alert's cancellation. This was especially critical in the case of a weapons system as awesome as an Ohio Class submarine. Capable of taking out a good part of the Soviet Union with the launch of a single load, the *Phoenix* carried as much destructive power as all the bombs dropped in World War II.

On a day already filled with miscalculation after miscalculation, the brigadier general knew that they could take nothing for granted. If there was a one in a million chance that the *Phoenix* had survived the eruption and indeed received its war orders, they had to presume that the sub's commander was already well aware of the S.I.O.P. CINCNORAD had just completed interpreting. That would leave them with less than five hours to contact the sub before it began its mission of nuclear death and destruction. Walter Craig was certain that the next three hundred minutes would be among the most critical spans of time that the modern world was ever to know.

Chapter Ten

Unaware of the alert orders their captain had just received, the majority of the USS *Phoenix*'s complement went about their daily routine without any knowledge of the critical state of world affairs. This was especially evident in the boat's recreation room. Here a light, jovial atmosphere existed. Positioned between the officers' mess and the crew's quarters, the compartment was currently witnessing a spirited game of ping-pong. To the harmonic strains of the Richard Rodger's soundtrack, "Victory at Sea," blaring forth from the two, elevated stereo speakers, a pair of crew-cut sailors utilized their rubber-coated paddles with an expertise sharpened by hours of practice. Behind them, separated by a thick acoustic partition, was the vessel's library and study area. It was toward this particular section of the boat that Thomas Kraft found himself drawn.

Disturbed by the abrupt manner in which the captain had ordered him from the control room, the shaggy-haired lieutenant anxiously searched the book-lined cabinets for any reference material that could help him prove his point. A good third of the library was composed of current and classical novels. The rest of the books were primarily of a technical nature. This included several dozen college-level texts covering such subjects as nuclear engineering, physics, astronomy, and higher mathematics. Recognizing several familiar volumes in the geology section, Kraft's eyes brightened when he spotted just what he was looking for.

Entitled *All About Volcanoes*, the book was written primarily for the lay reader, and included a chapter explaining the general physical characteristics that caused and accompanied such phenomena. The usual basic information about plate tectonics and the composition of the earth's crust was presented with the aid of various charts and diagrams. The majority of the text was reserved for a rather detailed history of actual volcanic eruptions. Beginning with the destruction of Pompeii in 79 AD, it took the reader right up to modern times. Individual chapters dealt with the disastrous explosion of Mt. Pelee, which had completely destroyed the French Caribbean city of St. Pierre in 1902, and the eruption he had personally witnessed, that of Mt. St. Helens on May 18, 1980. Filled with excellent, firsthand pictures, the book would definitely fulfill his immediate needs.

To determine just what information he would choose, Kraft seated himself at the wall-mounted, simulated-wood table and began thumbing through the volumes pages. As he settled into his chair, he couldn't help but notice the curious stare of the young seaman who was the table's only other occupant.

"Excuse me," greeted the ruddy-faced sailor. "But I don't believe I've seen you on board the *Phoenix* before. Are you that newcomer that scuttlebutt rumored we were taking aboard?"

"That's me," Thomas replied discreetly.

"Well, welcome aboard, Lieutenant. I hope you're finding our little home away from home comfortable."

Kraft managed a sociable smile. "That I am, sailor.

What are you reading?"

"International law," he answered. "If everything goes as planned, I hope to apply for law school when my tour of duty is up in three more years."

Before Kraft could respond, his attention was diverted to a tall, solidly built familiar figure who rounded the acoustic partition.

"Good afternoon, gentlemen," Pete Walsh said. Angling his line of sight down toward the seaman, the XO added, "Sailor, will you excuse us?"

Taking this hint, the young man quickly stood and saluted. "Yes, sir, Mr. Walsh. I was just about to break for chow, anyway."

Hastily gathering his books, he turned to exit after leaving Thomas Kraft the briefest of nods. The exec seated himself in the newly vacated chair.

"I hope I'm not disturbing you, Lieutenant Kraft?"

Thomas studied him cautiously. "Not at all. In fact, you're just the person that I wanted to speak to. What in the world is going on around here? I thought the *Phoenix* was supposed to be assisting me complete my experiments, not hindering me?"

"I can imagine how confused you must be, Lieutenant, but unfortunately, something quite extraordinary has occurred that has drastically altered our mission's goal."

Thomas strained to control himself. "If you're referring to that explosion we just monitored, I think I can explain its actual source, if you'll just give me a couple of minutes. The captain is jumping to a much too hasty conclusion with his assumption that the blast was nuclear in its origin. An underwater volcanic eruption would produce a shock wave almost identical to that caused by a NUDET. Have you forgotten already that it was because of an unusual amount of seismic activity here that I was sent to this sector?"

Walsh responded icily, "It's not just that explosion that's worrying us, Lieutenant. Only seconds after the *Phoenix* rode out that wall of compressed water, we received a top-priority transmission from Naval Operations. In effect, this coded message informed us that a state of war existed between the United States and the Union of Soviet Socialist Republics. To the best of my knowledge, this is no mere wargame."

"You've got to be kidding," Kraft returned, his face etched with astonishment.

"I wish I was," answered the XO. "In my fifteen years of service aboard boomers, this is the first time the emergency, extra-low-frequency radio system has been used to contact us. All attempts to confirm the transmission on our part have been met with nothing but static."

Thomas managed a single question. "Will we be leaving the Tonga Trench area now?"

Walsh was quick to respond, "The great depth of the ocean here offers us the perfect area for us to carry out the next part of our S.I.O.P."

Aware of the perplexed look on Kraft's face with the mention of this last phrase, the XO added, "S.I.O.P. stands for the *Phoenix*'s Single Integrated Operational Plan, or simply put, our prearranged war orders. Since all communications with submarines are kept to a minimum for security reasons, a simple code has been worked out to let us know when a DEFCON 1 alert status prevails. In the event of a subsequent Soviet strike, which resulted in the destruction of command's ability to communicate with us, the receipt of this single code word would be sufficient to give us authority to proceed with the attack plan. At present, the *Phoenix* is running deep and silent. Using the waters of the Trench to our best advantage, we will attempt to remain anonymous, rising to launch depth in less than five hour's time. At this point, we will again initiate various communications attempts. If the results are still negative, we are to assume the worst and launch our load of Tridents."

Thomas Kraft appeared unable to comprehend the scope of the XO's narrative. "Do you really think that we're at war?"

The lieutenant commander looked him straight in the eye. "Mister, I learned long ago to leave the thinking to those guys back in Washington. Right now, I only know what we're ordered. I guess you understand now the reason for the skipper's harsh words earlier. After all, he's the one who's bearing the brunt of this predicament."

"I'd say that this is one plight that all of us share in. I just can't believe that this whole thing is really coming down."

"I know what you mean, Lieutenant. We kept on building one more sophisticated weapons system after another, and somehow, we really never believed that they would ever be used. I'm afraid it's a nightmare of our own making. In the end, we've got no one to blame but ourselves."

Most aware of the somber course of their imaginings, the XO attempted to divert their mood. "We've still got plenty of time left for Command to contact us and call this whole thing off. Who knows, perhaps it's all some sort of ultra-realistic exercise."

Sensing that his hopeful words were still ineffective in lifting Kraft's melancholy, Walsh tried a different tack. Noticing the book open before him, the XO pointed to the large black-and-white photograph printed on one of the pages. It showed the remnants of a Caribbean city that appeared to have been blown apart by a massive bomb attack. Occupying the desolate landscape of burnt-out buildings was a single, tattered child.

"And you think we got problems. What in the hell happened there?"

Thomas Kraft slowly stirred. "This photo was taken on the island of Martinique two days after the eruption of Mount Pelee. That city was once the thriving metropolis of St. Pierre. On the morning of May 8, 1902, Pelee erupted with a boom heard clearly on islands fifty miles distant. Along with tons of airborne ash, stinging pumice, and smouldering lava, the volcano issued a cloud of glowing incandescent gas called the nuée ardente. Superheated at over 1,300 degrees Fahrenheit, this mist billowed down the mountainside and completely engulfed the city. Minutes later, over 30,000 men, women, and children lay dead. Miraculously, there were two survivors."

Astounded by this tale, Walsh shook his head. "My lord, I never even knew that such an event took place before."

"Few people do," added Thomas. "There aren't many forces on this earth that are as strong as an erupting volcano's fury. It has been estimated that a single major volcanic eruption can release as much energy as an entire nuclear war. I don't have to remind you that we are currently cruising in one of the most seismically active spots on this entire planet. Features such as the Trench we are currently following are indicators that the crustal plate here has been warped drastically downward. When this crust is cracked, molten rock — or magma, as it is commonly called — is expelled under great pressure to the surface. When this release takes place under the seas, inrushing water cools the magma, causing solid plugs to block the cracks. Yet below, the superheated molten rock is still releasing gases. Imagine closing the safety valve of a steam boiler, all the while increasing the size of its heat source, and you can begin to comprehend the reason that these eruptions can be so violent."

Kraft abruptly cut off his discourse as the book that lay flat on the table before him suddenly slid down onto his lap. Immediately aware of what this meant, the XO wasn't surprised when two soft electric tones sounded from the boat's p.a. Compensating for the unexpected tilt of the sub's deck, Walsh stood and carefully made his way over to the nearest wall-mounted handset. Taking in the rapid string of words that awaited his ear, he acknowledged the message, hung up the phone, and turned to face the bearded geophysicist.

"I'm afraid that I've got to get topside on the double. Sonar has just picked up an approaching Soviet attack sub. Things could be getting a little bit rough during these next couple of minutes. If I were you, I'd get off to our stateroom and hole up there."

As a loud, harsh tone began sounding in the background, sending the men off to General Quarters, Walsh began his way around the acoustic partition. Seconds later, Kraft was all alone in the rec room. Conscious of the steepening angle of their ascent, he could have sworn that he could pick up the sensation of rapid acceleration.

If a state of war indeed existed, all of them would soon know this fact for sure. A Soviet sub attack would leave little room for doubt in this matter. With his book firm in his grasp, Thomas cautiously stood to follow the XO's suggestion.

Two floors above the deserted rec room, the *Phoenix's* command center was filled with frantic activity. Captain Charles Blake barked out orders with unquestionable authority as he took up a position behind the central sonar console. With his hands firmly gripping the tubular steel railing set behind this unit, Blake addressed the heavyset individual seated immediately before him.

"Canova, what does Big Brother tell us about our bogey?"

The headphone-wearing sonar operator double-checked his monitor, and without turning from its rounded, circular face, spoke out roughly. "The probability is up to ninety-eight percent that she's the same Alfa, Skipper. I don't know how in the hell they found us, but they're sure churning up the ocean something fierce."

Turning his head to the right, Blake called out to the dark-haired diving officer at the bank of consoles on the room's opposite side. "Peterson, launch that external buoyant thermometer and find us the limit on this thermocline. We're going to need the cover of that warmer water on the double!"

"Aye, aye, Captain," the lieutenant replied alertly.

Without hesitating, Blake turned back to the sonar unit. "Canova, what's their range?"

"Three-seven nautical miles and still closing, Skipper," snapped the bald-headed New Yorker.

Aware of the fact that the Alfa's SS-N-15 subroc wouldn't be effective until they closed this gap to twenty-five miles, Blake turned to his left and again cried out. "Damn it, engineering! Throw some more logs into the boiler and get us moving!"

The officer responsible for the boat's nuclear propulsion unit responded guardedly, "Reactor's up to ninety percent, Captain. We're still building steam."

Blake's jaw tightened. "Well, you'd better find a quick way to coax some more knots out of that pile of uranium, or we're all going to be fish food."

Focusing his attention back on the sonar screen, Blake mentally sized up their situation. The Soviets had been apparently prowling around in their baffles for a good time now. Like a blind man groping in the dark, they most likely knew the *Phoenix* was close, yet hadn't been able to put a definite tag on them until their ping had reflected off the *Trident's* stern less than two minutes ago. With this certain fix, the Russian skipper had opened his throttle full. Even though the result was noisy as all hell, the Alfa was already doing better than forty knots. The *Phoenix* would have to equal this speed and then some to keep out of the subroc's lethal range.

While calculating the seconds that they had until this range was attained, Charles Blake cursed to himself at the irony of it all. Here he was, planning to make this the final cruise of a career that had lasted well over two decades, and the superpowers had to pick this very moment to finally release the long contained nuclear genie. The approach of the Alfa only made this unbelievable fact more of a reality.

The moment that they had ridden out that NUDET and received the Cocked Pistol alert had signaled that the long journey to Armageddon had finally ended. Authorized to draw up their S.I.O.P., Blake found himself faced with a single goal. Using every trick that he had absorbed in his years of intensive training, he had to make certain that the *Phoenix* survived for at least five hours. Otherwise, his entire life's purpose would be wasted in vain. With his clammy hands still gripped tightly onto the steel railing, Blake sensed that time was not on their side the way things currently stood. The arrival of his executive officer snapped him back to reality.

"What's the Alfa's range, Tony?" The XO queried coolly as he positioned himself at his captain's side.

"Two-nine miles and closing, sir," returned the busy sonar man.

204

Pete caught Blake's anxious gaze. "How in the hell did we fall into this trap, Skipper?"

"It's that damn anechoic hull of theirs," answered Charles. "Sonar was practically useless, until our hydrophones picked up the sound of seawater rushing through the Alfa's free-flowing limber ports. That was followed by their ping, and they were off to the races."

Turning to his right, Blake's voice shot up an octave. "Peterson, where does this damn thermocline end?"

Ten seconds passed before the lieutenant excitedly answered. "I've got it, Captain! XBT shows an unusually thick band of warmer water starting at a depth of one hundred and sixty-five feet."

Since the colder the water is, the further and more distinctly sound travels through it, submarines were more vulnerable to acoustic detection the deeper they dove. Most conscious of this basic fact, Blake shouted out accordingly.

"Helm, bring us up to one-five-zero feet! Engineering, where's that speed?"

Before he could receive an answer, a high-pitched squeal pierced the compartment. Anthony Canova was quick to identify it.

"That's the WLR-9 Acoustic Intercept alarm! We show a definite launch of a single, subroc-type weapon, headed straight for the surface."

As Blake's hand shot out for the intercom, he issued a single query. "Peterson, what's our depth?"

"Two hundred and ten feet and rising, sir. We're at full planes."

Absorbing this info, the captain spoke rapidly into the handset. "Chief Crowley, ready that Mk-70 for firing on my command."

Covering the transmitter with his palm, he turned to face the XO. "Pete, get over to the helm and call out when we hit the one-seven-zero threshold. Then, ready us for a quick stop, followed by a scram."

Cognizant of Blake's desired tactics, Walsh nodded and made his way over to the diving console. Seating himself behind the tubular railing behind the helmsman, the XO scanned the bank of instruments he now faced. With eager eyes, he focused his attention on the digital display depth counter. As they broke two hundred feet, he visualized the progress of the lethal weapon currently on the way toward them.

The SS-N-15 was part missile and part homing torpedo. Launched from one of the Alfa's forward torpedo tubes, it would arch toward the ocean's surface, where its rocket engine would ignite. Once airborne, it would travel at supersonic speeds until the preprogrammed motor shut off to send the warhead slicing back into the water. At this point, a targeting device would activate, directing the weapon toward the Trident by homing in on the sub's sound signature.

Blake was attempting to negate this threat by initiating a combination of unconventional escape maneuvers. The Mk-70 MOSS (Mobile Sub Simulator) was designed to emit a sonar signature exactly like that of the *Phoenix*. They would launch this torpedo-like decoy as soon as they reached the thermocline's upper limits. The quick stop and scram maneuvers would immediately stop the sub's forward momentum and abruptly shut off the boat's nuclear reactor. Floating silently in the sea under the veil of the warmer waters, some one hundred and fifty feet from the surface, the *Phoenix* would be practically invisible as the Mk-70 continued to draw the Soviet subroc deep into the ocean's depths.

Walsh expertly conveyed these desired tactics to the helmsman. Seated rigidly before him, Mark Peterson took in these instructions, all the while pulling back on the sub's steering yoke. This effort soon had the desired effect.

206

"One-seventy, Captain!" cried out the XO.

"Fire the Mk-70," Blake ordered.

With a slight shudder, the decoy streaked out of the *Phoenix*'s port launching tube.

"Quick stop!" continued the captain.

The XO looked on as Peterson eased up on the yoke, and working closely in conjunction with the propulsion officer, initiated the series of frantic adjustments that would bring the massive vessel to a sudden halt. To accomplish this, a full reversal of the sub's power train was necessary. It was most vital that this reverse power be terminated at the precise instant that the boat's forward motion had ended; otherwise, the reverse pull of the screw would send the *Phoenix* totally out of control. It was the XO's responsibility to determine this exact moment and to signal the propulsion officer to cut all power.

The *Phoenix*'s depth counter showed a readout of one hundred and forty-eight feet when Pete made his move. Instantly reacting to his command, the engineer terminated the screw's biting reverse surge. Timed perfectly, the sub now found itself dead in the water.

"Scram reactor," added a relieved Walsh, then turned his attention back to the sonar console.

With the propulsion system now totally deactivated, the constant whirl produced by the spinning turbines was conspicuously absent. This unnatural silence was broken only by the steady voice of Lieutenant Canova. Hunched over his sonar screen with his headphones cupped securely over his ears, he monitored the all-important events taking place outside their hull.

"MOSS has taken our place like a true trouper. Her signature remains strong . . . I've got a splashdown, right on top of us. There's a single screw activating, steadily gaining intensity. . . . It's coming right down on us!"

All attention was riveted to the sonar console where Captain Blake now stood, anxiously perched above its heavyset operator. Forehead beaded with sweat, the captain studied the glass screen that displayed the SS-N-15's imminent approach. The subroc's advance took on a dimension of additional reality as its swirling propellor became audible in the near distance.

A single nagging doubt dominated Blake's ponderings. Was the Soviet subroc being drawn to its target by data other than the *Phoenix's* sound signature? If so, his desperate tactics would be completely futile. He should have attempted to outrun and outdive the weapon, instead of floating here like a sitting duck. It was because of firsthand intelligence information that he had committed the *Phoenix* as he had. Any second now, he would know if this strategy was indeed the correct one.

Just when it appeared that the SS-N-15 would smack right into the Trident's bow, the sonar screen began indicating a drastic alteration in the warhead's course. Blake caught the senior operator's relieved glance, as this diversion became evident to the others with the decreasing hum of the subroc's engine.

"It's taking the bait!" acknowledged Canova, who quickly refocused his attention back to his headphones.

While he did so, Pete Walsh scurried over to the captain's side. "We did it, Skipper!"

Blake responded cautiously. "Let's just hope that the MOSS can hold on a bit longer. I'd like to have as much distance between us and that exploding warhead as possible. Then, we've got to pray that the Alfa buys the kill. Otherwise, we're going to have to slug it out, torpedo against torpedo."

Though primarily designed as an offensive missile platform, both officers were well aware of the fact that the *Phoenix* could hold its own in the midst of such a battle. Yet, because vessels such as the Alfa were created solely to hunt down other submarines, the advantage would be slightly in favor of the Soviets. Anthony Canova's voice brought the two back to more immediate concerns.

"I'm picking up a sudden increase in the SS-N-15's rev rate. I believe she's going in for the kill."

"What's its range?" quizzed the captain.

"We've got approximately nine and a half miles of water between us, Skipper."

The sonar man's observation did little to relieve the lines of tension that etched Blake's face. "Rig the boat to meet a concussion, Pete. We'll soon learn for certain if their kill radius is limited to four miles."

The XO hurried over to the keyboard access unit set beside the sonar station and entered the captain's directive into the computer. Seconds later, the entire boat filled with a muted, pulsating tone, informing the crew to brace themselves for an anticipated concussion. It wasn't long after the XO had secured his own firm handhold on the railing set behind the helm when an ear-splitting boom rumbled through the command center. This was followed by the almost-instantaneous arrival of a massive shock wave. Striking the *Phoenix* with an intense jolt, the compressed wall of water tossed the 18,700-ton vessel upward and hard onto its starboard side.

Pete Walsh found himself straining to remain upright as the sub rolled over on its keel and then abruptly righted itself. As the light blinked off and then on again, the XO determined that the captain and the majority of those occupying the compartment had also managed to keep their footing. Except for the buckling groan of the boat's superstructure as the vessel again settled itself, an almost-eerie quiet prevailed. This silence was broken by Charles Blake.

"Damage control, what's our status?"

From an opposite corner, a strained voice replied, "Hull integrity is intact, sir. All stations appear operational."

Pete Walsh joined the captain as he directed his next inquiry. "Okay, Canova, what's going on out there?"

Still increasing the hydrophone feed, the junior officer responded somewhat hesitantly, "Except for the commotion caused by that shock wave, there doesn't seem to be anything else out there."

For a full minute, Anthony Canova deftly manipulated the controls of his sensor panel. Scanning the seas a full three hundred and sixty degrees, a pensive look emanated from his eyes as he shook his head despondently.

"They're waiting out there silently, just like us, Skipper," offered the XO. "After all, that Russian captain's going to want to confirm a certain kill."

"Or perhaps he didn't even fall for this whole charade," reflected Charles Blake. "If this warm water fails to veil us, we're going to really have our hands full."

A moment of contemplative silence again possessed the two officers, when suddenly Anthony Canova's pudgy hands shot up to press down on his headphones.

"We've got 'em! I'm picking up a single screw, bearing one-niner miles, due north of us, at about five hundred feet. She's moving this way."

"They're going to pass right under us," observed the jubilant XO.

A satisfied grin finally broke the corners of the captain's mouth. "It looks like this round goes to Uncle Sam, gentlemen."

Turning to face Walsh, he added, "Now, do you have any doubts as to the validity of those war orders? That NUDET we rode out earlier was only the tip of the iceberg. In approximately four more hours, we'll be able to throw in our two cents' worth. I'd say that 184 hundred-kiloton warheads will wreak just enough havoc to revenge the loss of Delta Base. How about it, Pete?"

Still finding himself unable to comprehend the full scope of the situation they found themselves in, the XO didn't respond. Blake noticed this distraction and directed his next request firmly.

"Mr. Walsh, I want to schedule a meeting in the wardroom, with the boat's senior officers, as soon as we're safely on our way again. Please include Chief Crowley."

"Aye, aye, sir," the XO replied flatly.

The exec's unemotional response was accompanied by a dull, unfocused gaze. Charles Blake was surprised by this. It was very out of character. Most likely, the reality of this whole mess was finally sinking into Walsh's head. This reaction of shocked disbelief was only natural. Many of the other officers, who had knowledge of their Cocked Pistol status, were probably going through similar mental distress. A one-hundred-percent effort on behalf of each man on board the *Phoenix* would be necessary if they were going to survive this fated day. This effort would be especially needed from the officers. As captain, he would have to set an example of unflinching strength before the others. Yet, deep inside, Charles Blake trembled at the thought of what would happen once they let their Tridents go. For only the end of the civilized world as they knew it would rise from the radioactive ashes of ground zero.

Seated at the wall-mounted desk of the cabin he shared with the *Phoenix*'s executive officer, Thomas Kraft found his gaze glued to one of the photos that graced the library book he had just borrowed. This representation was the same one that Walsh had asked about earlier. It showed a single, rag-torn child, standing in the burnt-out rubble of what had only two days earlier been a bustling city of 30,000. The eruption of Mt. Pelee had demonstrated with frightening reality the sheer, lethal power of a natural phenomena few men were willing to admit existed.

As if man alone had the right to kill indiscriminately, the geophysicist pondered with a disgusted shake of his head. How very puny the species to which he belonged was. Their utter ignorance and insensitivity to the gift of life was inexcusable.

The explosion that had sounded outside only minutes ago was proof positive of the attainment of a level of culture bordering on that of sheer barbarism. Yet Thomas doubted that even a crude savage would stoop so low as to spoil the entire planet, so that not even the lowest form of life would be able to flourish.

If the S.I.O.P. the XO had recently explained to him indeed came to pass, the nuclear madness would have reached a level of acceleration impossible to turn back. Blanketed by thousands of nuclear warheads, the planet itself would shiver and die. Yet, perhaps this trial by fire was what the species needed. Mutated to a state of pure madness, mankind had failed to pass the final judgment.

While one portion of his mind weighed such absurdities, his other sphere was still locked on the photograph before him. With unblinking eyes, Thomas studied the cloud-shrouded mountain that dominated the setting's foreground. Was Mt. Pelee nature's instrument in a judgment mankind instinctively deserved? How very similar was this burnt-out countryside to the photos he remembered seeing of Hiroshima and Nagasaki. Stirred by this comparison, a mental image locked deep in his consciousness rose with the swiftness of a dawning sun. In a heartbeat, he was suddenly swept back to a moment, a virtual lifetime ago, when he had sat on the porch of his fales overlooking Tutuila's Cape Taputapu. Soaring above him was the majesty of the crystal-clear, moonlit sky, while caressing his ears was the voice of his beloved.

In an unearthly octave, Telsa Vanua told him the tale of the fire goddess, Pele. Walking the planet once a year to search humankind's hearts, this tempestuous deity was provoked to utter madness upon finding man needlessly wasting the gift of life. The price she extracted from her subjects took the form of massive earth tremors and boiling waves of bubbling lava. It was most evident that her vassals in St. Pierre had failed to heed the warnings of the goddess. Would all of mankind soon share this very same fate?

Thomas Kraft was not a superstitious fellow. After his parent's tragic death, he had even stopped attending mass. Throwing himself into his studies, he had entered a realm far from the mysteries of the spirit. But less than twenty-four hours ago, a cup of the native brew called kava had brought him back to a secret world he hadn't tapped since childhood. For several hours after consuming the milklike, peppery substance, everything had seemed so clear. The entire universe had appeared to have a single, all-prevailing purpose. Why, he had even believed Telsa when she explained that the elders would be dedicating the evening's kava to the goddess, who they planned to petition with their prayers to have mercy on mankind. How very totally had these elders failed!

In approximately four more hours, the world would be facing a calamity from which it would never return. Pele would have her final laugh as thousands of nuclear blasts cracked the earth and released the ultimate fury. If Thomas was a praying man, he'd lose himself in meditations of pity and forgiveness. Unfortunately, he would have to leave that task to Telsa and her people; he could only follow his instincts. Strange as it seemed, however, as if a voice were calling to him from the grave, he somehow had the distinct impression that the book before him held a single clue that could reverse the judgment. A scholar and a fool to the very end, he thought, as he turned to the first page to initiate a study he knew he might very well never live to complete.

Chapter Eleven

For a day which started so ominously, Captain First Rank Victor Kalinin couldn't believe how well things had turned out. Earlier this morning, when the *Magadan* had lost track of the American Trident, he'd known how slim the chances were that they'd ever locate them in the immediate future. Yet now, not only had they tagged them, but the Alfa had also blown the Yankees away to meet their makers. How quickly moved the hand of fortune in the struggle known as war!

Only minutes ago, Victor had left the *Magadan*'s cramped control room, where a joyous celebration was taking place. Why, even the stuffy zampolit was joining in this jubilation. Their alert orders had been received only moments before their sonar pinged the immense Trident as it plunged for the safe waters of the Tonga Trench. And the message had been preceded by a massive blast, which their computers had identified as being almost certainly nuclear in origin. Most probably targeted at one of their surface ships, this explosion had signaled that the real fight was only just beginning.

Not having much time to contemplate the real significance of the situation they found themselves in, Kalinin decided he needed a few minutes to be on his own. Since the relatively tiny vessel was jam-packed with both equipment and crew, his goal had been the cramped confines of his quarters. Located on the floor below the control room, his compartment was placed toward the sub's bow, directly behind the forward torpedo room. Accepting the hearty congratulations of several members of the crew, he gratefully utilized his plastic key card to gain entry to his private domain. Only when the door shut closed behind him did he issue a breath of relief. One by one, he slipped off his shoes, unbuttoned his tunic, and laid down on his stiff bunk. Closing his eyes, Victor allowed the steady throb of the *Magadan*'s engines to clear his mind of the morning's tense events. Relaxed by the monotonous whirling tone, the forty-seven-year-old line officer was able to place these events in their proper perspective.

The receipt of the Red Vulcan alert signaled the end of an era. The tense detente that had characterized the relations between the superpowers since the end of World War II had ended in the inevitable nuclear showdown. Only the strong would prevail in this nightmarish conflict. His years of intense training would now speak for themselves.

Although Victor had never ordered a deliberate attack before, he had done so earlier without a second's hesitation. Barely conscious of the fact that he would be sending one hundred and fifty-seven men to their watery graves, Kalinin had done his duty unflinchingly, a lesson he had learned well during his years of naval study.

Born into a family with a firm tradition in the Russian Navy, Victor Kalinin had had little doubts as to what his future would hold. And with the completion of his first military training course at the tender age of thirteen, the youngster had become completely infatuated with the armed forces. It was with great anticipation that he had joined the DOSAAF (All-

Union Voluntary Society for Assistance to the Navy). This paramilitary club offered him his first courses in basic seamanship. By the time he was eligible for naval service, Victor was already an expert sailor. Because of his natural intelligence and high-placed relatives within the Party, he had been accepted at the Nakhimov Black Sea Higher Naval School at Sevastopol. For five strenuous years he had learned all aspects of engineering, navigation, electronics, and nuclear propulsion. Graduating first in his class, he had found himself with his choice of duties. Though both his father and grandfather had been officers aboard fleet battleships, Victor had chosen the submarine services. Transferred to Leningrad, he had excelled in his studies at both the Leninsky Komsomol Higher School of Submarine Navigation, and the exclusive Grechko Academy.

His first duty had been as a junior lieutenant aboard a primitive Foxtrot Class, diesel-electric attack sub. A year later, he had been promoted to the rank of lieutenant and given service on a nuclear-powered Echo Class boat. His first senior command had been as a captain third rank aboard a Victor Class attack sub. One of the fastest and most sophisticated vessels of its day, it was while serving on such a boat, that he had been groomed for his present assignment.

The *Magadan* was designed with one purpose in mind: to hunt down and destroy the American Trident. To do so, she was equipped with the most sophisticated technology available. This included a radically new, compact, liquid-metal-cooled nuclear reactor, which allowed an unprecedented speed of over forty-five knots. To dive to depths no attack sub had previously dreamed of entering, a titanium alloy hull was utilized. Not only did this allow them to dive below 3,000 feet, but the nonmagnetic nature of the titanium veiled them from the imperialists' ever-probing magnetic anamoly detectors. Such MAD devices were mounted on the enemy's planes and surface ships to pick up a submarine's natural magnetic field and thus open them up to subsequent attack. Of equal importance was the anechoic, Clusterguard tiles that coated this hull. With the use of such a unique substance, opposing sonar units would have great difficulty picking up their signature.

Victor would never forget the glorious morning that he had been allowed to run under an entire NATO task force in the Magadan. With its throttle wide open, the attack sub had shot beneath the waters of the North Atlantic where, immediately above, the forces of darkness had been in the midst of a major exercise. Traveling at a speed that would have made it impervious to the enemy's latest torpedoes, the *Magadan* had proved that the Soviet Navy was a potent force not to be laughed at. And now that one of the Americans' most sophisticated submarines lay in scattered pieces on the ocean floor below, they had proven themselves completely.

If only he could inform Admiral Kostromo of their triumph. It was because of this old-timer's foresight that vessels such as the *Magadan* had been built. As father of the modern Soviet Navy, Kostromo could rest proud today, knowing that his years of hard work and sacrifice were finally paying off.

Victor wondered how the bald-headed, fifty-year Navy veteran had reacted upon first receiving the Red Vulcan alert. Hopefully, his flagship, the *Minsk*, was still safe. As fate would have it, his brilliant, timely exercise, Operation Lenin, had set the Soviet Union up in a perfect position to respond to the imperialists' initial aggression. Perhaps the war was already over. Having no doubt as to who the winner would ultimately be, Kalinin stirred excitedly.

Until further ordered, the *Magadan* would follow its predetermined war plan exactly. Their first duty had been to eliminate all enemy Trident submarines stationed to patrol the waters of the Southwestern Pacific Basin. Intelligence had determined that only a single such craft was currently positioned here; a single SS-N-15 had sent this same boat to the bottom only minutes ago. Ever-watchful for any stray subs, the *Magadan* would then resume its search for the top-secret American sub-refitting station known as Delta Base. Presumed to be located in the hollowed-out core of a nearby seamount, this base supposedly held vital stores which the surviving Tridents would need to continue the battle. By knocking it out, the Motherland could be assured that it would no longer have to fear any future aggression from the depths of the sea.

Aware that it was time to begin their search for this illusive station in earnest, Victor fought his tension-worn body's natural desire for sleep. Issuing a wide yawn, he wiped his eyes and sat up stiffly. At his washbasin, a handful of cool water splashed full onto his face helped awaken him completely. While staring back at the tired, bloodshot eyes that met his gaze from the mirror's reflection, he plotted their next move. Utilizing the *Magadan*'s computer-enhanced, three-dimensional mapping capabilities, he'd draw up an exact picture of the waters they were now entering. Their first area of intensive search would be that geological feature known as the Vavau Seamount. With the aid of their hull-mounted sensors, they'd study each cubic foot of the ocean here, ever on the watch for temperature anamolies, alien sounds, and new masses of land not on their charts. Delta Base would soon be theirs for the taking, just as the Trident submarine had been.

Rebuttoning his tunic, Victor Kalinin found himself filled with new purpose and vigor. Like a lad just out of naval school, he hurried over to don his shoes and make his way back to the control room. For the sooner the imperialist threat was nullified, the sooner the world could grow to new-found heights under the glory of pure Communism.

To properly celebrate the *Magadan*'s recent glorious victory, Sergei Vengerovo passed out a single round of vodka to each member of the sub's command staff. Though recent Party directives had warned all political officers of such alcohol's debilitating effects amongst the men, this was certainly not applicable in this instance. The handful of men who presently surrounded him were some of the best soldiers the Motherland had ever nurtured. Tried and true warriors, they had gone about their dangerous duty without a thought to their own safety.

Angling the shotglass upward, the zampolit tilted his head and poured the clear spirits down the back of his throat. With a stinging bite, the raw grain alcohol found its way to the pit of his stomach. Inspired by this drink, Sergei smoothed down his shiny, blond hair and surveyed the equipment-packed compartment he currently shared. When his eyes reached the navigation console set at the control room's rearmost corner, he found himself doing a double take. For, unbeknownst to him, their captain had returned. Busily hunched over the lucite screen of the mapping device, Kalinin seemed totally involved with that which he studied.

How in character it was for the captain to enter their midst with a minimum of fanfare. One other trait that was most obvious was the line officer's total knowledge of the complicated vessel that they sailed within. His resplendent elimination of the American Trident sub had been the act of a pure tactical genius. And to think that—earlier that very day!—he had actually doubted the man's competency to command. It was strange how the incident that promoted these doubts seemed to have taken place years ago.

At that time, Operation Lenin had been just about to be initiated. Sergei would never forget the captain's ire upon being informed that the Trident sub that they had been following for almost a week had somehow slipped out of their sights. Why the man had gone absolutely crazy! Screaming at the top of his voice, he'd angrily castigated the *Magadan*'s senior lieutenant, yelling at the embarrassed officer as if he had been the stupidest of conscripts. Sending the young man off to the isolation of his quarters, Kalinin had then orchestrated a frantic search pattern to begin. At top speed, oblivious to the ever-present threat of a reactor meltdown, the captain had guided the *Magadan* on what had appeared to be the most fruitless of courses. Not even stopping to respond to the massive blast that they had determined to be of nuclear origin, Kalinin had seemed driven by a madness that the zampolit was only now understanding. The receipt of the coded Red Vulcan alert orders had pushed the man even further. Fortunately, it wasn't long afterward that their sonar ping had reflected off the American's stern.

With his eyes gleaming demonically, the captain had prepared the *Magadan* to attack. Without a second's hesitation, he'd commanded them to join a war that minutes ago, they hadn't even known existed. It was at that instant that Sergei had begun to understand just what made their captain tick. He had read Kalinin's service record, and was most aware of his well-schooled background. Vengerovo had assumed that Kalinin's knowledge was strictly of the book variety. And the manner in which he had castigated Lieutenant Gribovka before the others had seemed to offer certain proof that the fellow didn't know the first thing about dealing with subordinates.

What Sergei had been confusing with a severe personality weakness—which was a by-product of the Captain's birthright—was instead another quality altogether. Driven by the relentless needs of a hunter, Kalinin had treated both his crew and his vessel as mere instruments for the attainment of the ultimate quarry. The man's goals had been the same as those of the Motherland all along. Sergei had only been misinterpreting the methods being used to meet these difficult objectives.

If the rest of the Soviet Union's officer corps acted in such a cold, ruthless manner, the war would soon be over. Buried under the rubble of their own greed, the United States of America didn't stand a chance. Buoyed by these observations, the zampolit decided it was time to offer Victor Kalinin a victorious sip of their great country's lifeblood. With vodka bottle in hand, the immaculately groomed political officer began his way to the control room's rear.

Watching Vengerovo cross the compartment was Senior Lieutenant Yuri Gribovka. Only recently allowed to leave his cabin, the lanky, red-haired young officer was assigned a relatively minor position, assisting the *Magadan*'s radio operator. Though the captain still wouldn't look him in the eye, Yuri knew that just to be released from detention was a very good sign. Perhaps soon, with their new predicament and all, Kalinin would even reinstate him totally to his former responsibilities. The thirty-seven-year-old had certainly learned his lesson. Never again would he hesitate to inform the captain if something unusual was occurring during the midst of his watch.

As things had eventually turned out, his incompetency really wasn't that costly. The Trident had been found soon enough, and at present lay in a million, scattered pieces on the floor of the Tonga Trench. Currently, there was a much greater problem for them to concentrate on.

The arrival of the Red Vulcan alert code meant that the *Magadan* was to assume that a state of war existed between the Motherland and the imperialists. Unless they were informed otherwise, they were to proceed with their sealed war orders. This strategic operational plan was in the sole hands of their captain. Yuri could only guess, from their current speed and course, that they were continuing southward into the Pacific Basin. Here they would sink all bogey subs and disrupt enemy surface movements whenever possible.

Their only link with the outside world would be the radio. So far, it had been of little help. Since receiving the alert call, all that they had been able to pick up was a throaty band of static. No matter which frequency they tried, the results were always the same. Even a specially designed VLF buoy, launched to the surface, had been unable to pick up any sort of manmade communications. This included the frequencies that the Americans utilized. Knowledge of such top-secret bands had only come to them recently, as a result of a high-placed spy in the imperialists Pentagon. When the buoy had been launched on previous occasions, it had never failed to pick up at least some sort of chatter.

Yuri knew that if they were indeed in the midst of a nuclear war, that communications relay stations would be among the first targets. His present duty was to carefully scan each available channel, in the hopes that at least one of them would provide a hint as to what was going on. To accomplish this task, he was fitted with a pair of bulky headphones. Seated next to the petty officer responsible for their radio operations, the senior lieutenant monotonously switched the selector from channel to channel. Tuning in each frequency with the help of a special filter mechanism proved to be a time-consuming task in itself. Yet it was certainly better than being confined to his stuffy quarters. Such a position would also allow him to be one of the first members of the crew to make contact with the outside world.

Certainly, there had to be at least one radio transmitter still operating. What would he hear upon first making contact? Would it be one of their own commentators bragging about a total Soviet victory, or would the Americans be the ones to prevail? If all that he had been hearing lately was true, he doubted that either country would be in very good shape. Even if the Motherland did rise victoriously, the price extracted for such a triumph would be a severe one.

And what of his own loved ones? His Katrina and their two infant boys had been living outside the naval installation at Vladivostok, home of the Pacific Fleet. He seriously doubted if they had survived more than the first few minutes of hostilities. In this respect, they would be among the lucky ones, for the country they loved so before would be a vastly different one. With hundreds of millions dead or dying, a good part of all industry blown to bits, while clouds of deadly radiation rained down from the heavens—such would be the spoils the winner of such a conflict could enjoy!

Somehow he found himself unable to believe that such an unthinkable calamity could have possibly occurred. Chilled by such thoughts, Yuri's hand proved to be shaking when it again went out to turn the frequency selector. Twisting this dial a single notch, he grimaced with pain when a deafening blast of raw static burst from the headphones.

"Yes, Mikhail, I understand the difficulties that you're encountering. Both our satellites and ground-control transmitting stations are experiencing similar problems. We must keep trying, though."

The general secretary was forced to press the telephone receiver up to his ear to hear the deputy defense minister's response. Nodding in agreement to Antonov's words, Vladimir Kirensk responded in a firm voice, "Please give the admiral my personal regards, and good luck with that typhoon and all."

Hanging up the handset, the bald-headed chief executive caught the icy stares of the two men sitting immediately before him. He addressed these aides with a somewhat reluctant tone.

"I'm afraid Kostromo has also had no success in contacting the *Magadan*. Currently, the *Minsk* is entering the Celebes Sea. As we feared, they will be forced to sail through the tail end of that typhoon that is moving up toward the Philippines."

"That storm is a nasty one," replied Pyotr Altyr. "I've been monitoring its progress on the Lenin I weather satellite. Not even an old salt like Admiral Kostromo will be able to penetrate it at top speed."

"What about the point vessels that have already reached the Melanesians?" D. F. Pavlodar quizzed. "Surely they must be in a better position to contact the sub?"

Kirensk exhaled a long, worried breath. "They have also met with no success, Comrades. For some strange reason, the *Magadan* is completely deaf to our calls."

Altyr's gaunt frame stirred as he stood and began nervously pacing the study. "I tell you, I'll bet my life that the American Trident is responsible for all of this. Why, I'd say the chances are good that our Alfa Class vessel can't respond to our transmissions because she doesn't even exist anymore."

"I agree," added Pavlodar. "I still think this is a clever imperialist ploy."

Vladimir Kirensk sat forward, pinching the upper bridge of his nose. "I think idle speculation will get us nowhere. We can only go by the facts. We can be thankful that General Kupol's son was successful in knocking down the cruise device. We also know for certain that not long after that volcano erupted in the Tonga sector, both our Alfa and the American Trident sub ceased responding to any type of communications attempt. I can't help but feel that somehow that eruption is responsible for this entire mess."

"Perhaps the subs eliminated each other, seconds after receiving their war alerts," observed Altyr.

Pavlodar turned his thick neck to respond to his coworker directly. "And if it proved to be the Trident that did the eliminating, then what, Pyotyr?"

The hollow-eyed advisor suddenly stopped his pacing. "Then, I'd say, in about four more hours, that the Soviet Union would be opening itself for a barrage of one hundred and ninety-two MIRV'd nuclear warheads. Most likely targeted to air defense and naval installations in eastern Siberia. I'm certain that cities such as Vladivostok and Petropavlovsk would also feel the Tridents' sting. Andrew Lyons says that he's impotent to call off such a strike. So are we to merely sit back and watch as millions of our fellow comrades are needlessly burnt to a crisp? No, we can not allow this!"

"But what can we do?" queried Pavlodar sullenly.

Altyr walked over to put his bony hands on the back of his chair, his eyes sparkling. "We must call the president's bluff. If the hour approaches and Lyons still pleads that he's unable to reach his sub, the strategic forces of the Motherland, already in place with the help of Operation Lenin, will strike accordingly. The second that our recon satellites pick up one of those Tridents as it breaks the water, we will launch a weapon of equivalent throw weight. I think their cities of San Diego, Seattle, Jacksonville, and Norfolk, plus various defensive early-warning stations spread out on their west coast, should offer us sufficient revenge."

"Such a plan is brilliant!" offered Pavlodar, whose eyes went to implore those of Vladimir Kirensk. "Comrade General Secretary, since you are hesitant to order a full-scale first strike to respond to this lunacy, at least consider Pyotyr's proposal. If this is all but a clever bluff, the imperialists will quickly back down. If it is not, and the Tridents indeed fly, the very least we will be able to do is revenge the lives of our unfortunate countrymen who find themselves at ground zero. Please, Comrade, there is no other way!"

Silently absorbing this emotional plea on behalf of his chubby aide, Victor weighed the consequences of such an unorthodox response. Almost certain that Andrew Lyons was being one hundred percent truthful, he was well aware that if the United States were unable to reach their sub in four hours time, its captain would launch his lethal load regardless of the actual state of world affairs. Millions of Soviets would die a horrible death in return. Even though he believed Lyons's sincerity — accepting that this was all a tragic mistake — could he just sit back and do nothing in return? Sure, he was all for world peace, but there came a point where one had to defend himself. If the Tridents flew, the American people would have to pay the price, of this fact Vladimir was certain.

Still aware of the intense stares of his two aides, who waited anxiously for some sort of response, Kirensk pushed his chair back and stood up. With his arms cocked at the small of his back, he walked slowly over to one of his study's huge picture windows. Focusing his gaze on the copse of trees that lay before the spotlight-illuminated Kremlin wall, he deliberately cleared his dry throat.

"The picture that you paint, Comrades, is a grim one. Unfortunately, reality doesn't always follow the course that we would like it to. Thus, we must not delude ourselves. Your plan indeed has some merit. It warrants further study. If we are forced to make such a rash decision, we still have until the dawn to do so. Until then, we must do all that is humanly possible to reach those subs. Elements of Admiral Kostromo's fleet are in the best position to initiate such contact. If communications remain impossible, I will order the admiral to hunt down both vessels and eliminate them. Such a move would incur a minimum loss of life. Let's just continue to hope that the Soviet Union will not be placed in the awkward position of having to hunt down and sink one of its own submarines.

"I think it would be best for me to contact the admiral at once, to inform him of my decision. It has been a long evening, Comrades. I sincerely thank you for your continued support."

The two aides knew that it was time to get to work on their own plan, for there were targets to determine and missiles to ready. With the pensive general secretary still standing firmly before the window, they excused themselves to begin the long walk back to their offices.

Alone once again, Vladimir Kirensk angled his gaze upward, to survey that part of the night sky visible over the immense brick wall. Outside, it proved to be a crystal-clear evening. Dominating the heavens was a blood-red, full moon. Noticing that its ragged craters had never appeared so visible, he looked on with awe as a shooting star shot past the shining lunar orb. Conscious of time's rapid passing, he pivoted to return to his telephone. As he did so, he found himself issuing a single wish. If the spirits of the Motherland continued to be at his side, the call he would now initiate would end this nightmare once and for all.

Deputy Defense Minister Mikhail Antonov had never prided himself as being the best of sailors. For the first hour or so, his voyage aboard the *Minsk* had been perfectly enjoyable. Why, most of the time he hadn't even realized that they were at sea. Nestled comfortably in the admiral's stateroom with a bottle of excellent potato vodka between them, they had monitored the tense situation caused by the errant cruise missile. It was right after they had gotten the word that this threat no longer existed, that the first massive sea waves had begun to crash into the giant carrier's bow. Since that moment, the ocean's state had progressively worsened. At present, it was all Mikhail could do just to make his way out of the comfortable lounge chair he was seated in, and progress the few feet to the restroom. After emptying his stomach for the sixth time that morning, Antonov gingerly left the confines of the lavatory.

Most aware of this old friend's distress, Admiral Kostromo watched the green-faced bureaucrat settle back into his seat. "Feeling better, Comrade?"

Mikhail took a second to regain his breath. "Ah, I tell you, Alexis, I don't know how there's anything left to throw up!"

Chuckling at this, Kostromo braced his hands on the edge of his desk when a particularly nasty wave sent the *Minsk* rolling on her keel.

"My heavens, that was a bad one," observed the admiral, who followed this remark with a healthy swig of vodka. "Radar shows that the worse is yet to come.

Are you certain that you won't reconsider and have a sip of this, Mikhail? It will settle your stomach."

Shaking his head adamantly, Antonov waved away the silver flask. "That would do me in for good, Alexis. What was that phone call all about, when I went running off to the lavatory last?"

"It was no one but our illustrious leader, once again." remarked Kostromo coldly. "You'll never believe what he wants from us this time."

His words were abruptly interrupted by the loud beep of the intercom. Shrugging his solid shoulders, the bald-headed, seventy-five-year-old picked up the red handset before it could ring a second time.

"Yes, Captain Markova, I'm most aware of the agitated state of the seas we're currently crossing. . . . No, I don't think that's a good idea at all. Until I notify you further, we will remain on our present course and speed. That will be all!"

Slamming down the receiver, Kostromo's face turned a brilliant shade of bright red. "These young officers today are nothing but a bunch of pampered pansies! Can you imagine him having the nerve to ask me, on behalf of the crew, if it would be all right to turn back to the shelter of the South China Sea? What is this younger generation made out of?"

Almost in response, the deck beneath them pitched violently to port. Both men grasped the edges of their chairs tightly. As the *Minsk* precariously steadied itself, the deputy defense minister found his sour stomach still rolling. Only his piqued curiosity kept him from crawling off to the bathroom.

"The phone call, Alexis. What did Kirensk want this time?"

Regaining his composure, Kostromo continued. "It is our esteemed leader's opinion that as long as both the *Magadan* and the American sub remain at large, the world's peace will be unnecessarily threatened. In order to negate this menace, I have been ordered to notify the elements of our flotilla who have already penetrated the Melanesians that it shall be their responsibility to make contact with these subs. A failure to establish communications with them shall be followed by a single course of action: Utilizing every available antisubmarine weapons system at their command, they're to locate and eliminate both parties without further hesitation.

"Do you realize what this means, Mikhail? That fool is ordering us to blow away our own submarine!"

Abruptly thrown forward as the *Minsk*'s bow was buried by tons of frothing sea water, Antonov swallowed back his rising bile and managed a weak reply. "I'm sure that the general secretary has his reasons. Though the man is a bit soft on defense matters, his ability can't be questioned. Under Kirensk, farm and industrial output have never been higher. For the first time in years, the people seem genuinely content."

"Oh, come now, Comrade, are you forgetting who you're talking with? You an I go back many years. Why, both of us were already in uniform, defending the Motherland, when Kirensk was still suckling at his mother's breasts. A strong, unyielding manner is the only way to stand up to the power-hungry imperialists. Sinking our own submarine would be the ultimate folly, even more foolhardy than the weak-willed Khrushchev's actions during the Cuban fiasco.

"The cruise missile threat has been negated by our own hand. Must we be responsible for cleaning up the Americans' own messes now? Instead, we should strike the Yankees with every usable warhead. With our strategic forces positioned like they are, Operation Lenin can evolve into much more than a mere exercise. Just think of it, Comrade, a world totally free from

231

capitalist aggression!"

With the *Minsk*'s superstructure straining in protest around them, the deputy defense minister vainly attempted to make sense out of the admiral's peculiar logic. "So does this mean that you're going to ignore Kirensk's directive?"

Kostromo returned his old friend's serious gaze and spoke out thoughtfully. "As much as I would like to, Mikhail, insubordination is not in my make-up. I have never deliberately gone against an order from a superior, and I'm not about to begin such foolishness at this ripe old age. If this damn typhoon permits us, I'll relay the general secretary's instructions at once."

Relieved that the admiral had come to his senses, Antonov dared a single question. "Is it reasonable to assume that your ships can even locate these two submarines, let alone destroy them?"

Kostromo sat forward. "Again, you forget who you're talking with, old friend. Who do you think personally trained the captains' of those surface vessels that are presently entering the very waters the subs are reported to be sailing in? If they're out there, my men will find them. As to destroying them, just listen to the concentrated firepower that we have available.

"Leading the way into the Southwestern Pacific Basin are a pair of Udaloy Class destroyers. I don't have to remind you that these ships are among the most potent, sophisticated antisubmarine platforms that have ever sailed the seas. Equipped with a pair of sensor-laden, Hormone helicopters each, the subs will be spotted long before the destroyers are even within range. It is at this point that their exceptionally powerful ASW armaments will come into play. These take the form of two quadruple SS-N-14 launchers, a pair of RBU-6000 rocket launchers, and two quadruple, twenty-one-inch torpedo tubes.

"If for some reason these Udaloys fail to do the trick, they are being closely followed by the command ship of this mini-flotilla, the Kara Class cruiser *Azov*. At the helm of this last ship is an officer of a most exemplary nature. He is none other than my own son, Josef. Having my boy out there will be like having my own eyes and ears in those waters. Surrounded by such a task force, the submarines won't stand a chance!"

With the conclusion of these words, the admiral seemed suddenly drained of all energy. Sitting back in his command chair, he put the flask to his lips and downed a healthy mouthful. Mikhail Antonov sensed the old-timer's exhaustion and commented compassionately.

"You know, I didn't realize Josef had command of his own ship already. I still picture him as a mere lad, running through the woods that surrounded your dacha outside of Yalta. Where have the years gone to, Comrade?"

Shaking his head in response, Kostromo drained another sip from his flask while Mikhail continued, "Well, we still have several hours before we even have to worry about such things as hunting down those two submarines. Hopefully, we will establish contact with them long before hostilities are necessary. Until then, we mustn't upset ourselves needlessly. We are getting too old for such nonsense. Let's leave the worrying for youngsters like Vladimir Kirensk and Andrew Lyons. We have certainly sacrificed our share of sleepless nights to the cause. Speaking of the devil, shall I continue my explanation of the reason for my delay earlier this morning? I think that you will find it most refreshing."

Warmed by Kostromo's sudden smile, Mikhail Antonov sensed that the ice had at long last been broken. Though the two had seen less of each other as the years progressed, they were still the closest of friends. Taking a few seconds to regain his balance after a massive swell had tossed him about in his chair, the white-haired bureaucrat continued with the tale he had started much earlier in the day. Spurred on by his host's total attention, Mikhail carefully chose his words, to describe that moment in the hotel room, back in the Vietnamese city of Cam Rahn, when he had first laid his eyes on that magical piece of femininity called Black Jade.

Chapter Twelve

The office of Admiral Richard Burnhardt, Commander in Chief of the Pacific Fleet, was located in a white, two-story stucco building overlooking the naval installation at Pearl Harbor. Perched on a hardened ledge of volcanic basalt, the structure offered an excellent view of the dozens of warships currently at port, and of the southwestern tip of the Hawaiian island of Oahu.

It proved to be another gorgeous, tropical afternoon as the distinguished, white-haired admiral exited the office building. At his side was Commander Bob Walker, a stocky, crew-cut representative of the Office of Naval Research. With slow, purposeful strides, the two walked up a narrow gravel pathway. Surrounded by stately coconut palms and thick, lush vegetation, the trail led to a small clearing cut into the hillside's lip. Placed here was a solitary bench, providing a spectacular overlook of the crystal-blue waters of picturesque Mamala Bay beyond.

Taking positions in front of this bench, the two naval officers scanned the horizon. Their gazes seemed to simultaneously lock on a pair of sleek gray destroyers in the process of slicing their sharply angled bows into the open sea.

"Those are the two newest Spruance ships," the admiral observed proudly. "You can clearly see why their ill-informed critics were so quick to criticize them. With the only visible weapons being those pair of 5-inch, Mk-45 guns fore and aft, and that single ASROC box launcher forward of the bridge, the ships appear very lightly armed indeed upon first look. In reality, the Spruance's ASW capabilities are largely hidden. That ASROC launcher, for example, has a magazine beneath it holding 24 reloads. In that large hangar set to the port of the afterfunnel is room for two LAMPS III choppers, while triple Mk-32 torpedo tubes are hidden behind sliding doors. With the addition of four LM-2500 gas turbine engines, geared en echelon to provide nearly silent operations, and the powerful SQS-53 bow sonar arrays, which can operate in a variety of active and passive modes, the Spruance has more than proved itself."

"Where are those two headed?" quizzed Walker, whose hand went up to his brow to help cut the glare of the noon sun.

"Where else but American Samoa," replied Burnhardt. "Though it's more than a 2,600-mile voyage to the Southwestern Pacific Basin from here, I'm going to sleep a lot better knowing that we've got those guys on the way."

With a clear view of the wide patch of white-foam turbulence bubbling up from the destroyer's blunt sterns, the khaki-clad commander shook his head appreciatively. "I know what you mean, Admiral. I just wish that they were down there already."

Burnhardt's response was delivered firmly. "The *Phoenix* can take care of herself, Bob. That's the way she was designed to operate."

"So you think that they're still operational," Walker commented, a hint of doubt accenting his words.

There proved to be not a trace of vacillation in the admiral's tone. "Until I receive solid proof otherwise, I'm going to stick with that Trident all the way."

As the pair of destroyers continued on their southward courses, Richard Burnhardt took a seat on the wooden bench. With a practiced gaze, he scanned the harbor that lay to his right. Clearly visible were a variety of docked surface vessels. Dwarfing these warships was the huge steel-gray figure of a single aircraft carrier.

"Do your boys have the final word on that eruption yet, Bob?"

Walker pivoted to seat himself beside the admiral. "We've got a P-3 Orion due in at Auckland shortly. They were able to pick up a bagful of volcanic ash. A laboratory analysis of this substance will tell us exactly what's been spewn into the air above the Tonga Trench. The crew's visual scan showed a thick, mushroom-shaped column of venting material, estimated to already extend some fifteen miles into the earth's atmosphere. That would indicate that some 275 million tons of airborne ash has already been released.

"Incidentally, because of the thickness and height of this cloud, the chief scientist on board the aircraft compared it favorably to the Mount St. Helens eruption. If this is indeed true, that would make this eruption one of the most powerful blasts of modern times."

Focusing his attention on the line of tall antennas placed on the opposite hillside immediately above the spot where the carrier was docked, Burnhardt continued to probe. "Could this ash be responsible for the difficulties that we're encountering in establishing communications with the *Phoenix*?"

Walker stirred. "I'd bet my reputation on it, Admiral. Why, even the Orion experienced difficulties cut-

237

ting through that cloud. When they eventually did reach Pearl, the signal was extremely weak and diffused with static. It's believed that the superheated nature of the volcanic sulfur oxide and hydrogen sulfide gases produces an effect much like that of a nuclear explosion's electromagnetic pulse. Such a disturbance would be especially bothersome in the sending and receipt of radio signals occupying the low frequency ranges."

"Wonderful," Burnhardt responded disgustingly. "That's just the frequencies we use to communicate with our subs. Although I'm most aware of our attempts to harden our radio equipment against EMP, I don't believe I've ever read anything about seriously considering volcanic interference."

"The Office of Naval Research has tossed around this very problem," the commander said. "The issue first came to our attention in the spring of 1980. Immediately after the eruption of Mount St. Helens, commercial airline traffic experienced all sorts of radio interference in the routes directly downwind from the volcano. Unfortunately, the study of this ash's influence on low frequency transmissions only reached the theory stage."

"Well, how soon until that stuff clears out of the area?"

Walker hesitated before answering. "That will depend on a number of factors, such as the velocity and direction of the prevailing winds, and whether or not the eruption continues its present intensity. When the Orion lands, I'll be able to make a much more accurate projection, but for the moment, I'd say that the worse interference has only just begun."

Expecting just such an answer, Richard Burnhardt audibly sighed. "If this means that our land- and satellite-based transmitting stations will be unable to reach the *Phoenix* within the next four hours, we only have a couple of alternatives. First off, there's TACAMO. As Murphy's Law would have it, both C-130s especially assigned to cover the Tonga area are out of commission. One is down in Guam, the other in San Diego. Both are on the ground waiting for critical spare engine parts to be shipped in by the manufacturer. That leaves us with a single operational aircraft to cover the Pacific, based at Subic Bay in the Philippines. Initially delayed by the approach of that typhoon we've been watching form for the last couple of days, the plane is currently on its way into the South Pacific. Even at its maximum speed, I'm afraid it won't reach the range of its transmitter until well after the time arrives for the *Phoenix* to launch its Tridents.

"The only other communications device that has a chance of broadcasting through that muck is the Emergency Rocket Communications System. Launched into a suborbital trajectory by a Minuteman booster, the ERCS carries a UHF radio transmitter in its nosecone."

"I thought that the ERCS was specially designed to broadcast a preprogrammed, thirty-minute set of launch orders to the other Minuteman crews in the event that a Soviet decapitating strike took out SAC Command," the confused commander interjected.

Burnhardt was quick to reply, "It was, Bob. Fearing just such a snafu like we're currently experiencing, I gave Missouri's Whiteman Air Force Base a call about a quarter of a hour ago. Although it's going to take a couple of hours to make the necessary adjustments, a specially adapted, VLF radio transmitter is being prepared to be fit into one of the Minutemen. The nosecone's trajectory will then be targeted to penetrate the airspace directly above that damned Trench. Its preprogrammed message will order Blake to pack up and proceed homeward on the double."

Walker issued a breath of relief. "That sounds like it should do the trick, Admiral. You're going to get the Congressional Medal of Honor for that one."

"Hold on, lad, not so quickly. Those rocket boys still have to complete refitting that Minuteman. The way things look, it's going to go right down to the wire. Then, we just got to pray that the signal is strong enough to pop through that ash."

With this, Bob Walker checked his wristwatch. "What kind of man is the captain of the *Phoenix*, anyway? Would he initiate a launch even though he received only a single set of Cocked Pistol orders?"

Refocusing his angle of sight to include the line of supply vessels docked beside the carrier, Richard Burnhardt took some time before replying.

"One thing that you can be certain of, is that Captain Charles Blake is one hundred percent Navy. I got a chance to work directly with him during the Vietnam days. Do you remember that Sturgeon Class sub that we lost in the Pacific back in '71? Well, Blake was her XO."

"Was he the guy who swore during the Naval Board of Inquiry that the sub hadn't experienced a major structural failure of its hull like it was reported, but was instead rammed by a Russian cruiser?"

"That's the fellow," Burnhardt returned with a grin. "Though he never could accumulate enough substantive evidence to prove his case, Charles Blake was even starting to make a believer out of me. I was the one who shipped him back to New London not long afterward to begin training for his present assignment. I was afraid that if he kept raving on about that mishap aboard the *Orca*, that he'd completely throw away a most promising naval career.

"I'm certain that it was the intense training program

that helped him to forget that traumatic incident and get on with his life. As it turned out, Blake didn't disappoint me in the least.

"His first command position was aboard a Benjamin Franklin Class ballistic-missile-carrying submarine. Responsible for a load of sixteen Poseidon C-3s and a crew of 167, Charles proved to be the definitive skipper. He was well thought of by both seamen and officers, and posted a decade of superb service. As an award, he was granted his present assignment.

"Though we bump into each other infrequently nowadays, I feel that the man has changed little since we worked together back in the late 60's. He'll follow through on his launch orders, all right—just like he's been trained to do."

Their attention was suddenly drawn to the skies immediately behind them when the familiar chopping sound of a helicopter rose in the near distance. It didn't take them long to spot the quickly advancing, shiny white Sikorsky Seahawk. Sweeping through the blue skies only a few hundred feet above the two officers, the chopper angled sharply to the right as it began its descent to the deck of the docked carrier. As the commotion caused by this vehicle's two turboshaft engines faded, Commander Bob Walker of the Office of Naval Research spoke out crisply.

"Of course, there's always the possibility that my man on board the *Phoenix* will figure this whole thing out. Thomas Kraft is a highly intelligent, intuitive young man. He can also be quite persuasive when he wants to be. If he can make the association between the ash thrown into the air by that volcano and the *Phoenix's* inability to transmit or receive any outside communications, I'd say there's an outside chance that he'd be able to convince the captain of this fact."

Admiral Richard Burnhardt waited until the

Seahawk had safely completed its descent onto the carrier's deck before turning to meet the commander's hopeful gaze. "I wouldn't put any money on it, Bob. Even if the youngster figured this whole mess out, his chances of swaying Blake are about a hundred to one. You don't know the man like I do. It's going to take one hell of a case to persuade him to ignore those war orders. This is one instance when a skipper is allowed to act solely on his own initiative. Like I said before, Charles Blake is one hundred percent Navy. If he feels that there's even the barest of chances that the United States is in the midst of a nuclear strike, he'll hit the Soviets with every single warhead that he can muster."

This statement was punctuated by the deafening crack of a jet airplane as it broke the sound barrier. Angling their eyes skyward, it proved to be the Admiral who first caught sight of the thin, milky contrail that the lone Grumman F-14 Tomcat was leaving behind.

"Well, I think it's time for me to get back to my desk, Bob. I'd better be checking both Whiteman's progress with that ERCS, and that of our TACAMO. I'd appreciate any info that you derive from your Orion flight as soon as it's available. I've got a feeling that I'm going to be hearing from our commander in chief before this day is over with. At least I can do is give him his money's worth."

Returning Walker's salute, Richard Burnhardt stiffly stood and turned to make his way down the narrow gravel walkway leading back to his office. Still seated on the bench, his younger subordinate contemplated the intense conversation just completed.

The situation that he had been briefed on earlier was even more dangerous than he had been led to believe. In less than four hour's time, an American Trident submarine could very well put into motion a series of tragic events from which the world would never re-

cover. And to think that at the center of this predicament was a geological phenomenon that had been an
integral part of the earth's history from its very beginning. Would the volcano also be responsible for the
planet's end?

Shivering with this thought, Walker looked out to
the glass-smooth waters of Mamala Bay. Beyond, the
two Spruance destroyers were now tiny dots on the
southern horizon. The commander found himself pon-
dering that, in a way, he was indirectly responsible for
their current, hasty sailing orders. For that matter,
responsibility for this whole dilemma could be placed
upon his shoulders.

When Thomas Kraft had first called his office to
warn him of the unusual seismic activity taking place
in the Tonga region, he could have stopped this whole
thing in its tracks. A single call to the Pentagon's
National Command Center would have put him on the
record as warning that a volcanic eruption, with all its
possibilities for interrupting strategic communications,
was almost certainly imminent in this region. Not only
would all naval vessels have been directed far away
from the Tonga area, but a vastly different manner of
transportation for Thomas Kraft would have been
arranged.

There was no way that he should have allowed the
navy to use one of its Tridents to taxi the young
scientist down into the waters surrounding the Vavau
Seamount. Even if Delta Base was directly threatened,
a much safer means of transfer should have been
found. Yet, who could have ever foreseen the nightmarish series of events that would eventually occur?

Walker could only pray that Admiral Burnhardt's
observations weren't accurate ones. If Kraft indeed
figured out the real reason for the *Phoenix*'s communications blackout, somehow he'd find a way to convince

the captain of this fact. Faced with the possibility that the *Phoenix*'s load of Tridents could be launched in error, surely Charles Blake would listen to Thomas. No man alive would do otherwise, of this Bob Walker was certain.

2,470 miles to the south of Hawaii's Oahu Island, the USS *Phoenix* cautiously continued with its S.I.O.P, veiled by the deep, quiet waters of the Tonga Trench. Finding himself with barely three and a half hours until he would have to issue the orders sending their Tridents skyward, the sub's captain sequestered himself behind the locked door of his stateroom. Charles Blake knew that the next couple of hours would be his last opportunity to rest for an indefinite period. Not sure what would occur after the launch, he knew it would be best to have a clear head and rested body to face it.

Confident that the boat's XO could handle all contingencies until he returned to the command center, Blake seated himself behind his desk. With his stare locked firmly on the photo of his family, the captain's thoughts drifted far away from those of his immediate duty. Once more, he became conscious of the blank piece of stationery that still lay before him.

Hadn't he promised himself earlier that he would complete this letter to Susan at the very next opportunity? Yet that seemed to be an entire lifetime ago! Since that time, he had found himself suddenly faced with an entire new load of responsibilities. No longer was he accountable for merely keeping the peace at home. Right now, it was their very lives that were at stake.

Mesmerized by the innocent smiles of his children, Charles faced the question that had been haunting him for the past hour and a half. What were the chances that his family was even still alive? If the Russians had indeed struck first, Seattle and its environs would have been one of the first areas to be hit. With practically no advanced warning, the Soviet Delta Class submarine that perpetually patrolled off America's western shores would have launched its load of SS-N-18 missiles. Targeted at both the naval bases and military-industrial complexes that made this area their home, the warheads would have dropped in a matter of minutes. And since their home was located well within the boundaries of the sub base at Bangor, it would have been among the first to go. In a way, Blake found some solace in this macabre reflection.

Although the gift of life was the most precious of God's gifts, who would want to be one of the survivors of a full-scale nuclear holocaust? Such a world would be vastly different than the one mankind had forsaken. Plagued by disease, lawlessness, food shortages, and the ever-present threat of radiation poisoning, human civilization will regress to a state similar only to that of the Neanderthal era. It was certainly no place that he would want his children to grow up in. Thus, he felt almost fortunate that his family was spared this time of deprivation, pain, and longing for a world that could never be returned.

Because of the very nature of his present means of transportation, Blake knew that the odds were about even that he'd be one of the survivors. The unusual quiet that possessed the planet's radio waves made it most obvious that the first warheads had already taken out the superpowers' relatively fragile communications abilities. Blake visualized similar total damage to the world's military bases and command posts. His stomach soured as he wondered how many of the great population centers had already been hit. Had New York, Los Angeles, Moscow, or London shared the fates of San Diego, Omaha, Seattle, Vladivostok, and Kaliningrad?

Certainly, the *Phoenix*'s own missiles would herald the struggle's bloody climax. Targeted primarily on Siberia's air-defense centers, the warheads would free the way for the ponderous B-52 bombers that were currently passing their fail-safe coordinates. Guided by the accurate hand of man, the arrival of the massive, swept-wing jets would provide the ultimate clean-up bombardment. Hard targets that had somehow escaped destruction by the ICBMs would soon be nothing but deep radioactive craters.

It would be in the wake of such an attack that the *Phoenix* would eventually be forced to surface. With their original port long gone, and emergency bases such as that which graced the insides of the Vavau Seamount along with them, the men would be totally on their own. Afloat on a scarred planet that afforded more questions than answers, the true odyssey of the *Phoenix* would only be just beginning.

Drained by such a grim projection, Charles Blake issued a wide yawn. The time for halting this madness had slipped from their hands. Since each one of them was responsible, there was no use in finding blame. He could only follow out his duty and pray that America somehow prevailed.

With his weary gaze struggling to keep its focus on the photo of his family, Charles found his thoughts spinning incoherently. It proved to be the hypnotic hum of the sub's engines that carried him off totally. Slumped in his chair, with his head pointed downward, Blake surrendered to a sudden, deep sleep.

His dreams didn't take long to form themselves. In a single heartbeat, he found himself transferred to a time over a decade ago. With frightening reality, he identified his surroundings as belonging to a boat that no longer existed.

The bridge of the attack sub *Orca* was packed with both equipment and all-too-familiar faces as Blake positioned himself beside the vessel's periscope. Bathed under the protection of their red night lights, the crew seemed to take on a ghostly appearance as the dignified, gray-haired officer who stood beside Charles notified him of their unusual mission.

The sub rose to the surface of the South China Sea, and directed by a pulsating homing beacon, picked up a solitary, black, wet-suited individual. Only when the *Orca* returned to the shelter of the depths was Blake introduced to this dark-eyed diver. He was a civilian, working for the Central Intelligence Agency. His mission had sent him deep into Viet Cong territory, at the delta of the Mekong River. Because his only escape route was out to sea, the *Orca* had been sent to pick him up.

Charles continued to look on silently as the CIA man began issuing a rapid series of requests to the captain. As the boat's executive officer, Blake was not used to seeing anyone speak to their captain so brusquely. This was especially true of a civilian.

With convincing tones, the agent begged the captain to allow the *Orca* to again surface. Only in that way could he deploy the special antenna linking him to his cohorts in Saigon. His top-secret assignment had led to the discovery of a previously unknown enemy build-up in the Delta. This signaled that a Viet Cong offensive would almost certainly take place soon.

Charles looked on neutrally as the skipper argued that it would be much safer for them to head for more southerly waters before again surfacing. Stressing that there was no time for this, the civilian warned that the

lives of thousands of American G.I.s were being needlessly threatened by the captain's hesitance.

Though he was most aware that he should be
speaking out in support of his captain, Blake watched
as the gray-haired commander hesitantly walked over
to the sonar console. With words of warning locked in
his throat, Blake heard the sensor operator indicate to
the captain that their hydrophones picked up no other
ships in the immediate vicinity.

Again the civilian argued that time was of the
essence. All he would need was a few minutes to deploy
the antenna and convey knowledge of the enemy build-
up back to command.

Struggling now, to warn the captain not to change
his mind, Charles found his voice nonexistent. He
could hardly believe his ears as the order to blow
negative and prepare to surface sounded out reluctantly.

The next part of the nightmare seemed to take place
at an even more ponderous pace. As if his feet were
cast of lead, Blake remembered plodding over to the
periscope. Placing his eyes against the glass range-
finder, he slowly swept the surface of the seas above,
halting only upon spotting the jungle-filled expanse of
tiny Con Son Island lying directly to their stern.

He knew what demon haunted this island! Why
couldn't he shout out the proper warning?

Heedless to his plight, the *Orca* surfaced. Another
heartbeat followed as Charles was transferred to the
sub's conning tower. With day-glow binoculars in
hand, he again studied the jungled hell lying to their
rear. Most aware of the dangers that waited them
there, he vainly attempted to spur on the deck crew,
who were deploying the antenna with laborious,
drawn-out movements.

It was at that moment that the cursed sound began.

Amplified over the *Orca*'s intercom, the characteristic grinding of powerful, turbine-powered, twin shafts pierced their hydrophone. This was followed by the terrified cries of the sensor operator. "Surface screws! One hundred and eighty degrees and closing!"

As if his waist were set in concrete, he fought to pivot and set his eyes on this threat. When he eventually did so, Blake took in a sight that sent his heart pounding. Streaking around the shelter of the island was a six-hundred-foot, eight-thousand-ton cruiser! The staccato chugging of its geared turbines rose to an almost ear-splitting level as he watched the sub's deck crew scramble to clear the deck. As the diving claxon called them below, the startled XO viewed a sight that chilled his blood. The CIA agent was actually trying to keep the men from halting their deployment of his antenna! Still unable to voice his frustration, Blake turned just in time to see the knifelike hull of the cruiser slice into the *Orca*'s stern.

The dream took on an additional degree of realism when it transferred him next into the warm, oily waters of the South China Sea. Fighting to keep his head above the surface, he remembered setting eyes on the cruiser's rounded stern. Lit there by the light of a crimson full moon were two objects that would haunt his nightmares for all eternity: Standing next to the stern railing was a single, white-suited individual. Charles swore that he could actually make out a thick mop of red, curly hair and a pair of dark, beady eyes emanating from this person's head. And beside this figure, who seemed to be mocking him, flapped a large red flag, complete with the hammer and sickle of the Union of Soviet Socialist Republics.

As the cruiser disappeared to the north, the chugging sounds of its turbines faded also. Cast adrift in the silent waters, Charles recreated the moment he had spotted the *Orca*'s other two survivors. Steadied by a piece of flotsam, he gathered together the remaining crew, one of which would turn out to be a physical vegetable and the other a catatonic schizophrenic.

Fortunately, he didn't have to live out the next portion of the dream in its entirety. This conveyed him to a Naval Board of Inquiry. Frustrated and angry, he was in the process of hearing the admiral in charge reading the Board's findings. It was just as this stiff personage was speaking the words, "probably hull stress failure," that Charles Blake was abruptly called back to waking consciousness.

Clouded at first, his mind registered a thunderous explosion nearby. This reverberating boom was followed by the sound of straining steel as the *Phoenix* was lifted up and thrown on its keel. Pitched accordingly, Blake was violently thrown from his chair. With hands and feet sprawling, he plowed headfirst into the forward bulkhead with a painful jar. This blow was of sufficient strength to knock him temporarily unconscious.

Twenty seconds later, the captain awoke. Weakened by the excruciating ache that throbbed from his forehead, he vainly attempted to gain control of his limbs. This attempt was spurred on by the raucous blare of the alarm siren sounding General Quarters. Realizing that his long legs had somehow managed to get tangled under the supports of the desk, Charles carefully rolled over on his back to free his lower torso from this obstacle. Upon doing so, he slowly sat up. This movement was met by a wave of nauseating dizziness. Swaying backward, he found himself completely disoriented.

My God, the *Orca* has just been rammed by a Soviet

cruiser! This was no case of mere hull failure. He had to warn the others!

Fighting to stand, he found himself on his hands and knees. On the floor directly before him was the photograph of his family. Though its glass frame was shattered, Susan could be clearly seen, her calming stare locked firmly onto his own frantic eyes. This was all Charles needed to snap him from his state of confused shock. With one hand on his bruised forehead, and the other one gripped firmly onto the edge of the wall-mounted desk, he gradually made his way upright.

The ringing of the room's intercom quickly redirected his attention. On shaky legs, he crossed the debris-cluttered compartment and picked up the red plastic handset.

"This is the captain," he muttered groggily.

"Charles, it's Pete. Are you okay?"

"I'm fine," Blake answered a bit more strongly. "What in the hell was that blast all about?"

"They must have hit Delta Base again," returned the XO. "That NUDET was significantly stronger than the first one. That shock wave really walloped us."

Suddenly conscious of several elements of the disturbing dream he had just experienced, Charles questioned. "How's the *Phoenix*?"

"She's fine, except for the forward torpedo room. Two of those damn O-rings have apparently failed again. Crowley is on his way to size up the damages."

"Since that compartment is directly underneath my own, I'm going down there to take a good look at one of those infernal seals myself. Can you manage things upstairs, Pete?"

"Can do, Skipper. Just take care and give us a call if you need a hand."

Disconnecting the intercom, Blake took a deep breath. Taking another look at the jumble of debris that covered the floor, he set eyes on the cracked photograph of his family. Once more it was Susan's glance that triggered the deep recesses of his mind.

Vietnam, their picking up of the CIA diver, the sinking of the *Orca*—though re-experienced in dream, these events had actually happened. Yet one element of the nightmare continued to haunt him. Was his viewing of the Soviet cruiser a figment of his shock-torn mind, as the Navy doctors hinted, or did this phantom vessel indeed exist? Knowing this was a question that would most likely stay unanswered until his dying day, Charles Blake turned to make his way out of his stateroom.

The *Phoenix*'s forward torpedo room was situated on the left side of the hull, positioned directly behind the reinforced fiberglass dome housing the BQQ-6 sonar system. This compartment featured four tubes, each slightly angled outward at five degrees, each was capable of firing the Mk-48 advanced-capability torpedo, the Harpoon missile, and the Mk-70 MOSS decoy.

By the time Charles Blake finally made it to this room, the boat's senior weapons chief was already at the scene. The potbellied Missourian had the stem of his all-too-familiar unlit corncob pipe gripped firmly in his teeth as he used his solid shoulders to pry the torpedo room's door open. This gave the two corpsmen just enough room to squeeze their way out of the compartment. Between them they carried an unconscious and totally soaked young sailor.

Charles Blake arrived in time to watch the medics load this youngster onto a stretcher. Before he could question them to determine the sailor's condition, he noticed the steady stream of water gushing out into the hallway from the torpedo room's hatchway. Sensing that Crowley was about to seal this doorway from the other side, the captain rushed over to the forward bulkhead just as the hatch was about to shut tight.

Shouting out over the sound of rushing water, Blake screamed, "Crowley, it's the captain, let me through!"

There was a slight moment's hesitation, then the hatchway began reopening, ever so slightly. Not needing it to open fully, Charles squeezed his big frame inside. Once this was accomplished, he quickly turned to help the senior petty officer seal the door completely.

They found themselves in a room covered by nearly four inches of icy water. The sound of dripping liquid allowed the two to quickly pinpoint the exact spot where this leakage was emanating from.

The torpedo compartment was dominated by four large steel racks. Running the length of the room, these tubular frames were designed to transfer the desired weapon into its launching tube. These armaments were conveyed with the help of thousands of mounted ball bearings. It was from the two circular tubes, fed by the empty racks on the right side of the room, that the water was emerging.

Following the chief's lead, Blake used these frames to steady himself as he began his way toward the forward bulkhead. Ever conscious of the treacherous footing below, he found himself taking small, shuffling steps. Halfway down the rack's length, Crowley's voice boomed out distinctly.

"The port tube was the one that popped earlier. To seal it properly, I was forced to permanently shut its outer induction plate. You just should have seen that inner O-ring when I stripped it off. That damned sucker was as rotten as a September peach!"

"When was it replaced last?" the captain queried as he continued his slow progress forward.

"I changed all four of 'em personally, less than three weeks ago. I know what we're going to find when we strip off those others. Some money-hungry manufacturer sure put one over on us this time."

With this observation, the chief reached the portion of the room directly below the leaking tubes. Seconds later, he was joined by the captain.

"Jesus, Lou, I didn't know it was this serious," commented Blake, whose pants were soaked well above his ankle.

"Neither did I, Skipper," Crowley admitted as he prepared to reach up to turn the hand-sized steel wheel placed under the tube farthest to the right. "I didn't beat you down here by much. Fortunately, the first thing I spotted was that kid, laying on his back unconscious beneath this rack. Must have slipped and hit his head. Whatever, if I was a minute later, that boy would have drowned."

Standing on his toes, the chief was just able to put one of his hands on each edge of the induction shut-off. Grunting, he strained to turn the valve clockwise. When it failed to move after several tries, Blake squeeze in beside him.

"Let me take a side, chief."

Gesturing the captain to be his guest, Crowley moved his grip over to concentrate pulling up on the left portion of the rim, while Blake got ready to yank the right side downward.

"We'll move her on the count of three," directed Charles, whose expression tightened with determination. "One . . . two . . . *three!*"

The combined strength of both men strained to budge the stubborn valve. When it appeared that their effort wouldn't be a successful one, Blake interceded.

"Hold it, Chief. Let's take a second before giving her one more try."

Releasing their grips, they readied themselves for another attempt. While drying his hands on the tail of his shirt, the captain notice that the volume of water spraying out from the closed tube above them was gradually increasing. Sensing that the water level was already up to his mid-calf, he spoke out firmly.

"We've got to do it this time, Lou. Are you ready?"

Accepting the chief's nod, Charles reached up to grasp the circular valve's right portion. As Crowley gripped the left side, the captain called out.

"One . . . two . . . *three!*"

To a chorus of strained grunts, the two red-faced men gave it all they had. With soaked muscles straining, both continued applying pressure, until, unexpectedly, the wheel turned free. Quickly taking up the resulting slack, the chief was now able to turn the valve all by himself. Ten seconds later, the current of water that had been issuing down from the tube above abruptly ceased. That left only the tube immediately beside it still leaking.

"One down, one to go," the chief observed triumphantly. "I hate to have to seal up those tubes permanently like we're doing, but it doesn't appear that the spare O-rings we're carrying will do us any better."

Blake followed him over to the neighboring valve. "I understand, Lou. We've just got to do what we can to keep the *Phoenix* afloat. At least we still have one tube in operation."

"I don't know about that," Crowley commented. "The way those O-rings are failing, I'd say all we got is one good shot left in her. We can't even think about launching one of the Harpoons or a MOSS. The concussion would blow right through that seal and we'd have water in here up to our necks. She just might hold up to a single Mk-48, though."

With these cautionary words in mind, Charles prepared himself to have a go at the remaining valve. When a try on his own failed to move it, the chief was quickly at his side. This time, four combined shoves proved to be ineffective.

"This one's going nowhere fast," warned Crowley. "We're going to need a wrench."

"Do you still keep one above the hatchway?"

"It should be there, Skipper, unless some hotshot back in Bangor needed one for his own garage."

Scoffing at this last remark, Blake took off for the tool. With his hands on each one of the rails, he cautiously began his way toward the door that he had entered through earlier. Yet this time his progress was even slower, held back by the icy water that was about up to his knees.

By the time he finally got to the bulkhead, his pants were thoroughly soaked. It didn't take him long to locate the twelve-inch steel wrench that sat on an elevated ledge, beside an emergency flashlight. With this object in hand, he pivoted to return to the last of the leaking tubes. As he did so, his right foot slipped out from beneath him, and Blake went splashing down, rear first, into the awaiting water.

The first sensation that the captain was aware of was an icy, numbing chill. Because the seawater had already desensitized his lower torso, the moment his upper body and head dipped beneath the surface, the alien cold knocked the wind from him. Floundering uncontrollably, he found himself unable to regain his footing. Submerged in the oily, frigid waters, a single thought rose in his shock-torn mind. He was in the sinking *Orca* once more—this time, though, he would not survive.

It was while he was preparing to accept the inevitable darkness that surrounded him that his consciousness registered a strange pressure gripping his body from behind. This was followed by a brilliant shaft of light as he found himself yanked upward. A sharp slap between his shoulder blades cleared the water from his throat and lungs. Gagging, he spat this liquid out, replacing it with sweet, pure air.

"Jesus, Skipper, are you all right?"

Slowly, the face of the individual responsible for this concerned query came into focus. "I think so, chief. What in the hell happened?"

Gingerly, Crowley leaned his commanding officer up against one of the rails. "You were on your way back with the wrench when you took a little unscheduled dive. I'd better get that damned tube sealed, and get you out of here and into some dry clothes, before you succumb to hypothermia. Can you hold on for a couple of more minutes?"

"I'll be fine, Lou. Just stop that leak before we lose this whole compartment."

Blake looked on as the chief bent over and plunged his arms deep into the water at the captain's side. His brief search proved fruitful as he stood upright with the steel wrench held firmly in his right hand. Without hesitation, the potbellied petty officer took off for the bow bulkhead.

Charles watched Crowley's progress, ever alert to the pounding, incessant pain that radiated from his own forehead. As the chief positioned himself under the valve and began tightening the wrench onto its circular control stem, Blake's mind began clearing. Like a summer's mist lifting off a country pond, his thoughts sharpened. While watching Crowley channel the strength of his thick arms and shoulders in an effort to stem the leak that was threatening them, Charles realized how very close he had come to losing his life. Suddenly conscious of the time, and of a responsibility that could possibly turn the tide of history, he gratefully sighed when the chief's exertions proved effective, as the sound of dripping water disappeared completely.

Wasting no time in celebration, Crowley went over to the intercom and punched in two numbers. "Mr. Walsh, it's the chief. The forward torpedo room is secured. We're going to need a clean-up detail down here on the double. Some blankets would be appreciated also."

While absorbing the XO's response, the chief's hand went instinctively to his top shirt pocket. Fumbling to unbutton its flap, he removed his faithful corncob pipe and placed its stem firmly between his lips. Watching him biting on it like a pacifier, Blake felt oddly relieved. Faced with this new lease on life, he was certain now that fate had bigger things in store for him yet.

One floor above the flooded torpedo room, Thomas Kraft sat at the wall-mounted desk of the stateroom he was sharing with the *Phoenix*'s exec. Completely oblivious to Charles Blake's plight, the geophysicist found himself skimming the library book with even greater determination than before. That blast and shock wave they had just experienced certainly verified his theory. That was no nuclear detonation. Emanating from the exact same location from which the previous explosion had originated, it had to have been caused by a volcanic eruption. To verify his suspicions, and to help him prove their legitimacy, he planned to present portions of the book he was studying to the sub's officers.

To clearly demonstrate a volcano's awesome might, he decided to emphasize the chapter he was currently reading.

This section was entitled, "The Eruption of the

leeping Giant—Krakatoa." It concerned the explosion f one of the most powerful volcanoes that modern man ad ever observed. In the Sundra Straits between Java nd Sumatra, Krakatoa had been an active geological ormation for many centuries. Native tales told of lumes of thick smoke and fiery lava capping the nountain's summit for dozens of generations. Yet on he morning of August 22, 1883, only one-third of the 2,000-foot peak would still be remaining above sea evel. It was at this time that a thunderous volcanic xplosion virtually ripped the mountain apart. So ncredibly loud was the initial burst that it actually ould be heard some three thousand miles away. Tons f fine, white ash fell in such varied locations as ingapore, some six hundred miles to the north, the Cocos Islands, over seven hundred and sixty miles to he southwest, and was even reported covering the lecks of ships over seven thousand miles to the west-orthwest.

Darkness covered the Sundra Straits for two solid lays as giant sea waves surged outward, devastating verything in their path. As a result, over 36,000 eople died and 165 villages were completely de-troyed.

Thomas Kraft found the paragraphs dedicated to Krakatoa's worldwide effects most interesting. Particu-arly fascinating was the fact that every recording barograph in the world had documented the passage of his explosion's airwave, some as many as seven times, s the wave bounced back and forth around the world or five days after the eruption. Each of the planet's idal gauges had been equally as effective in recording he passage of the resulting sea wave. This same wave eached the Arabian country of Aden in only twelve ours. This was quite an accomplishment, considering t took a steamship twelve days to complete this 3,800-

nautical-mile trip.

Equally as astounding were the blue and green sun observed worldwide on the days that followed. This optical phenomenon was created as Krakatoa's fine ash and superheated gases were launched twenty miles into the stratosphere, completely encircling the equator in thirteen days. Three months after the eruption, this veil spread to the higher latitudes. So intense were the resulting sunsets that in the city of Poughkeepsie, New York, fire engines were called out to quench an apparent blaze, so realistically etched upon the western horizon.

The volcanic dust also acted as a solar filter. Global temperatures dropped as much as one-half a degree centigrade. It took over five years for the world's thermometers to return to normal.

But it proved to be the paragraph that followed which caused the hairs upon the back of Thomas Kraft's neck to stand up and take notice. In an addendum to their formal report on the eruption, the Royal Meteorological Society postulated a relationship between the eruption of Krakatoa and difficulties being experienced in a series of experiments they were currently sponsoring. Complaining that a mysterious blanket of static was interfering with his previously undisturbed tests in the new science of wireless telegraphy was the brilliant physicist Heinrich Hertz. This static had begun haunting his research in the infant science of radio in late August of 1883. It would continue for over a year, until it just as mysteriously dissipated, at about the same time that the sunsets returned to normal. It was the society's esteemed presumption that this static was directly attributable to the high degree of magnetic iron ash launched into the atmosphere by none other than Krakatoa!

With knowledge of this unbelievable incident in his

head, Thomas Kraft put the book down and pushed back his chair. No wonder the USS *Phoenix* was unable to send or receive any type of wireless communications! Veiled by a cloak of magnetic ash and super-heated gases over one hundred thousand feet thick, not even the lowest of radio frequencies would be allowed entry. Just to think that such a natural phenomenon could be responsible for the outbreak of World War III sent shivers down the young geophysicist's spine. He had only one purpose now: to convey this possibility to those commanding the submarine. Surely they'd listen to him, giving him the chance to prove that this was indeed the case. Yet, how could he make this argument an airtight one, and just who could he approach?

For some strange reason, the captain was totally deaf to his suspicions that the blasts were volcanic in origin. Why, the man wouldn't even give Thomas a second of his time. Of a much more approachable nature was the executive officer, Pete Walsh. This likable individual, whose quarters he was currently sitting in, seemed to be much more open-minded. As second in command, his support would be invaluable.

Kraft's training as a scientist made it most obvious that concrete physical proof was the best way to verify a theory. The book that sat before him would be most helpful in explaining the scope and past history of the subject. But to push the officers further, he would need actual, tangible evidence.

Not having any idea as to how he could possibly get his hands on such proof, Thomas reached forward and slammed shut the library book with a frustrated wave of anger. Staring him in the face was the full-color photo that made up the volume's cover. This shot was a most familiar one. It showed the smoking summit of Mount St. Helens only hours after its initial eruption in May of 1980.

Closing his tired eyes, Thomas visualized those exciting days. Even though the mountain had been responsible for the deaths of several colleagues, it had been able to teach him more about the science of volcanology than any of the hundreds of textbooks he had previously studied. This had been true for the rest of the scientific establishment also.

Not only had old theories been proven and new ones proposed, but an entire new division of field research had been developed practically overnight. This included not only laser-guided surveying techniques to monitor the bulge of the rising magma visible from the surface, but also remote-controlled sensors, such as the ones Commander Walker had ordered him to activate in the Tonga Trench. Able to relay to its operator the sound of the magma as it rushed up from the earth's mantle, it was hoped that such devices would warn scientists when a dangerous eruption was imminent.

Sophisticated, high-tech gear of this type hadn't existed in the time of Krakatoa. Thomas doubted if such equipment had even been dreamed of back then. Just think what the scientists of the Royal Academy could have done with the likes of the gear he presently carried in his duffelbag. They would have labeled such instruments as being miraculous!

Thomas suddenly sat forward, completely stunned by the thoughts his musings had just triggered. How blind he had been — the answer to this entire dilemma was within his reach!

Standing, he turned, and quickly made his way over to the metal locker set into the room's far wall. Inside the stuffed, green canvas duffelbag on the locker's floor were two instruments that would put into his hands just the solid proof that he needed.

If the *Phoenix*'s course and speed had remained constant, Thomas knew that the harmonic-tremor sensor monitors should be well within the range of the remote-control unit he carried. By activating this device, and recording the audible results the undersea hydrophones would transmit, he could relay to the captain concrete evidence of speedily moving magma, proving that a nearby volcano was indeed in the midst of a major eruption.

By deploying his bag's other mechanism, evidence of a completely different nature would be attained.

The air-scanner device was designed to capture a low-altitude air sample. Mounted on the end of a two-thousand-foot-long nylon tether, the scanner was sent skyward with the help of a self-inflating, rubberized balloon, which would deflate as soon as the sample was snared.

Since this experimental instrument had proved most effective during his recently completed research cruise in these same waters, Thomas didn't see any reason why it couldn't do the job today. By launching it through the *Phoenix*'s escape hatch, he could demonstrate that a nuclear detonation was positively not responsible for that series of explosions. A simple test would show whether or not radioactive residue was present; another test would break down the exact nature of the sample. If his suspicions were correct, he was certain just what they'd find: minute shards of jagged pumice, millions of microscopic pieces of whitish basaltic ash, high-density levels of sulfur oxide and smelly hydrogen sulfide—and all this would prove without a shadow of a doubt that the *Phoenix* shared these waters with an exploding volcano. With such a point made, it wouldn't take much more to convince the captain that this residue could just possibly be responsible for the sub's communications difficulties. With this doubt in his mind, the captain wouldn't dare go ahead with the launch of the Tridents until he was absolutely certain that such a desperate course of action was necessary.

Gripping the strap of his duffelbag firmly in both hands, Thomas carefully placed it on his bunk. Who would have ever thought, when he had hastily packed it back on Tutuila, that the fate of the entire world would lie within this green canvas bag's confines? Trembling with this thought, the young geophysicist took a series of calming deep breaths. More than anything now, he would need a calm, clear mind.

Chapter Thirteen

"Mr. Walsh, we've got some traffic upstairs!"

Canova's words broke the XO from his intense study of the damage control board. Confident that the chief had things well under control in the flooded torpedo room, he crossed the command center's floor to monitor this possible new threat. Taking up a position behind the bald-headed sonar man, the exec questioned him matter-of-factly.

"What have you got, Lieutenant?"

The portly New Yorker pressed his headphones tightly over his ears. "Sounds like a single, unidentified surface ship, sir. It's about fifty-five nautical miles to the west-northwest, and headed our way. I'm presently feeding the sound signature into Big Brother for an I.D., but I think she's still too far out for a positive."

The XO's brow tightened. "That would put it smack in the North Fiji Basin. I didn't think that we had any warships in the vicinity of Melanesia, but the way things are going topside, who knows what's going on up there?"

The arrival of Kraft in the command center broke the XO's contemplations. "Call out when you've got anything, Canova," the exec directed the sonar man. "I'll be close by."

Walsh beckoned the serious-faced geophysicist to join him at the deserted navigation table. Set in the room's rear corner, this console was dominated by a flat, lucite screen. Projected beneath this covering was an intricate three-dimensional map of the Tonga Trench.

"What can I do for you, Lieutenant?" quizzed Walsh.

Thomas Kraft opened the book he had been carrying to a pre-marked page, and set it down on the table before the XO. Pete glanced at the black-and-white photo showing the smoke-filled summit of an erupting volcanic mountain.

"If you'll just give me a couple of minutes of your time, I think I can prove to you that those blasts we've been experiencing aren't nuclear detonations. I can also provide concrete evidence linking the real source of those blasts to the *Phoenix*s present difficulties in establishing communications with the outside world."

With this, Pete let out a skeptical sigh. "You're not going to give up, are you, Mister? All right, shoot, but make it snappy. Not only are we currently having technical problems on board, but we've also got a surface bogey headed our way."

Relieved at this chance to present his case, Thomas spoke out rapidly. "In August of 1883, the world witnessed one of the most violent volcanic eruptions of modern times. This photo shows what was left of the mountain called Krakatoa a week after the initial blast blew away two-thirds of its mass. What is important for you to be aware of about this particular eruption in the straits between Java and Sumatra, is the effect it had worldwide. For years afterward, the millions of tons of ash sent soaring into the stratosphere by Krakatoa not only tinged the planet's sunsets in shades of fiery reds, but also lowered its average temperatures.

266

"This airborne debris was reported to be comprised [o]f unusually high amounts of magnetic iron. As a [di]rect result, scientists in Europe reported a quite [u]nexpected by-product. The respected physicist [H]einrich Hertz reported that mysterious waves of thick [a]tmospheric static interrupted his experiments, in the [n]ew science of radio, during the late summer of 1883.

"Do you understand what this could mean to the *[P]hoenix*, Mr. Walsh? I'm certain that you're well aware [o]f the phenomenon labeled electromagnetic pulse. [C]reated when a nuclear weapon is detonated at high [al]titudes, EMP is formed when intense energy released [b]y the explosion interacts in the upper atmosphere. [D]eflected downward, this energy would bathe the [e]ntire world in a massive electrical storm, playing [p]articular havoc with the planet's communications [n]etworks.

"In our instance, a nuclear warhead is definitely not [re]sponsible for this deflected interference. As Hertz [w]as later to learn, a thick blanket of ionized volcanic [a]sh can be the culprit. This is the reason our radio [w]aves are so mysteriously empty."

Taking his eyes off the photograph, the XO linked [h]is gaze to that of Thomas Kraft. "All this is most [in]teresting, Lieutenant. But I still don't understand [w]hy you're so certain that we've got a hot volcano [n]earby."

Thomas pushed the book aside and pointed to the [to]pographical map clearly visible beneath the lucite [sc]reen. With his right index finger, he encircled the [n]orthernmost section of the undersea mountain range [th]at snaked down the chart's center.

"Have you forgotten already the reason that I was [ca]lled out here? Hitching a ride on your submarine [w]asn't my idea, Mr. Walsh. I assume that the com-[m]ander I answer to back in Pearl Harbor put us together.

"This particular patch of seafloor is extremely activ
seismically. Such activity can only mean that, beneatl
these waters, various crustal plates are rubbing u
against each other. Such movement provides the per
fect conditions for a volcanic eruption. And once m
seismographs recorded what would prove to be the firs
of dozens of unusually strong earthquakes here, w
could be certain that these shifting plates were th
cause. To find out if they were accompanied by movin
magma, though, I was ordered to trigger the burie
sensors that would indicate if this was indeed the case

The XO shifted his weight impatiently. "I still don'
see, short of surfacing, how you're going to convinc
the skipper that we've got a volcano out there *and* tha
it's responsible for our communications problems."

Thomas Kraft prepared to set the hook. "This i
where I'm going to need some help. First off, I've t
activate my remote-control unit. This will trigger th
sensors buried in the seafloor directly beneath us. B
interfacing their audio signal with the *Phoenix*'s com
puter, we will know if harmonic earth tremors ar
present. If we are successful in picking them up, there'
a ninety-nine-percent probability that an active vol
cano is close-by.

"Secondly, in order to obtain certain proof that th
resulting ash is responsible for our radio blackout, I'
like to launch a specially designed air-scanner devic
that I'm also carrying. Does the *Phoenix* have a reusabl
escape hatch?"

The XO carefully answered, "There's a hatch in th
forward compartment designed to accommodate sev
eral different sizes of weather and communication
buoys."

"Excellent," Thomas said. "I'll only need enoug
space for the scanner itself — which is about the size of

standard weather vane—a self-inflating balloon, and several hundred feet of coiled nylon cord. In less than five minutes' time, I can provide an accurate sample of just what the air is comprised of above us. A simple test will show if there's any radioactivity there. If so, I'll rest my case. Upon finding it free of artificial radiant energy, another test will confirm both the presence and composition of any volcanic ash. Only if this sample indicates a significant density of such debris can we assume that we've located the cause of our communications difficulties.

"I'm not asking for much, Mr. Walsh—only some assistance in carrying out these two, basic experiments."

The XO was hesitant with his response. "You're asking more than you think, Lieutenant. Such authorization would have to come from the captain."

"But he would never agree to allow them!" Kraft shot back passionately. "He's already got his mind made up. That's why you've got to help me obtain this concrete evidence that will show him otherwise. Please, the fate of the entire world is most likely resting on your decision."

This last, emotional point seemed to hit home as Walsh considered the global implications of the S.I.O.P. they were currently being guided by. In approximately three more hours, their deadly load of Tridents would be on the way. Impossible to call back, such a launch would be the final commitment. Could he possibly rest until that time came, knowing that the orders scrubbing this attack had been issued, but that the *Phoenix* had been unable to pick them up? Although the sub was outfitted with a variety of redundant radio frequencies to convey such a cancellation, what if the whining scientist's pleas were based on fact?

While searching the geophysicist's face for any sign

of insincerity, Pete realized that if he side-stepped the captain in this matter, he'd be guilty of a serious breach of command. The XO wasn't one to go against the rules, but he couldn't help but be cognizant of the extraordinary circumstances that made this situation a unique one. Mentally calculating just what would be needed to complete these experiments, Walsh knew that he wouldn't have to provide much. Conveying a simple password would open the computer to Kraft's needs. An unauthorized use of the escape hatch could be a little more difficult to carry off, yet it was certainly well within the realm of possibility.

An unexpected look of concern in the scientist's glance diverted his attention, and Pete turned to see what had suddenly caught Kraft's eye. Just emerging from the hatchway at the command center's opposite side was the tall, solid figure of the man who had a good part to do with his current dilemma.

Walsh couldn't help but notice that although Blake's uniform seemed dry, his hair was soaking wet. Dominating his forehead was a nasty looking, swollen bruise. Beneath this discolored wound, the skipper's gaze seemed distant and preoccupied, focused on thoughts far away from his present duty.

Anthony Canova's strained voice redirected the attentions of all of those present. "I'm picking up a second set of surface screws, approaching us from the west-northwest. Range is fifty-three nautical miles and closing fast."

"What do you mean, second set of screws?" Blake asked sternly as he marched off to the sonar console.

Before the confused sonar operator was forced to answer the captain, Pete Walsh intercepted him. "I was just about to inform you of the first detection, Skipper. We picked it up several minutes ago, headed in from the North Fiji Basin. I'm afraid that we're going to have to wait for them to get closer before we can get an accurate I.D. on those sound signatures."

"Jesus, Pete," barked a disgusted Charles Blake. "You know that I like to get word on any possible bogeys as soon as they're picked up. These contacts could be *especially* significant because of our present alert status and all."

"I'm sorry, Skipper. Next time you'll be the first one to be informed. Say, that's a nasty gash on your forehead. Has the doc taken a look at that?"

"It's nothing," mumbled Blake, who turned to face the helmsman. "Peterson, take us out of this thermocline once again. A new depth of one hundred and forty feet should do it."

"Yes, sir," responded the diving officer, who instantly began pulling up on the steering yoke.

Meanwhile, the XO stuck close to the captain's side as Blake positioned himself behind the sonar screen.

"My gut tells me that we got troubles coming," offered Blake. "Canova, I want those sound signatures analyzed by the time they reach the forty-mile threshold."

Reacting with a hearty thumbs-up, the big sonar operator didn't look up from the green-tinted screen before him. As Blake's eyes focused in on this same object, the XO questioned, "What's the forward torpedo room look like, Captain?"

Not bothering to meet Pete's inquisitive gaze, Blake retorted, "The last glance that I got of the compartment, it appeared more like a wading pool. Crowley's almost certain that those O-rings failed because of a manufacturer's defect. That would have been one hell of a way for us to lose the *Phoenix*. We're fortunate, though, to have at least one tube still in operation. It won't fire a MOSS or a Harpoon, but one of our Mk-48s can most likely be utilized."

Now knowing part of the reason for Blake's rotten mood, the XO grimaced upon noticing that Thomas Kraft was approaching them. Pete's worst fears were verified when the bearded scientist anchored himself at the captain's other side.

"Captain Blake, if you'll just give me a minute, I'd like to show you something very important."

Opening the book he had been faithfully carrying to the photo showing the eruption of Krakatoa, Kraft bravely shoved it into the captain's hands.

"If you'll take a look at this, I think I can explain just what is going on in the waters outside the *Phoenix*'s hull, and how it is affecting the vessel's communications gear."

His thoughts far away from any such esoteric rambling, Blake took a quick, annoyed look at the picture before him, and found his face reddening with anger. What in the world was this high-brow trying to prove? Did he think that this was all some sort of game? They were at a state of war, not researching a college science paper!

Slamming the book shut, Charles handed it abruptly back to Thomas, all the while staring him maliciously in the eye. For some unknown reason, a vibrant vision captured the captain's thoughts. At the snap of a finger, he was transferred back to the bridge of the *Orca*. He found himself as the boat's executive officer once again, in the process of watching his captain in the midst of a fruitless argument with the CIA agent. Damn it all, an outsider had no business on a submarine's bridge! If the captain would have only stuck to his own beliefs, one hundred more men would have survived that fateful night.

Inflamed with this realization, Blake returned to the present with his temper fuming. "Listen, Mister, I thought that I ordered you once before to stay out of this command center. Take your high school book, and consider this area off limits! And while you're at it, get that damned beard trimmed, and cut that hair. You're supposed to be a naval officer, not a fucking beach bum!"

It didn't take any more abuse for Thomas Kraft to begin wisely backing off. Managing a shaky salute, the geophysicist pivoted and, with his head down, rushed off for the forward hatchway.

Watching this whole encounter was an impotent Pete Walsh. Even though he felt genuinely sorry for the young lieutenant, the XO dared not challenge the tempestuous captain.

"Okay, everybody, back to work!" ordered Blake loudly. "Canova, start running that signature I.D. Mister Walsh, I want you to get down to the torpedo room and to supervise the loading of a Mk-48. You'd better bring along your knee boots."

Snapping a salute, Pete turned to initiate this directive. As he proceeded toward the same doorway from which Thomas Kraft had just exited, he pondered the strange expression so clearly etched upon the captain's face, deciding it was most probably influenced by the swollen bruise that capped Blake's forehead. The man appeared totally out of character. Gone was his pleasant, easygoing smile; in its place, an angry, menacing scowl.

Sure, they were all under pressure, but was this any way to act? The man was their commanding officer and thus had to set an example. If they were indeed able to survive the next three hours, much calmer attitudes would be needed by all. A bunch of guys running around with uncontrollable tempers would only insure a certain disaster. Promising himself that he would keep a close eye on the skipper, Pete ducked through the hatchway that led toward the *Phoenix*'s bow.

It took the XO less than five minutes to make his way to his stateroom. Once inside the shut doorway, he found a single, despondent figure seated on the spare bunk.

With his eyes full of longing, Thomas Kraft looked up and greeted his host emotionally. "I told you that he wouldn't listen! That man is nothing but a stubborn, pig-headed old fool."

"Easy now," advised Walsh, his voice filled with a calming tone. "I admit that the captain is being a bit harsh with you. Lord knows the man is under enough pressure. Give him a chance to calm down, and then I'll see about having a talk with him."

"Some good that will do," interjected Thomas.

Quite mindful of Kraft's dismay, Pete shook his head powerlessly. Without further hesitation, he crossed the narrow room and opened his recessed metal locker. From inside this compartment, he pulled a pair of knee-length rubber boots. Grasping them firmly in his left hand, he shut the locker and turned to face his guest.

Thomas Kraft continued to sit on the mattress, his gloom-filled gaze cast downward. Walsh couldn't help but sympathize with the young man. More than anyone else aboard the *Phoenix*, the scientist had been through quite a lot these past few hours. The transfer to the sub from his isolated jungle research station was a traumatic experience all its own. Now, to be faced with the reality of World War III staring down at them only made his plight that much more difficult. The words that next flowed from the XO's lips were generated more by a spirit of patronization than an actual belief in the theories the lieutenant promoted.

"Say, Kraft, where's that equipment of yours?"

Without looking up, Thomas reached down and pulled out his duffelbag from beneath the shelter of his cot. Walsh watched this sluggish movement, and he attempted to stifle a smile.

"Say, lieutenant, I've just been ordered to personally check out the status of the forward torpedo room. By the strangest of coincidences, the compartment holding that escape hatch happens to be located right next door. Are you coming along, or have you decided to stay locked up here sulking until doomsday?"

Hardly believing what he was hearing, Thomas looked up discreetly. Captivated by the warm grin that met his eyes, he couldn't help but find himself smiling. He had found that much-needed ally after all! Not wasting a second, he carefully draped the straps of his duffelbag over his shoulder and beckoned the XO to lead the way.

Seated at the compact computer keyboard, Thomas Kraft felt like a pilgrim who had at long last returned home. Set up exactly like the one he had back in Tutuila, the console was a snap to operate. While he busily fed in a long stream of data, he couldn't help but overhear the XO's noisy puttering behind him.

The forward emergency compartment that he presently occupied was a cramped, narrow room. It held little else but the terminal Thomas was working on, and its main feature, the escape hatch, which was placed to his rear. Set into the starboard bulkhead, this bulky device was connected directly to the vessel's outer shell. Appearing like a large, steel bank vault, it utilized tons of concentrated air pressure to allow not only the launching of buoys, but also the transfer of the submariners themselves in times of emergency.

Walsh had briefly described such a procedure. Designed to accommodate a single, kneeling sailor at a time, the hatch would be sealed and pressurized. A submersible rescue vessel would then couple its own emergency hatch onto the *Phoenix's*. The pressures would be equalized, and the seamen free to climb the short distance to safety. Although the system had yet to be tried in times of actual crisis, the sub's complement gained a certain amount of added confidence just knowing that such a device existed. It was, however, the hatchway's other capability that Kraft had a more immediate interest in.

Pete Walsh had opened the outer vent doors and pressurized the inner chamber long before Thomas had finished with his work on the keyboard. Clearing his throat, the XO spoke out.

"Lieutenant, I'm just about ready to launch. Can you give me a hand?"

Without hesitating, Thomas swiveled off the chair and approached the kneeling exec. "You don't waste any time, do you?"

Walsh responded dryly. "Mister, that's one commodity that's extra precious around here. Where's your gear?"

Bending down, Kraft removed a coiled ball of thin, white nylon cord from his duffel bag. Attached to one end was a two-foot-long, tear-shaped, red plastic buoy. He carefully handed this equipment to Walsh, who tied the other end of the cord to a small, winchlike device set into the inner chamber's wall. He then laid the rest of the tether line flat on the unit's floor, gingerly placing the buoy on the very top.

"That should do it," commented the XO as he sealed shut the heavy metal door. "I'll need you to monitor the inside pressure. The dial is on the wall to your right. Call out when it hits one hundred percent."

Nodding in compliance, Thomas found the proper readout. With his eyes glued to the glass dial, Kraft took in a deep breath as the hissing of rushing compressed air sounded out beside him. It took barely a minute for the inner chamber to fill completely.

"One hundred percent!" exclaimed Thomas, whose words were followed by an even stronger wallop of gushing air.

Swearing that he could almost feel the deck shake beneath him, Kraft visualized the journey his buoy would be taking as it shot to the ocean's surface, protected by this bulletlike capsule of air. Needing only a few seconds to complete this voyage, the canister would then split open as the altimeter-triggered helium cartridge filled the balloon designed to carry the air-scanner skyward. Both men agreed that five minutes would be plenty of time to let the scanner reach its maximum height. Once this had been achieved, all they had to do was activate the mechanical winch and wait for their sample, which would be encased in a watertight capsule, to be drawn back to the safety of the escape hatch.

"How are you handling that computer?" queried Walsh, breaking Thomas from his reverie.

"So far, so good," returned Kraft, who was suddenly reaware of the work that still had to be done. "I'm just about finished with completing that audio interface with the harmonic sensors. Then I'll be able to trigger the remote-control unit and use the *Phoenix*'s computer to tell us exactly what's going on under the earth's crust here."

"Well, let's get moving," spurred the XO. "We'd better be keeping our visit here as brief as possible."

Taking this hint, Thomas returned to the keyboard. Emptying his mind of all outside distractions, his fingers efficiently completed the link between man and machine. When all of his desired data was entered, he reached down and removed a shoebox-sized, black plastic case from the interior of the duffelbag. From this object's topmost corner, he pulled out a three-foot-long telescoping antenna. Briefly catching the XO's glance, Kraft depressed the large red button set into this case's center. Several seconds of anxious silence followed, and then a steady stream of coded information began filling the computer's central monitor screen.

Chapter Fourteen

The bridge of the Soviet Kara Class cruiser *Azov* was a spacious, comfortable compartment, equipped with the latest in sophisticated hardware. Perched beneath the ship's dual fire-control radar cones, and set overlooking the pointed bow, it offered its occupants an unobstructed view of the seas before them. At present, these waters belonged to that portion of the South Pacific known as Melanesia. Stretching out in gentle, undulating swells, the placid ocean allowed the cruiser to proceed virtually unimpaired by natural obstacles. Most appreciative of this fact was the *Azov*'s captain, Josef Kostromo. The tall, red-headed commander was well aware of their good fortune. Several thousand miles to the west, the character of the waters was drastically different. The last report from his father had told of typhoon-tossed waves rising almost one hundred feet above sea level. Though Josef was no stranger to such storms, he could certainly live without them.

Conscious of the distant grind of the *Azov*'s dual gas turbines, Captain Kostromo paced the bridge's breadth. With his eyes ever alert to that portion of the ocean visible through the compartment's rectangular observation windows, he found his thoughts focused on their present mission.

Because of the initiation of Operation Lenin, the day had started off full of expectations. Josef had trouble accepting the fact that what had started as a mere exercise had evolved into an actual state of war. His father's most recent orders to him made this most apparent. What was so confusing, though, was the scope of this directive. Not only was he instructed to eliminate an American Trident vessel, but, strangely enough, also one of their own Alfa Class models.

When Josef first heard this, he couldn't help but question the sanity of such a move. Had his father gone completely crazy? The elder Kostromo's words of response were icily brief and most firm: An unprecedented situation had developed, totally out of the admiral's control. Originating right from the lips of General Secretary Kirensk himself, the orders to sink the two subs had apparently been issued in a last-minute attempt to save the world from a conflict of a much larger scale.

Yet wouldn't the flagrant attack of a Soviet cruiser on an American warship directly lead to just such a worldwide confrontation? And why, in the name of Lenin, was one of these targets to include one of their own boats?

"Do not bother yourself with such needless ponderings," his father had advised. "Just do as you are told. Believe me when I tell you that we have very little choice in this matter."

Accepting the last known coordinates of these subs, Josef had broken contact with the *Minsk* still totally perplexed. As a thirty-year veteran of the navy, the fifty-three-year-old officer had received some strange directives in his day, yet this beat them all. If they hadn't come directly from his father, he most likely would have called Vladivostok to have them confirmed.

Yet, in this instance, they appeared most legitimate, so what else could he do but obey them?

Josef had to admit that the first half of his target list was a most anticipated one. How many nights had he dreamt of actually stalking and attacking one of the American Trident submarines? One of the most advanced missile platforms of its kind, the Trident carried almost two hundred nuclear warheads. Able to be sent on their missions of death and destruction deep into the Motherland, such missiles and the vessels that carried them were the imperialists' most-feared weapons system. The cocky Yankees had thought these subs to be practically invulnerable. Josef couldn't wait to show them otherwise.

There was no way that he was about to focus the same degree of enthusiasm when it came time to hunt down the Alfa. Veiled by its anechoic hull and able to dive to depths far beyond the threshold of any other sub on this planet, such a target would be a most difficult one to locate and eliminate. Thus, it was very likely that this would be one part of their mission that would be impossible to carry out.

It hadn't taken Josef much thought to determine what the *Azov*'s first course of action would be. They would locate the Trident, and utilizing their varied load of depth rockets, torpedoes, and SS-N-14 missiles, blow it to the ocean's bottom. Only then would he seriously consider his next target.

With this plan firm in his mind, Josef had already begun the hunt for the Americans. Their initial search pattern would be limited to the sector known as the Tonga Trench. Since the Trident had last been spotted south of the island of Tutuila, he could only guess that they were still in the area. By drawing up a topological map of the region, Josef was able to pretty well guess the patrol route the American skipper would most likely frequent. This course would probably take the Trident down the spine of the trench's north-south meander, where the deep waters would provide an excellent spot to crawl along silently, at barely five knots, waiting for the orders that would send their Tridents skyward.

If the American captain had indeed chosen this likely course, Josef knew that his plan to trap them would have an excellent chance for success. He had set his snare by stationing the pair of Udaloy destroyers on each end of the trench. With the *Azov* headed smack toward the trench's midsection from the west, this would leave the surprised Americans with little choice when it came to finding a quick escape route.

The waters to the immediate east of Tonga spread out in a wide, flat basin, which had few geological features to hide a submarine in. Aided by the four Ka-25 helicopters that the Udaloys carried, and the *Azov*'s single Hormone chopper, the Trident would be unable to escape their sensors. Josef stirred expectantly as he pondered the type of weapon he'd use to send the Americans to their graves.

Even though he had never served in an actual war before, he had had the distinct pleasure of "unofficially" being responsible for the elimination of a solitary enemy attack sub. This had taken place over a decade ago, only months after Josef had first received command of the *Azov*.

It had been during the time of the imperialists' bloody occupation of South Viet Nam. Though Moscow had taken on the Viet Cong as their "silent" allies, little direct involvement by the Soviet military had been desired. That was why, when a Soviet Army advisory team had found itself trapped in the Mekong Delta, the *Azov* had been called in to discreetly pick them up. Josef had accomplished this without incident,

282

and had just been ordering the cruiser to pick up steam and head for the open seas to the north, when the chance of a lifetime had presented itself. Sitting motionless on the surface, immediately behind the small island that had served as the rendezvous point, was an American submarine! Could he help it if the Yankee vessel, lying there in international waters, had not even had running lights?

He would never forget the face of the helmsman as he had ordered the stocky Uzbekian to point the *Azov*'s bow squarely into the submarine's conning tower. After instructing the engineer to open the throttles of their geared turbines fully, Josef had positioned himself outside on the exposed catwalk to witness the collision firsthand.

Lit by a luminous full moon, he had watched the scene with bated breath. Had it been his imagination, or had he actually seen the face of one of the shocked American officers as he first set his gaze on the rapidly approaching cruiser? Regardless, the *Azov* had neatly cut the sub in half, just as he had planned it to. And as things had worked out, the doomed Yankees hadn't even had time to radio knowledge of the attack before the sub went down with a supposed loss of all hands. Never making the headlines of the Soviet newspapers, this sub's loss had only been reported to their top leaders. Apparently, it had been blamed on a structural failure of its hulls welds. Josef supposed that just like his own government would have done, the families of the deceased sailors had merely gotten notices that their sons had been lost in an accident.

Escaping with only minor scrapes on their bow, the *Azov* had returned to Vladivostok. Only the helmsman and a handful of other sailors had known the ramming had been intentional. To the rest of the crew, it had been only a routine collision with an undisclosed surface object. Not knowing how his superiors would react to his actions, Josef had been somewhat hesitant to make his official report. When he had finally done so, he hadn't been surprised when he received the call ordering him to his father's office.

Upon first entering the old man's stateroom positioned deep within the bowels of his flagship, the *Minsk*, Josef had found his father's face drawn and strained. Only when his own facial expression wilted correspondingly, had the elder Kostromo broken this charade. With eyes wide and a beaming smile, he had stood and taken his son in his arms.

"You're merely a younger version of myself," Alexis had greeted warmly.

Proud of his accomplishment, and certain of his motives, the old-timer's only advice to his son had been to redraft the report to remove any intentional designs on his part. The old navy veteran had known there were weaklings in Moscow who would misinterpret Josef's ambitions. But if the *Azov* had just happened to slice across an unidentified surface object in open waters, surely Josef couldn't be faulted? And to those on board who had had knowledge of his original motives, ways were found to insure their silence.

In such a way, the incident had been closed. This was only one of the benefits a fellow secured when his father was Admiral of the Fleet.

Josef was proud of the fact that, throughout his career, his dependence upon his father's rank had been kept to a minimum. When his old man's advice was needed, he had the wisdom to listen to it closely — which was why he had taken care to alter the report of the ramming incident off the coast of Viet Nam, just like Alexis had advised him to do.

Earlier today, when the admiral's orders had arrived Josef's first instinct had instantly been to dispute that portion which dealt with the elimination of the Alfa vessel. Even if the admiral in charge *hadn't* been his own father, Josef would have immediately called the *Minsk* to verify this directive's legitimacy. The icy response that Alexis had given him couldn't be ignored, yet he could also take the initiative to read between the lines. He would concentrate his full ability on knocking out the Trident sub. As for the Alfa, who could say what he'd do when it was time to hunt it down.

Pacing the *Azov*'s bridge, Captain Josef Kostromo felt each of his fifty-three years of age and more. As his practiced gaze surveyed the blue expanse of water stretching endlessly eastward, a loud blast of static sounded out behind him. Turning with a start, he saw the communications officer trigger a single filtering mechanism. Instantly, the static emanating from the radio receiver transformed itself into a strained, nasal, male voice.

"Red Banner leader, this is Shooting Star. Do you read us, Red Banner?"

Without delay, the *Azov*'s radioman spoke into his headphone-mounted microphone. "Shooting Star, this is the leader, copying you loud and clear. Go ahead with your transmission."

"We've spotted . . ."

A burst of raw static made the rest of his words inaudible. The radio operator vainly tried his various filters, but all resulting in a similar, garbled response. Josef Kostromo was quick to get to his side.

"What's gone wrong with our radio?" he firmly queried.

The communications officer glanced up, clearly concerned. "I'm afraid the interference is not being caused on our end, Captain. The helicopter must be having problems with its transmitter."

"It was working fine, earlier," Josef shot back. "Try the emergency bands."

Just as the operator was about to switch frequencies to carry out the captain's orders, the static mysteriously cleared. "To repeat, Red Banner leader. We've spotted some sort of weather balloon. She's soaring at about two thousand feet, mounted to a tether line which leads back beneath the surface of the ocean. Coordinates are nineteen degrees south, one hundred and seventy-one degrees west, bearing due south . . ."

Again a burst of static completely veiled the transmission, yet this time Josef Kostromo didn't seem to care.

"They've found them!" the captain exclaimed joyously. "Navigation, plot us a course for an immediate intercept! Weapons, ready our SS-N-14s! Engineering, give me more steam!"

This last request echoed out commandingly as Josef began the mental calculations that would precipitate this attack. In the back of his mind, he was already transcribing the message to notify his father that the Trident had been eliminated.

"Skipper, we're picking up something on AUSEX."

Anthony Canova's words brought Charles Blake over to the sonar console. Without a second's hesitation, the captain donned the extra set of headphones. Closing his eyes to help channel his attention, he strained to pick up a cluttered, chopping noise barely audible in the distance. This alien sound was conveyed to his ears with the assistance of the AUSEX device, a specially designed hydrophone towed from a deployment pod set into the center of the sub's rear stabilizer fin.

"Those are the contra-rotating blades," observed Canova. "That would make her a Ka-25 Hormone helicopter."

Blake's eyes opened as he picked out the sound of the dual, Glushenkov turboshaft engines. He pulled off the headphones and set them back on the console.

"It must be stationed on one of the those two surface bogeys. What's their current status, Lieutenant?"

Alertly, Canova switched frequencies and glued his eyes to the map visible beneath the glass of his sonar screen. "They've split up, Skipper. One seems to be steaming northward, and the other to the south. They're still a good forty-five nautical miles distant, but I think Big Brother can get a positive I.D. now."

"Well, let's do it, lad," urged Blake, who looked on as the heavyset sonar man began feeding data into his computer keyboard.

Several anxious seconds passed before the readout screen began filling with the desired information. Anthony Canova interpreted it.

"We show an eighty-seven-percent probability that they're Udaloys, Captain."

Charles Blake was extremely familiar with this class of warship. Designed primarily for use against submarines, each destroyer carried an exceptionally powerful complement of ASW weaponry, including depth rockets, homing torpedos, and SS-N-14 subrocs. Each also had space available for a pair of Hormone helicopters, which the Udaloy would rely on to initially spot the quarry. The Hormones would use chin-mounted search radar systems, towed MAD (magnetic anomaly device) sensors, and dunking sonar units. Though each chopper carried a variety of depth charges and bombs, Charles doubted that they'd be sent in to attack. Rather, it would be the mother ship that would do the dirty work. If the *Phoenix* was indeed spotted, the first weapon that they'd most likely face was the SS-N-14. Since the subroc's range was limited to thirty-four miles, they could breathe easy for the moment.

"Let's just pray that we haven't been tagged yet," the captain prompted.

Canova's eyes remained locked on the sonar screen. "I doubt it, Skipper. Those Udaloys are continuing on to the north and to the south."

"I just don't like the idea of being sandwiched between them, even if we are still out of their range. What's the sea like east of here?"

In response to this question, Anthony leaned forward and changed the direction of his sonar scan. Instantaneously, a new section of map showed itself on the screen. "This portion of the Southwestern Pacific Basin looks clear as a bell, Captain."

After a moment's deliberation, Blake turned his head and addressed the helmsman. "Peterson, chart us a course due east. Be prepared to heat up the reactor. We're going to need some speed."

From the opposite side of the command center, the diving officer responded cautiously, "Captain, we won't be able to get any speed until the boat's forward escape hatch is sealed. I show a red light in that portion of the *Phoenix*, sir."

"That's impossible!" Blake returned, as he quickly crossed the compartment to check the status board for himself. "I haven't authorized the launch of any buoys. Check to see if there's a short circuit in the sensor mechanism."

Peterson reached up and depressed a series of toggle switches. "All circuits check out, sir."

Gently rubbing his bruised forehead, Charles attempted to figure out what else could cause such a faulty reading. Unable to come up with anything, his hand shot out for the nearby intercom. He punched in three digits, and waited a full minute before hanging up the handset disgustedly.

"No one is answering in the forward escape hatch. I'd better get down there and check out the situation for myself. It's got to be a crossed circuit of some sort. Peterson, chart me that new course and get us ready to move out of here in a hurry on my command."

"Aye, aye, sir," the helmsman replied as he swiveled back to his keyboard.

Meanwhile, Charles Blake walked back over to the sonar console. "Canova, keep your eyes and ears open. I'll be down in the forward hatch compartment. Notify me the second that one of those Udaloys alters its course by even the slightest of degrees."

"Will do, Skipper," answered the sensor operator with a nod. "You're not thinking of stepping out on us, are you, sir?"

"Canova, you won't be getting rid of me that easily. Now, get back to that screen!"

Taking in the New Yorker's smart salute, Blake began his way to the forward hatch, his stride determined, his thoughts focused on a single goal.

Pete Walsh issued a deep breath of relief when the green light popped on signalling that the scanner instrument was secure back inside the hatch. He had had second thoughts about his involvement in the scientist's scheme all during the long five minutes that the device had been airborne. Such an act on his part was a serious breach of trust between himself and the captain. By not informing Blake, he had even opened himself to possibly disciplinary action. Yet the XO wasn't even sure what had convinced him to go along with such a desperate plan. Even though Thomas Kraft's pleas were very sincere, surely their captain should have had the final say in this matter. Knowing that it was too late to turn back, Walsh now only wanted to finish this procedure as quickly as possible and get back to his original duty.

"Lieutenant, we're ready to open her up."

Thomas rose from the computer console and joined him beside the hatchway. "The harmonic sensors seem to be working perfectly," Thomas said. "I've got it all down on tape inside the computer."

"Great," the XO returned half-heartedly. "If you'll just depress that red decompression button set above the pressure gauge, we can remove that air sample and get the hell out of here."

Quite aware of the XO's strained tone, Kraft hit the button with his right index finger. A loud hissing sound followed as the water inside the hatch was purged back into the open sea. When this noise completely dissipated, Walsh waited ten seconds before gripping the hatch's circular steel handle and turning it counter-clockwise. With a resonant, sucking pop, the hatchway opened.

Oblivious to the several gallons of remaining seawater that splashed out onto the deck, Pete reached inside and pulled out the instrument, which was sealed in a narrow, two-foot-long plastic pod. He handed it to the beaming scientist.

"I'll never be able to thank you enough for your help, Mr. Walsh."

"Forget it, Lieutenant," returned the XO. "If what you're saying is true, it's us who owe you the thanks. You can continue your experiment back in my cabin. Right now, we'd better be getting out of here."

Slamming shut the hatchway, Pete Walsh had turned to lead the way out of the room when his startled eyes caught sight of the captain. Standing squarely, his hands set tightly behind his back, an expression was etched on his face that not only hinted at disbelief, but also was indicative of a rising inner fury.

"Going somewhere, gentlemen?" Blake said icily.

The XO met his gaze sheepishly as the captain continued. "Spare me the excuses, Mr. Walsh. I think I'm quite aware of what's going on here. Lieutenant Kraft, I believe you're the one responsible for this unauthorized breach of the *Phoenix*'s integrity."

"If you'll just let me explain," stuttered the geophysicist.

"Save it for your court-martial, Mister. As of this moment, you can consider yourself under house arrest. That means that you're to be confined to your quarters at once. Can I trust you to find your way there and stay put, or am I going to have to assign an escort and put you in handcuffs?"

"But, Captain," pleaded the scientist.

"No, buts!" Blake shouted angrily.

Realizing that Blake wasn't going to budge, Thomas took a quick glance at his accomplice.

"You'd better get moving, Lieutenant," whispered Walsh.

"I'm sorry I dragged you into this, sir," Thomas replied softly.

Pete shook his head. "I can take care of myself. Now, you'd better be listening to the Captain before he follows through with his threats."

Answering him with a sorrowful gaze, Thomas Kraft saluted, and with the buoy still firm in his left hand, began his way toward the exit. When the captain failed to move out of his way, Kraft was forced to halt. He looked up, puzzled, as Blake again addressed him.

"I don't think you'll be needing that contraption."

As Blake held out the palm of his hand, Thomas reluctantly surrendered the sealed plastic buoy. Only then did the captain step out of the way to let the scientist continue on. This left the *Phoenix*'s two senior officers alone in the cramped compartment. Several seconds of strained silence followed, then Blake cleared his throat.

"I could expect such a thing from anyone but you, Pete. What in the hell got into you?"

"I'm sorry to upset you, Skipper. It just seemed like the right thing to do at the moment."

Charles took a step forwards. "Aw, come on, Pete. What's with this crap? You know as well as I the order of command that allows this vessel to operate. If everyone went around doing their own thing, we'd never manage to get out of port."

Walsh managed to reply a bit more strongly. "Kraft's theories were making a lot of sense. Since you wouldn't even give the kid a chance to explain himself, I thought a little hard evidence would help show if he was right or not. After all, he is our guest."

Blake's expression softened. "I admit that I may have handled the lieutenant a bit harshly, but at the moment, I can't help but feel that we're faced with much more important responsibilities. My God, Pete, we're at a state of war! What kind of time is this for you to go making command decisions on your own?"

The XO shrugged his shoulders. "I'm sorry, Captain. I should have asked your permission first."

"I'm sorry too, believe me. You've left me no alternative but to write you up, Pete. You would have made one hell of a fine captain."

Blake's words were interrupted by a single, harsh, ring from the intercom. Catching the XO's sullen glance, the captain reached over to pick up the handset.

"Captain here."

The voice on the other end replied sharply. "Sir, it's Canova. We've just picked up a new bogey. She's a big one, Skipper, headed right at us from the west, with a bone in her teeth."

292

With his eyes still locked on the slumped figure of the XO, Blake questioned, "What's her distance?"

"Approximately seventy nautical miles and rapidly closing, Skipper. She's still too far out to get a definite sound I.D."

"Well, stay with her, Canova. Any change in the course of those Udaloys?"

"Negative, Captain. Both targets remain constant."

"Very good, Lieutenant. I'm counting on you to keep us out of harm's way. For any further updates, I can be reached in the forward torpedo room. Call Chief Crowley and have him meet me there on the double."

"Aye, aye, Skipper. By the way, Peterson shows a green light on that escape hatch. Should he proceed with that new course you requested?"

Blake made some hasty mental calculations. "Have him hold our present course and speed until further notified. Before we go running for it, I'd like to know exactly what's chasing us. Relay to me that sound signature I.D. as soon as it's available."

"Will do, Captain."

Thoughtfully, Blake hung up the intercom. With a deliberate slowness, he angled his line of sight to gradually catch that of the concerned XO.

"I've got a gut feeling that the Russkies are up to something topside. We've got a little over two hours to go until we're due to launch. Until then, I'd like us to stay nestled in here, under the shelter of the Trench, for as long as possible. The next one hundred and twenty minutes are going to be critical, Pete. I'm going to need a one-hundred-percent effort on the part of each crew member if the *Phoenix* is going to ride this thing out."

"Does that mean that I get a reprieve, Captain?" Pete quizzed hopefully.

"Consider yourself under probation," shot back

Blake. "Now, how about accompanying me to the torpedo room to see if this lady has still got some sting left in her?"

"Yes, sir," the XO replied with a crisp salute.

Only when the captain answered Walsh with a salute of his own did his expression significantly lighten. Pete knew that he was lucky. Under any other circumstances, he would have most likely been confined to his quarters, right alongside Thomas Kraft. Yet for the moment, their situation made his presence imperative. Issuing a sigh of relief, he watched Charles Blake turn and casually toss the plastic buoy he had been holding into a nearby wastebasket. Walsh watched it land with a thud, and fighting the impulse to retrieve it, followed the captain outside into the surrounding hallway.

Chapter Fifteen

President Andrew Lyons wasn't the type of man who was easily intimidated. Yet, the longer the current crisis persisted, the more noticeable were his rising anxieties. These worries expressed themselves internally with a splitting headache and a tight, painful knot in his stomach. Because of his position of command, he did his best to mask his exterior appearance with an "all is well" expression. But he was struggling to keep even the hint of a calm smile on his face as he walked down the interior passageway of the flying White House.

Crossing through the deserted briefing room, he entered the E-4B's central compartment reserved for a large portion of Kneecap's ninety-person battle staff. Seated in their high-backed leather command chairs, busily at work at their individual consoles, the majority of these black-jumpsuited figures wore the insignia of the Strategic Air Command on their chests. Those men and women whose attentions weren't locked to their computer screens welcomed Andrew with a salute. To these, Lyons answered with sincere nods of encouragement, trying not to disrupt their important activities whenever possible.

Continuing toward the E-4B's tail, the president

couldn't help but notice that every one of the windows was securely boarded up. He had learned from General Sachs only hours ago that this was done to shelter the staff's eyesight in the event of a nuclear explosion nearby. Even the flight crew had blinds of solid steel, which they would slide into place when the first warheads started dropping. A pilot whose retina was burned out wouldn't do them much good.

This fact only served to make Andrew that much more aware of the precariousness of their present situation. Quickly checking his watch, he saw that they had less than two hours to reach the *Phoenix* before it was scheduled to launch. As he ducked through a doorway that sheltered a long bank of data processing equipment, he found himself intercepted by an attractive young woman wearing the dual silver bars of an air force captain on the shoulders of her jumpsuit.

"Mr. President, I just got word from the flight deck. It looks like we're going to be encountering a little rough weather as we head over Lake Superior. It would be best if you had a seat and buckled yourself in."

"I appreciate the warning, Captain," replied Lyons. "You know, things were going so smoothly, I almost forgot that we were even airborne. How's the staff holding out?"

The young officer smiled. "We're hanging in there, sir. Are you comfortable?"

Andrew patted his thighs. "Except for stiff old legs, I'm doing fine."

A rough pocket of air buffeted the plane, and the fuselage rattled and shook accordingly. Thrown off balance by this vibration, Lyons was steadied by the firm, warm grasp of the woman he faced. Conscious of the light, sweet scent of her perfume, Andrew's senses slightly stirred.

"Thanks for the helping hand, Captain. I think it's

time to take your advice and find refuge under a seat belt. See you later on."

Taking a deep breath, he turned to make his way back to that section of Kneecap set forward of the E-4B's wings. He was just entering the conference room when Secretary of Defense Russell Tate entered the compartment from the opposite doorway.

"Ah, Mr. President, I was just checking for you in your stateroom. You've got a call from Admiral Burnhardt holding."

Settling himself in the tall-backed chair set at the head of the wooden table, Lyons looked up expectantly. 'I hope Pearl Harbor has some good news, Russell. Have a seat, and let's hear what the admiral has to say over the squawk box."

Taking the chair on the president's left, Tate reached forward and punched two of the dozen, clear plastic buttons set into the base of the red telephone. In response, the slight static of an open line filled the cabin.

"Admiral Burnhardt, it's Andrew Lyons. Are you with us?"

A firm, slightly distorted male voice answered, "Yes, Mr. President, I'm here."

Andrew's glance linked to that of his secretary of defense. "Well, Admiral, I hope you have a good report for us."

"It appears that way," returned Burnhardt. "I just received word from Whiteman Air Force Base. That specially adapted Minuteman belonging to the Emergency Rocket Command System is ready for launch. We can have its radio transmitter penetrating the atmosphere directly over the Southwestern Pacific Basin in less than twenty minutes' time. There's practically no way that the *Phoenix* can help but receive its signal calling them off alert."

297

"Excellent," Lyons replied hopefully. "What's the status of TACAMO?"

The admiral's response was a bit more hesitant. "The C-130 is continuing to make up the time it lost when they had to side-step that typhoon. Even with their excellent progress, they won't be within range of the *Phoenix* for another two hours."

Lyons watched as Russell Tate checked his wristwatch, then shook his head worriedly. Most aware of the time, Andrew met his concerned glance with one of his own.

"I'm afraid that won't do us much good, Admiral. That Minuteman is going to have to do the trick. Please hold off on the launch of the ERCS until I get back to you. It shouldn't be long from now."

"Very good, sir. I'll be awaiting your call."

Lyons reached forward and disconnected the line. As the president sat back, Russell Tate queried, "Why the delay, Mr. President? The sooner that Minuteman gets down range, the sooner we can all breathe more easily."

"I understand that quite well, Russell. Yet I think that it's important that I make one more phone call before we send that missile up. Please get ahold of the National Military Command Center in the Pentagon. I'm going to need the hotline to Moscow activated at once."

Before initiating this directive, Russell Tate again questioned, "Why's that?"

Lyons answered him directly. "I think there's two good reasons why I must personally inform Vladimir Kirensk before I give the launch order. First off, you know as well as I how skittish the Soviets are at the moment. I don't want one of their satellites mistaking that Minuteman's heat signature for that of an entire flight. Secondly, I want the general secretary to know

xactly what's mounted inside that ICBM's nose cone.
 sure would be a tragic waste if one of their surface
 ssels in the South Pacific tagged it as containing a
 uclear warhead, and blew it from the skies before it
 ompleted its mission."

Impressed with the president's logic, Tate's serious
 xpression softened. "That call sounds most prudent,
 Ir. President. I'll get in touch with the Pentagon at
 nce."

While the secretary bent forward to initiate this
 ookup, Andrew Lyons angled his line of sight to the
 nbossed seal of his office that graced the cabin's
 pposite wall. Focusing on its design, he found his
 oughts drifting back to a time of much more inno-
 nt worries.

It had been during his only-recently concluded
 ggressive campaign for this office that the sharp
 ifferences between himself and his incumbent oppo-
 ent had become a matter of public record. This
 isparity was most noticeable in the fields of arms
 ontrol and military policy. Whereas his adversary
 romulgated a hardline program of confrontation
 rough the practically unlimited development of new
 eapons systems, Andrew swore that he would put an
 d to such wasteful madness. Though the old-guard
 ad labeled such thoughts as bordering on treason, the
 ation's population rallied to his cause in unprece-
 nted numbers.

Elected to office in a landslide victory, Andrew had
 ut his theory to the test when he issued the summit
 vitation to Vladimir Kirensk. When the general
 cretary had accepted, Lyons had taken it as a certain
 gn that the Soviets were just as fed up as his own
 ople with the unwarranted size and attention past
 dministrations had devoted to the military.

Both man had sworn that the Space Arms Treaty

they proposed would only be the first step to th
eventual elimination of all nuclear warheads from th
face of the planet. This announcement had been me
with relieved cheers from the world's populace an
skeptical grunts from its military planners. It had onl
taken Andrew a couple more months to find out th
true reason behind this skepticism.

The crisis he found himself presently embroiled i
was proof positive that the nuclear threat had bee
allowed to grow completely out of proportion. Me
were no longer the guardians of their own destinies; th
malfunction of a single microchip could issue the ale
sealing the planet's doom.

If his constituents could only see their candidat
now, he thought. Less than two hours away fror
witnessing just the type of catastrophe he had sworn t
eliminate, Lyons realized how totally helpless thei
situation appeared.

Swallowing a wave of nausea as the E-4B plummete
downward in a gust of vicious wind, Andrew coul
only pray that mankind's overextended luck had yet t
run out. Grabbing onto the arms of his chair as th
plane's engines strained to regain the altitude that the
had so suddenly lost, he petitioned a Lord he was onl
now rediscovering, to lead them away from the brink c
self-destruction.

Approximately 5,700 miles away from the aircra
known as Kneecap, the leader of the world's othe
superpower found himself reflecting on thoughts fa
away from the grave predicament in which mankin
found itself entangled. With his sturdy frame perche
solidly before his office's massive picture window, Vla
dimir Kirensk looked on as a stiff evening breez
ruffled the limbs of the simple copse of trees set befor

the Kremlin wall. For some mysterious reason, this movement triggered ponderings of a much simpler time, as he recreated that afternoon he had first arrived in Moscow, seemingly a lifetime ago.

A mere lad, fresh off the farm, he would never forget that chill wind that had greeted him as he stepped onto the capital city's train platform. How intimidating the city had seemed as he wandered the frozen, snow-covered streets, carrying his few earthly possessions at his side, vainly searching for the building housing the Bureau he had been called to.

What would his life have been like if he had listened to his first instincts and returned to Kiev? Would he still be a farmer like his father, or would another calling have drawn him away? Of a more significant nature, he wondered what the world would be like if he hadn't stuck it out here and become general secretary. Catching his reflection in the window, he decided that the planet's destiny wouldn't be much different that it was currently. For all his dreams and lofty ideals, his presence at the head of the Soviet Union meant little.

Feeling frustrated and totally powerless, Vladimir came to the conclusion that it wasn't individuals who shaped political destinies, but rather events long set into motion. Thus, they were presently facing a quandry left to them by a generation long retired from positions of power. He could only guide the ship of state on what he considered the smoothest and safest course available.

Kirensk recalled both the phone call that he had just received, and that which he had initiated soon afterward. President Andrew Lyons had sounded tired and strained. In a flat, emotionless tone, he'd reiterated that he was doing everything within his power to contact the lost U.S. Trident submarine, including sending up a Minuteman missile in whose nose cone was placed a powerful radio transmitter. In such a manner, they hoped to contact the vessel, and to rescind the orders authorizing it to launch its warheads.

Vladimir had had to admit that this was a clever move on the part of the Americans. And he had been about to give the project his full blessings when both of his advisors, who had heard the conversation while seated beside him, signalled the general secretary to be more cautious. Putting the president on hold, Vladimir had allowed Pavlodar and Altyr to voice that which was so urgently on their minds.

It was just like these old-timers to be instantly suspicious of Andrew Lyons's plan. Both had warned him that this launch could very possibly mask a full-scale attack on behalf of the crafty imperialists. Under the authorization of their own leader, elements of Admiral Kostromo's Fleet could be among the first to feel the bite of such a diabolical tactic.

Watching these two hardliners whining on like a pair of washerwomen, Vladimir had known that these were just the type of individuals responsible for their current fix. Feeling wise beyond his years, Kirensk had silenced his advisors with a single, harsh gesture. Beckoning them to leave his office, he had sat back alone—and had decided that this was an instance when only he could chose the country's course.

Reconnecting the hotline, he had wished the American president the best of luck with his endeavor. Accepting the young man's relieved thanks, Vladimir had placed one more phone call.

The line to the carrier *Minsk* was static filled, and he found himself practically shouting to be heard. His call found Admiral Kostromo valiantly riding out the full brunt of the typhoon. Seated in his stateroom, the father of the modern Soviet Navy was speaking to

Vladimir while Assistant Defense Minister Mikhail Antonov was perched nearby. Accepting the news of the approaching ICBM without comment, Kostromo promised to immediately inform the elements of his fleet currently penetrating the Southwestern Pacific Basin of the Minuteman's peaceful intentions. With his terse response, the line went completely dead.

Satisfied that he had gotten his message across, Vladimir stood and found his way back to the window. If the Americans' aim was true, their problems would soon be over. Called back from the brink of nuclear annihilation, the superpowers would have more reason than ever before to ratify treaties — such as their Space Weapons ban — and to consider more comprehensive legislation eliminating nuclear warheads all together.

Glancing back at the stand of trees planted before him, the general secretary found his spirits lightening. Perhaps his years of hard work and toil weren't about to be wasted after all. Buoyed by this thought, his attention was abruptly diverted to his office's front door. There, his beloved wife Olga had just entered, carrying a silver serving tray securely in her grasp. Infatuated by her innocent smile, Vladimir couldn't help but derive a spurt of much-needed strength from her mere presence.

"I thought some tea and cakes would do you no harm, husband," she warmly greeted. "It seems that none of us will be afforded any sleep on this fated night."

As she placed the tray on his desk's corner, Vladimir swept her into his arms and squeezed her tightly. Fighting the impulse to let her know that there was a very good chance that they could all be snug in their beds within the next hour, he kissed her instead, hard on the lips.

"My goodness, husband, what's gotten into you? I

haven't had a kiss like that since our honeymoon!"

Meeting her tender glance, Vladimir was speechless. All of his hopes and dreams were locked in those two, baby-blue eyes. Like an angel from above, Olga came to him when he needed her the most. Could he have risen to his current position without her invaluable assistance during those formative years in the Bureau of Agriculture? And would his life even be worth living today, if he didn't have his beloved at his side to share in his triumphs and to soothe his defeats?

It was during rare moments such as this one when life's purpose seemed so crystal clear. Man would escape the nuclear snare, and somehow, the world would persevere. Of this fact, he was certain.

On the other side of the world, the general secretary's optimism was not being shared. Inside the carrier *Minsk*, the atmosphere permeating Admiral Alexis Kostromo's stateroom was a dank, sour one. The figure most responsible for this sickly tone was his guest, Mikhail Antonov. Laying prone on the room's narrow couch, he had long since abandoned all efforts in making it to the toilet to deposit his typhoon-induced vomit. Merely rolling his head to the side, he gagged up strand after strand of milky vomit, as the nine-hundred-foot-long vessel they sailed upon was tossed to and fro like a toy.

The admiral took pity with his comrade's plight, yet knew there was little that he could do for him. A veteran of fifty years on such rough seas, he had seen many a man empty his stomach in such a manner. Somehow, these past few years, his body seemed to have gained an immunity to the ravages of seasickness. Of course, when a storm threatened, he was always careful to have plenty of his special "medicine" nearby.

Seated at his desk with the deck pitching wildly beneath, Alexis removed a pint-sized bottle of potato-distilled vodka from his top drawer. Putting the neck to his lips, he angled it back and consumed a hearty dose of the fiery liquid that calmed his stomach and soothed his nerves. After he had digested it with a burp, Alexis looked up, and met the pitiful gaze of the deputy defense minister.

"Are you certain that you won't change your mind and join me, Mikhail? My trusty tonic is guaranteed to cure your misery."

Weakly, Antonov shook his head. "Thank you, Comrade, but I don't think that my stomach could handle it at the moment."

"It genuinely hurts me to see you suffer so," offered Kostromo. "Yet, you aren't alone. The doctor informs me that over ninety percent of the *Minsk*'s complement is sharing your plight. I must admit that these seas are a bit rough, but I've experienced worse storms before."

To emphasize these words, the ship pitched hard to port. Forced to grab onto the arms of his chair to steady himself, Kostromo watched as various unsecured books and office supplies rolled off their counters and ended up on the floor on the cabin's left side. These objects slid to the opposite wall when another wave pushed the carrier's keel over on its starboard.

"If you could only have seen some of the seas that I've crossed before," the admiral continued as the *Minsk* righted itself. "Why, there was one hurricane off the coast of Cuba that made this typhoon appear more like a spring shower!"

"I can just imagine," managed Mikhail, whose pallid complexion had a slight green tint to it. "Tell me, Comrade, did you have any luck reaching your son, to convey the general secretary's most recent directive?"

Kostromo sat up straight, and consumed another sip

from the vodka bottle before answering. "We're still trying to get through to the *Azov*. For some reason, all that we're able to pick up is a heavy band of static."

"Could this typhoon be the culprit?" questioned Antonov.

"I doubt it. Radio communications with other elements of our fleet are still possible. We are greeted with this unusual atmospheric interference only when attempting to transmit in the direction of the Southwestern Pacific Basin. I tell you, Comrade, EMP is the reason for this disruption. Even though Kirensk won't admit it, I'm certain that the Americans have exploded a nuclear weapon in this area."

Mikhail managed to pull himself up into a sitting position. With the help of a towel, he wiped a line of saliva from his lips and then asked, "But what could be their intended target?"

Kostromo answered thoughtfully. "Who knows, perhaps it was the *Magadan*, or maybe our Udaloys. One thing that I'm certain of is that Josef will get to the bottom of it all. In a way, I'm not really sorry I wasn't able to contact him. This entire incident with the American Trident is just too unbelievable. Who ever heard of such a thing as wasting an ICBM to send up a simple communications device. This is all a clever imperialist trick, my friend. Our gullible young leader can't see the forest for the trees."

"Your observations are most astute," offered Mikhail, his tone a bit stronger. "I was afraid that the American president was up to something devious when he initiated that hasty summit meeting. The way Lyons accommodated our premier made it most obvious that he was setting Kirensk up. The true nature of this underhanded scheme is only now coming out into the open."

Kostromo smiled. "Isn't it strange how destiny has

nterceded on our behalf? Without having to disobey the orders of our misdirected general secretary, it appears that I won't have to instruct my son to allow the Yankee Minuteman to penetrate their airspace. Not only have the fates spared the lives of Josef and his men, but also the continued existence of the Motherland."

Antonov sat up with his posture slouched forward. "Then you indeed feel that this strange maneuvering by the Americans is a ploy veiling an intended nuclear first strike?"

The admiral's eyes gleamed. "That is only most obvious, Comrade. How fitting that this should all come to pass during the midst of Operation Lenin. Never before have our strategic forces been so ready to strike. The present global positioning of our fleets will ensure that the Soviet Union will survive any U.S. sneak attack. If our high-minded young leader would only come down from his cloud, he could take advantage of the situation and grab the initiative. Before too many innocent Soviet lives are needlessly threatened, Kirensk should order an immediate launch of our own. Our ICBMs and submarine-based warheads can quickly cripple America's ability to answer with a counterstrike. In less than a half-hour's time, Andrew Lyons would be begging for mercy."

Kostromo's emotional discourse was interrupted by the arrival of a massive swell that pounded into the *Minsk*'s bow. To the jarring rattle of the ship's superstructure, the deputy defense minister fought back a wave of rising nausea, while Alexis helped himself to another mouthful of vodka. Invigorated by this drink, the admiral watched as his white-haired guest doubled up in a fit of uncontrollable gagging. Mikhail Antonov looked every bit his age, and then some.

Conscious of an alien soreness in his rheumatic

307

joints, Kostromo couldn't help but feel the year's toll on his own worn body. Now, more than ever before, he realized that his time left for service was at a minimum. Contemplating the legacy he'd leave behind, Alexis allowed his thoughts to soar back to those of the past. Closing his eyes, he visualized those early formative years, over six decades ago, when he had first gotten the call to go to sea. What a great adventure each day had seemed!

Sent off to exotic ports in the far corners of the planet, he had gotten a firsthand lesson in the world's colossal size. As big as the Motherland may have seemed, it was only one small segment in the true scope of things. One fact that had become most apparent from his very first voyage, was that if the Soviet Union were to take its inevitable place as the earth's dominate leader, it would have to secure control of the seas. The importance of an effective navy had been proven in the Great War.

Although the Soviet Union had had a considerably larger Navy than that of Germany when hostilities had begun in 1941, its performance had been pitifully ineffective. Weakened by an inexperienced officer corps, the fleet had seen little action — and the army had had to take on the brunt of the responsibility for stopping the Nazi hordes.

Alexis had sworn at the war's conclusion that their country would never be in such a position of weakness again. Single-handedly, he had initiated the design and procurement of an entire new generation of naval vessels. To properly man these ships, he had focused great attention on the training of both officers and noncommissioned ranks alike. Afloat on a variety of sophisticated carriers, cruisers, destroyers, and submarines, the Soviet Navy had been transformed from a weak coastal-defense force into a strong, oceangoing fleet, able to hold its own on any sea.

Operation Lenin was designed to show this fact to the world. It also represented the pinnacle of his long career. The fruits of his thousands of hours of selfless toil had thus been finally realized. It would be up to young men such as his son, Josef, to keep this legacy intact. Only with such a sacrifice could the power-hungry imperialists be contained.

And if the Americans were to choose this day to launch their missiles, it would be the Soviet Navy that would make the difference between a tragic defeat and a glorious victory. Even if Vladimir Kirensk didn't have the nerve to order a first strike beforehand, the Motherland would persevere because of this fleet's strength. Confident of this certainty, the admiral's lips turned up in a smile, as his weary body slipped off into a deep, dreamless sleep.

Watching Kostromo drift off into this slumber was the prone figure of Mikhail Antonov. From his position on the narrow couch, the deputy defense minister found himself wondering what the strange smile etching the admiral's wrinkled face was all about. Was the old man recreating an old romance, or gloating over some sort of personal triumph? Whatever, the aged, bald-headed sailor certainly deserved this moment of rest.

Astounded at the way the admiral had ridden out the typhoon's fury without a hint of seasickness, Mikhail admired his old friend that much more. Unable to demonstrate any sort of bodily self-control of his own, the white-haired bureaucrat felt like a foolish child. Too weak even to lift himself up and clean up the sourish mess he helplessly floundered in, Antonov wished that he too could be whisked off into the carefree hands of a sound slumber. Yet, the still rolling deck made any such a repose an impossibility.

This was certainly a very difficult environment for a landlubber like himself to cope with. Perhaps he should have taken the admiral's advice, and tried a sip of the vodka. Her seriously doubted that he could be much sicker than he presently was, anyway.

Unable to concentrate on anything but the nauseating dizziness that possessed him so, Mikhail tried desperately to project his meditations elsewhere. Contemplations of the tense political situation that they found themselves in only made him sicker. It proved to be a single, magical vision that eventually diverted his ponderings away from himself. By recreating the exotic face and voluptuous figure of the woman known as Black Jade, Antonov temporarily escaped his physical distress. So powerful was this pleasing mental image, that he was hardly aware of the jarring concussion that rattled the cabin around him as the *Minsk* plowed into a towering, typhoon-induced swell.

Captain Josef Kostromo anxiously paced the narrow metal catwalk that surrounded the *Azov*'s elevated command bridge. Stopping occasionally to angle his binoculars out toward the eastern horizon, the red-haired officer found the distant ocean deserted. Yet, his hunter's instinct warned him otherwise. Somewhere close by, veiled by a few hundred feet of water, their quarry awaited. Such knowledge made it impossible for him to stand still for long. His senses totally aroused, the cruiser's master was pumped full of nervous energy. Only a single action would allow this blood-lust to be satisfied.

Now he understood what the German u-boat captains had felt as they waited in their wolf packs for the ever approaching convoys. No other feeling in the world was quite like that experienced in those minutes that preceded the moment of actual armed combat. When the hatchway leading into the bridge opened, and the tall dignified figure of his senior lieutenant approached, Josef was certain that the time had come.

"Captain Kostromo," greeted the white-uniformed officer urgently. "Our top-sail radar had just picked up a projectile believed to be a Minuteman warhead, descending toward this sector at an altitude of 80,000 feet."

"Are you sure that this object isn't of Soviet origin?" the captain quizzed.

"We are positive, sir. Its trajectory indicates that it originated in the American Midwest."

Sobered by this information, Josef ordered a single course of action. "Ready a pair of SA-N-10 pop-up missiles. We must intercept this warhead at once!"

As the senior lieutenant clicked his heels and then pivoted to hastily return to the bridge and initiate this directive, Josef scoured the skies above them. Cursing to himself, he tried not to visualize the lethal damage a nuclear warhead could wreak on the *Azov*. Exposed in the mid-ocean as they were, such a blast would be instantly fatal.

Well aware that each passing second brought such a tragic outcome closer to a reality, he stirred expectantly when a loud grinding noise sounded from the deck before him. Surveying that portion of the ship immediately behind the bow, he gratefully caught sight of two hinged, circular, manhole-type covers slowly popping open. Barely a second after they were fully erect, he was forced to shield his eyes as a brilliant ribbon of flame shot from beneath these covers.

The entire ship shuddered as the two SA-N-10s blasted upward, one after the other. Leaving a thick trail of black smoke in their wakes, the rockets arched into the air in a blinding burst of supersonic speed.

311

Their ascent was so quick that Josef had trouble following their progress with his binoculars. Just when it appeared that they were out of the range of his amplified sight, a blindingly bright ball of flame lit the heavens. This brilliant light was followed by a distant, muted boom. Straining to view the results of this explosion, Josef jumped nervously when the senior lieutenant's voice cried out behind him.

"The Minuteman has been eliminated, Captain! Our radar shows absolutely no more threats in the skies above us."

"My compliments to the missile team, Comrade. Now, it's time for us to once more resume our role as the hunter. Call in the Udaloys and have them tighten the snare. That Trident is close, I just know it!"

Returning his captain's salute, the officer disappeared back into the bridge. Most satisfied with the manner in which they had disposed of a very difficult target, Kostromo angled his line of sight back to the sea before them. Laughing at his silly fears, Josef felt invulnerable. Of course, he knew precisely who to thank for the sophisticated antimissile system that had just won them a reprieve.

It was his father's vision, that had originally prompted the SA-N-10's development. Why even the cruiser they currently sailed upon had been designed and produced to the old admiral's specifications. Proud of his patriarch as never before, Josef swore that he would never let him down. Utilizing every ounce of hard-earned skill, he'd track down the Trident and blow it to the bottom.

Never forgetting the indescribable feeling that had coursed through his body when he made his first kill, the namesake of the Kostromo line craved for this incredible high to be duplicated.

How very frustrating it had been when the *Azov*

sliced through the American attack sub and he had found himself unable to take the credit for its subsequent sinking. Cooled at the time by his father's cautious warnings, Josef now knew how important it had been for him to keep knowledge of this event from the ears of all but a precious few. To do otherwise would have incurred drastic after-effects on both his own career and the very integrity of the Motherland. As his father had so wisely saged at the time, "The imperialists may seem slow to anger, but pity their poor adversary when their wrath has been needlessly aroused."

Faced with a humiliating defeat in Southeast Asia, the Americans would have rallied around such an unwarranted ramming. Since their masses desperately sought a legitimate enemy, Josef's rash actions could have provided them a focal point to voice their frustrations. A full-scale nuclear war could have easily been the result.

At that time, the Soviet Union had still been in the midst of a frantic program to achieve nuclear parity. Today, their efforts had achieved this parity, and much more. Weakened by social unrest and a succession of moronic leaders, the United States was far from the unrivaled power it had been in the 60s. Unwilling to pay the price a modern arsenal demanded, the greedy imperialists had grown fat and overconfident.

In the meantime, the peoples of the U.S.S.R. had done just the opposite. Most aware of the sacrifice military security asked from its beneficiaries, the citizens of the Motherland had agreed to give up a few material advantages to achieve this desired goal. Thousands of new planes, ships, and rockets had rolled off their assembly lines. Never before had the earth seen the likes of such a military build-up.

Exercises like Operation Lenin were only the beginning. To have permitted it to take place, and now to have actually ordered the *Azov* to eliminate the Trident, their leader, Vladimir Kirensk, must have finally seen the light. Josef thought that the crafty general secretary had had something else in mind when he'd agreed to meet Andrew Lyons in that hastily called summit. Their premier must have been baiting the American all this time! Now, they'd show the world the true strengths of the Socialist way of life.

Excited to be on the forefront of this initial confrontation, Captain Josef Kostromo felt proud of the blood that coursed through his veins. With renewed intensity, he lifted his binoculars and scanned the waters before him, fully aware that it was from these depths that he would meet his destiny.

Chapter Sixteen

One hundred and fifty feet below the waters of the Tonga Trench, the muted sounds of the exploding ERCS was barely audible. Conveyed through the sensitive hydrophones of the AUSEX towered-array unit, this blast was picked up as a mere *pop*. Hardly distinguishable from the myriad of other noises that perpetually haunted the seas, it took an experienced sensor analyst to determine its significance.

Lieutenant Junior Grade Anthony Canova was faithfully manning the *Phoenix*'s central sonar position as the Minuteman was intercepted. Hunched tensely over his console with headphones clamped securely over his ears, he was in the process of using the AUSEX device to monitor the approach of unfriendly helicopters. It was while scanning the airspace directly over the sub that the muffled discharge caught his attention. At first, he thought it was just another atmospheric anomaly. To make certain, he rewound the taped recording of the alien noise and played it back at twice its normal volume. Still unable to clearly interpret the sound, he again rewound the tape, this time playing it back at a quarter of its normal speed. With this technique, he was able to pick out the characteristic crack of a high-altitude explosion underlaying the initial signature. Having only heard this particular intonation one time before, Canova felt that it warranted the captain's attention, also.

Charles Blake was in the midst of studying the topological maps of the seafloor to their immediate south when he heard the sonar man's rough voice boom out behind him.

"Skipper, we've got something on AUSEX!"

Without hesitation, Blake broke away from the navigation table, and made his way over to Canova's side. "What have you got, Lieutenant?"

Anthony held up the auxiliary set of headphones. "You'd better take a listen first, Skipper."

Anxiously, Charles put on the headset. The first recording that he was to hear contained a single, distant popping noise. The second was a slower, distinctly louder noise. Puzzled by what he was hearing, Blake pushed back the phones and looked down at the sonar operator.

"Could it be a sonic boom?" the captain guessed.

"I don't think so, Skipper," returned Canova. "At first, I didn't think anything of it—until my curiosity demanded that I play it over at one-quarter speed and twice normal volume. That's when I realized that I've heard that sound before. Do you remember last winter, when we participated in those antiballistic missile tests in the Marshall Islands? Well, that noise you just heard matched almost exactly the signature created by a high-altitude interception of a descending warhead."

Blake replied cautiously. "If it was an ABM, it had to come from those Udaloys. I believe those ships are fitted with the new SA-N-10 missiles that are designed for just such a job. Yet, that would mean that the descending warhead was from one of our Minutemen. What in the hell was its intended target?"

Before Canova could answer, the senior seaman seated on his right turned toward him and spoke out excitedly. "Mr. Canova, our passive acoustic detection system has a definite on that bogey we've been monitoring coming in from the west. It's increased its speed significantly, and continues headed straight for us."

"What's its range, lad?" shot back Canova.

The seaman cleared his throat. "Forty-five miles and closing, sir."

"Forty-five miles!" exclaimed the captain. "How in the hell could we have let them close in on us like they have?"

"Those Russkies must be flying over that water," observed Anthony as he hit the switches allowing him to tap into the sensor system directly monitoring this bogey's approach. It didn't take him long to lock onto it.

"She's got a bone in her teeth, all right!" cried Canova, who pressed down on his headphones. "Must be doing a good thirty-five knots. She's a big one too, with some strange-sounding geared turbines. Hit the signature I.D. recorder, seaman."

Preoccupied with his study, the potbellied junior lieutenant noticed that the captain was tightening his own headphones, and signaling Canova to patch him in also. Flipping a single toggle switch, Anthony accomplished this task.

With the connection complete, Charles Blake was able to listen to the racket the quickly advancing vessel was leaving in its wake. As his attention focused in on the turbulence, his pulse unexplainably quickened. Stirred by the characteristic grinding of powerful, turbine-powered, twin-shaft engines, his body tensed as he picked out the staccato chugging of its geared turbines. Engulfed by a wave of *deja vu*, he was instantly transferred over a decade into the past. For it was from the conning tower of the doomed attack sub *Orca* that he had last heard this very same sound.

The urgent voice of Anthony Canova brought him abruptly back to the present. "We've got that positive

I.D., Skipper. Big Brother shows a ninety-nine-percent probability that she's a Kara Class cruiser. I'm drawing up her specs on the screen now."

Blake looked on, pale and unblinking, as the computer readout flashed alive with this requested data.

Subject: Kara Class cruiser
Displacement: 9,700 tons full load
Dimensions: overall length, 571 feet; beam 60 feet; draught 22 feet.
Propulsion: Four gas turbines, 120,000 hp, two shafts, maximum speed 35 kt.
Armament: 2 quadruple SS-N-14 launchers, 2 RBU 6,000 and 2 RBU 1,000 launchers, 2 retractable SA-N-4 installations, 2 twin 3-inch guns, four 23mm Gatlings, 2 quintuple 21-inch torpedo tubes and silos for SA-N-10 ABMs being fitted.
Aircraft: 1 Ka-25 Hormone helicopter
Complement: 540
Strengths: Vessel is packed with an array of sensors and weapons the likes of which no ship currently in any Western Navy can even remotely begin to match. It is a particularly effective ASW platform. To facilitate this chore, both a hull-mounted LF sonar array and a towed VDS unit is utilized. By combining the pinpoint targetting ability of the Ka-25, plus its more than adequate load of subroc SS-N-14s, the Kara Class cruisers offer a significant threat to submarines.
Weaknesses: none available.

Absorbing this information, Charles Blake couldn't help but be aware of the potent threat this adversary offered. Though he knew his prudent course should be to hightail it to the relative safety of the waters to their east, the captain inexplicably hesitated in issuing any such directive. With his total attention refocused on the sound emanating from his headphones, Blake allowed himself to slip back in time once again. In the midst of recreating the humid, musty smell of the South China Sea, he didn't even notice it when the *Phoenix*'s executive officer entered the command center and rushed to his side.

It didn't take long for Pete Walsh to notice the captain's blank preoccupation, and to size up the situation they currently found themselves in. Meeting Anthony Canova's concerned glance, the XO skimmed the data displayed beneath the glass computer monitor.

"How far is she?" queried Walsh.

"Approximately forty-two miles and closing, sir," answered Canova, his tone flat.

"Then what in the world are we doing just sitting here?" exclaimed the XO. "We've got just enough distance between us to make good an escape run. Otherwise, we're going to be tagged any second now. Those SS-N-14s can be awfully unforgiving!"

Jarred from his stupor, Charles Blake noticed the XO's presence, yet barely acknowledged him. Rubbing the swollen bruise that painfully throbbed on his forehead, the captain shouted out like a man possessed. "Navigation, chart us an attack course! Mr. Walsh, have Chief Crowley ready that Mk-48 at once!"

Barely believing what he was hearing, the exec dared to challenge these orders. "Captain, you can't be seriously considering taking on that cruiser! Even if we did have all four torpedo tubes operating, she's just too powerfully armed for us. Have you forgotten about our present orders already? At least wait until we get our Tridents off."

Staring icily at the XO, Blake replied with a directness most out of character. "So, now you want to add dereliction of duty to your growing list of charges. Must I remind you, Mr. Walsh, that you are merely

319

under probation at the moment. Carry out that order, or I'll have you locked in confinement with that lily-livered scientist friend of yours!"

Resisting the impulse to further challenge the captain's command, Pete hesitantly backed down. Whatever Blake was up to, the XO wanted to be absolutely certain that he was around to personally witness the officer's further actions. Getting himself locked up would gain him nothing. As he reached out for the intercom to page the weapons chief, Walsh found his hand slightly shaking. This nervousness took on an added dimension as the captain's renewed directives boomed out behind him.

"Blow negative! Bring us up to periscope depth. It's time for the *Phoenix* to prove what she's made of!"

Busy at work two floors beneath the command center in the cabin he shared with the XO, Thomas Kraft barely noticed the *Phoenix*'s gradual ascent. Though he did hear the loud, raucous roar of venting ballast, he found the experiment in which he was currently involved much too important to give this alien sound much second thought.

Five minutes ago, Thomas had been sprawled on his bunk, his hopes of proving his theory completely dashed. Frustrated and angry at himself for allowing the captain to intimidate him, Thomas had given up. The whole world could go blow itself up as far as he was concerned.

Such were the nature of his glum thoughts when the door to the cabin had suddenly popped open. Standing beneath the door frame, a devilish grin cutting his face, was Pete Walsh.

"I thought you might be able to put this to good use," the XO had said as he tossed the compact plastic buoy toward Thomas.

Instantly recognizing the familiar object, Kraft had grabbed onto it tightly, as if it were made of the most delicate of crystal. Sitting up, his belief in mankind abruptly reaffirmed, the geophysicist had barely had time for a question.

"How did you ever convince Blake to give this up?"

Walsh had smiled. "Tact, my boy, and also a little old-fashioned thievery. Now, I'd better get topside before I'm missed. Good luck, and let me know the second your tests are completed."

With this, the XO had pivoted and disappeared back into the hallway. Finding himself alone once more, Thomas felt as if a great weight had been lifted from his shoulders. He jumped from the cot, and rushed over to the room's wall-mounted desk. With the help of a compact tool kit that he removed from his duffelbag, he swiftly went to work.

First, he broke open the seal, splitting the buoy into two separate halves. He allowed himself a sigh of relief only after finding the air-scanner device in perfect condition. Shaped like a weather vane, it held a pair of walnut-sized capsules on each of its spindly rotating arms. Inside these containers were the samples he so desperately needed.

Emptying the contents of the duffel bag at his feet, Kraft covered the desk with a thick, rubberized cotton tablecloth. Next, he donned a set of translucent surgical gloves. Opening a compact hinged case, he removed the instruments he would need for the first of the tests. These included a heavy plastic specimen container, into which one of the air samples would be introduced, and three vials of differently colored solvent solutions. An interaction of these fluids would show if the air above them held any noticeable amounts of radioactivity. If this test proved negative, he would

proceed with a second experiment, which actually
broke down and identified all but the most minute o
airborne particles that the sample held. It was at this
point that he hoped to find the pumice and ash to
provide the solid evidence proving his theory.

Thomas was well into the first of these tests when the
bubbling sound of what he assumed to be venting
ballast momentarily caught his attention. His assumption appeared to be a correct one, when, seconds later,
the hinged case that had been lying flat on the desk
began sliding toward him. Oblivious to the fact that the
Phoenix was gradually ascending, the scientist surrendered himself to a much more immediate concern.

"Periscope depth, Captain."

Mark Peterson's words seemed to have a hollow ring
as they echoed out into the tensely silent command
center. All attention seemed riveted on the tall figure o
Charles Blake as he positioned himself behind the
rising steel column of the periscope. Yanking down this
device's two, short collapsible arms, he turned along
with the rotating tube until it provided him an unobstructed view of the western horizon.

Pressing his eyes snugly against the hard rubber
coupling, Blake fine-tuned the lens to meet his specifi
cations. Even with the weakest magnification, it took
him less than a minute to focus in on the cruiser's
sharp, angled bow. Still forty miles distant, he had to
increase the power of the lens ten-fold in order to get a
decent view of the forward superstructure. Characterized by a massive top-sail radar array set before a
single, huge square funnel, the vessel appeared sleek
and fully armed.

"What do you think of this little baby, Mr. Walsh?"
the captain quizzed as he backed away and beckoned

he XO to have a look.

Pete stepped forward and gripped the scope's stubby djustor arms. He needed to take only the briefest of lances before standing erect and replying.

"I think that cruiser is way out of our class."

"Oh, come now, Mr. Walsh. For all of your brave alk, you disappoint me. Where's your spirit of adventure?"

As the XO looked on, puzzled by the captain's esponse, Blake again positioned himself behind the eriscope. This time he reached up and activated its naximum magnifying lense. As a result, the cruiser eemed to jump up and practically be running right ver them.

Charles carefully fine-tuned the adjustor mechaism. Slowly, he inched the lens's directional hairs to ncompass that portion of the superstructure visible eneath the dual fire-control radar cones. What he saw here made him weak in the knees. Standing on the xposed walkway set in front of the boxlike bridge was single, white-uniformed figure. Like a phantom from he past come suddenly alive, this individual's dark, eady eyes and red, curly hair could belong to but one erson.

"Prepare to fire the Mk-48 at the following coordiates," responded Blake, his eyes still snuggled up aside the coupling. "Mark, one-nine-zero degrees est, three-seven-six degrees north. Set for passive coustic homing."

"But that would make it a bow-on shot," rebutted the XO frantically. "If you're going to go through with this nad scheme, at least let's position ourselves to put our sh smack into that cruiser's midsection."

"Stow it, Mr. Walsh!" the captain returned angrily. "I aink I'm quite capable of directing this attack. If you eel otherwise, you can voice yourself now."

Fighting to restrain himself, Pete's silence was all that the captain needed. Reaching for the intercom handset, Blake personally conveyed his orders to the forward torpedo room.

"Chief Crowley, targeting by the use of passive acoustic signals has been completed. If the Mk-48 is ready, you are free to launch."

Walsh counted ten, long seconds, when the *Phoenix* seemed to gently shudder. This movement was followed by a distant surge of *swooshing*, compressed air.

"We've got a strong propellor!" shouted Anthony Canova. "So far, her course seems right on the mark."

A tense stillness possessed the compartment as Charles Blake took one last look at their target and almost reluctantly, backed away.

"Down scope!" he ordered firmly. "Mr. Peterson, take us down to the threshold of the thermocline. Our course will remain the same, at patrol speed."

"Aye, aye, sir," replied the helmsman, who began cautiously pushing down the steering yoke.

Watching all this as if he were in a daze, Pete Walsh could only pray that their captain knew what he was doing. By not putting the sub into an immediate evasive dive at emergency speeds, he was almost taking it for granted that their torpedo would hit home. How unlike this was from the cool, collective, "play it by the book" skipper he had known for the last three years. Why, it was almost as if an entirely different man presently stood inside Blake's shoes.

Perhaps that bump on the captain's head had done more damage than he originally admitted, pondered the XO.

To be in the best position to monitor their situation, Pete began making his way over to the sonar console. Conscious of the unnatural quiet that permeated the compartment, he found himself taking light, careful steps so as not to upset the delicate equilibrium that was present here. Only when he was solidly set behind the portly figure of Anthony Canova, did Walsh turn to see where the captain had positioned himself. To his continued amazement, he found Blake still standing beside the drawn-up periscope. His hands folded tightly in front of his chest, the *Phoenix*'s commander had his vacant gaze angled down at his feet.

"Propellor whine remains good," instructed the sonar man, breaking Pete from his observation. "Range is one-nine miles and continuing to close."

Most cognizant of the variety of obstacles that the Mk-48 would still have to overcome in order to penetrate its target, the XO figured that it had about a fifty percent chance of doing so. That was why attacks such as this one were much more effective when at least a pair of torpedoes were utilized. For good measure, he would have liked to throw in a couple of Harpoons. With a range of over thirty miles beyond that of the Mk-48s, the subrocs would have practically guaranteed a kill. Yet, they had lost the chance to use these effective weapons with the untimely failure of the torpedo tubes' O-ring sealant gaskets. Fortunate to have been able to launch the Mk-48, Walsh was very aware that unless the O-rings could somehow be salvaged, the *Phoenix* was now totally defenseless.

Scanning the compartment, Pete studied each member of the command team. Equally concerned, the men sat by rigidly. Only an occasional cough and the constant mechanical hum of the boat around them broke the silence. When his gaze returned to the captain, the XO realized that Blake had yet to alter his position. The Exec was wondering what the man's thoughts could possibly be, when Canova's voice boomed out loudly for all to hear.

"I've got an increase in whine frequency. . . . I'm

325

beginning to lose her in the turbulence churned up by the target. . . . The two signatures are indistinguishable."

Since this could indicate that the Mk-48 had either initiated its final attack surge, or had merely run out of fuel, Pete knew that the next couple of seconds would be most critical. After wiping a thin line of sweat from his forehead, he glanced down to check his watch. Twenty-five long seconds had passed when a muffled series of explosions boomed in the far distance.

"We got her!" Canova cried as he reached to turn down the volume feed to his headphones. "It sounds like the Mk-48 hit them right in the forward ammo magazine. The whole ship is breaking up!"

Glancing up to check the effects of this report on their captain, Walsh found Blake's stare glued to his own.

As a wide, warm smile broke his weary face, the skipper looked almost like his old self once again. Just as if a curse had suddenly been broken, Charles Blake's entire body seemed lighter and more full of life.

Suspicious of his own sanity, the XO hardly noticed the cheering of the men around him. Confused and fatigued, he didn't bother to join in on this celebration, as his mind considered a single fact. In less than an hour from this exact moment, the *Phoenix*'s rear, outer superstructure would open, and twenty-three Trident C-4 missiles would begin their apocalyptic journey to the northwest.

Cheer well, my friends, the XO thought morosely. In sixty more minutes, there will be nothing left to celebrate.

Chapter Seventeen

Senior Lieutenant Yuri Gribovka, of the Alfa Class attack sub *Magadan*, sat stiffly at the sub's radio panel. His back sore and legs cramped, the thirty-year-old officer couldn't wait to be relieved. Well into his second consecutive round of duty, he was not only physically tired, but was also bored of his routine task and hungry as a bear in spring. Ever since he had been allowed back inside the control room, his job had been the same. Monotonously switching the radio receiver's frequency dial, he vainly monitored the bands reserved for the world's communications relay stations. Except for a short burst of puzzling telemetry data, which he had picked up less than an hour ago, his efforts had been fruitless. Streaming into his bulky headphones was a seemingly endless blast of throaty static. Not sure how much longer he'd have to continue this dull chore, Yuri supposed it was a better way of passing the time than being locked inside his quarters.

Although his confrontation with the captain had taken place only hours ago, it seemed apparent that Kalinin was already forgetting the incident. Earlier, after the Trident was sunk and the zampolit had shared some vodka with the *Magadan*'s commander, Kalinin had actually looked him right in the eye and managed a bare smile. Surely this meant that the man's attitude toward him was softening. Of course, their present situation could be responsible for this sudden change of heart.

Isolated beneath the seas, without the benefits of outside communications, the *Magadan* patrolled the depths while the superpowers waged war around them. Each member of the crew shared a common concern: Had their loved ones survived the initial hostilities? Certain that his apartment inside Vladivostok would have been one of the first to be hit, Yuri had already come to the conclusion that he would see his Katrina and their two infant sons no more. Yet, until he knew for certain, that nagging doubt persisted. Had they had sufficient warning to get to one of the dozens of well-stocked bomb shelters that dotted the city? — or perhaps the imperialists hadn't hit them at all. Hoping that the radio receiver he was presently operating would give him at least a clue to their condition, the senior lieutenant continued scanning the frequency bands with a renewed sense of urgency. He was just repeating a survey of the VLF wavelengths when a firm hand grasped his right shoulder. Startled by this unexpected touch, Gribovka turned with a start, and set eyes on the sub's political officer.

"Any luck, Comrade?" greeted the immaculately groomed figure of Sergei Vengerovo.

Warily, Yuri pushed his headphones back off his ears. "I'm afraid that there's nothing to report but that endless static."

The zampolit shook his head. "This lack of communications is most nerve-wracking, Senior Lieutenant. It was assumed that EMP would disrupt the airwaves for the first couple of hours following a nuclear attack, but nothing to this extent. Surely, there must be a radio station operating somewhere."

"Not only am I unable to pick up our own signals, but also those of the Americans. Both South America and Australia as well, appear similarly silent."

With this dismal report, Vengerovo calmly smoothed down his shiny blond hair. "We mustn't lose hope yet, Comrade. I am most confident that the Motherland can survive even the most dastardly of Yankee sneak attacks. Just the fact of our own survival means that others like us have prevailed as well."

This response was followed by the sound of a series of distant, muted explosions, barely audible outside the sub's hull. Meeting the political officer's concerned glance, Yuri no longer felt like they were alone. He looked on as the zampolit hastily made his way over toward the sonar console. Also headed quickly toward that portion of the crowded control room was the captain. Wishing that he could join them there also, to find out firsthand the causes of those blasts, Gribovka instead reluctantly refitted his headphones. Reaching forward, he began switching the frequency selector to those bands reserved for ships in distress.

"What in the name of Hades is going on up there?" Victor Kalinin questioned brusquely. He had to wait several seconds for the sonarman's reply.

"I've rewound the audio tape and I'm presently feeding it back into the computer," returned the petty officer in charge of the *Magadan*'s sonar operations. "I believe we picked up a screw pattern, similar to that of a torpedo, immediately before the blast itself."

This information caused the color to drain from Kalinin's face. Aware now of the zampolit's intense, puzzled stare, Victor continued to ignore him. Concentrating his attention on the seated petty officer, the captain watched him busily address the computer's keyboard.

"Run that section of tape back at full volume, over the control room's public-address system for added clarity," ordered Kalinin. "We must know exactly what's going on here!"

After hitting a series of switches, the sonarman looked up as a loud, electronic hum echoed from the two elevated speakers mounted in each of the room's corners. Gradually, this hum faded, to be replaced by a distant, staccato chugging sound. Though this grinding noise predominated, a buzzing, high-pitched whine could be heard, slowly gaining with intensity. The strength of this alien tone built for a full minute, when it suddenly seemed to merge with that of the stronger chugging sound. Another thirty seconds passed, and a thunderous, ear-splitting blast poured forth from the speakers. This deafening explosion was followed by a distinct series of at least a half-dozen reverberating detonations. After the last of these discharges faded, the rending sound of splitting steel signaled that whatever had been hit was quickly breaking apart. Kalinin beckoned the petty officer to cut the feed when the cries of the vessel's doomed sailors could clearly be heard, screaming in agony in the distance.

Hesitantly, the sonar operator addressed the two senior officers standing behind him. "The computer analysis is completed, Captain. Both of the sound signatures that preceded the explosions have been positively identified. The dominant sound belonged to the geared turbines of a Kara Class cruiser, while the secondary noise source came from an American Mk-48 torpedo."

These words had a sickening effect on both of the men who stood behind him. The zampolit finally dared to question the shocked figure standing on his left.

"But I thought that these waters were clear? Could you have been somehow mistaken when you assumed that the Trident had been eliminated?"

Unable to respond, the captain could only shrug his shoulders. Taking in this pitiful gesture, the political officer found his thoughts filled with nothing but isdain for the men who stood beside him. Once again, e doubted Kalinin's very ability to command the essel on which they sailed.

Their captain was nothing but a weak-willed, spoiled mbecile. How could he possibly have allowed them to e fooled so by the imperialists? And just look at this nisjudgment's disastrous results!

That Kara Class cruiser could only be the *Azov* erself. Commanding this ship's complement of five undred and forty was Admiral Kostromo's own son! Iauseated by such a realization, Sergei felt his belly oil in stunned protest.

If only he had trusted his original instincts, and had omehow relieved Kalinin of his command earlier. His nprovoked outburst of anger against Senior Lieutennt Gribovka, for not calling him when the Trident ave them the slip, had just been the first indication of heir captain's instability. When the man had ordered hat frantic search to begin, at speeds dangerous to heir very survival, Sergei should have been certain of is gross incompetencies.

To think that he had actually toasted to Kalinin's rilliance when the Trident was presumed sunk! Most kely, their subroc had only hit a mere decoy. What ools the Americans must think that the Soviet Navy as comprised of.

Angry and frustrated beyond belief, Sergei Iengerovo took in one last glimpse of their moronic aptain. Sneering in utter contempt, he studied the vay Kalinin slovenly stood there, staring out dumbly oward the sonar screen. Such were the inevitable esults when one was brought up without knowing the rue toil that life was made of. Kalinin's service record aade it most obvious that he had never had to really ork for anything in his entire life. Handed his comiission on a gold platter because of the previous duty

of his father and grandfather, Victor Kalinin was proof
positive of the weakness of the bourgeoise.

Turning in disgust, the zampolit managed to hold
back his temper. Sounding off now would only upset
the crew's already poor morale. Better that the channel
his rage into the pages of his official diary. At least such
a documentation could point out this weakness in their
system for all to see. Hardly aware of the curious stare
of the crew as he silently crossed the compartment, the
political officer hurried toward the shelter of his state
room.

Watching Vengerovo disappear out the forward
hatchway, Victor Kalinin tried hard to stir himself into
action. Unfortunately, the traumatic after-effects of the
macabre tape that they had just heard made any
movement impossible. Shocked into inaction, all he
could do was mentally replay the cries of the doomed
crew as their ship broke up around them.

No one was more aware of his shortcomings than he
was. The sinking of the *Azov* and the certain loss of her
crew were his direct responsibility. This was a realization that he would take with him to his grave.

By being too hasty in his assumption that they had
eliminated the Trident, Kalinin had failed both his
country and his bloodline. That once-proud naval
tradition handed down by Victor's father, and to him
by his father, was now tinged by the cowardly veil of
disgrace. This dishonor would haunt him eternally.

Only minutes ago, how well he had thought things
were going. Certain that he had carried out the first
part of his war plans, and that he shared these waters
with no other Western submarines, he had just been
beginning to make some progress with the second half
of his orders.

As the *Magadan* had continued its way southward
down the Tonga Trench, their sensors had been picking

up a series of anomalies which could very well mean that Delta Base was close-by. These readings had reached the sub while it was approaching the sector dominated by the Vavau Seamount. The first hint that something out of the ordinary was occurring outside their hull came in the form of a temperature inversion. Even though they were cruising at a depth well within the thermocline, their external thermometers had picked up temperatures much more indicative of the warmer surface waters.

At their depth of over six hundred feet, the surrounding water should have been icily cold. Yet instead of finding a continued temperature drop of at least one degree centigrade with each meter of increased depth, the thermometer was actually rising! This could only mean that they were approaching an area warmed in an unnatural manner. Delta Base's nuclear reactor could well be the cause of this.

Of an equally interesting nature were the series of strange noises that their hydrophones were picking up from these depths. Far from being produced by the creatures that normally made these oceans their homes, the strange crackling, hissing sounds could also be attributed to man.

Victor had just been comparing their topographical map of the trench's bottom with the information their sonar was currently beaming up when the first explosion had diverted his attention. He had been hoping to find an altered landmass to provide Delta's exact location, but the captain now knew that such activities would have to be placed on the back burner for the meantime. At the moment, they had a much greater responsibility: the souls of five hundred and forty of his comrades begged from their watery graves to be revenged. To accomplish this task, he had to regain control of his shocked senses. Taking in a deep breath, he spurred himself into action.

"Comrade Kungrad, is it possible to determine the direction that the Mk-48 approached from?"

The sonarman alertly nodded and issued this request into his keyboard. Seconds later, he read the answer from the computer's glass monitor screen.

"It appears to have been following a northwesterly course at the moment of intercept, Captain."

Kalinin made some hasty mental calculations. "I want you to determine the exact fix of that intercept point, and transfer these coordinates into the map gracing the navigation table."

Nodding in response, the petty officer began this task while Victor made his way to the counter that held a computer-enhanced, three-dimensional map of the northern portion of the Southwestern Pacific Basin. Starting at the island of Tutuila, he traced a narrowing band of dark blue water as it followed the eastern wall of a vast, subterranean mountain range southward. Approximately halfway down this sector was a small isolated mound, cut off to the east from the rest of the range. This he knew to be the Vavau Seamount.

Kalinin looked on as a tiny red dot began blinking some thirty-seven nautical miles to the northwest of Vavau. Tracing an imaginary line to the southeast, Victor considered what he knew of the Mk-48's maximum range. A straight, bow-on shot could have been launched from a position forty miles distant. If this had indeed been the case, he had a pretty good idea exactly where he'd find the murderers responsible for the sinking of the *Azov*.

Because the *Magadan*'s current position put them a good fifty miles away from this spot, he knew that they'd need every last bit of power to get into striking range within the next hour. Deciding that a pair of SS-N-14s would be more than sufficient to finish off the

Trident once and for all, Victor Kalinin turned to issue the orders that would at least temporarily clear his guilty conscience.

At the exact same moment that the *Magadan*'s Captain issued the orders sending them at full power northward, President Andrew Lyons convened a meeting with his top two military advisors. The E-4B's conference room was deserted except for these three individuals. Lyons sat at the head of the rectangular table, his gray pin-striped jacket removed, his vest unbuttoned, and sleeves rolled up. On his right sat Secretary of Defense Russell Tate. To his left, General Barton Sachs. Both of them sat stiffly, with their jackets still in place.

In the midst of jotting down a series of notes on his legal pad, the president looked up, concerned, when the plane around them violently shook. The General noticed this and responded.

"We shouldn't have much more of this rough air left. Radar showed a large Arctic high-pressure system moving down over Hudson Bay. The last report from the flight crew put us just about over the southern portion of the Bay."

"The smooth ride will be appreciated," returned Lyons. "Especially during the next sixty minutes. I'm sure both of you are aware that Admiral Burnhardt called me approximately five minutes ago. I'm afraid that he had some bad news. The Minuteman holding the ERCS exploded only seconds before it was to begin transmitting its message to the *Phoenix*."

Both Tate and Sachs appeared genuinely shocked by this information. The Secretary of Defense asked, "Did he know why it went down like it did?"

Andrew massaged his forehead, where a splitting

headache persisted. "That's the puzzling part. The rocket was long out of its booster phase. With engines jettisoned, it was initiating its descent through the stratosphere when we lost contact with it. The best guess is that it burned up during re-entry."

Barton Sachs alertly sat forward. "Sounds to me like it could have been knocked out by an ABM. It's believed that several Soviet surface ships have been fitted out with the new SA-N-10 interceptor. This missile is reported to be extremely effective against our ICBMs."

"Although that's possible, I seriously doubt it, Bart. I talked with Kirensk personally, only minutes before the Minuteman was launched. The first secretary was very supportive of our plan. He even promised to immediately inform elements of their fleet in the South Pacific to allow the warhead to penetrate the atmosphere."

"You know my feelings on trusting a Russian, Mr. President," the general retorted icily.

Clearly irritated by this remark, Lyons strained to control himself. "Your suspicions are noted, General. No matter what the reason was for the ERCS to fail, we are still faced with our dilemma."

"What about TACAMO?" Russell Tate queried.

Andrew checked his watch before answering. "The C-130 is still a good hour away from the area where it can begin effectively transmitting. Unfortunately, it's being further delayed by a stream of powerful headwinds. The *Phoenix* will be facing its S.I.O.P. launch orders in a little less than fifty-five minutes. Right now, it doesn't look like that plane is going to catch them in time."

"Has everyone here forgotten about Milstar?" challenged Burton Sachs. "The first step of this same S.I.O.P. instructs the *Phoenix* to launch its number one Trident independently of the others. Inside the nose cone of this missile sits one of our finest little communications satellites ever produced. Only if the sub is unable to receive orders countermanding the original Cocked Pistol alert, after this satellite is activated, will Captain Blake proceed with the launch sequence."

"Exactly what are we going to use to contact this satellite?" quizzed Russell Tate.

The general's eyes gleamed. "Earlier, I took the liberty of placing a call down to the Consolidated Space Operations Center near Colorado Springs. We just happen to have an all-military space shuttle orbiting the planet at the moment. In an hour's time, they'll be smack over the South Pacific. By tapping into the Milstar using their extremely high frequency transmitter, the shuttle crew can convey the coded message that will send that sub back to Bangor."

Andrew Lyons caught his defense secretary's hopeful gaze. "That sounds too good to be true. You know, I was almost ready to throw in the towel. I hate to be a spoilsport, but since everything that has possibly gone wrong has done so today, how do you think the Soviets would react if Milstar failed and those Tridents were launched?"

After a thoughtful pulse, the general was the first to attempt an answer. "If I know the Russians, one thing that they're certainly not going to do is just sit back and let those one hundred and eighty four, 100-kt MIRV'd warheads blow apart a good chunk of their country. At the very least, they'll demand to eliminate an equal amount of U.S. territory."

"Surely, we'd never allow them to do such a thing!" Tate returned vehemently.

As calm as he could manage, Lyons responded. "Wouldn't you expect me to do the same if that was a Soviet sub out there, ready to launch its load of SS-N-18s? What else can we do?"

Barton Sachs pushed his chair back and spoke out forcefully. "We can launch an immediate, bolt-out-of-the-blue, surgical nuclear attack! By taking the initiative, I can almost guarantee you that our warheads can cut off the Russians' ability to order any type of counterattack. With a minimum of civilian casualties, we could strike a crippling blow aimed at eliminating their military command posts, communications relay stations, and ICBM fields. This, Mr. President, is the only way that we can be certain that needless American lives won't be taken."

Rebutting this emotional outburst was Andrew Lyons. "That's no answer to our problem, Bart. It would only put us in a worse of a mess. How in the hell did we get ourselves into such a predicament, anyway?"

"Defense Department directive one-three-nine," returned Tate. "Fearing just such a Soviet decapitating attack, we decided to give our submarine commanders authority to launch their load of missiles if no other communications is received after the initial alert is given. This would guarantee an answer on our part to any attack that would cripple the other two elements of our triad."

Lyons shifted his weight uneasily. "I guess, with all the redundant communications systems, we never considered something like a simple volcano cocking things up. This has certainly been one hell of a day for screw-ups!"

Grasping the edge of the table as the plane's fuselage was buffeted by a strong gust of wind, the president held on tightly. He somberly addressed his two assistants.

"We can only pray that Milstar does the trick. I want to thank you both for your continued support. In this desperate, dark hour, the world's population is counting on us to make the right decision. We can not let them down. Now, if you'll excuse me, I think I'd like to have some time for myself."

Taking this cue, both Barton Sachs and Russell Tate excused themselves. Alone in the conference room, Andrew looked at the seal of his office as his thoughts struggled for some sort of overall perspective.

Less than six hours ago, he had looked at vehicles such as the Boeing E-4B on which he presently rode as mere instruments in a readiness exercise. One call from General Theodore Bowman had changed all this, and what had started as a test run turned abruptly into a legitimate crisis. The second DSP North had picked up the signature of that heat flare outside the Siberian city of Vankarem, a series of seemingly unrelated events had followed, each driving them ever closer to the actualization of the ultimate nightmare. First there had been that mistakenly targeted cruise missile, and then, DSP South's activation. And what had appeared to be a NUDET in the South Pacific had turned out to be something much different. Who could have ever guessed that a mere volcano could be indirectly responsible for leading the superpowers to the brink of World War III?

Astounded by such a realization, Andrew was once more aware of the tight, painful knot that had gathered in the pit of his stomach. Would General Sachs's hopeful observation indeed come to pass, and the *Phoenix*'s own Milstar satellite convey to them the orders diverting them from war? After what had happened to their ERCS, Lyons knew that he could take absolutely nothing for granted.

The only thing that he was sure of was his countrymen's overwhelming desire to prevent a nuclear confrontation if at all possible. Yet, just by having such weapons available made such an exchange inevitable.

His summit meeting with Vladimir Kirensk had put

into motion the first initiative to the eventual banning of such weapons from the face of the planet. Unfortunately, such a move had come too late; the planet's luck had worn out, just as it was bound to have happened at some time or another.

To reaffirm his commitment to the principles of world peace, Andrew knew that he must call the first secretary one more time. He would tell him of the failure of the ERCS, and explain the manner in which they hoped to use the Milstar to diffuse their shared dilemma.

As to what would occur if the satellite failed to achieve its mission, Lyons could only emphasize America's abhorrence of unprovoked nuclear warfare. This was one principle of which both men had a common understanding. Yet how would the Soviet leader react if the worst-case scenario prevailed and the Tridents were launched? Would Kirensk issue his own attack, as General Sachs believed would be the case, or would he have the strength to merely turn the other cheek? Gambling that Kirensk was a man of compassion, Andrew prayed that the first secretary wouldn't be forced to make such a decision.

Conscious of the smooth drone of the E-4B's engines as they sucked in the cold air above Canada's Hudson Bay, the president reached out to pick up the handset of the red telephone. Hastily checking his watch, he saw that they had less than fifty minutes until the first of the Tridents were scheduled to break the surface of the Pacific. Trapped in a snare of its own making, humankind was getting just what it deserved, as its very survival now depended on the fickle whim of destiny.

Chapter Eighteen

Of all the compartments aboard the USS *Phoenix*, none were as unique as that one fondly labeled "Sherwood Forest." Set behind the sail, between the forward section of the vessel and the reactor room, it was here that the sub's twenty-four missile tubes were located. Positioned in two linear lines of twelve apiece, the circular steel launch silos indeed resembled the trunks of an ancient forest. Yet this was as far as the resemblance went, for inside these tubes were the sophisticated devices that the boat had initially been designed to carry.

Some 13 inches smaller than the silo itself, each Trident C-4 missile rose 34.1 feet high, with a 74-inch diameter. Each of the 24 SLBMs weighed over 70,000 pounds. To keep the missiles from shaking around, and to stabilize their trajectory during launch, a protective elastomeric liner pad was bonded to the inside of each tube. Set down the length of this pad was a line of explosive charges, to be triggered at the moment of launch to allow the Tridents unobstructed liftoff.

Currently responsible for this lethal load was Chief Petty Officer Louis Crowley. A fifteen-year navy veteran, the chief had begun his career aboard a Lafayette Class strategic-missile carrying submarine. Acting as the Trident's predecessor, the Lafayettes had been the definitive U.S. subs of the 1960s and 70s. Originally fitted with Polaris A-2 missiles, such vessels continued serving their country, even today.

As Louis ambled his solid, six-foot frame down the metallic catwalk that divided Sherwood Forest in half, he found his thoughts returning to those early days of service. How proud he had been to serve his country in such a manner. The Polaris A-2s had been the most advanced weapons of their type available at that time. Yet compared to the Trident, they were almost primitive. Not only was the C-4 able to go over twice the distance, it also carried a significantly larger load of warheads, delivering them with a much higher degree of accuracy. Well aware of the amazing technological advances that he had witnessed in his years of service, the chief was just as proud of his present assignment as he had been of his first.

Like a nightmare come abruptly true, today's unbelievable activities were allowing the years of hard work and incessant training to finally pay off. Only when the captain had actually given him the command to launch the Mk-48, had the reality of it all come into focus. By the time the torpedo had plowed into the Soviet cruiser's bow, this reality had completely sunk in. The world was at war once again. The unthinkable had occurred just as he always feared would eventually happen.

Having remained a bachelor throughout the years, and with little family still alive to speak of, Louis had no one in particular to worry about but the country as a whole. If everything went as originally scheduled, the *Phoenix* would be doing its bit to punish the enemy in less than a quarter of an hour. The captain had included him in the briefing that covered their present S.I.O.P. Even with this information, he still had trouble distinguishing their present war plans from one of the hundreds of exercises he had been involved with in the past. Only a gathering tightness in his gut made their current situation different.

Louis had just completed his cursory inspection of Sherwood Forest, and was standing in the compartment's rear, when he noticed that he was not alone. From the room's forward hatch, an indistinct figure could be seen gradually approaching. Positioned between tubes number one and two, the chief peered down the catwalk's length trying to identify this figure. The person's face hidden by the shadows of the twenty-two remaining silos, all that Crowley could positively distinguish were the crisp tones of the stranger's footsteps as they echoed off the metallic walkway. This visitor was able to proceed nearly halfway down the corridor before the chief finally identified him.

"Captain Blake," the surprised chief greeted with a crisp salute. "I wasn't expecting you, sir."

Dwarfed by the surrounding silos, the tall officer halted between tubes three and four. Returning Crowley's salute, he firmly answered him.

"I realize that, Chief. Just wanted to check things out personally before the big moment dawns on us. How do things look?"

"Excellent, sir. All fire-control systems are armed and functioning perfectly."

Blake winked. "That's what I was expecting to hear from you, Chief. I want to thank you again for getting that Mk-48 off like you did. It certainly did its job. How did that O-ring hold out?"

"Like I expected, it blew immediately after the launch. This time, though, we were ready for it. We had the tube sealed without further leakage in less than a minute. Say, Skipper, that bruise on your noggin is getting awfully nasty looking. Have you had the doc take a look at it yet?"

Charles waved him away. "It's nothing to worry about, Chief. Only a little scratch. I'll have it looked at as soon as we get these little ladies off."

Taking several steps forward, the captain carefully pressed the flats of his palms against the smooth, rounded surface of launch tube number one. "Ever put a Milstar into orbit before, Lou?"

"This will be my first, Captain."

"Ditto for me, Chief," returned Blake. "We'll handle her just like she was one of the warhead-carrying varieties.

The chief bent over to check the silo's pressure gauges. "How long will we wait afterward, until we fire off the rest of them?"

Charles hesitated. "That depends on how much time the satellite takes to become operational, and what it picks up once it does. If my suspicions remain correct, we'll be able to start emptying the rest of the magazine approximately ten minutes after this baby is sent airborne."

Patting the silo for good measure, Blake stepped backward and turned to study the rest of the compartment. Angling his line of sight down the catwalk's length, he took in the forest of other tubes ending at the distant hatchway leading to the sub's bow. The chief finally broke the moment of contemplative silence.

"It sure is hard to believe that this whole thing is really coming down like it is. Funny how I never actually thought that this day would ever come."

With his glance still surveying the room's depths, Blake responded. "I know how you feel, Chief. It appears that our days of being the peacekeepers are over. We've got a new duty now. We're going to have to hang tough to make sure that this revenge force gets off in A-1 condition."

"I wonder what took place topside to precipitate this crisis?"

Slowly, the captain met the chief's concerned glance. "I think specifics don't really matter. Each side carries just as much blame as the other. Eventually this day just had to come. What matters now is that the United States prevails in this madness. At the moment, we'd better one step of our S.I.O.P. at a time. I'd better be getting back to the command center to check on how the last-minute targeting procedure is going. Are you going to be all right down here, Chief?"

Flashing the captain a thumbs-up, Crowley responded without hesitation. "Don't you worry about a thing, Skipper. Just give me the word, and I'll get these little ladies skyward one way or the other."

Following these words with a salute, the chief looked on as Blake began his way back up the catwalk with a quick, fluid pace. As the sound of his captain's footsteps faded in the distance, Louis Crowley found himself contemplating the conversation he had just completed.

The captain seemed tense, yet totally in control. The great strain he was under showed itself in the dark circles that painted his eyes. Certainly, the nasty gash on the forehead that he had received earlier didn't make this stress any easier to cope with.

Louis was glad that he had made the decision, years ago, to keep from becoming a member of the officer corps. Though such a commission had been offered to him on several occasions, he had always felt that the added responsibilities were not for him. The pressures of his duty were great enough, without having to worry if the rest of the sub's crew were doing their jobs or not.

With this thought in mind, Crowley noticed that the compartment's forward hatch was in the process of being sealed shut. Alone again, he reached into his top pocket, and removed his trusty corn-cob pipe. Placing it securely in his mouth, he began his way up the catwalk one more time, taking a second to double check the series of gauges placed at the base of each of the twenty-four launch tubes.

Pete Walsh was in the process of updating the *Phoenix*'s Mk-98 FCS fire control system when he noticed the captain enter the command center and proceed immediately to his side. Not stopping to acknowledge his presence, the XO continued his complicated task as the time for the first scheduled launch quickly approached.

When the first missile left its tube, the Mk-98 FCS system would have to know two precise positions: that of the *Phoenix* and that of the target. This information would allow a CEP, or Circular Error Probable, of a mere 300 meters. This CEP was the measure of the warhead's accuracy. The more precise this figure became, the greater the chance that the target would be destroyed.

Since their S.I.O.P. had instructed them to empty their first tube independently of the others, Pete was currently tapping into the sub's Mk-2, MOD 7 Ship's Inertial Navigation System, or SINS for short. This data would provide the initial Trident with the *Phoenix*'s precise fix by using interconnected gyroscopes, accelerometers, and computers to relate the *Phoenix*'s present position to that of true north. Walsh was waiting for the computer to complete this computation when the captain quietly said, "How's it coming, Pete?"

Surprised with Blake's informality, the XO softened the tone of his response. "We just need SINS to do its job, and we'll be ready to go up here."

Charles managed a bare smile. "Well, the chief

prepared to launch when we are. Look, Pete, I want to thank you for riding this thing out with me. I know I've been a little difficult to put up with these last couple of hours."

"Forget it, Skipper," returned the exec. "I can just imagine the pressure that you're under."

"That's something all of us share," added Blake. "It's the not knowing what's happening upstairs that makes it so damned difficult. Once we get Milstar in orbit, events should be much clearer. Until then, I think that it's time that I had a word with the crew."

Accepting the XO's compassionate nod, Blake reached over to pick up the intercom handset. After he punched in a single digit, three loud, interspaced electronic tones sounded forth from the *Phoenix*'s public-address system. This was followed by the captain's steady voice.

"All hands, this is your captain speaking. I'm sure that by now, each one of you has gotten wind of the scuttlebutt pertaining to the *Phoenix*'s present alert status. Though I wish that I could tell you otherwise, for the past five hours we have been under a state of alert analogous to that of an actual war. In the next few minutes, we will be emptying the first of our missile tubes. Loaded inside this Trident's nose cone is a Milstar communications satellite. By the use of this device, we will be afforded actual proof that a state of hostilities exists between ourselves and the Soviet Union.

"If countermanding orders are not received at this time, the *Phoenix* will proceed with its predetermined attack plan. By the grace of God, we pray that such a course of action is not necessary. Yet if it is, you can rest assured that we will strike the enemy a crippling blow! Your thousands of hours of diligent service have allowed such a counterattack to be possible. Though

347

your thoughts are most likely to be focused on the fate
of your loved ones back home, your one-hundred
percent effort is needed now to revenge the dastardl
actions of our enemies. To your stations, men, an
may God bless America in this hour of need!"

A full thirty seconds of tense silence followed; th
portion of the crew present in the command cente
watched their captain breathlessly. Breaking this spell
Blake called out sharply.

"Sound General Quarters! Mr. Peterson, bring u
up to launch depth. Lieutenant Canova, what's th
status of those two remaining bogeys?"

Tony Canova replied loudly over the harsh, persist
ent tone sending the crew to their action station
"Those Udaloys are continuing to slowly move in o
our present position from the north and south. Bot
ships are still well over fifty nautical miles distant."

Reacting instantly to this information, Charles Blak
stepped over to join his XO at the fire-control pane
"We've still got plenty of time to launch, Pete. What
the status of SINS?"

Walsh skimmed the data visible under the monitor
screen. "We've got more than sufficient data to plac
Trident number one in a geosynchronous orbit abov
the South Pacific, Skipper."

This response was followed by a report from the
helmsman. "Launch depth, Captain!"

Well aware that the fated time had arrived, Pe
Walsh joined the captain at the launch panel. Slidin
out the pair of portable seats that were stored beneat
the consoles when not needed, both officers sat dow
Each removed a single key from his breast pocket. Bot
readied these keys before the set of dual unlock mech
nisms placed a full arm's length away from each othe
Charles Blake initiated the coordinated movemen
that followed.

"Key inserts! Key turn!"

This simultaneous action opened the two panels fully. Each officer faced a set of identical controls. These were dominated by twenty-four individual red-plastic switches. Beneath each of these unlit buttons was a single toggle mechanism.

"Arm tube number one."

Both men hit the toggle switch located beneath the first of the buttons. In response, its red light began blinking. Before initiating the next order, the captain met the XO's gaze. Trading a second of silent concern, Charles spoke out curtly.

"Fire number one!"

Imitating Blake's hand movement, Pete depressed the flashing button with his right index finger. In return, the switch stuck in, while its light abruptly stopped blinking. Still anxiously hunched over the firing panel, he visualized the series of events that they had set into motion.

Outside, above on their hull, the port rear hatch belonging to the missile superstructure had popped open to unmask the launch tube of Trident number one. Inside this silo, two blasts would be taking place almost simultaneously. One explosion originated from a network of linear charges mounted on the underside of the Trident's dome-shaped, protective urethane-foam shell. The other blast came from the steam ignition system as a small, fixed rocket engine ignited. As the resulting exhaust was directed into the cool water stored at the base of the tube, the resulting steam pressure expelled the Trident upward as the *Phoenix* violently yawed onto its keel. Shaken in this manner, after suddenly losing one of its 70,000-pound missiles, the vessel began steadying as the now-empty tube was backflooded with water to re-establish its trim. Following this reballasting, the outer hatch would close.

Issuing a breath of relief, Pete again caught the captain's gaze as Anthony Canova screamed out for all of them to clearly hear, "AUSEX indicates that Trident number one has broken the surface. We have a first-stage booster ignite!"

The XO followed Blake as he relocked the firing panel, stood, pushed his chair back under the console, and quickly made his way over to the sonar operator. Standing at his rear, they watched the big man tighten his set of bulky headphones.

"You should just hear that solid propellant booster roar! It's pure music to my ears—"

Canova cut his words short as he hunched forward, a look of puzzlement clouding his previously triumphant expression. Noticing this abrupt change in mood, Blake questioned, "What in the hell is the matter, Canova?"

Angling his hand up to silence the captain, the balding New Yorker strained to pick out the alien sound that was barely audible far in the distance. It was only as the Trident continued to ascend that he was able to identify this sickening, high-pitched whine.

"Holy Mother Mary!" exclaimed the astonished sonar man. "That's some kind of ABM! It appears to have been launched from the direction of that Udaloy to our north."

Soaking in these words, Blake grimaced as his hands went out to massage his forehead; the XO's heartbeat instinctively quickened. Anxiously, both officers listened as Canova again spoke out.

"I'm sure of it. It's an interceptor, all right, and it's vectoring in right on our Trident."

His tone tinged with doom, Blake addressed his XO "You see, didn't I tell you that we were at war?"

These apocalyptic words were punctuated as Anthony Canova disgustingly pulled his headphones off

350

and rubbed his pounding ears. "Jesus Christ, she's gone! A single fucking explosion and Trident number one has been blown away!"

Charles Blake started to pivot back toward the fire-control panel. "Mr. Walsh, prepare to launch the rest of our magazine. In order to insure their survival, we'll utilize a ripple-fire pattern. I want every last Trident out of its tube in six minutes."

Meekly, the XO balked. "But captain, without Milstar, we still don't know for sure if there's a shooting war going on out there."

Astounded at what he was hearing, Blake turned to face his executive officer. "Wake up, man! What do you think those Russkies are hunting up there, tuna? Let's get on with it, before those Udaloys get any closer and we lose our entire load."

Just as he was about to give in reluctantly, Pete became aware of a sudden commotion behind him. Angling his line of sight toward the forward hatch, he quickly set eyes on the individual responsible for this disruption. Standing inside the hatchway, his bushy hair disheveled and his eyes wild, was Lieutenant Thomas Kraft. Waving a compact, white plastic case over his head with his left hand, he spoke out bravely.

"The guessing game is over, Captain. Inside this box, I've got that solid evidence that I needed to prove my point. That was no nuclear detonation that we witnessed earlier on the surface of these waters. Instead, I believe that we're sharing these seas with one of the most powerful underwater volcanic eruptions this planet has ever known. Wait until you see the high degree of magnetic ash and pumice that lies in the air above us!"

Barely had these words escaped the scientist's mouth when Blake shouted out commandingly, "How dare you merely walk into this command center like this!

Have you forgotten, Lieutenant, that I've confined you to your quarters? You're to consider yourself under arrest, Mr. Kraft, for insubordination. Now get out of my sight!"

"But, Captain!" pleaded Thomas. "I can prove why the *Phoenix* has been unable to receive any communications for the last five hours."

His face flushed, the captain took a step toward the forward hatchway. "I've had it up to my balls with your incessant whining. This is no game that we're playing, son. We've got Soviet warships topside firing live ammunition! Now, are you going to get out of here on your own, or am I going to have to drag you out myself?"

Heedless to this threat, the geophysicist stubbornly stood his ground. "Captain Blake, sir, I'm not budging until you at least give me the courtesy of taking a look at what I've found."

Blake seemed prepared to physically manhandle the scientist when the strained voice of Pete Walsh stopped him in his tracks. "Skipper, I think Lieutenant Kraft deserves a bit more respect on our part. After all, he is our guest. At least give him a chance to express himself."

The captain turned to face the XO. "Mr. Walsh, must I remind everyone present that we've got a war to fight at the moment?"

Again Thomas Kraft bravely spoke out. "The only war that we're caught up in is a struggle against Mother Nature. Don't you understand that this volcano is veiling the Soviets' ability to communicate also. I don't know what initially provoked these hostilities, but I'd say there's a very substantial chance that they're of a regional nature only."

"I agree with Lieutenant Kraft," added the XO, who swiftly crossed the compartment to join him. "Wha did you find when you triggered those remote-controlled sensors buried in the seabed here?"

Thomas grinned, happy to have the support of this ally. "I just happen to have the audio results secure in the *Phoenix*'s computer. I can even play them back for you if you'd like. I've only heard such a concentrated flurry of harmonic tremors on one other occasion. That was in mid-May of 1980, while I was stationed outside of Mount St. Helens, Washington. I don't have to remind you of the awesome violence of the volcanic eruption that followed."

Faced with the opposition of his executive officer, Charles Blake attempted to regather his cool. "This is all very interesting, but what in the hell does it have to do with the *Phoenix*'s current situation? That volcano sure didn't send us that Cocked Pistol alert. You're gambling with the security of our entire nation."

"It's you who's very possibly threatening the world's fragile peace, Captain Blake," Kraft returned sternly. "All that I'm asking is that you refrain from launching the rest of the Tridents — at least until we know for certain that there's really a war going on."

Momentarily hesitating in his quick rush to judgment, Charles Blake was just beginning to reconsider Kraft's pleas when a familiar rough voice boomed out from the sonar console. "We've been pinged! I show a solitary underwater bogey approaching from the southwest at a distance of three-four nautical miles. The way it's trucking, it's got to be an Alfa."

Sobered by this threat, both the captain and his XO hurried over to Anthony Canova's side. Just as they positioned themselves behind the hefty junior officer, he cried out once again.

"I show a launch! And there's another! That bogey just shot out two torpedo-like objects, both of which are angling up toward the surface."

"They're SS-N-16 homing torpedos!" exclaimed the captain. "Of all the damn times to have been tagged!"

With his right hand gently rubbing his throbbing forehead, Blake strained to clear his cluttered mind. The one fact that was most obvious was that he'd have to make a choice between two alternatives, and make it quickly. Should he immediately launch his Tridents to follow his S.I.O.P., or should he run, and risk losing everything? Massaging his bruised wound, he looked at both his XO and the scientist who stood beside him. Both of them looked on worriedly, their concerned gazes seemingly trying to implore the captain to follow their stream of thought. It proved to be this expression that sent Charles spinning back in time. In a heartbeat, he was conscious of where he had seen such a look before. It had been on the *Orca*, and had emanated from the eyes of the CIA agent as he'd attempted to bend the will of their captain to surface the sub against his wishes. The influence of this outsider had had disastrous implications for each member of the doomed crew. Stirred by this memory, Charles knew that he could never fall into such a trap again. Roused into action, he spoke out firmly.

"Come on, Pete. If we launch now, we've still got time to empty our magazine before those two subrocs arrive!"

Not even checking to see if the XO was following him, he rushed over to the fire-control panel, pulled out the rail-mounted chair, and seated himself before the launch console. It was only as he reached inside his top pocket to pull out his key that he realized that his exec wasn't doing likewise. Turning his head, he saw that Pete was still anchored on the other side of the compartment.

"Jesus Christ, Walsh!" Blake spat angrily.

Sensing that the XO wasn't about to be moved, the

captain swiveled to the intercom handset and speedily punched in two digits. Breathlessly, he talked into its transmitter.

"Chief Crowley, it's the captain. On my authority, I need you to proceed with a manual launch override. I want the first of those Tridents out of here in thirty seconds, with the following missiles launched in fifteen-second intervals. . . . There's no time to explain, Louis. All I can tell you is that the very security of the free world is presently on the line. Now get moving!"

Hanging up the handset, Blake turned to address the XO and the scientist. "You spineless fools! If only you knew of the hundreds of millions of lives that you were about to jeopardize."

Responding to this, Thomas vainly pleaded to his ally. "Mr. Walsh, you've got to do something! That man's stubbornness is about to needlessly trigger the Apocalypse."

Without a second's indecision, the XO reached out and grasped the telephone handset mounted beside the sonar screen. Depressing two numerals, he expressed himself vigorously.

"Chief Crowley—"

A thunderous explosion sounded outside their hull. Walsh barely had any time to react to this blast when a series of even louder detonations caused him to drop the phone to protect his ears with the palms of his hands. It was at this point that the *Phoenix*'s command center was engulfed in total chaos.

Triggered by the arrival of a series of huge, underwater swells, the 18,700-ton vessel was thrown hard on its keel, as if it were a mere toy. As the sub strained to right itself, it rocked back violently in the opposite direction, then once again rolled uncontrollably over on a reverse incline.

Caught by this unexpected convulsive movement,

Walsh found himself thrown hard against the compartment's port bulkhead. Unable to see anything because of a temporary loss of the lighting system, he could clearly pick out the groans of the rest of the men, the rattle of loose equipment, and the frightening buckling noise of the hull around them. When the tilt of the deck suddenly reversed itself and shifted in the opposite direction, he lost his footing completely. Tossed painfully on his side, he slid shoulder first into one of the sonar console's sharply angled sides and an agonizing spasm numbed his entire upper torso. The angle of the deck shifted itself once more; sliding back into the bulkhead, Pete was unable to protect his temple from the concussion that followed. An instant wave of unconsciousness engulfed him.

Though he was only out for less than a minute, when his eyes finally opened, it was as if he had awakened from a long, sound slumber. Groggily, the XO struggled to orient himself. Stunned by the sharp pain that coursed through both his shoulder and the side of his skull, Walsh found his vision clouded at first. As it gradually cleared, he could see that the room's lights had snapped back on. Carefully, he sat himself up, propping his bruised back against the smooth, cold surface of the bulkhead. It was from this angle that he was able to survey the rest of the command center.

In the process of recovering from the abrupt shock wave, the dozen sailors who manned this area were slowly coming back to life. Those sailors who hadn't been securely strapped in their chairs were stiffly rising from the debris-strewn floor. Individuals such as the helmsman and sonar operators had been able to keep their seats, yet it was evident that their necks and backs had taken a beating. Then Pete set eyes on the Captain. Slowly crawling on his hands and knees, Blake could be seen headed back toward the fire-control panel.

Shocked by this sighting, Pete's mind cleared. Completely reaware of the tense situation that had possessed the room in the seconds preceding the explosions and the arrival of the first wave, the XO struggled to make it to his feet. Hanging from its cord, the intercom's handset beckoned him to complete the frantic conversation he had been in the midst of when he was so rudely interrupted.

Pete stood, and a wave of nauseating dizziness almost sent him back to his knees. Yet this lightheadedness soon passed, and he found himself able to complete the half-dozen steps that would lead him back to the sonar console. Just as he was preparing to bend over and regrasp the handset, his eyes caught sight of the lower half of a man's torso partly exposed behind the bank of sensor equipment.

Oblivious to the pain that throbbed in his shoulder, Walsh turned the corner and set eyes on the prone, still body of Lieutenant Thomas Kraft. Lying flat on his stomach, the scientist appeared to have been knocked out cold. It was only when the XO spotted the rapidly gathering pool of blood beneath Kraft's forehead that he screamed out commandingly, "Canova, give me a hand back here! We've got a seriously injured officer!"

It took the portly sonar operator only seconds to slip out of his chair and reach the XO's side. Carefully, the two men turned the geophysicist over to check the extent of his injuries. Though a deep gash was etched into the side of his skull, they breathed sighs of relief upon seeing that Kraft's eyes were open and alert.

"Were we able to halt the launch?" he mumbled feverishly.

Reaware of their predicament, the XO hastily reorganized his priorities. "Jesus, the Tridents!"

Pivoting, the turned the corner, to again pick up the

intercom. Only when he put the handset to his ear did he realize that it had already been activated.

"Crowley, are you awake down there? Launch those missiles, damn you!"

Taking in this frenzied directive, Pete caught sight of the person responsible for it. Standing before the fire-control panel, the tail of his shirt hanging sloppily over his waist, was their captain, telephone firmly in hand.

"Crowley!" continued Blake, furiously.

The XO listened as the chief petty officer's voice shakily broke from the speaker. "Captain, I'm afraid there's going to be no launch today. That concussion has knocked out the superstructure release mechanism. With their hatches unable to open, those Tridents won't be going anywhere."

The moment of silence that followed this disclosure was broken by the excited shouts of one of the two remaining sonar operators. "We've got our sonar back! Both that bogey sub and those two subrocs are nowhere to be seen! Even the Udaloys are gone!"

"All right!" added Anthony Canova, as he stood beside the XO. "Since they were closer to that blast's origin, the concussion must have wiped the sub and those SS-N-16s completely out. There must have been one hell of a tidal wave upstairs to bring down those cruisers."

A gentle tugging on his pants legs redirected the XO's attention. Having raised himself to a sitting position, Thomas Kraft meekly looked up, appearing pale and drowsy. A thin trickle of blood continued flowing from his head wound.

Pete bent down to comfort him. Utilizing his handkerchief as a compress, he covered the wound, yet the white, cotton cloth was all too soon blood soaked.

"Canova, you'd better get the doc up here on the double."

As the potbellied sonar operator went off to fulfill this request, Walsh found himself gently holding the scientist's head in his lap when Kraft abruptly keeled over. The XO studied his bearded, blood-speckled face. Taking on an almost-angelic quality, Kraft's tense features softened as his eyes once more opened and gradually focused themselves. His renewed gaze locked to Pete Walsh, Thomas managed a weak query.

"Did we do it?"

Before Pete could answer, a raucous blast of static shot out from the nearby radio receiver. This was followed by a distant booming male voice.

"USS *Phoenix*, this is TACAMO zero-two-Alpha. Cocked Pistol has been scrubbed. I repeat, cocked pistol has been scrubbed. . . ."

As this transmission repeated itself, Pete looked down to share his joy. It took him only a glance to realize that Thomas Kraft had slipped off into a sleep that he'd never return from.

The XO wasn't sure how long his gaze remained on that of his expired ally. So moved were his emotions, that time no longer mattered. When he eventually did return to reality, Pete couldn't help but identify the tall, trim officer who now stood before him. Looking old and tired, Charles Blake addressed him calmly.

"Pete, if you can manage all right, I'd like you to take over here. Under the circumstances, the quickest route back to Pearl would be most appreciated. Right now, I've got one very important letter to finish and an overextended career to wrap up. Susan was right—I *am* getting to be a narrow-minded, stubborn old fool."

Leaving him with these puzzling words, the captain wearily plodded out the forward hatchway. Conscious of his new responsibility, Pete was preparing to rise, to get back to work, when Anthony Canova approached him.

359

"The doc will be up here as soon as he's able. It seems that the guys in the engine room really took a beating. He's setting a couple of broken bones at the moment."

Walsh responded grimly. "There's no rush now, Tony. Can you give me a hand?"

With the junior lieutenant's help, Thomas Kraft's corpse was set aside, and Walsh was able to stiffly stand. Ignoring the pains that throbbed in both his temple and shoulder, the XO straightened his frame and scanned the control room. Finding it none the worse for wear, he efficiently took command.

"Damage control, I need an immediate report. Navigation, draw up the quickest route to Pearl. Lieutenant Peterson, prepare the helm to get us on our way."

Satisfied to hear that their hull integrity was intact, and that all systems appeared operational, the XO was preparing to issue the orders sending the *Phoenix* northward when Anthony Canova beckoned him excitedly.

"Mr. Walsh, there's something strange going on that I think you'd better know about. Unless our sonar has gone out of whack, or those shockwaves carried us way off course, we got us some kind of landmass to our immediate south that sure wasn't there earlier."

Checking this sighting firsthand on the sonar screen, Pete met Canova's puzzled glance. Giving this discovery some second thought, he turned to face their helmsman.

"Mr. Peterson, bring us up to periscope depth."

"Aye, aye, sir," shot back the alert diving officer.

To the characteristic bubbling sound of venting ballast as the *Phoenix* lightened its load, Walsh crossed to the corner of the command center reserved for the periscopes. Barely aware of the sensation created from the vessel's gradual ascent, he waited to hear from the diving officer before issuing the next order.

"Periscope depth, sir."

"Very good, Lieutenant. Lower the scope."

Somewhat awkwardly because of his bruised shoulder, the XO clamped down the two short arms attached to the periscope's central column. Bending over, he slowly positioned his eyes inside the rubber coupling, careful not to bump his sore temple. As he swung the scope to scan the southern horizon, it didn't take much effort to view the thick, billowing, mushroom-shaped cloud that dominated the sky here. Stretching from the surface of the sea upward to a height he couldn't begin to measure, the thick band of smoke had a familiarity he at first couldn't place. It was only when he increased the magnification tenfold that the association came to him with a spine-tingling start.

Gracing the surface of the sea, seeming to be only an arm's length away, was the massive black cone of a newly risen volcanic island. Appearing to match almost exactly the photograph Thomas Kraft had shown him only hours ago, it was from this jagged summit that the dense, black smoke belched.

Only then did Pete realize how deadly accurate his fallen comrade had been after all. He looked on unblinkingly as a huge ribbon of fiery lava burst skyward in a jagged, glowing line.

In such a way the earth was born, pondered the XO somberly. How fitting it would have been for such an eruption to be responsible for mankind's ultimate demise.

Epilogue

For a reason she at first couldn't rationally explain, Telsa Vanua, eldest daughter of the *matai* of the village of Amanave, found herself drawn to the fales overlooking Cape Taputapu. The sun was just setting in a veil of crimson magnificence as the long-legged Samoan beauty made her way out of the forest of stately coconut palms and breadfruit trees that fringed the clearing in which the oval-shaped, thatched hut was situated. Even though she wasn't sure if her lover was even present, an inexplicable longing drew her here.

The day just completed had been a most busy one, yet Telsa had been impatient for the sacred Kava ceremony to end. Carrying out her duties as the server with impeccable exactness, she had gone through the intricate motions by rote, yet her heart had been far from in it. How shocked she had been when her father confronted her with this very fact.

"My dearest, child," he'd said warmly. "It is most obvious that the Goddess is not with you on this special day. Do what you must to find her, for it is through your heart that her judgment is passed on."

Taking this as permission to leave the ceremony, she'd handed the Kava pouch to the next girl in line and darted off for the path leading to Cape Taputapu.

Not certain what she would find there, Telsa had printed the entire way, her long, flowing brown hair creaming out behind her.

She was hardly out of breath as she climbed onto the porch. Taking in the empty furniture, Telsa's memories returned to a time barely twenty-four hours ago, when her strong, hairy mate had made love to her on this very same rattan lounge chair. Tingling with renewed excitement, she pushed open the hut's door, and to her dismay, found it completely deserted.

Somehow, she knew that she wouldn't even find him here later this evening. Probably called to duty by the powerful State that he served, he could be absent for hours, days, or even months.

Making her way back to the porch, Telsa seated herself on the lounger, and directed her gaze over the white beach to the sea beyond. Becalmed by the dusk, the blue waters stretched to the western horizon like a smooth plate of silvery glass. Though the sun had been down for some time now, its radiance was hinted at by the fiery, crimson fingers of color that branched upward from the distant ocean like points on a crown.

Never could she remember seeing such a vibrant sunset. Surely, this was a sign that the Goddess had finally returned. Opening her heart to this wonder, she shivered with the realization that the color of this dusk and that of Pele's eyes were certainly the same. Both shone with a fiery iridescence. Both spoke in similar tones.

Lulled by the song that only the worthy could hear, Telsa understood the true meaning of sacrifice. It was because of this offering that mankind would have its reprieve.

Feeling as if a part of her had been cut off and tossed into the sea, she knew without a doubt that Thomas Craft had been the oblation that the Goddess had demanded. Taken before his rightful time, his passing would but temporarily calm Pele's anger. But would the world be so lucky next time?

With tears rolling down her cheeks, Telsa Vanu whispered her good-byes to a love with whom she had only shared the shortest of times. Ever mindful that the memories of this relationship would have to last her for a lifetime, the eldest daughter of the *matai* of Amanava swore to keep this vigil an ever holy one, as nightfall descended upon the island of Tutuila.

THE WORLD-AT-WAR SERIES
by Lawrence Cortesi

COUNTDOWN TO PARIS   (1548, $3.25)
Having stormed the beaches of Normandy, every GI had one
dream: to liberate Paris from the Nazis. Trapping the enemy in
the Falaise Pocket, the Allies would shatter the powerful German
7th Army Group, opening the way for the . . . COUNTDOWN
TO PARIS.

GATEWAY TO VICTORY   (1496, $3.25)
After Leyte, the U.S. Navy was at the threshold of Japan's Pacific
Empire. With his legendary cunning, Admiral Halsey devised a
brilliant plan to deal a crippling blow in the South China Sea to
Japan's military might.

ROMMEL'S LAST STAND   (1415, $3.25)
In April of 1943 the Nazis attempted a daring airlift of supplies
to a desperate Rommel in North Africa. But the Allies were lying
in wait for one of the most astonishing and bloody air victories of
the war.

LAST BRIDGE TO VICTORY   (1393, $3.25)
Nazi troops had blown every bridge on the Rhine, stalling
Eisenhower's drive for victory. In one final blood-soaked battle,
the fanatic resistance of the Nazis would test the courage of every
American soldier.

PACIFIC SIEGE   (1363, $3.25)
If the Allies failed to hold New Guinea, the entire Pacific would
fall to the Japanese juggernaut. For six brutal months they
drenched the New Guinea jungles with their blood, hoping to live
to see the end of the . . . PACIFIC SIEGE.

THE BATTLE FOR MANILA   (1334, $3.25)
A Japanese commander's decision — against orders — to defend
Manila to the death led to the most brutal combat of the entire
Pacific campaign. A living hell that was . . . THE BATTLE FOR
MANILA.

*Available wherever paperbacks are sold, or order direct from the
Publisher. Send cover price plus 50¢ per copy for mailing and
handling to Zebra Books, Dept. 1789, 475 Park Avenue South,
New York, N.Y. 10016. DO NOT SEND CASH.*

ASHES
by William W. Johnstone

OUT OF THE ASHES (1137, $3.50)

Ben Raines hadn't looked forward to the War, but he knew it was coming. After the balloons went up, Ben was one of the survivors, fighting his way across the country, searching for his family, and leading a band of new pioneers attempting to bring America OUT OF THE ASHES.

FIRE IN THE ASHES (1310, $3.50)

It's 1999 and the world as we know it no longer exists. Ben Raines, leader of the Resistance, must regroup his rebels and prep them for bloody guerilla war. But are they ready to face an even fiercer foe—the human mutants threatening to overpower the world!

ANARCHY IN THE ASHES (1387, $3.50)

Out of the smoldering nuclear wreckage of World War III, Ben Raines has emerged as the strong leader the Resistance needs. When Sam Hartline, the mercenary, joins forces with an invading army of Russians, Ben and his people raise a bloody banner of defiance to defend earth's last bastion of freedom.

BLOOD IN THE ASHES (1537, $3.50)

As Raines and his ragged band of followers search for land that has escaped radiation, the insidious group known as The Ninth Order rises up to destroy them. In a savage battle to the death, it is the fate of America itself that hangs in the balance!

Available wherever paperbacks are sold, or order direct from the Publisher. Send cover price plus 50¢ per copy for mailing and handling to Zebra Books, Dept. 1789, 475 Park Avenue South, New York, N.Y. 10016. DO NOT SEND CASH.